P9-BZT-057

The Carpathian Novels

Anthologies

EDGE OF DARKNESS
(with Maggie Shayne and Lori Herter)

DARKEST AT DAWN
(includes Dark Hunger *and* Dark Secret*)*

SEA STORM
(includes Magic in the Wind *and* Oceans of Fire*)*

FEVER
(includes The Awakening *and* Wild Rain*)*

FANTASY
(with Emma Holly, Sabrina Jeffries, and Elda Minger)

LOVER BEWARE
(with Fiona Brand, Katherine Sutcliffe, and Eileen Wilks)

HOT BLOODED
(with Maggie Shayne, Emma Holly, and Angela Knight)

Specials

DESOLATION ROAD

CHRISTINE FEEHAN

JOVE
New York

A JOVE BOOK
Published by Berkley
An imprint of Penguin Random House LLC
penguinrandomhouse.com

ISBN: 9780593099759

First Edition: July 2020

Printed in the United States of America
1 3 5 7 9 10 8 6 4 2

Cover design by Judith Lagerman
Cover art by Neils Antone

For Carol Cridge. This one's for you.

FOR MY READERS

Be sure to go to christinefeehan.com/members/ to sign up for my private book announcement list and download the free ebook of *Dark Desserts*. Join my community and get firsthand news, enter the book discussions, ask your questions and chat with me. Please feel free to email me at Christine@christinefeehan.com. I would love to hear from you.

ACKNOWLEDGMENTS

As with any book, there are so many people to thank. Kathie Firzlaff, thank you for always being there for me when I need you. Leslee Huber, I know I talk your ear off about Torpedo Ink. Thanks for listening. Brian and Sheila, thanks for competing with me during power hours for top word count when I wanted to move fast on this one. Anne Elizabeth, thanks for letting me know some books are important even when others just don't get them.

TORPEDO INK MEMBERS

Viktor Prakenskii aka *Czar*—President

Lyov Russak aka *Steele*—Vice President

Savva Pajari aka *Reaper*—Sergeant at Arms

Savin Pajari aka *Savage*—Sergeant at Arms

Isaak Koval aka *Ice*—Secretary

Dmitry Koval aka *Storm*

Alena Koval aka *Torch*

Luca Litvin aka *Code*—Treasurer

Maksimos Korsak aka *Ink*

Kasimir Popov aka *Preacher*

Lana Popov aka *Widow*

Nikolaos Bolotan aka *Mechanic*

Pytor Bolotan aka *Transporter*

Andrii Federoff aka *Maestro*

Gedeon Lazaroff aka *Player*

Kir Vasiliev aka *Master*

Lazar Alexeev aka *Keys*

Aleksei Solokov aka *Absinthe*

NEWER PATCHED MEMBERS

Gavriil Prakenskii

Casimir Prakenskii

PROSPECTS

Fatei

Glitch

Hyde

ONE

Aleksei "Absinthe" Solokov loved books. He loved the smell of them. The sight of them. The information in them. He especially loved the places he could go in them. Books had saved his life on more than one occasion. He'd originally come to this place needing the quiet and peace, needing the scent and the words. And once again, books had led him to find something so unexpected, so spectacular, he still hadn't accepted the offering, the gift, not quite believing yet, but he couldn't walk away.

He sat in his favorite place right in front of the tallest stacks. The table was smaller and less inviting due to the crowded space. He didn't like being disturbed. He came to the library to get respite from the continual bombardment of other people's thoughts and emotions. He could command with his voice, and sometimes the temptation to tell everyone to not think or speak for five minutes was brutally hard to resist. He needed to feel normal when he wasn't. He wanted to see if he could fit in somewhere, but he knew he couldn't. He needed to stand on his own, but it was impossible.

His small table, nearly hidden there beside the taller stacks, not only protected him from unwanted company but gave him a direct view to the desk where the librarian checked out books, recommended reads and sometimes—make that often—helped teens with their homework. He had been coming for over a month. Six weeks to be exact. And he just watched her. Like a fucking stalker. The librarian. She was so damn sexy he was shocked that the place wasn't overrun with single men—because she was single. He'd made it his business to find out.

When he first came to the library, he hadn't worn his colors. It was more to be anonymous than for any other reason—at least he told himself that. Sometimes, he just got a feeling. Whenever it happened, he acted on it, and he'd had that feeling—the one that often saved his life—so he'd removed his colors and gone into the library feeling a little naked without them.

He didn't want to be noticed, although he was covered in tattoos and scars that couldn't be seen beneath the tee that stretched tight across his chest. Just his sleeves showed, those tattoos that meant something to him but wouldn't to anyone else. Memorials to his lost family and the children who hadn't survived that nightmare he'd lived through.

Now, he still didn't wear his colors for the same reason, although he felt a fraud, because he was Torpedo Ink. His club colors were tattooed onto his back, but it was more than that. His identity went beyond skin and sank right into bone. He knew with absolute certainty that he couldn't live without his club, nor would he want to. Torpedo Ink was his identity. His life. His family—brothers and sisters—and their lives were bound together irrevocably.

They were woven together like an old tapestry, and nothing could take them apart, and yet, he felt as if he had betrayed them. Skulking away. The members rarely went off alone, certainly not daily for six weeks. And they didn't go six weeks without wearing their colors. It wasn't done.

He might as well have gone naked. He didn't know why he kept this place to himself . . .

He did though. It was the librarian. The little redhead. She moved like poetry. Flowing like words across the pages of a book. One moment she could be a lady in a historical, taking the hand of a gentleman and gracefully emerging from a carriage; the next, a modern-day woman striding down the busy street in a business suit with her briefcase. Or a sexy librarian dressed in a pencil-straight skirt that hugged her curves and gave him all kinds of very dirty and graphic thoughts, like bending her over that desk of hers when the rest of the world went away.

Still, that feeling of staying anonymous, of keeping his identity secret, so that no one had a clue what or who he was, persisted while he unraveled the mystery of the woman who ran the library so efficiently.

~

He was back. Oh. My God. The most gorgeous man in the entire world and he just walked in off the street like he owned the place. Like the library was his home and gorgeous men came in every single day. He was tall with broad shoulders and a thick chest and arms. Really great arms. Muscles. Really great muscles. Scarlet Foley spent a *lot* of time perving on his muscles. And all those delicious tattoos. Who knew she'd fall for tattoos when she'd never been all that fond of them?

He had thick blond hair, a lot of it, and it spilled across his forehead, making her fingers itch to smooth it back. His eyes were very different. Blue. But not. More crystal blue. But not. Like two really cool crystals. She couldn't decide. When she wasn't perving on his muscles or fixating on his fascinating mouth, she was definitely wondering how to describe his eyes, and she was really good with words as a rule.

She knew she shouldn't be around him. He left her breathless and tongue-tied. If she had girlfriends, she would be over at their houses every night after work so she could share the mythical pictures she would secretly sneak of him like a crazy stalker. They would have dropped by the library to see him and giggled like schoolgirls.

Instead, she acted the part of the librarian. Dignified. Hiding behind the glasses she didn't really need. She had that role down perfectly. No giggling. No snapping contraband pictures to stare at in the middle of the night and fantasize over and pretend she might actually have some sort of a love life. Worse, get out every single toy known to single women that wouldn't help because he was *too* gorgeous, and nothing *ever* was going to match the real thing. But as long as he kept coming to her library, she was going to do some daydreaming; no one could take that away from her.

He liked science fiction. He read psychology books. Not self-help books, but the real thing, industry books. He also read a lot of obscure reference books on the pyramids of Egypt. The building of them. She knew because she watched his every move, and sometimes she helped him find the books he wanted. Up close, he smelled like sandalwood, and at night, when she was alone, she couldn't get that scent out of her mind. She knew she would always associate it with him. Man. Muscles. And sex. Worse.

Yes. It did get worse because she'd looked down his body. It wasn't her fault. She didn't mean to. She practiced keeping her eyes up on his chest. But she handed him the book and her gaze just dropped and there it was . . . in all its glory. Hard as a rock. The full ultra-impressive package. So now, she had it all to take to bed with her. And quite frankly, it sucked that the man wasn't in bed with her as well.

He would ask her for help in finding a particular book, and when he did, his voice was mesmerizing. Velvet soft. She swore she felt the sound sliding over her skin. Stroking her. An actual physical sensation. A little shiver always slid down her spine and a very inappropriate flutter in her sex accompanied that shiver. Now that she knew what he had, her wayward gaze strayed often and her panties went damp more than they should have. She had no respect for herself. None. But that didn't stop her.

She'd never had that kind of reaction to any man, not in college and not when she'd traveled to other countries. His voice was always pitched low, very soft, but it was commanding, and she heard a little twist of his words as if he had an accent under the English pronunciation, but she couldn't place it. She'd never heard a voice like his before, and she'd traveled extensively. He was very much a gentleman, and yet he gave off an extremely dangerous vibe. She'd been around dangerous men and she would have placed him right there with them, but she didn't know why. He seemed as if he'd be more at home in a suit and tie than casual clothes. And he wore his clothes like a model.

She had a lot of time—too much time—to think about him when she went home from the library and sat alone in her reading chair, surrounded by her books and little else. He was the fastest speed-reader she'd ever seen in her life and she knew he was for real. At first, she thought he was faking his ability to read that fast, but then she realized after time that he clearly was reading the books and must be comprehending what he was reading.

She was impressed. She'd taken several speed-reading courses and, in the end, had gone with the advice of the fastest reader in the world, learning from his books. She picked up things fast, she always had. The more time spent, the faster she learned. It was a gift she had, and she used it often, which made it all the more readily available to her.

She'd made certain to touch him. The first time had been a brief brush of their fingers as she handed him a book. Frankly, she hadn't been certain if he'd made that initial contact or if she had, but she would never forget it as long as she lived. The spark had gone up her finger to every nerve ending in her body, spreading like a wildfire, bringing her to life as if she'd been asleep—or dead—her entire life and it had taken him to wake her up.

She *had* been dead. She'd chosen to be dead. She'd shoved the woman in her aside out of necessity and become what she had to be. Now she was simply surviving. Until he walked in. She had no idea what to do with him—but she wanted him. She'd sworn she would never—not *ever*—go there again. Put herself in a situation where the dark things inside of her had a chance to escape. She'd seen the results of that, and yet she couldn't stop thinking about him . . . wanting him.

Touching him was dangerous, but she couldn't seem to resist no matter how hard she tried, and every touch brought something new. She couldn't get to him, couldn't uncover him or strip him in layers like she did others, but something connected them so strongly, melding them so tightly together that there was no going back, and she knew it. Every time he was close to her, he melted away that shell of a hardened human being that wasn't real and, for a moment, she felt alive and genuine—and vulnerable.

Right now he sat in her library, disturbing her beyond all measure. She hadn't thought it possible. She thought she was stone-cold when it came to the opposite sex, but she lit up around him. On fire. Hot as Hades. She apparently had red hair for a reason, and it wasn't her temper. Okay, maybe it was that too. She hadn't made up her mind how she felt about Mr. Aleksei Solokov. That was the name on his library card. She didn't know if her body coming to life was a good thing or a bad thing. If fantasies were wonderful or a curse. There was a lot to think about, but then she had a lot of time to think.

"Miss Foley?"

She jerked her head up, her breath exploding out of her lungs. No one had managed to sneak up on her in years, and yet just by perving on Aleksei Solokov she had failed the first lesson in survival. She turned slowly, already knowing who was behind her, identifying him by his voice.

"Hi, Tom." He was sixteen and trying desperately to learn to read at his age level. His English teacher was no help, giving him assignments far beyond his comprehension. It made Scarlet angry that the man couldn't take the time to help the boy.

"I was hoping you'd come in today. I have plenty of time to help you." She flashed him a reassuring smile.

The boy's face flooded with relief. "Thanks, Miss Foley."

She waved him toward the table where they often worked together, and where she was most comfortable. She could see out the windows, but no one could see her or the boy she tutored. She was always careful just in case, so no one could ever harm any of the teens just because of her. She put aside the rest of the evening's work and settled down to help Tom do his homework. She would have plenty of time to finish her own work before the close of her shift.

꠷

The librarian moved, drawing Absinthe's attention. It was growing late, and she walked the boy she'd been helping with his English paper to the door, reassuring him he was getting better with every paper and she was proud of him. She moved like someone who could handle herself, always balanced, even when she was carrying stacks of books. He'd noticed that about her almost immediately. When you were as fucked up as he was, you always assessed the men and women around you to see who the fighters were. Under that sexy prim-and-proper librarian façade she could handle herself.

She wore her hair up in an intricate, twisted bun, but twice, after work, he'd seen her let it down. It was bright red, shiny red. There was no other word for the color. Just red, and that color hadn't come out of a box. It was a waterfall of true, thick, silky red. Her hair, once let loose, refused to be tamed. It snaked down her back to her waist, drawing attention to just how small her waist and rib cage were and how curved her hips were. She had an ass, and tits that were high and firm, and very generous. Her curves were deceptive considering she was very fit.

Absinthe's entire body reacted to her in an entirely unprecedented way. He didn't have normal erections. Those had been beaten or raped out of him when he was a child. To achieve one, he had to command his body to cooperate, and why the hell bother? To sit in the library—that quiet and peaceful place—and feel his body respond to a beautiful woman was a form of magic. He enjoyed the feeling, knowing he would never take it for granted—and it happened every damn time he looked at her.

He had experimented after he'd had a reaction to her, going to various bars and even the market, in the hopes that his body would respond to someone else after it had come to life, but it seemed it was only the little librarian with her bright red hair that did it for him. That was just fine with him. He liked her. He liked the way she was so gentle and calm—so patient with the kids who came in asking her homework questions. If she noticed there was a much higher percentage of boys than girls, she didn't make a big deal out of it. She spoke in soft, melodic tones, but hushed, in keeping with the library rules.

After seeing the boy out, she turned and looked straight at him. He could never quite interpret the expression on her face. He was always careful not to touch her for too long. He didn't want to read her thoughts. He was enjoying their dance around each other too much for that. She was fascinated, but nervous—anxious even, which he found interesting as well. She was always so calm with everyone else. She couldn't know he was in a club, so it wasn't that.

She came toward him, flowing across the room. She was breathtaking. Beautiful. All woman wrapped up in that sweet package. Her name was Scarlet, and he loved that name. It said Scarlet Foley on her nameplate, and she'd finally introduced herself formally to him three and a half weeks earlier. It had taken quite some time before she actually spoke to him. She'd smile, but she didn't come near him at first. Even now, she was extremely reserved with him.

"You've been here for hours. Are you doing research again? I might be able to help you," she offered. "Although we're closing soon."

He glanced around. The library was empty. It was definitely near closing time. He decided to take a chance. "I stayed late on the off chance you'd have time to have dinner with me. Nothing fancy, just across the street there." He indicated the more upscale restaurant facing the front of the library.

He liked the location of the library. It was on a block that was also quieter than most of the town's streets. Foliage was abundant, in fact the front and sides of the library were covered in ivy so that it appeared to drip down the brick walls and fall like a waterfall over the second story to the first. Everything about the place proclaimed it was cool and inviting.

Scarlet stood very still, her large green eyes behind her glasses moving over his face slowly. For a moment she looked scared. Not scared exactly. That wasn't the right word. Leery, maybe. Assessing the risk? He wasn't certain but she wasn't jumping at his invitation. She glanced over her shoulder toward the restaurant. Absinthe stayed silent, letting her make up her mind. He needed her to feel safe with him—and he wanted her to *want* to spend time with him the way he wanted to spend it with her, just the two of them. Walking across the street with her vehicle close by was a good start.

"I think that sounds fun," she said finally. Almost reluctantly.

He could hear lies. She wasn't lying, but there was something he couldn't quite put his finger on. For the millionth time, he glanced at her hand to see if she was wearing a wedding ring. She wasn't. There was no faint tan line that might indicate she'd worn one. She had very pale skin. A dusting of freckles was across her nose, spreading out just a bit, very faint, but he had the unexpected urge to kiss each one.

"I'll wait here for you while you close up and we can walk over together," he said. He made it a statement. She more than likely would want him to go out the door first. She didn't walk outside with anyone, even if one of the teens stayed late. Not one time in the six weeks he'd been coming. She always stood at the door for a long period of time, scanning the entire block, the buildings and even the rooftops.

Her small white teeth caught at her lower lip for a moment and his heart nearly stopped. Why he found that sexy, he had no idea, but he did. His body stirred, and heat rushed through his veins like a drug. Just being close to her was addicting. Her eyes did that reluctant drop, as if she couldn't help herself. He fucking loved that. For just one moment her gaze rested on the bulge at the front of his jeans and he hardened even more. She turned red and averted her eyes. He resisted grinning.

"I have a few things to do. You could grab us a table and I'll meet you there."

Yeah. She didn't want to be seen with anyone. That was a red flag. He held up his cell phone. "I'll text them to hold us a table. I scoped it out earlier and they have a few tables for two. They're kind of in the shadows, but if you'd rather sit on the main floor . . ."

"No, I think a table for two sounds excellent."

She jumped at that. A little too fast. She didn't want to be seen with him. Fuck.

"I'll make us a reservation and you finish up."

She hesitated again, but then turned away with a little nod. He watched her go back to her desk. He'd already made the reservation. If she'd said no, he simply would have canceled it. He kept an eye on her while he made a show of writing down a few facts from the book he had pulled out to reference. Truthfully, he didn't need to write anything down. He could read and absorb over twenty thousand words per minute. He retained everything he saw or read. He could compel truth and make suggestions that others would follow. He had highly developed gifts. Some were a curse, no matter what others thought. Most were. Or maybe it was how he'd had to use them.

He was uneasy without his fellow Torpedo Ink members close by, and even more so now that he could see just how nervous she was. They had survived their childhood—and then later, as teens and adults—by sticking together. The rule had always been one or two stuck close to a third. Sometimes they were unseen, up on a rooftop with a rifle; sometimes they were in the shadows, but there was always someone close to protect one another.

Absinthe knew if the pull toward the librarian hadn't been so strong, he never would have continued to come without at least one of the others. He wanted them close. Eventually, he would have to ask them to ride with him, but there would be so many questions and he wanted this time with her to be real. He wanted to unravel the mystery of Scarlet Foley alone. If he enlisted the aid of his club, Code would be involved, and her life would instantly be an open book. No one escaped Code's ability to uncover their past with his genius computer skills. There was something to be said for the old-fashioned way of conversation and courtship.

He drummed his fingers on the table, reminiscent of Czar, their Torpedo Ink president. When Czar was thinking, he often kept time with his fingers. Absinthe found himself with the same habit and he'd never bothered to try to break it. Twice, there in the library, his little redhead had sent him a small frown. Now he often drummed his fingers on the table just to see that frown because he found it provocative. Sensual. Hell, everything she did was sensual.

He waited for her to turn the lights off before he got up and made his way down the aisle between the tall stacks to her. She knocked her purse off the desk and then when she picked it up, she dropped it again. Absinthe recovered it and handed it to her. That was absolutely, entirely unlike her, especially the fact that she hadn't caught it before it hit the floor. He'd seen her catch dozens of books and other objects over the last six weeks even when others had dropped them.

Scarlet took the purse with a rueful expression. "I'm a little nervous," she confessed, not looking at him. "I don't go out very often."

He'd already guessed that. He also was very sure she was afraid of someone. "Does your family live here?"

He held the door open for her. He wasn't used to making conversation with an ordinary citizen, and certainly not one that made his cock feel so diamond hard he was afraid he might not be able to walk. Wasn't that a perfectly ordinary question? One any man might ask a woman on a first date? Date. Hell. He didn't date. He'd never been on a date in his life.

She had dropped back, not walking with him, and he just stood there, waiting for her to exit. Scarlet's gaze slid up and down the street before she reluctantly stepped outside and allowed him to close the door behind her, take the keys from her hand and lock it and then hand them back to her.

"No, but my grandmother did. I used to visit her here. I had a lot of good memories, so I came back and was able to get the job at the library. What about you?"

He shook his head. "No, but now I live in Caspar, which isn't all that far from here." It was by some people's standards, but he found it peaceful riding his motorcycle, and the roads were perfect for cruising between the coast and inland, so distances didn't matter to him.

Her face lit up. "I've been to Caspar. It's on the coast, right? I love it there. The sea is always changing. One day it will be quiet and calm, and the next, it's wild and crazy. You're lucky to live there, although I imagine there aren't very many jobs available."

Was there a wistful note in her voice? He hoped so. He needed the stars to align and let him have this miracle of a gift. He needed her in his life. He just had to find a way to make it happen and have it be real. He was most afraid of that—needing her too much and creating a false relationship.

He opened the door to the restaurant for her, scanning the room quickly for potential trouble before allowing her to do the same thing while he turned back toward the street and gave that another quick once-over. Certain no one was paying attention to either of them, he closed the door and followed his librarian's amazing ass. She was in a black skirt with small white polka dots scattered over it. The material clung to her curves. He appreciated that particular skirt very much.

Absinthe held the back of her chair for her, ignoring the waiter, who looked as if he might conk him on the head and abscond with the girl. She looked regal as she took the seat, smiling up at Absinthe, nearly taking his breath away. Whatever it was that she had affected him like some kind of aphrodisiac. Her small teeth. That mouth with her full, pouty lips that were made for a man's dirtiest fantasies. He hadn't had them until she came along. Not like this. Mostly he'd had nightmares. The erotic, very graphic dreams were a welcome change.

"Are you a wine drinker?" Absinthe didn't know the first thing about wine. He could make her any kind of drink she wanted, or talk beer, but wine eluded him. If she loved wine, he was going to be taking a crash course. It wouldn't take him long to catch up.

She shook her head. "I actually don't drink very much. Once in a while, if it's really hot out, I'll have an ice-cold beer. But other than that, it's a very occasional drink and usually I go for something girly like a cosmopolitan."

"I don't drink wine," Absinthe admitted. "Like you I'm not a big drinker, but mostly that stems from wanting to be alert all the time."

"You don't put your feet up, relax and have tons to drink?" There was the merest hint of amusement in her voice. Mostly she was serious.

He loved the look on her face when she gave him her full attention. He focused completely on her once he was certain the few couples already eating or waiting to be served weren't interested in them in the least.

"No, that wouldn't work for me. I do like to put my feet up though," he admitted. "I'm going to be very up-front with you." It was confession time. If he didn't say it straight up, she'd find out anyway. "I'm not good at this. I never know what to say and I come off stilted and awkward, but I don't want to be that way with you."

Her green eyes were hard to stay still under. She seemed to see right through his skull into his mind, where chaos reigned—thanks to her.

"I'm not so great at this either," she declared. "I guess we're going to have to learn. I'm very competitive and I have a fast learning curve. Very fast. Wait." She frowned at him. "You weren't reading a help book on dating, were you?"

"Do they have those in the library?"

Her lashes swept down and then back up. A small smile teased the curve of her mouth, causing his heart to accelerate. He found himself staring. Shit. He was going to lose before he got started because he couldn't stop staring at her.

She laughed. "I'm not telling you. I'll read them and turn into a scintillating conversationalist in minutes, leaving you in the dust."

He instantly learned three things. There were multiple self-help books on dating, she read extremely fast and she really was competitive. He flashed a small grin, looking at her with hawk-like eyes, giving her the predator look just for a moment. Just to the see the shiver that crept down her spine.

"I'll have to be there first thing in the morning before your shift."

"You know my shifts?" The smile faded, and she sounded uneasy.

He shrugged. "How was I going to ask you out? I went multiple times without seeing you, so clearly you had a shift and only came into the library during those times. I kept having to trade work with friends, and drive here from the coast, so, I found out when you worked. I came as often as I could, and just waited until we'd established a very tentative woman can charm the socks right off a shy man any day of the week."

"Is that what we established?"

Her laughter got him every time. He found himself actually relaxing. The waiter hovered, and both guiltily studied the menu. She ordered a pasta dish and he ordered a steak. Fresh-baked bread was put on the table, and he suddenly realized he was very hungry.

"I watched you right back," she admitted as she buttered a small piece of bread. "You're quite fascinating."

"I am?"

"The way you read. Even the books you choose. They're reference books on just about every subject. Three were language books. All on Hindi. Are you planning on going to India?"

He shook his head. "I like languages. I study the various ones to see how alike they are, and how different. There are at least seven hundred and twenty dialects spoken in India, but most speak one or more of the official twenty-two languages."

"Do you speak other languages?"

"Yes, I've studied them so much over the years, I've picked them up. Some more than others. You know how some people are good at mechanics? I've got a gift with languages. I can pick them up easily."

"How did you learn to read so fast?"

She really had been watching him. He liked that, although it could be dangerous.

"I started practicing when I was really young. I practiced every single day for hours. I have a gift there as well. I read and absorb very quickly now, and I never miss a day that I don't keep up the practice. I like books."

"That's so awesome that you started so young. I read this really cool article on the Internet about speed-reading and how to comprehend what you were reading at the same time," she explained. "It's funny that you speed-read too. I started practicing about seven years ago. It comes in handy when you want to learn about various subjects."

"That and YouTube."

She nodded. "Right? I've found help from a tremendous number of videos. I rent this little house out in the middle of nowhere and it's always falling apart. Repairs are my responsibility, so I just read or YouTube whatever I need."

She was so fucking perfect for him. She made him ache inside. It was a good kind of ache after a lifetime of nothing but bad.

"Tell me about this boy you work so much with. Tom. He seems like a nice kid. What's his story? You work with a lot of the kids, but he seems very special to you."

She shrugged and buttered another piece of warm bread. He liked that she didn't stint on the sweet, salted butter and worry too much about her figure. She had curves and he wanted her to keep them.

"He's a nice kid. He has a great mom. Single. She works all the time. She came in once to thank me for helping him and even brought me some cupcakes she'd made. They were delicious."

She flashed him a grin that said he'd missed out. His cock jerked hard at that mischievous grin. He could fall hard for her. He thought maybe he already had. Six weeks staring at her and she'd cast her spell.

"He was deaf the first few years of his life and then they operated on him, but he's had trouble hearing sounds correctly and so has been slow reading and identifying words. He fell behind and she can't help him because she works nights and isn't home with him."

Scarlet shrugged again but he had the feeling she wasn't as casual as she tried to sound. She was upset on the boy's behalf.

"He puts in the time, but he needs a tutor. I work with him after hours sometimes and he's catching up now. He's getting it."

He knew immediately she was tutoring him as well as working with him in the library. He didn't bother asking but knew she didn't get paid for it. She didn't want him to ask. He liked her all the more for it. He dipped his bread into oil and balsamic. "I'm glad the kid's picking it up and that he wants to learn. That's really what it takes, the desire."

"You know what I do—the library. What do you do?"

He made a point of sighing. "I was afraid you'd ask. It's very boring. I'm an attorney."

She stiffened. She tried not to, but she did. He could see she had a major aversion to anyone with his particular career choice. He thought perhaps that would gain him some points, but he just lost any advantage he might have had.

"Hate it. Don't work much. Looking for another career. Kind of fell into it because I like to debate but feel like criminals always get off and no justice is ever served. So I'm kind of a lousy attorney." He kept his voice low and pushed a little persuasion into it. Just the slightest bit to see the effect on her. She was different. He'd noticed that right away when he was with her in the library just observing her, and then later when he would ask for various books.

She was susceptible to his voice, and yet he could see

she could build a resistance fairly quickly to things, she reacted so fast. He wasn't going to let her find a way to stop his subtle influence on her until he had already managed to get her to fall completely under his spell. He intended to put everything he had into this war and win. She already admitted she had a fast learning curve. She had gifts, the same as he did, and they were strong in her, already developed. He had to be cautious. This was one war he was determined to win.

Scarlet visibly relaxed a little, taking a breath, studying her bread before she took another bite and washed it down with a sip of water. "What kind of lawyer are you?"

He shrugged. Now that was a very good question. He was whatever he had to be. In the days of specialization, Code's paperwork was invaluable. Absinthe's ability to devour law books and keep up with the latest on whatever was needed for Torpedo Ink was equally as valuable. "I'm kind of a jack-of-all-trades, the fill-out-papers, boring kind of work."

She relaxed even more. "Do you have your own practice?"

He nodded. "I get by. It's not my passion though."

"What is?"

He wanted to say he'd walked into the library and found it, but he knew that wasn't going to fly. "Books. Languages. The written word. Dead languages. History. Art. Martial arts from around the world. Legends. Weapons. Poetry." That was all true. He didn't bother to hide the enthusiasm because he actually felt it and that was who he was. If he wanted the real her, she had to want the real him.

A slow smile spread across her face. "You are an amazing man. I can't imagine you as a lawyer."

"Neither can I," he agreed. "I should have been a librarian, although I did volunteer in a library once. I read all the books and then had to quit." That was sort of true. He worked there, read as many of the books as possible, assassinated a member of the ministry and then returned to Sorbacov's hellhole. That had been in Russia. "Do you like the outdoors?"

She nodded and looked up as the waiter returned to place a salad in front of her and then one in front of Absinthe. The waiter stood a little too close to Scarlet and she shifted in her chair slightly, edging away from him. She waited until he was gone before she spoke.

"I actually prefer to be outdoors if the weather's good. Well," she hedged, "sometimes I find the most amazing places and take a book when it's storming just to be outside when it's raining. I love storms."

She was perfection. Who knew that it was possible to have a woman be perfection for him? He didn't think it was. He hadn't thought one was made for him. He could look at her all day. He knew he could because he had. He'd sat in the library and studied every single inch of her body. She was clothed, but often, her clothing was tight and moved with her body and he had mapped every curve, every valley, every sweet inch of her that he could.

"I really love storms as well. I particularly love to sit above the ocean and watch the storms move in while the waves rise up to meet the lightning. There's something very freeing in the wildness of it."

She regarded him over a forkful of romaine lettuce. "That's poetic, Aleksei. I haven't experienced that, but now I want to."

"What about motorcycles? How do you feel about them?"

Scarlet took a sip of her water and then smiled up at the water boy who rushed to fill her glass. It was already mostly full. Absinthe thought the boy just wanted an excuse to be closer to her. He couldn't blame the kid. Even the waiter was trying to find excuses to visit their table. He didn't have to like it though—and he didn't. The boy he didn't mind. She didn't either. The waiter was a different story. He actually seemed to brush his body up against Scarlet's when he got close to her. Absinthe had never been a jealous man, but then he'd never had a reason to be jealous. He wanted her attention centered on him, which was childish. He was a grown man and very confident. He didn't whisper "Go away" to either of the two servers, but he thought it.

"I take it you like motorcycles."

"You could say I'm passionate about motorcycles. I love the freedom of riding on them. The way the road opens up and you become part of the world around you. You can't get that in a car or truck. Even a convertible doesn't give you that same feeling of being part of the landscape and highway around you as you ride. You can see everything. The road stretches out in front of you and it's like the entire world is yours to see."

"You make riding motorcycles sound very different than I ever thought about them."

"What did you think about them?" He braced himself. Most people were very judgmental about motorcycles and the men and women who rode them. He was prepared for her poor opinion and knew he'd just have to work to change her mind.

She took off her glasses for a moment, blinking at him with her vivid green eyes. She had very long lashes, reddish-gold tipped with more gold. For some reason just looking at those lashes framing her large eyes made his cock come to life all over again. She had no idea what that meant when it was unheard of. The men of Torpedo Ink, his brothers, commanded their cocks. Women didn't do that. Nature didn't do that. The reality was, the ability had been beaten out of them so they could be trained to order their erections, to always be in complete control of every sexual response.

Until now. Until Scarlet Foley. The redheaded librarian complete with her black or purple or red square glasses framing her gorgeous eyes seemed to have taken command of his body. She was definitely his lady. His *literaturnaya ledi*, literary lady. He loved that she was as much into books as he was. That she loved the written word and she could read and comprehend what she was reading fast.

"I don't know exactly. I haven't been around motorcycles. I think I thought of them as death traps. One accident and bye-bye, brain." She pushed her salad away. She'd eaten most of it. "You don't like salad."

He looked down at his plate. "It's lettuce. Ruffled lettuce, but green all the same. Bugs thrive on this stuff."

She burst out laughing and that dark place inside of him that was so solid nothing could penetrate it cracked. It just cracked like an iceberg. The sound of her laughter was incredible. Low. Soft. Intriguing. The tones played over his skin like the dance of fingers. He felt the brush of the notes on his chest and down his spine, the stroke of them on his cock and balls like caresses whispering over him. He wanted to close his eyes, all the better to savor the sensation. He had to file it away to take out later, but he knew he would never forget it. She had given that to him, just as she'd given him the first natural erection he could remember.

"So, you're afraid of lettuce but not of motorcycles. I suppose, since you put your argument for riding motorcycles so eloquently, I'll have to concede it sounds pretty awesome, as long as you ride with a helmet."

"Babe, there's a law in this state that makes that mandatory."

The waiter arrived with their food, stepping very close to Scarlet so that when he bent to place her plate in front of her, his face was almost nuzzling her neck. She pulled her head immediately to the side, to get away from him, with a look of distaste. The move was almost reflexive.

"Step away," Absinthe commanded, his voice low, but there was no mistaking the threat. He "pushed" blatantly, although no one would know. Only the waiter would feel it—and the threat that was all too real. "She doesn't like you so close."

The waiter immediately complied. There were very few people who didn't comply when Absinthe used his voice at that level. It was rare and he was shocked that it came out so aggressively when the indiscretion had been a small one. There was silence as the man finished giving them their food. Once they were alone Absinthe reached across the table to gently cover her hand.

"I'm sorry, are you all right?" He removed his hand immediately before she could be the one to withdraw it. He wanted her to feel his touch, to be comforted, not offended by it.

"He just startled me, that's all. I don't like anyone I don't know coming so close to me. It's just a thing I have."

"It's not a bad thing to have, Scarlet. It's called self-preservation. You're a beautiful woman and men are going to find you very attractive. Most will just look. Others take advantage when they shouldn't."

"What do you do?"

"I ask you out and see if you're interested." He flashed a little self-deprecating grin. "I confess my worse sins, including not liking lettuce, and let you decide." He was a fucking liar and he was going to burn in the fires of hell, but she was worth it.

She flashed him a smile and pointed to his steak. "Eat up before it gets cold. Do you actually own a motorcycle? Is that what you ride all the way from Caspar to here on? Because it gets cold, you know."

It was his turn to laugh. They spent the next hour and a half talking and laughing together. He enjoyed every minute with her far more than he expected. He spent all of the time watching her every move, absorbing her as if he could just take her inside of him. It was interesting to be able to relax wholly in her company. He didn't know why he didn't worry about making mistakes with his voice, but he didn't. He just felt at peace, the chaos in his mind receding until it was gone completely.

After dinner, he walked her to her car and told her he had a great time and he'd see her in a couple of days. She didn't object or pull away when he brushed a light kiss across her forehead. Touching her skin was a mistake. Inhaling her scent was a mistake. Taking in her laughter and the poetry of her lyrics was even worse. It didn't matter. He'd done it and he'd do again. She was his addiction now and he would return again and again. He hoped she felt the same about him.

He walked the two blocks to the parking garage where he'd left his Harley. Parked on either side were two other motorcycles, and sitting on them were two familiar men. Both wore Torpedo Ink colors and they were grinning at him.

Maestro tossed Absinthe's vest to him. "You've been holding out on us."

He had been. Absinthe caught his vest and shrugged into it, his colors fitting over his body like a second skin. "How long have the two of you been following me?"

Maestro and Keys exchanged a long, amused look between them. "About two weeks now," Keys admitted. "We hung back, stayed up on the roof across from the library, just to make certain you were safe." He shook his head. "Even if she's yours, Absinthe, you know to be careful."

"*Especially* if she's yours," Maestro corrected.

Absinthe nodded and slung his leg over his bike. The moment he did, most of the chaos that had been returning in him settled. His bike. His colors. His brothers. His little redheaded librarian. "Yeah. What blows the most is I wasn't aware you were following me."

"We only had to stay close the first time. After that, we knew where you were going. You like books. You like to hang out in libraries. We weren't aware for the first week that the librarian was the big draw."

There was a questioning note in Maestro's voice. Absinthe nodded. "Yeah. She's mine. I don't have her yet. She's somewhat of a mystery and I'm taking my time with that." And enjoying it. He liked watching her. Uncovering her little secrets. Watching her with the teens that came in and the infinite patience she had with them.

She was attracted to him and shocked that she was. Shocked and a little embarrassed, yet at the same time, she wanted to go for it. He was certain she would have tried for a purely sexual relationship had he suggested it, but because he had asked her to dinner and kept it light, talking about himself and asking questions about her, pushing more for a relationship, she was confused and didn't know exactly what to do.

"Code look into her yet?" Keys asked cautiously.

"No. Tonight was the first real contact I've had with her," Absinthe said. "When I said I was taking it slow, I meant really slow. I would have lost had I gone too fast."

Maestro's head went up alertly. "You didn't use any influence?"

Absinthe shook his head. "No, of course not. If she comes to me, I want it to be because she wants me as much as I want her. Something's not quite right though. I did lift the fork she used tonight and got her prints. I also got a very good picture of her on my cell. Code should be able to give me the information I need if she needs protection, or if I do."

He sent them a brief grin, but he wasn't kidding. She had abilities. He was certain of it. He just didn't want to give Code the opportunity to find out about her yet. He wanted to take his time and uncover her himself, one layer at a time. He knew he was giving them the impression he was turning over the fork and picture to Code immediately, but he didn't intend to do it, not yet. He really did want to take his time with Scarlet.

"I'm just taking my time right now and enjoying myself." That was the best he could do, give them the truth of it. They seemed to understand, both nodding.

"Let's ride, gentlemen. It's getting late and we've got a distance to go," Keys said.

"She know you're in a club?" Maestro asked.

Absinthe should have known he wasn't going to get off that easily. He expected the question. "No. Not yet. I went into the library without my colors and kept it up. Didn't tell her tonight. I had a feeling . . ." He trailed off. Why hadn't he told her? He was Torpedo Ink. The club logo was inked into the skin of his back, but more importantly, he was part of his brothers and they were part of him. One didn't work without the other. It was that simple. It always would be.

"A feeling?" Maestro prompted.

Absinthe shrugged. "I just had a feeling I shouldn't. She's skittish, and I'm losing her. I'm reeling her in slow. Once I have her hooked, then I'll tell her. I just need to set that hook in good."

Maestro shook his head. "I hope to hell you know what you're doing, man."

Absinthe hoped so too.

TWO

"Who do we have watching outside?" Czar asked, indicating the door leading to the common room.

Savage was leaning casually against the inner door. He was a big man, with wide shoulders, narrow hips, a thick, muscular chest and glacier-cold eyes. He flicked a look at the president of Torpedo Ink. "Fatei," he answered, naming the prospect they all respected the most. Fatei hadn't attended the same school in Russia as they had, but he'd been in the next most difficult and he was a hardened, dangerous man.

Czar nodded and looked around the oval-shaped table. Including Czar, all eighteen of the original charter members of Torpedo Ink were seated for the meeting, along with Gavriil and Casimir, the two newer fully patched members. Both were Czar's birth brothers, and both had attended one or more of the four schools in Russia Sorbacov had set up to train children to become assassins for their country.

Czar believed in getting right down to business. "The Diamondbacks have reached out to us and asked us to help them with, and I'm a quoting, a 'small' problem they have. According to them, the Venomous club has been encroaching on their territory just this side of Sacramento. They bought a strip club there they knew the Diamondbacks were in negotiations for. This is the third club they've moved on in the last few months and stolen out from under them, meaning the Diamondbacks didn't offer enough money and gave the Venomous club the opportunity to take it. Again, according to the Diamondbacks, Venomous is running drugs, particularly heroin and cocaine, through these clubs. We know that the Diamondbacks have the territory and they aren't partial to sharing or to having any other club come in and start cutting up their territory."

"Interesting," Code said. "I get notifications any time Jeff Partridge's name shows up—he's president of Venomous—and he was in a photograph on a realtor's website in Fort Bragg. I just noted it and moved on. I'll have to go back and pay more attention. The fact that he was photographed with a realtor out of Fort Bragg means they could be looking to buy something in this area. If that's what he's doing, they'd be encroaching on Diamondback territory in this county as well."

Czar looked around the table, his gaze touching on Alena, one of the only two fully patched female members. "You need to be very careful of the relationship you have with Pierce, Alena. Always remember, he's a Diamondback. Just as you're fully loyal to Torpedo Ink, he's loyal to them. You always, always have to watch your back and protect your identity and your life at all times."

She nodded. "I'm aware."

"You're still doing it—looking for that adrenaline rush. Maybe all of us are. We lived so long in crisis, on the edge, we think we need that intensity of staying there, balancing right there on that edge, to feel like we're alive, but we have to find a way to stop. All of us do."

Absinthe looked down at his hands. Every member of

Torpedo Ink was so fucked up. They'd been that way since they were children. Czar had been made responsible for them at the age of ten years old. He'd been their parent, their instructor, their savior, all rolled into one. He was still that. He'd been a child raising other children in the worst possible environment, doing his best to keep them alive and keep them human. He was their moral compass back then, and was still leading them now.

"I'm aware, Czar," Alena admitted. "He's an addiction. A thrill." She sighed. "Okay, more than that to me, although I know better. And I know nothing can come of it. I'm ultra-careful. I promise. I never go near his other club members."

"Keep it that way. Don't let him lure you near them. And you never slip away from your guards. You understand me?"

"Ice has made that very, very clear, Czar," Alena said, indicating her older birth brother.

Absinthe glanced at Ice. Ice and Storm, Alena's twin brothers, watched over her even more closely than the other members of the club did. Ice's face was set in stone. He didn't like the relationship any more than the rest of them did.

Czar took Alena at her word. That was one thing about the club members—they didn't lie to one another. They had a code and they followed it to the letter. It was how they survived and how they lived. They were changing, trying to evolve, trying out a new way of living, but they kept to their original code. Anyone joining Torpedo Ink was expected to live by that same code, and if they betrayed it, the penalty was death. They had to live that way from the time they were children because they knew if they didn't, they wouldn't survive; they'd lost too many others to the other side.

"Essentially, the Diamondbacks want us to remove the managers of all three clubs permanently, both the night and day managers, and burn the clubs to the ground. Once Code establishes that Venomous did in fact encroach deliberately and are bringing in drugs, I have no problem with the request, although I don't want this done where there can be any blowback to us, so we plan carefully, and where we can't be seen by anyone," Czar continued.

That meant not wearing their colors or allowing the Diamondbacks to know when they were going in to fulfill the contract on the off chance—and in Absinthe's opinion it was a big one—that they were being set up.

"The fires are a different matter altogether. I want to know who owns the buildings. If there is insurance, and can we make certain no one else can get hurt? That's a pretty big order," Czar added. "We don't torch the building with anyone in it."

Alena dropped her hands into her lap, twisting her fingers together. Absinthe instantly covered her hands with one of his for comfort beneath the table. He didn't look at her.

Czar turned his attention to Code. "I want this researched very, very carefully. Take your time. If the Venomous club doesn't actually own the buildings, we don't take them down. We don't drag civilians into this. We can't afford to make a mistake."

"Diamondbacks could be setting us up," Steele, the vice president, commented. He always presented a good counterpoint and he was nearly always the calming influence. "All they need is good video of one of us and they think they'll have us in their pocket. A little blackmail and they think we'll do whatever they want."

"A little blackmail and we wipe them out one by one," Reaper corrected.

"True," Steele agreed, "and they'd never see it coming, or know where it's coming from, but the video would still be out there, and we all know how difficult it is to get that shit back. And they have no idea we'd react that way. They don't know us."

"I've got eyes on the Diamondbacks," Code said. "The moment Plank asked us to go after his wife and get her back and then he got a little weird on us . . ."

"Weird?" Keys asked.

"I stayed with them until they could get their own doctor, remember?" Steele reminded. "I think Plank would have liked to wipe us all out."

Reaper nodded. "He thought he'd set us up to get rid of us when we brought her back to him. He was leery then, still thinking we might have had something to do with her kidnapping in the first place. Pierce talked him out of it. Told him our club might be useful to him."

"Plank was still nervous," Steele said. "In the end, I think he just wanted us to fade away."

Czar shook his head. "We've added another chapter with twenty-five members. That's not fading away. And now there's the problem of Tawny."

There was a small silence. Absinthe shifted uncomfortably in his chair. Tawny had been one of the women who hung around the club, ready and willing to party all the time. She was up for anything, anytime, with any of them. She made it clear her goal was to be with all of them, including Czar, who made it equally clear he was off-limits.

It wasn't that they looked down on Tawny because she was so promiscuous. Hell, they partied hard when they wanted to. It was because Tawny had no loyalty at all. She lied to everyone and caused as much trouble as she could among other women who came to the parties. She tried to undermine friendships. She wanted to climb over the top of people, and if she was angry with anyone, she talked as much shit about them as possible—truth or lies, it didn't matter.

She had committed one too many sins, although they all had to take some responsibility in her last fiasco, but they were all relieved when she was told to leave. She'd gone straight to the Diamondbacks. All of them knew she would run her mouth about them, but she didn't really know anything about their club. It wouldn't stop her from making up stories though.

"So now we all know we have an enemy in the Diamond-back camp. Tawny has managed to become best friends with a woman by the name of Theresa," Code said. "Theresa just happens to be the old lady of one of the members, a man by the name of Terry Partridge. His road name is Judge. I think you all remember how Tawny can suddenly be best friends with someone if it benefits her."

"How do you find out all this stuff, Code?" Transporter asked.

"I monitor all correspondence between them. Tawny has a lot to say to Theresa, in particular about all of us. Now she has her sights set pretty high in the Diamondback club."

Czar looked around the table. "You should all remember Tawny and her scheming ways. She was hoping to be Reaper's old lady, and when that didn't pan out, I think Savage was her next target."

Savage lifted an eyebrow. "Yeah, she was all over me until I had her a couple of times and then she decided I wasn't the one for her." He shrugged. "Said she liked my kind of sex. I laid it out for her, spelled it out plain as day. She didn't like it after all."

"Your sex is extreme, Savage, even for someone like Tawny," Czar said. "I imagine you scared the shit out of her on purpose. You don't ever want anyone more than once anyway."

Savage didn't reply but he exchanged a look with Maestro that Absinthe couldn't interpret. Savage was brutal. And scary. And dangerous. Tawny shouldn't have tried lying to him. With a man like Savage, that was just plain stupid—especially when it came to sex.

Ice nudged Storm. "I'm pretty certain we were her favorites. She was all over us. We weren't rough."

"She was all over every single one of you and no doubt she's all over every one of the Diamondbacks," Czar said. "The point is, she's got the ear of one of Plank's close friends through his old lady."

Code nodded. He didn't look at Alena, but Absinthe did as Code continued. "Tawny has convinced Theresa, who in turn has convinced her husband, that Alena is not only using Pierce so she can spy on the Diamondbacks, but that her mission is to kill Plank. Supposedly, Alena wants to prove to Czar that she's every bit as good as one of the men in our club."

The fact that Code didn't look at Alena told Absinthe he'd already revealed the contents of the emails to her. He had her back. They all did. She and Lana were the only two female survivors of the school of horrors they'd grown up in, and all of them watched over them.

"Theresa has enlisted the aid of her husband in helping her get Pierce to see that Tawny is the one for him. She's whispering to all the club members how dangerous Alena is and how they need to watch out for her to protect their president," Code continued.

"And then they turn around and ask us to do their dirty work for them," Mechanic said. "What a crock of shit. It's probably a setup, just like Czar said. Or they're after Alena, trying to throw some heat her way."

"I am afraid of that," Czar admitted. "Have you been careful, Alena, when you're around Pierce? You haven't allowed him to see your gifts? Any of your abilities? You haven't told him about your childhood or how you were raised? The fact that you know more ways to kill him than he could ever have been taught with all his military training? Even hinted at it?"

"Of course I didn't allow him to see or suspect any of that," Alena snapped indignantly. "I'm no amateur, Czar, and I wouldn't get so wrapped up in him that I would forget who my loyalties belong with. He wanted to know what happened to Fred from the Venomous club on the last run we went to when the man keeled over at the table, but I told him I didn't know, that I had no idea why he died or how." She looked at Absinthe. "It's true. I don't know how you actually melt someone's brain any more than I know how I can burn the world down if I get pissed enough." Her tone suggested she was getting that pissed right then.

Absinthe shrugged. He rubbed his thumb along the top of her hand to soothe her. "We were all born with gifts. Probably everyone, everywhere, is. We needed ours and we worked until we could use them. Now we're stuck with them." He shrugged again, trying to make it all seem casual, trying to tell Alena he believed in her, that they all did.

Alena gave him a faint smile of appreciation and then turned her attention back to their president. "Don't worry, Czar. I follow protocol at all times. When I leave the safety of the clubhouse, I wear prints, and I never deviate from our scripts."

Czar nodded his approval. "Just know this is hanging over your head like a sword. Tawny is an enemy and she's capable of creating a force in that club against us and you in particular. She wants what you have. She wants to best you, Alena." He looked around the table. "She wants to best all of us. Once she gets Plank's ear, he'll likely grow even more uneasy than he already is."

"Pierce knows what I am," Ice confessed without one iota of remorse in his voice. His glacier-blue eyes met Czar's eyes across the table. "In Vegas. He came to see Alena. I didn't want him to think he could pull anything on her and get away with it. I let him see me. He knew I'd come after him and I'd kill him."

"He saw us that first time he met us when they came to talk about Plank's wife being taken," Reaper said. "It was in his eyes then. He knew what he was up against trying to protect his president. He might not realize Alena is every bit as lethal as we are, but if that's the case, he's more of an idiot than I've given him credit for."

"I think we should take the fucking job if Code says it's legit. Venomous club is becoming a pain in the ass," Transporter said.

Mechanic nodded his head. "I agree. I say we pull it off without letting the Diamondbacks see how we did it and they'll be all the more confused about us. Give them something to think about other than the gossip Tawny is spreading around about Alena."

"Vote on it then," Czar said.

Absinthe knew before he tapped his own yes on the table that they would go after the six managers of the clubs. One didn't invade another club's territory. It was against the code of every club, not just theirs.

Czar turned to Code. "The first part of the request is a go provided the information given to us is correct. The second is a go only if the Venomous club owns the buildings."

Code nodded. "I'll have that information to you along with everything I can get on the movements of our targets as soon as possible."

"Be thorough. If it takes extra time, I'd rather know we're not hitting at civilians," Czar reiterated. "If we decide it's a go, team one will take this one, both jobs. Alena, you'll need to make certain you're not seen at all anywhere near Sacramento. That goes for all of you. No bikes. No colors. We slip in and slip out. Mechanic, you'll disrupt all electrical systems anywhere near the clubs. Code, I'll need the blueprints and layouts, the latest you can get me. You know the drill. All information as quickly as possible. No possible trace as usual. We'll meet again as soon as Code gives us the information we need. At that time, we'll determine whether or not we'll do this job."

Czar led team one. Absinthe was on the first team with Reaper, Savage, Ice, Storm, Mechanic, Transporter and Alena. They had always worked together from the time they were very small children. Steele headed up team two with the rest of Torpedo Ink. Sometimes both teams worked a job, and others, they had to cross over, but for the most part, one team was on standby in case the other needed help.

"Second part of this business is the drugs," Czar continued. "We've got a line on the drugs moving into Sacramento through the Diamondbacks and now the Venomous club. Code uncovered a single pipeline both clubs are using that seems to originate from Mexico, but it isn't coming from there. He's been tracing that pipeline back to the source and, surprisingly, the drugs are coming in from Canada, not Mexico like it first appears."

"What does that mean?" Steele asked.

"Someone has deliberately made it seem as if the drugs have come in from Mexico," Code said. "But when I continued with the trace, the trail stopped dead. I had to go back and found a single thread, picked it up there and found the origins are in Canada."

Czar drummed his fingers on the table. "There's a possibility that the Ghosts are involved in this. There's one name that continues to come up. Louis Levasseur seems to be bringing in everything. Fentanyl, meth, heroin, cocaine. Code is looking into him. His name is new on our list so we don't have much on him."

"This is a huge job. I've asked my friend Cat to help out," Code said.

"We don't want to put an innocent in danger," Czar cautioned, frowning. "These people are extremely dangerous. They play for keeps and they're aware someone is looking for them."

"She's careful," Code said. "I told her not to take any chances, not to use her own equipment and to make absolutely certain her location can't be traced. She has orders to break off if they even start to trace her. She knows what she's doing."

"Any chance this man has anything to do with the Ghosts we've run into before? Didn't they have some origins in Canada?" Keys asked.

"They seem to be spreading their poison everywhere," Reaper said. His woman, Anya, had been targeted by the Ghosts.

"I have a bad feeling about the assassins the Ghosts are mixed up with," Absinthe said. He was reluctant to bring it up because his "feelings" hit on the mark every time now and Czar was aware of it. He didn't want another "gift" revealed. To him, those talents he'd developed as a child had become curses he couldn't shake, no matter how hard he tried. Still, they were in dangerous territory and his club needed all the advantages they could get.

Czar turned those piercing, assessing, all-seeing eyes of his on him. It felt a little as if the president of his club could get right through flesh and bone and see into one's soul. Absinthe didn't want anyone doing that, especially not the man he admired most in the world.

"What kind of 'feeling,' Absinthe?"

In spite of the fact that Czar probably knew whatever Absinthe was going to couch in terms of speculation, his voice was mild, simply an inquiry.

"We've talked about it before, but the assassins the Ghost club hire to intimidate the rival clubs by killing their women, the way the assassins work, is too reminiscent of the way we were trained. We've seen their work. We briefly considered that they might have been trained in the same schools as we were and then we dismissed it. I think we should consider it a very real possibility. We patched in twenty-five members of a club made up of members from a school Gavriil attended. He vouched for those men because he knew them. We got to know them, but just briefly. Now we've got another club, members of two schools made up of men who were trained just as we were. They want to be patched over like the others, to be part of our club."

Steele leaned in close, his eyes shrewd. "What are you saying?"

"We have to get to know those wanting to join. We're not just going to take them on faith. We have to invite them here, to our clubhouse. We've got to let them near our women. These men are trained assassins, just like us. They were trained in the schools in Russia, and like us, they have banded together. I believe that the assassins the Ghosts hire also are from these same schools, displaced children set free when Sorbacov was killed. I think the man running the largest pedophile ring we know of, the one we know only as the Russian, set them up here in the United States to do his work for him."

Once Absinthe had stated the possibility aloud, it made even more sense. There wasn't a lot any of those trained in Sorbacov's schools could do other than continue to kill. They didn't know any other way of life. Where could they go? There was so much blood on their hands. They'd started so young. Some had a taste for it, a liking. Others just didn't know how to stop. Some, like the members of Torpedo Ink, had no idea how to live in society. Absinthe figured those working for the Russian hiring out as assassins for the Ghosts and possibly others had a liking for killing.

"Keep going, Absinthe," Steele encouraged. "Sadly, I think you're making sense."

Czar nodded, steepling his fingers together, those penetrating eyes fixed on his face.

Absinthe kept his expression a mask. "What better way to penetrate our club? Send one or two to join the club patching over, and once accepted into the club—which they would be—hell, they're probably well-known to the others. They were in the school together. All they have to do is get information on us and our loved ones. They're assassins and they're coming after us. They're the ones who ride as the Ghosts when they want to convince another club they're legit."

He'd put it on the line. He'd been working it out for a while, the pieces of the puzzle moving around in his head, until he had them all locked into place. He could see the others catching up fast. Savage was already there, agreeing with him. Ice and Storm nodding. Maestro and Keys right there. Lana and Alena reluctantly agreeing, but not wanting to think that someone might infiltrate through a possible club. The rest of the members were just as fast once he presented the idea.

Something had nagged at the back of Absinthe's mind ever since they had first rescued Plank's wife, and it had finally come together as Czar was speaking. The president of the Diamondback's Sea Haven chapter had been grateful, but wary—and frankly, he had reason to be. Their club didn't add up. They seemed benign enough on the surface, but they had been able to do what the Diamondbacks hadn't. More than once they had caught the president in a tight squeeze. When Plank had first approached them in their bar, to tell them about his wife being kidnapped, he thought he had the upper hand, but they had him in a crossfire situation. Again, when they brought her back, they had too many weapons in their vehicles. He would have gone down in a blaze of gunfire no matter the protection he thought he had.

"I'm going to play devil's advocate here," Czar said. "The Russian had no way of knowing we make up Torpedo Ink. He wasn't aware of us, at all. Even when I assassinated Blythe's stepfather and he was part of that, all those years ago, he had no inkling that I would ever cross paths with him again. In order for him to put someone into a chapter asking to be patched into Torpedo Ink specifically, the Russian would have had to know about us. He would have had to know we were from Sorbacov's school and that we were a threat to him."

"You're absolutely right," Absinthe agreed. "He had no way of knowing that. This group of assassins for hire, what do they call themselves, Code?"

"According to their offices in San Francisco—and they do have offices in a very upscale office building right in downtown San Francisco—they are called Sword Security. Nice little graphic. They don't solicit business, nor do they take it from just anyone. You have to be recommended to them, and they don't come cheap."

"So, we have Sword Security set up in San Francisco and who knows where else. I'm guessing more than one place, am I correct?" Absinthe asked.

Code nodded. "Three cities, and they travel as well. I'm looking into them to try to find out how many they have on their payroll."

"The Russian runs them. They're his assassins. He took the reins when Sorbacov and his son died. These men wanted someone to tell them what to do and they needed the work and the money. They banded together, just the way the others did from Gavriil's school, the ones that we patched over from Trinity County into Torpedo Ink," Absinthe continued. "Sorbacov died, all of us were free and most of us had no idea what to do."

"That still doesn't mean the Russian would know enough to send one of his assassins undercover into a club just on the off chance that we had formed a club," Czar said.

"He most likely didn't," Absinthe said. "He had his assassins working for the Ghosts, remember? They were pretending to be a club, getting in with other clubs, getting information, riding with them, trying to find the gamblers. The Russian would be smart enough to stick a couple of his men in with those clubs whose members they already knew. They could get the information so much easier. Go on runs with them, no one would suspect anything. If they had to kill, they were in a perfect position with plenty of cover."

That much was true, and they all knew it.

"Once the Russian suspected he was dealing with us," Absinthe continued, "if he had his men already in place, he could easily get word to his assassins to start pushing for their club to follow in the footsteps of the Trinity one to patch over to Torpedo Ink."

"You put this all together when?" Czar asked.

"I've had this nagging feeling in my gut ever since the hit went out on Ice's old lady. It didn't make sense to me the way everything was so connected," Absinthe admitted. "I couldn't put things together, not until now. They just sort of clicked into place. That's how it works with me."

"It isn't like we can ignore whenever something clicks into place for you as much as we'd like to," Czar said. "You've never been wrong." He drummed his fingers on the tabletop. "Damn it. The Russian knows we're his enemy. He isn't likely to try to recruit us. He's very familiar with all of us. He had to be part of the school we were in, whether as one of the instructors—and he would have been one of the younger ones—or one of the students, and he would have been one of the older ones we thought had been killed."

"I'm sorry, Czar." Absinthe meant it. He didn't like the pieces of a puzzle to snap into place late and put his club behind. "I should have figured this one out sooner."

"I'm always amazed when you put things together, Absinthe. This was barely a thread to follow. I had my first hint of the Russian when I was ordered to take out Blythe's stepfather. Her stepfather was a pedophile. At the time, all the information on him was correct and he deserved to die. What I didn't know then, but since have learned, was her stepfather was part of a major pedophile ring and he'd crossed the Russian and the orders had come from him through Sorbacov. That was quite a few years ago and I've never even considered that he was behind these men."

"Shit." Ice shook his head. "He knows us. He knows every one of us."

"That's not true," Steele, always the voice of reason, disagreed. "He may think he has the advantage because he thinks he knows us, but we survived by sticking together. By becoming one person, a machine. A killing machine, if you will. We wove ourselves together and he can't know that's how we function. He can't know we took our psychic gifts, talents other people may have but ignore, and we practiced until we could do things no one would believe. He doesn't know us as adults. Or that we still train every day to be faster and more skilled at the things we were taught and that we deliberately learned even more once we were outside the walls of that hellhole."

"Steele's right," Czar agreed. "Even if he was one of us, and at one time received the same training, we never revealed to anyone but those of us right here in this room what we could do. Alena would share food with us telepathically, and suddenly all of us knew what cinnamon was and what it smelled and tasted like. Our bellies felt full even though we hadn't eaten. The crap they gave us to eat, she made taste good. No one else knew about that. Only we knew. No one else but those of us in this room knows that we crawled through the vents and assassinated those raping us. The Russian, whoever he is, can't know who we are, and he's afraid of us. We're not afraid of him. We're patient. We'll find him. We always find the ones we're looking for, no matter how long it takes us."

Czar looked around the table and they all nodded, in complete agreement, because it was the truth. They had learned patience in a hard school, and they took their time. Their two newest members, Czar's birth brothers and men trained as assassins in the other Sorbacov schools, had learned that same patience and had the ability to take their time to strike at enemies. They knew loyalty and called each of them brother or sister.

"It will be easy enough to contact the president of both chapters and find out who the newest members are. If there are any prospects. They'll obviously know them, because they will have gone to the same school, and they'll trust them," Absinthe said.

"But we'll have to be discreet about it," Steele pointed out. "These men are like us. We can't ever forget we're dealing with trained opponents. The slightest hint that we're onto them and they'll be in the wind."

"Can Code and his computers uncover that kind of information?" Ice asked, looking at Code.

Code shrugged. "I can. I just have a slight problem at the

moment because I've had my computers searching in so
many directions that they're on overload. I'm in the process
of building a couple more but need a day or two to get all
this going."

"I'll take this off your hands." Czar made the decision.
"I can come up with a plausible reason to get names and
how long they've been with the chapters. We've got a run
coming up in a few weeks. It won't be that difficult, especially if we're throwing a party here as well."

"Do we have any other business to discuss?" Ice asked.

Before Absinthe could make up his mind whether or not
to bring up his librarian, Czar stood up, looking a little sheep-
ish, something completely foreign to him. "I have a request.
This came from Blythe—the two of us. I'm in agreement."
He paused.

Absinthe kept a straight face, but Ice looked at Storm
and the two of them got some of the others around the table
grinning. Czar stared them down. When they were all so-
ber, he took a drink and set the glass carefully on the table.

"Our newest adopted boy, Jimmy, is having a difficult
time adjusting. He's lived his life in a cage, and you all
know what that's like. The world is too a big a place for
him. Even the bedrooms. We've kept visitors to a minimum
in the hopes that sheltering him for a while would give him
a chance to get used to us and the household. The other
children help, but he's fearful and doesn't believe he's safe,"
Czar admitted. "He won't really talk about his experiences
with us yet, and I don't blame him. He can't possibly trust
that he's safe this fast."

"What do you want us to do?" Lana asked.

Czar looked around the table. "The kids need a few lessons in survival training. They need to get out of the house
and have a little fun, but still learn. It's part of their home-
schooling. Blythe was hoping some of you would volunteer.
She doesn't want Steele or me to teach them. It has to be a
few of you. Volunteering is good. It prevents me from giv-

ing out orders. Jimmy has been around both of us, but Blythe thinks if you come around and the other children treat you like aunts and uncles, without fear, and are having fun with you and doing something that might make him feel safer, it might bring him a little more out of his shell."

"That's a little unorthodox," Preacher said. "Especially for Blythe to think up."

Czar drummed his fingers on the table. "He has to feel safe and proactive. Once we felt we could fight back, once we felt we had a little control, we were better. All of us. He's just a little kid and curls up in a ball at night in a closet. I can't reach him. Blythe can't reach him. Even Kenny and Darby aren't getting anywhere, and they've tried. He's so scared."

"But survival training?" Maestro echoed. "Blythe is really okay with that?"

"It worked for us," Reaper pointed out.

"Think of it this way," Absinthe said. "The kids are part of this club whether they're here at the clubhouse or not. When we're threatened, they are. If we ever have to pick up and move, they do. They have to follow the code of the club, just as we do. They need to know how to survive in any situation. I don't want them hurt the way we were, but they should know what to do if someone attacks them."

"That makes sense," Gavriil said. "Just know whoever is teaching that class is going to have to contend with that little devil, my brother Maxim's son, Benito. He's a mini Maxim, a little assassin in training."

"Is that a bad thing?" Savage asked.

They all looked at one another, clearly puzzled.

"It is when he's a bloodthirsty boy bent on revenge and Airiana, my sister-in-law, and Blythe are watching his every move—and ours. He'll try your patience to no end," Gavriil said.

"You and Casimir are the newest members," Preacher pointed out. "You should volunteer and take this project on."

"They nixed us," Casimir said complacently. "Some little complaint about Gavriil pulling Benito through the window by his hair and putting a knife to his throat. Airiana wasn't very happy with him. I don't think she's fully forgiven him. The woman holds a grudge and she's our sister-in-law."

Laughter went around the table and when they sobered, Transporter shook his head and nodded at Gavriil. "Got to hand it to you. You don't talk much, but you've got a way with women."

Another round of laughter went around the table. Gavriil shrugged, not in the least disturbed by the assessment.

Absinthe looked around. "Czar laid it on the table. All joking aside, Blythe really wants this, and we have to give it to her. She doesn't ask us often. That means we have to be serious about it and come up with a plan. We need to know what we're going to teach them. How much time it's going to take. That kind of thing. I'm willing to plan it all out, but there are a lot of kids and they're different ages. I'll need help with the actual instructing."

Czar shot him a grateful look. For Absinthe, it was all about Blythe. She had put up with all of them almost from the moment she met them—and they hadn't been easy on her. Not even Alena and Lana.

"Absinthe, sadly, is right," Lana agreed. "We're going to have to deal with those little monsters. *All* of us." She looked around the table. "You're not leaving them to us because Alena and I are women. Every single one of you can help. Absinthe, when you're making up the lesson plans, factor that in. Give everyone a role."

Groans accompanied nods, but no one was going to turn down a Blythe request.

"Put it to a vote?" Steele asked.

"We don't have to vote," Preacher said, "but if you want it official . . ."

Survival training passed immediately.

Ice looked around the table. "Any other business?"

Absinthe waited, but when no one spoke, he nodded his head. "I found my woman," he announced. He kept his voice low, matter-of-fact. He was always careful when he talked. He'd learned never to use his voice on his brothers. It wasn't always easy to stop himself, especially if something was really important to him like this. Like his little librarian.

Czar's head went up alertly, as did Steele's. Czar was back to using his razor-sharp, piercing eyes. He turned them on Absinthe. "When?"

"About six weeks ago. I went to a library in Sonoma for a little downtime and she was working there. It took me all of about two minutes of looking at her before my body reacted to her. I knew then but refused to believe it." He couldn't help but smile. "She likes books. She likes the same things I like. I just watched her for a while. She's good with kids, teens especially. She helps them with their homework, and I can see she really cares. She's got this bright red hair. And I mean fire-engine red."

"Temper to go with it?" Keys asked with a small grin.

"Probably," Absinthe admitted, his gaze lifting to Keys just for a moment, amusement creeping into his mind. Yeah, he was pretty certain Scarlet had a temper. "I haven't tested that yet. I asked her to dinner the other night and wasn't stupid enough to push her beyond that, although the waiter pissed me off. He made a play for her right in front of me."

"You weren't wearing your colors," Czar said. "If you were wearing your colors no one would have made a play for your woman. That would have been a big red flag."

There was a silence and several of his brothers straightened in their chairs. Mechanic and Transporter shifted closer to him as if they were ready to protect him.

Absinthe shrugged, careful not to look at Czar's piercing eyes. "I was playing the lawyer. Wanted her to think that was what she was getting."

"Why?" Storm asked. "That's not you."

"That's a part of me. One side of me. The thing is, she . . ." What could he say to make them understand? He rubbed his temples. The slow throbbing had gone from annoying to painful.

"I told you I get feelings sometimes, and I did while riding up to the library. I removed my colors because I knew something momentous was about to happen. It didn't feel like a threat, and I always follow my gut instincts. I was right this time."

He looked around the table. These were his brothers and sisters. He'd fight and die for them. They were his family. His world. He hated telling them the truth.

"All of us in this room have demons. We can't escape them. We all know that. Unfortunately, I have all your demons in my head along with my own. I have the demons of every man or woman I've had to question or kill in my head. I have the demons of the ones we couldn't save. They don't leave me or let up. They just are stuck there, driving me insane."

He couldn't look at them as he made the confession because he knew he was hurting them. It wasn't his intention, but he had to make them see that Scarlet was as necessary to him as Blythe was to Czar or Anya was to Reaper.

"Sometimes, when one of you is having a particularly difficult time and you're trying to deal with it, my brain feels like it's being shredded. I can't make that stop, no matter how hard I try. So, when it's particularly bad, I go to a library alone. I sit there surrounded by books and the people who read them. I sit in that silence and there's a semblance of peace."

There was complete silence in the room, almost as if everyone held their breath. Absinthe finally forced himself to meet Czar's gaze, the man he looked up to. That hurt, right in the gut like a hard punch.

"The times you thought I was using my voice on a member of our club, or on Blythe, it was to end the argument because I thought my brain was going to start bleeding from all the demons shrieking. It wasn't to get my way. It was to stop what was going on in my head."

"Absinthe." Alena whispered his name, her voice so filled with compassion, he could hear tears. Feel them on his skin. Feel them pounding like rain in his brain.

Lana put her hand on his arm, something she rarely did. "Honey, you should have told us. We could have tried to shield you more."

"This woman, the librarian, does she shield you? When you're close to her, does she quiet your mind?" Czar asked.

Absinthe frowned. "Not at first. She's different though. Her brain is different. When I touched her, I could tell immediately that she was different. She would hand me a book and I made certain our fingers would brush against one another. She moved away immediately, but I work at a very high level and far too quickly. The very first time I touched her, I connected and forged a path between us."

He shook his head. "I've never run across a brain like hers. She's very gifted. She works on an entirely different path. She switches gears fast and like I said, the learning curve is amazing. I think her brain adjusts for her without her even recognizing what's happening most of the time. The more we were together, the quieter my mind became until finally it was still. I took her to dinner, and it was still. Completely, utterly at peace."

Again, there was silence. Czar looked tired, and Absinthe hated that he was the one to put those deep lines in his face. Czar had done more for all of them than they could ever repay. He'd never asked for anything in return, not of significance. Absinthe rubbed the bridge of his nose again, but before he could speak, Czar did.

"You should have told me, Absinthe. You should have told all of us. I can't imagine what you've gone through all this time." Czar shook his head. Pushed back his chair and then hit the table with his fist. "Damn it. What I put you through forcing you to question so many of our enemies. Those fucking pedophiles in the school."

"I had already been touched by them and knew what they were and how they thought, Czar. I did my part the same as everyone here and I was glad to do it. I'll always do my part. My demons aren't any worse than anyone else's in this room. We have them, we all carry them, and we deal." He tried to be as matter-of-fact as possible. "The way I deal is through my books. I like the feel of a library. Now, it's led me to Scarlet. I want to take my time with her, let her get to know me, hopefully bring her in slowly. I want to be her choice."

He was asking his club to back off a little bit and give him room to maneuver. He mostly didn't want to risk any of them. Scarlet Foley was a puzzle and he needed more pieces before he exposed any of his brothers or sisters to any danger she might bring. He knew they wouldn't agree, but he was determined to find out any truths about her on his own, hopefully without using his gifts.

"Anything else then?" Ice asked. He looked around the table. "We're good then. This meeting is officially over."

THREE

Aleksei hadn't come back to the library for three days. Scarlet tried not to be upset or disappointed. She had to view it as a good thing. She had no business dreaming about being with a man, any man, let alone one like Aleksei. He was dangerous. She knew it the moment she'd touched him. That had been deliberate. She couldn't help herself. He'd walked into the library and her entire world had changed.

She had sex with men because it was necessary. She needed certain skills and she had to pay her dues. She accepted that she had few choices and she used her body to get the abilities that were absolutely crucial to carry out her plan. She had devised that scheme step by step. It had taken those first three years of her life in prison to plan.

She had consulted some very risky people and paid very high prices to do so, but in the end, those risks had paid off. Each person had given her names and places she needed to go to train, and those instructors were the best. Her preparation had taken another five years of brutally physical nine- and ten-hour days, seven days a week, but she'd survived, and she'd learned. She'd become very, very good at what she needed to be.

She was lucky she had a fast learning curve. She'd told Aleksei the strict truth. Her brain just worked that way. She'd trained herself to be fast at reading and comprehending what she read. She loved books and she needed information, so it was easy enough to get it from books. She listened to conversations and she remembered every word, almost verbatim, and that added to the wealth of information she accumulated. She learned to be careful. To be quiet and stealthy. Most men looked at her and never saw beyond what she wanted them to see. She had a body and she used it to her advantage, dressing in clothes that showed her figure but made her look as if she couldn't possibly move if she had to. No one ever seemed to suspect that a woman could wear clothing that was tight and yet concealed a multitude of weapons.

Aleksei had seen through her disguise almost immediately. She had no idea how she knew that, but she did. She had touched him and connected. Her body had immediately responded to his as if the chemistry between them had been designed just for that purpose. She'd never reacted to anyone no matter how hard they'd tried to get her to. She'd faked orgasms. She'd gotten really good at it, but she'd never had a real one. She'd gotten close just sitting at her desk there in the library staring at him. Fantasizing. That was a first for her.

He was a beautiful man. Really. He had broad shoulders and a really good physique. She'd been around a good many men who were all muscle and knew when a man was totally ripped even when totally dressed. Aleksei was. She knew dangerous, and Aleksei was beyond anything she'd encountered in that realm, although he always looked so casual, and that was what tipped her off. She'd been around dangerous, good-looking men before and not one of them had made her fantasize. He was in a league all his own.

Aleksei was also the real deal when it came to intelligence. Just the one little touch, that first time, had confirmed that his brain worked as fast as she saw him reading. Maybe she got off on what amounted to a brainiac. She paid attention to the books he was interested in—and his interests were very diversified. He had shocked her when he said he was a lawyer. She had a pretty good bullshit meter and he wasn't lying to her.

She was twenty-seven years old and thought any life she had ever wanted for herself wasn't a possibility. Not a single day. Not a single night. She didn't feel sorry for herself. She had made her choices every step of the way and she hadn't regretted a single one.

Scarlet was a deliberate thinker. She didn't make rash decisions. Her mind worked quickly, much like a computer, but she definitely thought things over before she made her choices. Still, it had been over a year since she'd heard anything, even a rumor that she was hunted. Maybe she had a chance to have a normal life. She might not deserve it, but Aleksei made her want one for the first time.

Why hadn't he come back to the library after their dinner? She thought they'd had a great time. She'd been careful. Guarded. She drummed the eraser side of a pencil on her desk, something she never did anymore. She had long since conquered every nervous habit she'd ever had, including fidgeting. The person she'd become on the outside wasn't always the one she was on the inside. There was the one of sheer steel and then there was the woman inside, hiding, rolled up in a little ball, afraid to ever show herself again. But she had for a brief evening. One time. To Aleksei. She'd let her out, and now that woman wanted out again. She wanted freedom—with him.

Part of her wished he'd never come into the library. She would have remained asleep, like whichever princess in the fairy tale she could never remember—or she'd blocked out. She'd read them all to her sister. Every single one of the stories. She pushed the memory away before sorrow swamped her. She couldn't go there. She'd drown.

"Ms. Foley?"

She smiled at Joan Miller. A sixteen-year-old girl who really could be mean as hell when she wanted to be or sweet as sugar when she needed something. Of course, she was never mean to Ms. Foley because, in spite of her age, Joan had already learned to read people and she'd marked Scarlet as someone to respect.

The door opened and a woman came into the library, catching her attention. She always looked. She had to. That was how she stayed alive. The woman was a stranger; she'd never been in the library before, at least not on Scarlet's shift, and she was generally the one who worked the most hours.

This woman was beautiful. Unique. Unlike a single person who had ever entered. She was elegant, with sleek, black hair, shiny as a raven's wing, just kissing her shoulders. She wore skinny jeans tucked into boots. Not just any boots, but boots that had to cost a good five hundred or up. They were leather, butter soft, and just as elegant as the woman, with several inches of heels, a tan color that matched her tight tank. The top stretched over generous breasts and emphasized a smaller waist and then showed off flared hips. Scarlet managed to catch all that in a single glance.

"Yes, Joan?" She kept her voice strictly neutral. The last thing she wanted to do was deal with a snippy child who could play mean girl in a heartbeat to some young girl in school.

Joan looked at her face for a moment, shrugged and turned away. "Never mind. It's no big deal."

Instantly, alarm skittered down Scarlet's spine. Something in that offhand tone set off her radar. "Joan, look at me." She poured enough authority into her voice that the girl turned in spite of the stiffness in her shoulders and back.

"Sometimes, even adults have bad days, and they screw

up. I apologize. I was having a private pity party and wasn't listening properly. Let's start over, please. I really would like to hear what you have to say."

Joan shook her head but remained standing in front of the desk. For the first time since Scarlet had known her—which was about eighteen months—the teen looked uncertain and on the verge of tears. She really was upset. Scarlet rose and moved around the desk to circle the teen with one arm and shield her as best she could from any others in the library. There weren't that many up close to her desk, but still, no teenage girl wanted to be seen crying, especially one like Joan.

"Let's go over to that table. It's far more private." It was in the shadow of two of the tallest stacks, where she could shelter the girl even more. "Sit down, Joan, and tell me what's going on."

"Are you sure you have time?" Joan sounded reluctant now that she had Scarlet's full attention, but she did pull out a chair and drop into the seat.

Scarlet took the chair beside her, caging her in and, at the same time, shielding her body from any onlookers. From her position she could see out the window as well as the door, making certain everyone was safe.

"I have all the time in the world, Joan. Tell me what's going on." Scarlet kept her voice low and persuasive. She rarely tried to use her voice to influence the teenagers, other than to have them lower their voices and be respectful of the library and one another, but there was something about the way Joan was barely holding herself together that alarmed her.

Joan shook her head again, as if she would refuse, but Scarlet's velvet-soft voice had slipped into her mind and already was pushing her to do as she was asked. "I want you to tell my brother none of this was his fault. He'll blame himself. He always does, but I wanted him to go on the trip with Mom. I did. He shouldn't miss out because I'm never good enough."

Scarlet's stomach knotted. She sent up a silent prayer to the universe. *Let me be wrong about her intentions.* But she knew she wasn't. Very gently, she put her hand on Joan's arm as if she could hold her there. "Tell me where your brother is right now, Joan. Where's Luke?" Luke was older by a year and, as a rule, he generally was hovering close to Joan, daring anyone to get ugly with her. The siblings were close, and it was rare to see one without the other.

"On another trip with Mom. As usual she said I didn't meet her requirements and couldn't go. This one was to Argentina. I've always wanted to go there, and she knew it. I did everything she asked of me. I studied, got the grades. I didn't talk to anyone she told me was beneath us even though it sucked, and everyone hates me because they think I'm like she is."

Scarlet knew she was in a minefield and she had to be very careful as she negotiated her way through it. "Who is at home with you?" Joan's father wasn't in the picture and hadn't been for so long no one ever spoke of him.

Joan shrugged carelessly. "I'm on my own."

That was Scarlet's greatest fear. Two teenage boys came in, both punching at each other, but stopped abruptly when they saw her eyes on them. They skidded to a halt, mouths dropping open when they caught sight of the woman who had walked in just as Scarlet was taking Joan to the private table in the corner. She couldn't blame them. The woman was looking through the books in the reference area on Egyptian pyramids. That, for some reason, sent a warning chill down her spine. It just happened to be the same reference books that Aleksei had been interested in. No one else had looked at those books in the entire time she'd worked there. What were the chances? A coincidence? She wasn't buying it.

"How long is your mother going to be gone this time, Joan?" Scarlet asked. She kept the boys in her line of vision and tried to keep the newcomer in sight as well while giving Joan the impression that her entire attention was on her. She had to keep her voice pitched low and tuned to Joan's exact energy path in order to keep the teenager compelled to answer her.

"Another few days."

Scarlet continued to look at her. Joan sighed. "Another two weeks. She's always gone, you know that. She never stays with us."

"Is Alison there?" Alison was the housekeeper. As far as Scarlet knew, Alison was the one generally looking after Luke and Joan.

"Mom fired her."

"Why in the world would Brenda fire Alison?" That shocked Scarlet, and few things shocked her. Luke and Joan came into the library almost daily, and sometimes Alison came with them. Never Brenda, their mother. For quite a while she had thought Alison was their mother.

"Luke made a mistake. He can't love anyone as much as he loves Mom. He was angry with her and he told her that she might as well just not come home at all. Sign papers and give us to Alison. We'd tell the judge we wanted to live with her. The moment he said it, we knew it was a mistake. We both love Alison and the way he said it, Mom could tell. She all but attacked Alison. I think if Luke hadn't interfered, Mom would have really hurt her. She fired her and made Alison leave right then." There was a sob in her voice. Tears glistened in her eyes, but Joan didn't shed them. She dashed them away and looked determined. Defiant. Petrified.

Again, Scarlet had a very bad feeling. Joan was afraid and she'd made up her mind that she wasn't going to be alive when her brother got back from Argentina.

"Joan, you really want to tell me what you're so afraid of." Scarlet lowered her voice even more, whispering directly into the girl's ear. She had worked and worked on this skill. Practiced hours and hours to use exactly the right tone.

She didn't always succeed, but quite a lot of the time, she could be persuasive, and right then, she knew she needed to be. If she wasn't, if she blew it, she might lose this girl.

Joan went white. She shook her head over and over. Tears trickled down her face. She looked down at her hands and then finally leaned close to Scarlet. "She lets him come when she's not home. She tells him I'll be alone. He gives her money so she can pretend we're rich and she can go on trips." Her hands trembled and she pressed them both over her lips as if she was telling a secret that should never have been said aloud.

Joan's revelation was the last thing Scarlet expected her to say, but she should have read the signs. She was certain Joan was considering committing suicide, but the idea that her mother was selling her daughter to a man so she could have money never occurred to her. Scarlet moistened her lips and took a steadying breath before saying a word. This was far too important to make mistakes.

"Is he coming tonight, Joan?"

Joan nodded. "He comes every night she's away."

Scarlet had excellent hearing, but she had to strain to catch that soft whisper. "You need to tell me his name, baby, and then let me handle it. You're going to spend the night with Alison. I'm texting her to come get you." She matched her actions to her words. "You'll be safe. You don't have to tell her what's going on if you don't want to, but you'll never have to see that man again."

"You can't talk to him, Scarlet. He's evil. He'll hurt you." A shudder went through her.

"You really want to tell me his name, Joan. You've wanted to tell someone for a very long time." That was safe. She was certain Joan had.

Joan was nodding, even as tears ran down her face. The door to the library opened, but Scarlet didn't dare look away from Joan. She kept her eyes on her, compelling her to answer.

Joan rocked back and forth. "Giles McCarthy."

She mouthed the name rather than even whisper it, but Scarlet was leaning close and watching her lips, careful not to miss what she was certain would only come once. She sat back, a little shocked. Giles McCarthy was perhaps one of the wealthiest and best-known philanthropists in their town. He gave to every charity and was always the first to be in front of a microphone endorsing a new youth project. He was considered a wonderful man. Everyone liked him. He was single, an eligible bachelor, and often dated some of the most beautiful women in town.

Scarlet didn't make the mistake of asking Joan to repeat the name or act in any way as if she didn't believe her. She knew if Joan went to the police and accused the man, no one would ever take her word over McCarthy's. Joan knew it too. So did Brenda, Joan's mother. She could take whatever sum he was paying her and continue her lifestyle while her daughter paid the price. Brenda wasn't the only single mother with a teenage daughter he was reputed to be "friends" with.

"All right, honey. Thank you for telling me. Alison will be here in a few minutes. You're going home, packing a bag and staying with her. What time do you usually expect him to visit you when you're alone?"

"He comes at eight," Joan whispered. "Always at eight. If I'm not there, he'll be angry, and he won't give Mom the money she wants. It's a lot of money."

"Never mind about that," Scarlet soothed. "You aren't going to think about that anymore. You're going to have a good time with Alison while your mom and Luke are away. I want you to repeat that to me."

"I'm going to have a good time with Alison while Mom and Luke are away," Joan said softly, with a little more confidence.

The door to the library opened again, and Scarlet flicked a glance toward it. To her utter relief, Alison hurried in and came straight toward the table. Joan nearly flung herself into Alison's arms, her face lighting up, although she was crying at the same time. Scarlet stood up as well.

"Joan's mother is out of town and she would like to spend a couple of weeks with you, Alison," Scarlet said. "I'm certain that would be all right with you." She pitched her voice low, but immediately she could see she hadn't connected with a path to Alison.

Joan had already scooted around both women and rushed to get her backpack and coat from the front desk where she'd left both items, leaving Scarlet and Alison for just a few precious moments. Alison shook her head in protest.

"I can't take her. If I do, Brenda will have me arrested."

"She can't stay there alone," Scarlet said hastily. "Please, take her. I'll make certain her mother won't do that. I swear to you. She's in danger staying by herself. I believe she'll harm herself if she's alone."

Immediately Alison's expression changed. She glanced at Joan, and Scarlet could see the indecision on her face. "I've been afraid for her," she admitted. Abruptly, she nodded her head. "Brenda will come after me," she warned.

"I won't let you down," Scarlet promised, looking the woman in the eye. It was the only way she could give her word and hope Alison took her at it. "Take her out of here before she changes her mind."

Alison nodded a second time, caught her hand, squeezed it and hurried to intercept Joan before she reached Scarlet. She put her arm around the teen's shoulders, and they hastened out of the library together. Scarlet was grateful to see that Joan was smiling. She glanced down at her watch. There was still an hour until closing time. She had quite a few things to set into motion. She hastily sent out a text of her own. She needed a car and an alibi. An unbreakable one. Only then did she feel she could actually take a breath and look around the library.

The gorgeous woman was still there, and she wasn't alone. Aleksei was standing face-to-face with her, shaking his head. They looked almost as if they were arguing, but if they were, they weren't speaking aloud. She looked at their hands to see if they were using sign language. There wasn't a doubt in her mind that they knew each other, and he wasn't the least bit happy to see the beautiful woman.

As if he was connected to her, Aleksei looked up and instantly smiled at Scarlet. The moment he did, everything feminine in her reacted to that smile. She felt her insides melt. He was standing very close to a gorgeous woman and it was very clear they knew each other—not only knew each other, but had some sort of relationship—and Scarlet still wanted to just fall at his feet and worship him. It was pathetic.

The fact that he would look at her, his face lighting up the way it did, those eyes of his so completely focusing on her as if he didn't see anyone else, thrilled her. And there was that smile, one she knew was rare because she'd watched him, studied him for over six weeks now, and he just didn't give those smiles to everyone, making her feel like the only woman in his sight, even though he was standing beside the most stunning woman she'd ever seen.

She found herself smiling back. He took that as an invitation and came right to her, even though she did her brisk librarian walk that usually discouraged men from approaching her. She was ramrod straight, her glasses on her nose, as she strode toward her destination. Aleksei fell into step beside her.

"Is everything all right, Scarlet? It looked very intense with that young lady, so I waited to say hello until you were finished talking with her."

His voice, that low tone, the way it played over her skin as if he were physically touching her, brushing her with his fingers when he spoke, sent a shiver of absolute awareness down her spine. She'd forgotten just how susceptible she was to him. When he walked, he was close, but he didn't touch her. It felt as if he were stroking those long fingers of his over her body, her breasts, making them ache for him. She inhaled him with every step she took, and the heat from his body reached her. Warmed her. Somehow managed to find its way inside her.

She couldn't allow herself to get distracted. She had a short window of time and Aleksei didn't factor into it, no matter how much she wanted to see him and spend time with him. "Joan has problems at home, but her housekeeper, Alison, is an angel. She's going to spend a few days with her, and all will be well."

She let herself look at him again. Just a very small glimpse out of the corner of her eye as he prowled along beside her. The gorgeous woman he'd been talking to walked out with a small lift of her hand, but Aleksei seemed wholly focused on Scarlet, or he just plain ignored her—and neither seemed likely.

Absinthe shook his head, hoping he hadn't blown his chances so early with Scarlet because he hadn't called ahead. He'd been too eager, thinking only about getting there. He didn't really know the rules of dating, because he'd never done it before, and truthfully, he hadn't wanted to warn her he was coming. He wanted to see her face when he walked in. Now he realized he should have called her.

"I was hoping you would have time to go out with me this evening. It's the first break I've had, and I raced here. I didn't know I could get this evening off until the last minute. One of my friends stepped up for me," Absinthe said truthfully.

Torpedo Ink was working hard to get the grocery store up and running so that Inez Nelson, who had lent her name to the business but had her own store in neighboring Sea Haven, could leave feeling they would make a go of the store without her. She couldn't work in Caspar forever. Absinthe had given his time there, but it wasn't ever going to be his thing and he told Czar that. He wasn't a man to spend all his time indoors and around so many people. He doubted that any of them could manage the grocery store. Not even Lana, and so far, she'd been the best at training under Inez.

They desperately needed a manager and it was very clear to all of them that it wasn't going to be someone from Torpedo Ink. Czar had finally agreed to look for an out-sider. The club had a lot of secrets. Too many. The more people they brought in who worked every day with them, the more dangerous that could be—particularly if that per-son was observant as any good manager would have to be.

"I'm sorry, Aleksei. Really. I'd love to. I'm not just say-ing that because it's short notice. I'm really booked tonight and can't get out of it. I swear, ask me any other time, and I'll make certain I'm free."

Scarlet not only sounded regretful, but she looked it as well. Absinthe couldn't believe the disappointment he felt. He had half expected to be rejected just because he'd asked her at the last minute and he knew women didn't like that. He'd counted on the fact that Scarlet didn't seem to be a bullshit kind of player. If she wanted to see him and she could—she would.

"Not certain I can get out of work tomorrow night, but if you can, I'll move heaven and earth to try. Might have to sell my soul," Absinthe promised, "but for you . . ." He trailed off and gave her a half smile, hoping to entice her into a conversation at least. "What time do you get off work?"

He knew her schedule. She wasn't working. He couldn't very well remind her of that. He could tell when he'd admit-ted he'd found out about her schedule the first time she hadn't been flattered. It hadn't occurred to her that he was coming from the coast and it took two hours or more. He could cut that down on his bike, but it was a bit of a risk at times.

"I'm off tomorrow, so whatever time works best for you."

The relief was tremendous. She'd answered immediately this time. She really did want to see him. "Will you ride with me tomorrow?"

He saw her hesitation and waited, closing his mouth against temptation. He didn't touch her. He wanted his relationship with her to be built on real emotion, not something he'd contrived. That was his problem—he could never tell what was real anymore. He needed Scarlet to be real.

He couldn't live without Torpedo Ink. He knew that. Torpedo Ink was there in his skin and branded deep in his soul. It was who he was. He was part of that tree and he couldn't survive without the others. They couldn't survive without him. That much he knew to be truth. But he feared sometimes that his relationships had been built on shifting sands. This one had to be on a solid foundation. Scarlet had to choose him. Had to want him, to know he was right for her, deep down in her gut, the way he knew she was right for him.

"I want to." There was reluctance in her voice. "That's a lot of trust to put into one dinner."

"We don't have to ride the bike." He sent her a small smile. "You tell me what you'd like to do. I can arrange a picnic basket. Alena, a friend of mine, is a dynamite cook. She'll make us something and we can go anywhere. I can find us a truck."

"You were going to bring a picnic?"

Absinthe could tell she really wanted to go on the bike. He wasn't going to push it. She had to feel comfortable enough with him to choose his ride.

She swallowed. Her hand came up. A delicate hand, fingers small, nails shaped, not long, but nicely trimmed. She stroked her throat. "I don't date, Aleksei, and I'm not used to being with a man for long periods of time."

The reminder was again the strict truth. He could hear it in her voice. He could also hear reluctance, as if she preferred not to be so honest, but she couldn't help herself.

"The idea of going with you on a ride is tempting, but I really would hate to blow it with you so soon because I'm awkward and don't have a clue what to say or do. And I could be out late tonight . . ." She trailed off.

He could tell a part of her was hoping he would walk away, thinking she was too much of an effort, while the bigger part of her wanted him to make the running for her. He knew, for him, she would be worth every hoop he had to jump through.

"You seein' another man tonight?" He tried not to sound possessive. Or jealous. He couldn't imagine either trait associated with him. He'd never felt emotions the way he did around Scarlet. In some ways, it threw him. He was a man always in control, and around her, he was that little bit out of control because emotions were unexpected, and he was uncertain how to deal with them, but he knew he had to get on top of them.

"A girlfriend is leaving the country. She was here on a work visa and is heading home. I won't see her for a long time so we're going out to dinner. She needs to come back to my house after. I've got things I've been storing for her. She might stay and just talk for a while." She answered without hesitation. "After, I'm going to be taking a very long, hot bath. It's been a long week."

"I apologize. That was juvenile of me." Absinthe rubbed the bridge of his nose. She had mixed truth with a lie. And she was—not nervous. Leery. But of what? Was she afraid he might find out who her friend really was? A man instead of a woman? If he—or she—was leaving the country, that wouldn't make sense. She genuinely wanted to see Absinthe again, he could tell that much was genuine. "I'm showing you a side of me I've never seen before. I hate that I'm thrown off a little by the way I feel about you."

She gathered books together and put them onto a cart, barely glancing at the titles, but seeming to put them in order by memory alone. "Since we're making fools of ourselves, you could tell me who that really gorgeous woman is, because it was very obvious that you know her, and you weren't all that happy to see her."

He sighed. "I made the mistake of telling her about you. Lana and I grew up together. You could say she's a sister to me. Alena, the one I told you about that is such an amazing chef, grew up with me as well. They were excited when I said I met someone special. I didn't realize I've never done that before, told them about a woman I met. Lana was curious. I wasn't happy that she came in to spy on you."

He could see that Scarlet was pleased. "I told her I was going to ask you out tonight but if you said no, I'd take her to dinner and give her a lecture about spying."

"I'd like to meet her."

He made a face. "Don't encourage her bad behavior."

"You're taking her out to dinner," she pointed out. "That might be considered encouraging bad behavior."

He found himself smiling again. He'd been twisted up in knots because he wasn't going to get to see her and he knew something was a little off with what she was telling him, but somehow, everything else she said was the truth. She was willing to go out with him the following day on a picnic and she wanted to meet Lana.

"That might be so," he conceded. "I hadn't thought of that. Lana and Alena always get their way. Too many brothers." Shit. Another mistake. He immediately covered it. "I'll be picking you up early tomorrow," he warned.

She groaned. "I'm not a morning person. And it's bound to be cool on a motorcycle in the morning. Come at eleven. If you're coming from Fort Bragg or Sea Haven . . ."

"Caspar," he reminded. He shouldn't have. It was getting around that Torpedo Ink had bought quite a lot of property in Caspar and had started a few businesses there. Still, he didn't want to lie to her. He'd already committed the sin of omission and that was as far as he was going to go. He should have told her he was in a club and that club was important to him.

"Caspar. Right. It's still a long way and you'll have to get up *very* early to make it over here by eleven." She suddenly stopped sorting books and regarded him with mock suspicion. "You're not a morning person, are you? Like get up at five-thirty, exercise and be all chipper?"

"Chipper?" he echoed. "The librarian uses a word like *chipper*?"

"It's a perfectly good word." She used her snippiest voice. "It means cheerful and lively."

"I'm well aware what it means, I just thought it was a dated word."

Her eyebrow shot up. "There aren't any dated words. They're all perfectly good if they're used properly."

Absinthe found himself wanting to laugh. He couldn't remember a time when laughter was part of his life. This woman with her cute square glasses—they were purple today, he figured to match the swing skirt she wore. It flowed around her legs and showed them off to perfection. A different look from her tight pencil skirt. He wasn't certain which one he preferred. This one was flirty and fun. The other was all business and sexy as hell.

The tight prim-and-proper skirt put all sorts of dirty thoughts in his head. He had too many fantasies of bending her over her desk and doing all sorts of wicked things to her. This skirt had him wanting to pick her up, sit her on that desk, scatter those books everywhere, and shove the skirt to her waist, yanking down her panties and devouring her right there. That made him wonder how she would taste.

"Stop." She sent him a smoldering reprimand. "The library is a sacred place. You can't think those thoughts in here."

She was either reading his mind, in which case his fantasies weren't scaring the crap out of her—and they should be because he had a lot of them—or she was adept at reading him, and no one had done that yet, not even his brothers.

"You think about those things in here," he whispered, his

tone deliberately wicked. He stepped closer to her. Crowding her right into that desk of hers. The one she thought she was so safe behind. The one he had used in very inventive ways in a great number of his fantasies.

She gave a little gasp. "Aleksei. You have to stop. Really." She looked around the library, saw that no one was close to them and lowered her voice until it was a bare thread of sound. "I'm very susceptible to you. I don't know why and I'm not certain even why I'm telling you the truth, but there's a reason I haven't dated very many men. I'm not normal. I don't do well with most men. I just want you to know that up front, so you don't waste your time on me."

Her skin had gone to a delicate rose color that spread like a wildfire from under the prim-and-proper blouse that was buttoned up the front with tiny little delicate butterflies to match the ones taking flight on her swing skirt. The same buttons fluttered up the side of the skirt, but all were closed, so there were no little glimpses of her thigh, which made it all the more enticing.

"Babe, I've got to confess, I'm as fucked up as they come. Never dated. Never been in a relationship. Had a lot of women for a few hours only, but none I wanted to keep. Thinking there's a hell of a difference with you. I don't know why, only that there is, and I want to pursue it. You make me want to smile when I haven't had a reason to in years. You talk and I don't want to blow my head off because you're really intelligent and you know what you're talking about. Just listening to the sound of your voice is something special."

Scarlet pressed her lips together and then shook her head. "You know this could end up bad, right? We're weird together. We have this . . ." She trailed off and her hand fluttered between them.

"Connection? Chemistry? Explosive chemistry? The ability to read each other?"

"Whatever it is, Aleksei, it could be dangerous to both

of us," she warned, still trying to dissuade him, or maybe it was herself she was trying to warn off.

He couldn't deny that. It was bound to be dangerous for both of them, especially because his woman was hiding something from him, and he intended to find out what it was. She was mixing truth with lies in telling him what she was doing tonight. He didn't doubt that she was meeting someone, but the rest of her story—that was suspect. He intended to follow her and see what she was really up to.

Lana had spent a little time observing her, and Lana was very, very good at observation. She had indicated that Scarlet was concealing several weapons under her blouse, the one that hugged her rib cage and full breasts. He couldn't imagine where her gun was, but he had known all along she was armed. He knew there were other weapons stashed in her beautiful boots, the soft leather ones, a light midnight-colored suede with chains wrapped around the ankles and going up the boot midway. He had a feeling that chain came off fast when she needed it.

"I can handle dangerous. So can you," he said with confidence. "I think we're going to be perfect for each other. Maybe a little explosive now and then, but that just adds to the chemistry."

"Any more chemistry and we really are in trouble," she muttered. She lifted her lashes and looked directly into his eyes. "Are you certain, Aleksei?" Her vivid green eyes searched his.

She was looking for reassurance. He wasn't letting her get away, no matter what was spooking her. No matter what her past was. He was her future. She knew it. She just wasn't accepting it yet.

"I'm certain." He poured conviction into his voice. "You have fun with your friend tonight and I'll see you at eleven tomorrow."

She had glanced at her watch several times. The library was emptying as the time to close neared. He didn't want to hold her up. He needed to be "long gone." Lana had used one of the several sports cars the club kept. This one, a fast little Porsche she liked to drive because she was a little addicted to speed, was going to be difficult to hide from someone experienced in watching for a tail. Absinthe was certain Scarlet was more than experienced. The last thing he wanted was for her to catch him following her. That would put an end to their relationship faster than anything else he could imagine. It was a very good thing both Lana and Absinthe were excellent at tailing someone. They weren't about to get caught.

FOUR

"You're really gone on this girl," Lana said, not looking at Absinthe but keeping her gaze on Scarlet through the high-powered binoculars.

They'd followed Scarlet to a very upscale, trendy restaurant downtown where she parked in the upper parking lot next to an older gray Honda. A woman with long black hair got out on the driver's side of the Honda immediately, smiling at Scarlet, and the two women hugged.

Lana frowned. "They aren't that good of friends. They're pretty stiff with each other."

"Scarlet doesn't like to be touched," Absinthe supplied, happy it was a woman she was meeting. There was something "off," but he wasn't certain what it was.

The two women exchanged a couple of pleasantries and started walking along the narrow path leading to the restaurant. Scarlet turned her head and took a casual look around. She was up two floors, but her gaze included the parking garage beneath her as well as the grounds she could see. She looked across the narrow strip separating them to the gardens where Lana and Absinthe were behind the tree weeping long limbs of purple flowers. They stayed very still as her gaze swept first one way and then another, crossing them twice before the two women disappeared inside the building.

One side of the restaurant was glass from floor to ceiling, facing the garden. A lighted patio separated the indoor section from the jungle of plants. Scarlet and her female companion appeared at one of the little tables for two right in front of the window, where any passerby might see them. Absinthe went very still inside. There was something *really* wrong. They might be two stories up, but Scarlet was in plain sight. She was beautiful and anyone would notice her.

"What is it, Absinthe?" Lana asked, immediately noticing his body language.

"She never sits where she can be seen. Never. In the library, she watches the door, every exit. Every window. She never goes outside until she checks her surroundings, just like she did as she walked toward the restaurant. Choosing that table is out of character for her."

Lana watched the two women carefully as they ordered food and talked together. "You said they were old friends and one is leaving for her home out of the country?"

He nodded, not taking his eyes off Scarlet.

"Her friend is named Josefa. She's from Chile. They definitely know each other, but I don't think they're really good friends. Scarlet is leading the conversation and the other woman is following her lead. They're speaking Spanish, but using a Chilean Spanish, their dialect. Scarlet is very fluent," Lana continued.

Absinthe could read lips as well. Neither had been able, in the library, to get a good angle on Scarlet and Joan because Scarlet was protecting Joan with her body. But here, Scarlet was watching out the window, rather than looking at her companion, exposing her face openly. She was laughing in all the right places and acting as if the two women were old friends who wouldn't be seeing each other for a very long time. Her friend was shading the upper half of her face, but not covering her mouth.

"It's possible Josefa is here illegally," Absinthe mused. "She's far more nervous than Scarlet. In fact, Scarlet is as cool as it gets. She's chatting away, carrying the conversation as if she's done this a million times. Josefa is following along, but she's sweating. She's not facing the window and she's keeping her head down. She plays with that scarf all the time, pulling it up around her eyes and forehead. See?"

"I think you're right, Absinthe," Lana said. "Mystery is solved. Josefa was most likely a victim of human trafficking and Scarlet's helping her get back home. I can see her doing that, using the library for the railway." She lowered the binoculars.

Absinthe didn't move. It was the right scenario for certain. It felt right and yet—it wasn't all right. Just like Scarlet's truth held a lie. Scarlet was in plain sight in front of the window. Did she have a partner? Was she signaling someone by sitting in the window? Was that what she was doing by acting out of character? He didn't think so. Why be in the restaurant at all? Why go there if she was smuggling the woman out of the country? That made no sense.

He took the high-powered binoculars off his woman and swept the restaurant, first paying attention to the other customers. The room was full. There were quite a few male customers. More men than women. Most wore suits and quite a few had their eyes on Scarlet. He couldn't blame them. She laughed often and he'd heard that laugh. Soft. Sexy. And when she tossed all that gleaming red hair, falling like a waterfall of silk down her back, it gave a man far too many fantasies. She'd taken her hair out of the sexy librarian twist she'd worn earlier and let it cascade down her back, thick and rich and unforgettable.

"Fuck." He whispered the obscenity out loud.

"What is it, honey?" Lana had the binoculars back up.

"Look around that room. That restaurant is filled with suits. Men on the rise. Salesmen. Stockbrokers. Hungry for power. You can see the way they're talking to each other, their conversations, but most of them are looking at my woman."

"Babe, I hate to break it to you, but she isn't yours yet."

"She's going to be," he said with confidence. Because she had to be. But she was up to something. "You notice anything else?" He didn't wait for her answer. "There's security cameras everywhere. Lots of money comes to that place. They aren't risking their customers. Scarlet's making sure she's seen on camera. By the customers. Anyone walking in the gardens or the parking garage. She *wants* to be seen." Which didn't make a whole hell of a lot of sense when she was always so careful. And now, when she was helping a woman leave the country, and he was half convinced she was, why would she choose to be seen?

"Lana, what the hell is she up to?" Absinthe was intrigued, worried and annoyed all at the same time.

He was good at puzzles. Even brilliant at them. His mind moved at a very high rate of speed and little pieces of information clicked into place for him fast, forming a much larger detailed picture until his mind grasped exactly what he needed. What was she up to? It was beginning to drive him crazy, looping in his mind over and over.

"You're going to have to tell me what you're worried about, Absinthe. At the most, I see a woman who might be helping another woman get out of a bad situation. That's my best guess and you know I'm rarely wrong." Lana turned to him, her dark eyes focused completely on his face. She couldn't see anything to set off her warning system, but she was willing for him to convince her.

"Scarlet is behaving entirely out of character. She isn't like this. She's cautious. So much so that I thought she was in trouble, that she might be in hiding from an ex-husband, boyfriend or stalker. She stays away from windows; she doesn't sit in front of them. She's looking right into those security cameras. She deliberately chose this place so she would be seen, and the other men here would remember her. She wants the waiters to remember her, she's engaging with them. That woman she's with is covering her face, avoiding the cameras. She's letting Scarlet do all the talking with the waiter. When she went out with me, she barely looked up at the waiter and she definitely didn't want him touching her."

Lana frowned and glanced back toward the restaurant. "Okay, I can see why that doesn't follow that she'd bring someone here if she's getting her out of the country. I could be completely off track. They're taking their time with dinner and Scarlet's doing almost all of the talking. She's looked at her watch a couple of times. Just glanced at it, but I caught it. I thought she might have a partner and sitting there was a signal."

"I considered that, but it doesn't make any sense. None at all, Lana. This place? Cameras? No, she'd do a better job of hiding that woman. Something else is happening that we're not catching."

Absinthe didn't like anything he couldn't figure out. His mind liked intrigue and puzzles and continually needed new learning experiences to keep him from boredom. Knowledge was power, and power meant Torpedo Ink would always be safe.

"Don't do that to her," Lana cautioned.

"Do what?" Absinthe studied the restaurant again, looking for anyone in the background that might give him a clue to what Scarlet was doing.

"If you're really interested in her, you can't make her into some giant puzzle, Absinthe. I know you. You'll obsess over her, figure her out and then you'll drop her and move on. I thought you wanted her because she quieted your mind and she was all about making your body come to life. Don't make it about solving some ridiculous riddle that probably doesn't mean a thing. We're so used to intrigue and everyone having some kind of hidden agenda that we forget most of the real world is made up of nice people. She's a librarian, for God's sake."

"She's a librarian who carries guns."

"Women believe in protecting themselves." Lana sighed. "So, okay, I think, based on what I've observed of her, that she's probably better than most women at it, and she's had training, but that doesn't mean she isn't a normal person, Absinthe, not some crazy assassin running loose. You're most likely looking for trouble where there isn't any."

Was he doing that? He shook his head because even she sounded doubtful. "I want her, Lana. I know that she's the one. I think about her so much I can barely go to sleep at night. She's the first thing on my mind when I open my eyes. She makes me laugh. She's so damn smart. I like her. I like just watching her, knowing she's in the world. I like hearing the sound of her voice. No, this isn't about mystery or solving it, although I have to know what she's up to, but I'll figure it out. I always do. I need this woman. There's something with the way her brain tunes to mine and when she's with me after a certain length of time . . ." He trailed off. There was no explaining what it was like to anyone, not even to Lana.

"All right then. We'll just wait. I've brought food. We might as well eat it. They're eating slow so it's going to be a while."

Absinthe eyed her warily. "Did you cook? Buy it? Or did Alena provide it for you?"

Lana glared at him. "Just for that I'm not sharing with you. I'm quite capable of putting a meal together. I can make a sandwich. I've been around Alena since we were babies. And Blythe is always in the kitchen cooking for her demon children."

Absinthe smiled. "That means Alena sent you food. You planned on spying on me."

"Well, naturally." Lana didn't bother to try to hide her intentions. "Your protection is placed above all else, even my own comfort, brother."

He rolled his eyes when she flashed a little smirk at him and sauntered away, making certain to keep out of sight of that very large window that gave Scarlet the ability to see the parking garage and the front of the sweeping, over-grown garden.

He stayed low, fitting the powerful binoculars back to his eyes once more, and studied his little librarian. She seemed at ease, carrying the conversation as the waiter brought salads. Josefa pushed her greens around on her plate while Scarlet ate and talked animatedly, occasionally waving her fork around to emphasize a point she was making. He watched her very carefully just as he had for the last six weeks. He knew her every expression. She appeared relaxed, attentive to the woman across from her, but in reality, she was on alert, watchful, even more so than when she was at the library and always so careful to stay away from the windows.

Scarlet didn't like exposure, but nevertheless, she was putting herself in the position. Once again, he swept the restaurant looking for clues, anything that might tell him what she was up to. He examined the parking garage and the street below. He tried to see what he could of everything that Scarlet might be able to see. By the time Lana had made her way back, he was more convinced than ever that the only reason Scarlet had chosen the restaurant was for the location, so that she could be noticed and remembered.

The moment Lana opened the picnic basket he knew Alena had been the one to not only do the cooking but also the packing. The aroma was so incredible his stomach growled. Lana laughed at him. Two plates and glasses were included along with real silverware and napkins. Alena always planned for everything. Absinthe was certain she could manage a seven-course meal in a picnic basket if you asked her for one. This one had one of Lana's favorites, a pork roast stuffed with cheese and tomatoes, that Alena had created from a recipe she'd adapted from their childhood memories of home. There was homemade bread, all warm from her hot packs, and plenty of butter and honey to put on the bread. She had included roasted potatoes and beets, which happened to be a favorite of his.

"That girl is brilliant." He accepted the lion's share of the pork, fanned out like a book, without even raising minimal protest. It was that good, and Lana would have given it to him anyway.

Lana heaved a pretend sigh. "Isn't she? It doesn't leave much left over for me to do. She's good at everything."

Absinthe looked up from his plate of food, fork halfway to his mouth. Lana's voice was filled with amusement, but her eyes weren't at all.

"Babe, that's ridiculous. You're good at everything too."

Lana's smile lost all pretense of humor. "Actually, I'm not. Not at the things Czar wants for us now. I'm good at killing. I'm fast, efficient and accurate. I can seduce the socks off anyone, even someone who thinks they see it coming. I'm good at cards. The things I need to be successful at in a different life, like Blythe and Anya—or even Breezy, and she was born into the life—I'm no good at."

Absinthe wanted to wrap her in his arms and hold her tight. He didn't dare. Lana had too many demons. They all did. He couldn't take them all on. Already, the ones he had were eating him alive. He couldn't keep adding more. She wouldn't let him anyway. The moment he gave her too much sympathy, she'd turn away from him.

"You choose all the furniture because you can make us feel as if we have a home when we sit in it no matter where we are. You know that."

She shrugged. "I suppose there is a use in that, but how often do we buy furniture?"

"Lana, we're all learning. It takes time."

"I'm not certain what we're supposed to be learning," she said, sounding serious. "I'm not ever going to be able to cook like Blythe, and no one can cook like Alena. That's one of her many gifts. We all know that."

There was love and pride in her voice. Absinthe could feel the genuine affection she had for Alena. "Babe, that doesn't mean a thing. Cooking or not cooking doesn't make or break a relationship. I couldn't care less if Scarlet can cook. I doubt if Ice cares if Soleil can make a pancake for him. He loves her. That's what matters. What's wrong? What's this really about?"

She shrugged and pushed the food around on her plate with her fork. "I'm restless sometimes, that's all. I have to fight depression, just like everyone else. It isn't easy being with everyone all the time. The reminders are . . . difficult. Some days are worse than others. You know how it is. All of us have to fight those times."

"Lana, you can put an end to it. You're capable of loving, you know you are."

"I can't. There is no way to end it. I don't have that second chance like Steele got with Breezy. Some things, when they're broken, can't be put back together. I want to make certain Alena is all right, and Savage. I'm so worried about him. If he takes off, I'm going with him."

"No." Absinthe had been sitting back, lounging almost, doing his best to keep Lana at ease so she'd talk to him, but there was no way to disguise his visceral reaction to her declaration. "You can't do that."

"Someone has to watch over him."

"If he leaves us, it's for a reason. You can't save him if he goes. He's leaving because he knows he can't be saved."

"He already thinks that, Absinthe. We all know that. It's a matter of time. If he leaves, it's because he's given up. If I go with him, he'll try to hold out longer."

"And what? Prolong his agony? Because that's what he's

going through. I feel it when I'm close to him. Not all the time, but, man, when the devil's on his back, when it sinks its teeth into him, that demon has him hard. You can't save him, Lana. I don't know what can."

She looked out toward the restaurant, blinking rapidly to stop any moisture from touching her eyes. "I hate what they did to us. To all of us. Czar tried so hard to give us something to live for, but I don't see how we're all going to come out of this whole."

"We aren't," Absinthe said truthfully. "We aren't, Lana. It's an impossibility. Look at Reaper. He loves Anya so much. You can see it every time he looks at her. He loves her with every breath he takes. He's damned lucky she loves him the same way back because they have to work to make it work. He isn't an easy man to live with and he knows it. He tries, but he can't undo the damage done to him. Steele is insane sometimes and Breezy is strong enough to call him on it. She chooses her battles, but she doesn't let him get away with being a dictator. Ice has it the easiest because Soleil is a pleaser, but then he gives her the world. He would stand on his head to give her whatever she wanted. The two of them are making their art work for them together in a business, but even Ice can get out of hand sometimes and Soleil seems to be able to bring him back. But the absolute bottom line is this, we can't be without one another, not even Czar. Blythe knows it. All the women know it. They choose to live close because they know we need each other."

Lana rubbed her left temple. "I want everyone happy, Absinthe, I really do. I want to see every single one of my brothers and Alena find that perfect person, but to be left behind, to be alone and know I always will be, it's just too much. I can't watch that. I'm not that big of a person. I wish I was, but I'm not."

"You have a headache, babe? I shouldn't have asked you to stay."

"No, I get them sometimes, just like all of us. It's nothing. I wanted to stay. I like your librarian. I think she's perfect for you."

"Stop overthinking all this. You've always done that. You're the one who likes to plan out every detail."

"Like you."

That wasn't exactly the truth and both of them knew it. His older brother, Demyan, had been the meticulous planner. Absinthe had always gone on his gut feelings. As always, when he allowed himself to think about his brother, his stomach churned and his lungs burned for air. His heart accelerated and the pressure in his chest increased until it felt like a thousand-pound weight was sitting on him. He broke out in a sweat. Shit. He was finished with that.

"Honey." Lana's voice was pitched low.

He forced air through his lungs when it felt impossible to make that happen. Movement at the window across from him caught his eye. Scarlet had risen from her chair and moved right up to the glass. She appeared to be peering out, looking out toward the garden, right at him. Night had fallen, streaking the sky with gray and then deeper bluish black, making it impossible to see through the draping trees and thick shrubbery where Lana and Absinthe were hidden, but he still felt as if she could see right through it all straight to him.

He made an effort to breathe, to push his brother behind the doors in his mind, close and lock them. He couldn't afford to think too much about him or what happened to him. Or why. "Damn it, Lana. Like I said, we're never going to be all right. The damage they did to us will always be there no matter what we do."

Lana had turned her head and was looking at Scarlet as well. "Is it possible that she felt you, Absinthe? That she felt you upset? Can you already be that connected?"

He took his time answering. "I don't honestly know. We definitely have something unexpected. It's growing stronger every time we're together. Our minds kind of tune to one another. I've never felt anything like it before. There's a definite connection and I know she feels it as well, but just because I'm upset . . . that seems a little farfetched."

Scarlet turned away from the window to take her seat. Dessert and coffee were served to the two women. She smiled up at the waiter and he responded with something that made her laugh.

"I don't know, gut-wrenching, visceral, not just upset, Absinthe. I would have to say there's a difference and if you're connected, she just might feel that. You feel it when any of us are upset even over a distance."

"I've known all of you since childhood."

"You said she's much like you."

Absinthe had to give that some credence. Scarlet was a lot like he was, at least the closest he'd ever met to anyone with the same gifts. They weren't exactly the same and she wasn't as adept at using them, but no one else had even come close to having anything like his talents. He had no idea what she could or couldn't do yet.

"I really like spending time around her," he admitted again. "She gives off this really low energy I find peaceful. The little teenage girl she was talking to today was very agitated, but the more upset the girl was, the lower Scarlet's energy was and that helped to calm the girl. I like that a lot about her."

"That's what you do with us, isn't it?" Lana guessed.

"Something like that," he admitted, flashing a slight grin at her.

She wadded up a napkin and tossed it at him. He caught it out of the air, although he was watching Scarlet and Josefa, making certain he didn't miss them leaving. He wanted to get out in front of them, just to make certain they could follow the two women home.

Scarlet had told him she lived some distance from town, and she did. The property she rented was out on its own private road. A single back road led to a highway, although he discovered two smaller dirt roads that also branched away from the house, hidden by orchards that could be used as escape routes. The owners had clearly used the property as an illegal grow for years but eventually, when things got hottest just before the marijuana industry was declared legal in some states, they had gotten out of the business.

The house was set back from the road by more than a mile, making it easy for the occupants to see anyone coming up on them. It was ideal for the previous owners, who could either take off or hide as much cash or evidence as possible inside the house before the cops got to the residence. The groves of fruit trees and nut trees made the long rows of enclosed warehouses nearly impossible to see until you were right up on them. Those had been the real cash cows, where the marijuana had been grown and processed.

He hadn't done more than look around and was careful not to leave any shoe prints. He hadn't gone into the house. Scarlet was very careful. Too careful. She had no cameras outside, which he found interesting since he thought she was very security conscious. She was bound to have more security inside. In any case, he was hoping to be invited in soon.

"They're on the move," Absinthe said abruptly the moment he saw the waiter come over with the check.

Scarlet gave the waiter cash while Lana repacked the picnic basket. She was careful because the basket was Alena's and they were always careful with Alena's things. Absinthe took the keys and the basket and went ahead to the Porsche, sliding in and waiting for Lana. She wanted to ensure that the women weren't meeting with anyone else. Like him, she thought the entire setup was odd, no matter what she'd said playing devil's advocate.

Absinthe spotted first Josefa's car and then Scarlet's drive past. Lana slid in and they were trailing after the women, allowing several cars to get in between. Josefa's car had distinctive yellow rings on her taillights. That made it easier to spot several car lengths behind. There was nothing distinctive about Scarlet's car. She disappeared into the lights of the others on the road. Still, Lana kept her in sight, just in case she turned off somewhere else.

After a few miles, it was very clear they were heading to Scarlet's home. Absinthe didn't want to take a chance that she would spot the Porsche following them. "We'd better break off and find somewhere to settle down above them to watch the house. Do you want to go on home? I can handle it from here."

Lana frowned and tapped her fingers on her thigh for a moment. "Absinthe. She's doing exactly what she said she was doing. Why is it you're still watching her?"

He pulled the car to the side of the road, made a U-turn and parked and cut the lights. "I've got that feeling I get when something's not right, Lana. Instead of getting better, it's gotten worse. Something's going on with Scarlet, and I need to know what that is."

"Another man?"

Absinthe frowned. He wanted to say no. He didn't think Scarlet wanted anything to do with another man. She was genuinely interested in him. He could tell easily when a woman was attracted, and she was. More, she was honest about it when quite a few women wouldn't be. She wasn't coy, she was very up-front, although reluctant. Still, he had a feeling a man was tangled up in there somewhere, he just didn't know how.

"Absinthe?"

"I don't know. I'm feeling my way with her. Whatever this is, she wanted to go with me tonight. She really couldn't. She wants to see me tomorrow and intends to. She said she was seeing an old friend and that friend was leaving the country. It was both the truth and a lie. I could hear both. She said there wasn't another man, but I *felt* another man and it wasn't a good feeling."

"An ex? A stalker?" Lana guessed.

"She's watchful. At the library, she's always careful in front of windows and she definitely looks before she goes out the door, and yet tonight she deliberately put herself in front of the window. So what the hell does that mean?"

"Maybe she's tired of running and is calling him out?"

Absinthe turned the car back toward Scarlet's rental property. He'd discovered a little knoll up above it where he could park and they could watch the house. As always, Lana was prepared for spending the night in comfort. She had a ground blanket and night goggles.

"Don't worry, I brought food, just in case you think you're going starve come three in the morning."

"I better not have to be here that long," he objected. "I'm picking her up at eleven. I've texted Alena and asked for another picnic basket. I'll have to get back there and return before eleven."

"That's silly," Lana said, lying on her belly, fitting the goggles to her eyes. "Just get a room to sleep in tonight, have one of the boys bring you the food and pick your girl up in the morning. I worry about all of you without Alena and me to think for you when it comes to women. I've got eyes on the two of them, Josefa and Scarlet. They're talking in her living room. She doesn't have much furniture in there."

"Great." He rolled over and stared up at the stars. "I'm probably out of my mind because I've never had to deal with emotions like this before."

"Sucks, doesn't it?" Lana said.

The sadness in her voice caught at his heart. Sometimes the sorrow in Lana was so overwhelming he couldn't breathe. He kept his gaze fixed on the constellation right above his head and forced the air to move in and out of his lungs, thinking about Scarlet and that long fall of glossy red hair. It was the only way to keep from letting the demons consume him.

"Yeah, babe, it does," he answered, striving to keep his voice light.

An hour later, the door opened and the two women opened the trunk of Josefa's car, stuck a few items in it and then talked for a few more minutes, hugged and then Josefa drove off. Scarlet stood there a moment, hands on hips, watching her go, waved again and then turned back and shut the door. She turned off the light in the living room and turned on the light in what must have been her bedroom, and then the bathroom light went on. The bathroom windows began to steam up as she presumably ran a bath.

"There you have it, Absinthe, exactly what your girl told she was doing tonight," Lana said. "Let's go get you a room at a hotel."

"Not yet," Absinthe said. He was more uneasy than ever. He sat up and took the night binoculars from Lana. "Something is really off. Can't you feel it? Stop looking with your eyes. You're good at this, Lana. You want to believe her because she's mine and you liked her."

Lana sat up as well, her shoulder nearly touching his, but not quite. None of them ever quite touched him, not if they remembered in time. She studied the house.

"She's taking a bath and getting ready for bed."

He stared down at the house. He wanted to believe it. More than anything, he wanted to believe that was exactly what Scarlet was doing. What else could she be doing? He waited. After thirty-eight minutes, the lights went off in the bathroom. He pulled out his phone and texted Scarlet.

He phoned her. Her message said she would call back later, that she was busy.

Babe, you up? Need to know if you're allergic to anything.

He waited. There was no response.

"Don't get crazy, Absinthe. It's very late. She might not want to answer you this late. She might have fallen asleep already."

"Her light's on."

"Haven't you fallen asleep with the light on?"

"I don't sleep." Absinthe put the binoculars down and turned to look at her. "She's not in there. She's gone. There were no shadows. Lights on. Lights off. Windows misted over, but no shadows. That was a mistake. She's not in there."

"We've been here the entire time. She didn't get in the car with Josefa and her car is right there, sitting in front of her house, Absinthe," Lana pointed out.

"You think she's in there?" he demanded.

She started to open her mouth and then closed it. She sighed. "Damn it, Absinthe. She *has* to be in there. We're both right here. Where else could she be? She's not in the car with Josefa, that's for certain. Do you think she went out a back door and we didn't catch that?"

"I don't know, but I'm going in."

She caught his arm as he unfolded his long frame. "If she's in there, you're blowing your chances for good. She won't forgive you."

"She isn't in that house." He knew it with absolute certainty. "You flash me if you see anything that leads you to believe she's coming back."

"Like that's going to happen when I didn't see her leave in the first place," Lana said. "Let me get the rifle from the car."

"I've got to work my way down to the house. Don't want to leave traces just in case she gets suspicious and looks up this way. Have to be careful. You have time."

He didn't waste time because he had no idea what Scarlet was up to and didn't know how long she would be gone. He made it as fast as he could, being as careful as he could not to leave behind evidence of his presence. Going back, he would have to erase his boot prints with a branch, but right now, he was going to have to hurry.

He walked around the house first. It was on the smaller side. No cameras hidden under eaves. None on the porch or up by the door. She had two exits. A front and back door. Both were locked, and the locks were new and very good. Clearly, these weren't the landlord's.

The deadbolts were new installs and really good ones. She knew what she was doing. He checked for small threads in the doorway that would let her know someone had breached her security. There were none. Shaking his head, he went through the front door. He was careful to move silently, just in case he was wrong, but he knew the moment he stepped inside that she was gone.

The entire house smelled like her. Every breath he drew, he took that scent deep into his lungs. He looked around the living room. There were no photographs or artwork on the walls. There was no television. Very little furniture. She had two chairs and a lamp. That was it. He moved stealthily into the bedroom, careful not to disturb anything.

It was the same in that room. Not one thing on the walls. She had blankets on the bed, and this time, on a small, scratched-up end table that had seen better days, under a lamp, was a photograph in a beautiful silver frame of a girl that at first he thought was her, but when she was younger. In her teens. He realized when he studied it under his penlight that it had to be a sibling.

He looked around the bathroom. Again, a very sparse setup. Everything could be dumped or picked up in one minute and run with. He spent the next forty minutes going through Scarlet's house. Closets were mostly empty. Drawers were as well. She lived as if she could pick up and go at any moment.

He made his way back to Lana, taking his time to brush out the distinctive prints of his motorcycle boots with a branch laden with leaves. Scarlet was far too careful not to notice prints around her house in the light of day. He knew he hadn't made any mistakes, he was too experienced, but just the idea that she was so good that she'd managed to elude both members of Torpedo Ink bothered him.

"She wasn't there," he greeted.

"No shit," Lana said. "I guessed that since you didn't come back and I didn't hear gunshots. Did you figure out how she got out of the house? If she went out the back door, wouldn't we have seen her making her way to either road?"

"I don't know what to think. She's a pro, Lana. You should see that place. She can be gone in seconds. Found a go-bag in the wall with a good hundred K in cash and a passport in the name of Libby Simon. Good forgery too. Costs a mint to get that kind of work."

"Did she have any kind of alarm system? Cameras set up? Anything at all to protect the property?" Lana asked. "I didn't see you protect yourself from a camera."

"That's the thing that puzzled me the most. The locks on her door were good. I mean really good. She knew what she was doing when she put them on her doors—and she put them there, not the owner. They were too new. The windows slide open and she had little round sticks in them to keep anyone out. That would work unless someone broke a pane, and she'd know. Simple, but effective. So great locks and a simple solution on the windows. No cameras. Not a single one. She doesn't have any kind of aid-using technology."

Lana nodded her head. "I guess that makes sense. She's obviously smart. Code is always saying that technology is a two-edged sword. He's made us very aware our phones can not only track us but put us in places we don't want to be when a crime goes down. Cameras are everywhere and they're more sophisticated. Devices in homes can record conversations and anything on social media is open season. This woman clearly doesn't want anyone to find her."

"Until tonight in the restaurant, when she wanted to be seen," Absinthe pointed out.

"And she left her phone at her house after telling you she was taking a bath and staying in," Lana mused. "Lights on in the right rooms. Lights go off when they're supposed to."

"Where the fuck did she go?" Absinthe asked.

"That's the million-dollar question, isn't it?" Lana said.

"It's interesting that you mentioned that Code made us very aware our phones can not only track us but put us in places we don't want to be when a crime goes down. Do you think my little librarian is out committing a crime somewhere?"

"I think she's smuggling Josefa out of the country. I still think she was a victim of trafficking. For whatever reason, Scarlet took her to that restaurant. Taunting the traffickers? But she didn't ever let Josefa's face show clearly," Lana argued with herself. "That doesn't make sense, no matter how I say it."

Absinthe sighed. "I guess I'm going to have to find out what she has to say in the morning."

"You can't confront her and let her know you were spying on her like a stalker, Absinthe. Seriously, if she has a go-bag, she's got one for a reason. She's got to be in some kind of trouble. Oh, God, what if she's coming after you? What if she's an assassin for hire?"

"And her cover is being a librarian in Sonoma for over a year just waiting for an assassination assignment?" Absinthe raised his eyebrow at Lana.

"You have to talk to Code and have him investigate her right away. I mean it. This isn't safe anymore."

He hated that she was right. He would have taken the chance for himself, but not for any of the other members of Torpedo Ink, and he knew after Lana talked to them that they would be sticking close to him.

FIVE

Scarlet couldn't help the way her heart pounded as Aleksei came riding up on his motorcycle, looking for all the world as if he'd been born on it. She thought she might chicken out, but the moment she saw him on his Harley she knew she had to ride on the back of the thing with him. Just once. God. Just at least one time. She'd done her best to prepare. Braided her hair. Wore jeans. A T-shirt, a denim jacket. Gloves. She had sunglasses.

She'd parked her car in the parking garage adjacent to the library in the space where she always parked it, grateful he hadn't insisted he pick her up at her house. She didn't want him to try to come in. There was no way to explain her home. She'd lived there a year. Even if she got a bunch of boxes and were to pretend she was moving to a new apartment, he'd more than likely offer to help her move— he was that kind of man.

He smiled at her in that way he had. Slow in coming. So she had to wait. It almost stopped her heart while she waited for that smile to reach his eyes. Those beautiful, crystal-blue eyes of his that seemed to focus so completely on her. To see no one else but her. Every time she was away from him, she told herself he wasn't real, that he couldn't possibly really look at her like that, but he always seemed to.

"Hi." She couldn't help the happiness in her voice. She didn't even try to keep it from showing. This was her day. If she never had another one like it, so be it. Today was all hers.

"Hi, *miledi*."

Just the way he said it, soft and low, in a velvet voice that seemed to slide right over her skin in stroking fingers, sent shivers of awareness down her spine.

"How's my beautiful librarian this morning?"

"Absolutely great." Because she was. She *so* was. His gaze moved over her from head to toe, a slow appraisal, dwelling on her curves. His look sent heat rushing through her veins. His gaze touched on her boots and his faint smile sent another slow burn through her body.

"Did you get your friend off?"

"Yes. We had a nice dinner, a good talk and she flew out last night, back to Chile. Did your friend pack us a picnic lunch?"

"She did. I've got it safely stowed away. Do you have anything you need me to put up for you?"

Keys and Maestro had shown up early at his hotel room with the lunch for Scarlet and Absinthe. The two were probably asleep in the room. Player and Master had gone ahead to the Avenue of the Giants after Lana had reported to the rest of his brothers. He'd texted them where he was taking Scarlet for their lunch so they would have the chance to reach it in advance and be able to look out for him. He didn't think it was necessary, nor did he want them there, but Czar and Steele both insisted, and he wasn't in a position to argue with them.

He had, with great reluctance, turned over the fork he'd taken from the restaurant with Scarlet's prints on it as well as airdropped her photograph to Lana's phone so she could give them to Code. He knew the second she told Czar, which no doubt she would do the moment she returned to Caspar, Code would be on his computer, dropping everything else he was doing to ferret out every bit of information he could on Scarlet.

Absinthe had this one day with her. One. After this, his club would really be interfering. He would no longer have the chance to find things out about her on his own. Depending upon what she was into, he might even lose her. He wanted to have this one day at least. She was wearing gloves and he was grateful for that. It would lessen the impact when she put her hands on him, but he would still feel her emotions. Hopefully, the good would outweigh the bad, just as they'd done in the library.

"No, I'm just really excited. I have no idea what I'm doing, so you'll have to tell me."

She sounded excited. He liked that. He smiled at her and handed her a helmet. "You need me to help you put that on?"

"I think I can manage." She suited action to words and checked to make certain it was on snug enough.

He indicated the foot peg. "Foot there. Swing your leg over. Right up behind me. Wrap your arms around my waist. You're going to follow my body movements. Don't anticipate, just go with me. If you get scared, just tap on me and I'll slow the bike. I've been riding for a long time, but I don't want you to get nervous. This is supposed to be fun. We're heading to the redwoods. It's beautiful riding there. If it gets to be too much, we can always pull over, turn around and head back. I won't be upset, Scarlet. I really won't. This is a long ride for a first time, so we can change to something shorter."

She loved that he obviously meant it. Were there really men like him? She hesitated. She would know in a moment. She almost didn't want to take that next step.

"Scarlet?"

Absinthe reached for her gloved hand and put it on his shoulder. "Seriously, babe, we can switch to another vehicle, your car and you drive, or we can do something here in town."

She wasn't giving up riding on the Harley with him for anything. She swung up behind him and wrapped her arms around him, closing her eyes, expecting to be swamped with all kinds of emotion. They'd been so careful not to touch each other. Just a brief slide of a finger here and there. That had been incredible, establishing such a strong connection, but now, when they were in such close proximity, when she had her body tight against his, and granted there were layers of clothes between them, and both wore gloves, she only felt happiness, His. Hers.

The bike roared to life. It didn't rumble. It roared. Powerful. Formidable. A beast coming to life. She felt that vibration between her legs and she gripped Aleksei tighter. He dropped a hand over hers, patted hers and then had both hands back on the bars and was taking them out of the parking lot.

She closed her eyes and let herself just breathe him in. He smelled the same, that faint, wonderful aroma of man and sandalwood that got to her every time. She loved the way the wind rushed at them and when she opened her eyes and got over the faint dizziness, the way the world was all around them. He was careful in traffic, not hurrying them or getting too close to cars, until he took the exit onto the freeway. Once on the highway, he picked up speed, but she could tell he was still very cognizant of her riding with him. The longer they rode, the faster they went and the more she loved it, but then she'd always been an adrenaline junkie.

Scarlet knew she could ride with him forever. She didn't want to go back. She wished they could just ride off into the proverbial sunset and she could escape her life. Riding with Aleksei felt more intimate than with any other man she'd been with. When his body moved, hers naturally followed.

Her breasts pressed deep into his back and every movement and bounce of the bike rubbed her nipples so that they burned, hot and tight, and her breasts ached.

She was aware of him with every cell in her body. It didn't help that she was so tight against him, and that with the vibration of the Harley, after a while all she could think about was sex and more sex. Her panties were damp, and her clit inflamed and throbbing. She thought about how close his cock was to her fingers and wondered if the power vibration and her close proximity had gotten him in the same sexual frenzy as it had her. She really, really hoped that wherever he was taking her was somewhere secluded where there were no other people around so he would jump her. Please, please let him want to jump her.

His hand had come back to cover hers. He hadn't done that in the last couple of hours, but now that they were off the well-traveled freeway and more and more of the redwoods were coming into view along with the Eel River running along the side of them, he was relaxed. Scarlet felt so much a part of him, as if she really belonged. They moved together, man, woman, machine, along those wide sweeping curves of the road and the shorter, tighter turns and bends running along the motorway leading up to the Avenue of the Giants.

The road narrowed and Richardson Grove came into view, the redwoods towering above them. Scarlet had lived in Sonoma for over a year, but she'd never made the trip up north, although she'd always promised herself that she would. Now, on the back of Aleksei's Harley, she could look up at the towering giants and just marvel, wondering why she hadn't made the trip. It was so worth it. The trees, she knew, could live over two thousand years. Just that would be an incredible thing in itself. They were beautiful.

Aleksei maneuvered the narrow, two-lane road through the park and came to a stop down beside the water where the bathrooms were. She hadn't even had to ask him to stop.

He offered his hand and she put her palm on his shoulder to steady herself as she got off his bike, surprised that her legs were a little wobbly. She was extremely strong. She ran every day and stayed in condition, ready for anything, her body fit, but she wasn't used to traveling on a Harley for hours. Clearly that was something she was going to have to get used to if she stayed with him.

What was she thinking? She turned away from him fast, facing the bathrooms. He had parked close. Only the wooden stubs and a short expanse of grass and picnic tables separated her from the little building. The women's side faced her. She took a couple of steps in that direction, afraid of her thoughts. She liked Aleksei too much and she didn't have the right to draw him into her life.

"Wait for me, *moya literaturnaya ledi*."

Russian. Definitely Russian. The way he said it in that velvet-soft, low but firm voice vibrated through her just the way the Harley had, sending little wicked flames licking over her skin, rushing through her veins and settling, burning unmercifully between her legs. She was so susceptible to him. That was good. He spoke multiple languages. He'd told her so. She loved languages. All of them. And his literary lady? Hell yeah. She'd take that any day. The way he said it was just plain sexy.

"I prefer to escort you, just to be safe." He wrapped his hand around hers.

Her heart clenched hard. He was such a big man, towering over her, and his hand was much larger. Instead of feeling threatened as she normally would have, she felt ridiculously safe. She could easily take care of herself. The bathrooms were only a few feet away, thirty at the most, and in plain sight. There were a few motorcycles parked close and two picnic tables with occupants between them, but she'd already sized them up. She could take them if she had to.

To Aleksei she was a librarian, and she hated to deceive

him. She wanted him to know the real woman, not the one she pretended to be, not the façade she showed to the rest of the world. On the other hand, for the first time in a very long while someone wanted to look after her and it felt nice. She smiled up at him. "I think I'm safe."

"I think you are too, but two things, Scarlet. One, I wanted to hold your hand. I like everyone knowing you're with me."

She liked that so much she didn't pull away from him. "And two?"

"I've always believed it's safer with two people looking out for one another than one."

She wouldn't know about that. She tilted her head to look up at him and frowned. "Maybe. But if you rely on the wrong person, you'll be expecting help and it won't come. You might hesitate that second too long. Then, where are you?"

His fingers tightened for just one second around hers. "My brothers and sisters have never let me down, so I've never had that experience. I'm sorry if you have. That would suck."

"It's never actually happened." That much was true. She'd never allowed herself to rely on anyone else. "I was just debating the other side. It's a bad habit of mine."

He flashed a small grin. "I like it."

She loved talking with him. She could do it all day. About nothing. About everything. It might be a minefield and she might eventually step on a bomb, but it was exhilarating just being with him.

They were at the little building and he let go of her. She didn't want him to, but she had no choice but to go inside. In any case, she really needed to go. He waited for her to close the door. She knew he moved around to the other side of the building to the men's side, although she didn't hear him walking. That was another thing about Aleksei. He wore motorcycle boots as if they were natural footwear and he never made a sound when he walked. She loved that he could do that. It freaked her out a little bit, but she still loved that ability.

There were so many things about Aleksei she admired. Mostly, it was his intelligence. She realized, the moment she knew he was capable of understanding everything he read in those enormous reference books he was always reading so fast, that she was pretty much gone on him. It helped that his muscles had muscles. Beneath his tight tees, the ones that stretched across his chest, he had those washboard abs. Muscles rippled when he moved. She felt his strength. She saw it. But another thing about Aleksei she loved was he was never obvious about his strength. He was quiet, he didn't need to be loud. He could take someone apart with his eyes. Those beautiful, crystal-blue eyes that could look right through someone.

She sighed. When, in the last six weeks, had she allowed herself to fall so hard for the man? Because she had. She wanted him and it had nothing to do with his motorcycle or sex, and she was desperate for sex with him—and she totally was in love with his Harley. Aleksei Solokov felt as if he'd been created to be her other half. She might have missed out on the best thing in her life through her own choices.

Scarlet washed her hands, dried them on one of the few remaining paper towels and tried to see herself in the strange little warped piece of metal that passed for a mirror. She looked happy. She couldn't remember being happy, not in a very long while.

"I'm taking the day for myself," she whispered, wishing she'd agreed to meet him very early in the morning. She was going to be Cinderella or whatever princess it was— she still got them confused, but she knew there were multiple princesses because she'd read all the stories to her sister. "Be happy for me," she whispered, hoping Priscilla could hear her. "Please be happy for me."

Aleksei was waiting for her outside. Her heart skipped a beat when she saw him there. She had expected him, yet still, just seeing him waiting, looking so casual, lounging against the corner of the building, not in the least bit impatient, that slow smile climbing to his eyes, turning the crystal to a wild blue flame, made her melt inside.

"Don't know if I mentioned it earlier, *literaturnaya ledi*, but you're fucking beautiful." He held out his hand to her.

No one had ever called her beautiful let alone fucking beautiful. And she liked the way *literaturnaya ledi* rolled off his tongue. She couldn't help smiling as she took his hand. "Thank you." Her voice sounded husky.

"You up for more of a ride? I wanted to take you through the Avenue of the Giants. It's a place not to be missed on a bike. There're more private places for a picnic. We'd be alone though, Scarlet, and if you're nervous at all, I want you to say so."

"Have you taken a lot of women there?" She wanted to bite her lip hard. What had possessed her to ask him that? Did it matter how many women he'd picnicked with there? She wanted to go with him. This was her day. Hopefully her night with him. Maybe her only opportunity. Eventually she'd blow it because she—wasn't right. And she had a sword hanging over her head.

"I told you, Scarlet, I don't have relationships with women. You're the first. You're the only. I'm feeling my way here so if I make a mistake, I'm hoping you'll give me a bit of room."

He tugged on her hand and brought her in a little closer to him as they maneuvered around the picnic tables. His body was between those at the tables and her. She couldn't help noticing the way other women watched him as they walked back to the Harley.

"I definitely would prefer somewhere with less people and I've always wanted to see the Avenue of the Giants," she said hastily. She was going to blow it because she hadn't ever really dated anyone. "That makes two of us feeling our way." She laughed because suddenly everything was perfect again.

Aleksei got on the Harley and backed it out before helping her on. The moment she wrapped her arms around him, she felt complete. It was weird to know this man made her feel that way, when the entire rest of the world put her on edge. She tightened her hold, feeling possessive. For a moment, unexpected tears burned in her eyes.

"Scarlet?"

That soft voice got her low in her belly. She'd forgotten their strange, but very strong connection. "I'm all right. It's just that this is such a perfect day. I didn't expect it."

He rubbed his gloved palm over the back of her hand. "I don't think you ever expect very much. I hope I change that for you."

She closed her eyes against the burn of tears she didn't shed anymore. She didn't deserve to shed them. Had she paid the price for her sins? Was there ever a time when it was enough? She didn't know. She felt like she had.

The motorcycle roared again, the pipes loud, machine vibrating between her legs, and they were once again continuing along the two-lane highway, away from the tourists and campers who were staying in the grove. She was glad they weren't going to stay. She wanted Aleksei all to herself. She hoped he did know some secluded places where she could talk to him, not interrogate him, but just talk to him, get to know him. Pretend she was normal. Let the woman inside of her who desperately wanted to come out and live, do so.

Once they turned off the highway onto the roads that wove around heavy forests of tall, impressive redwood trees towering above them, Scarlet found herself staring upward. She couldn't stop from tilting her head back. It was a little dizzying even though Aleksei rode slow and maneuvered through the tight curves easily on the motorcycle. The sun shone through the canopy in stripes, creating a strobe effect as they rode. There were countless leaves on the road and built up on the ground so one couldn't see dirt or rocks under the years of trees shedding the needles. Branches and limbs lay haphazardly in the forest along with some hollowed-out trunks. Some trees had fallen over time and lay, the trunks so large they looked taller than she was.

Clearly, Aleksei had come here often. He made his way through the avenue to a small turnout where there was water dripping over a large rock and several tree roots sticking out of an embankment. There was a very narrow trail that she wouldn't have even noticed and doubted if most people would have. He slowed their progress even more, taking them carefully along the surprisingly well-packed road to a little area with just enough space for him to turn the bike around.

He let her off, turned the motorcycle around and then parked it before getting off himself. Scarlet looked around her. It was eerily silent, reminding her she was off in the middle of nowhere with a man she'd *seen* in the library for six weeks but really didn't know. She had no friends. She hadn't told a single soul who she was going out with or where she was going. He could murder her and bury her body out here and no one would know. Where were all her amazing survival self-preservation skills she'd honed to perfection?

Aleksei pulled off his helmet and dark glasses. "This is it. When I can't find a library and I need to get away, this is where I come. I call it my cathedral. I'll show you why in a minute." He gave her that slow, devastatingly beautiful smile.

The burn started immediately in the pit of her stomach and just continued to move lower. She shivered, awareness of him in every cell of her body. "How did you discover this place?"

"Sometimes my head feels like it's going to explode when I'm around too many people for too long." He rubbed his forehead with his gloved hands. "That sounds bad. It isn't that I don't like people, it's just that sometimes their emotions are . . . overwhelming to me. I need quiet places. Even that makes me sound like I'm crazy."

It didn't. She understood completely. That was why she was a librarian. Libraries were quiet and most of the people who entered were there for the purpose of studying or finding books to read or reference. They weren't there for counseling. Unless you counted the occasional teen.

"I don't think you're crazy." She didn't remove her gloves either. She watched him take a blanket and a rolled-up small duffel from a compartment of his bike. There was the faintest of trails and he indicated for her to follow him. "This is still a long way from the library, Aleksei."

"My brothers, sisters and close friends call me Absinthe."

She was silent for a moment, processing that. "Like the drink?"

"Yeah. Like the drink."

For the first time he sounded wary, as if he didn't want her to question him on why his friends would call him that. It would be natural to ask.

"If I ask why your family and friends call you that, are you going to tell me?"

He gave a heavy, exaggerated sigh. "Because they think they're funny, that's why."

He walked a few more steps and she stayed silent, just waiting. She knew he was going to tell her. He didn't look back at her, but she could tell he was a little embarrassed. This wasn't about drinking too much. He hadn't drunk anything alcoholic when they'd gone to dinner the other night. But maybe that was the reason. Maybe . . .

"In the nineteenth and twentieth centuries in France, artists and writers were particularly fond of the drink. I like the written word. I sometimes write shit down. They know it and they just like to give me hell for it. So that's how it all came about."

She found herself smiling again. She could see family

doing that, particularly brothers. Aleksei did seem to be a
man who, on the surface, looked as if he could really take
care of himself, but she could see he had the heart of a poet.
She knew he read poetry. He never had her get those books
for him, he always got them for himself, but she saw them.
He seemed confident in himself, not someone ashamed or
embarrassed to be caught reading poetry, so more than
likely, it was about writing it, or just admitting how the
nickname came about.

"Do you prefer Absinthe or Aleksei? Because that matters to me."

He did look over his shoulder at her and something
moved in his blue eyes. Something deep. He turned away
from her before she could figure out exactly what it was, but
her heart immediately accelerated at what she'd glimpsed.

"Everyone I care about calls me Absinthe. Aleksei died
a long time ago."

The sorrow in his voice had her reaching out to him. She
pushed her fingers into his back pocket and kept pace with
his longer strides. It was an intimate thing to do. Scarlet
wasn't the type of woman to ever take the lead when it
came to intimacy between a man and a woman. First, it
wasn't in her nature, it wasn't what she preferred, but more,
she hadn't been attracted to anyone in years. She was learning that intimacy and sex weren't always the same.

Scarlet didn't know what to think about that declaration.
Aleksei died a long time ago. What did it mean? Everyone
had a story. She wasn't alone in hers. From the moment he'd
come into the library and chosen that table far away from
everyone else, looking so alone yet wanting to be that way,
she had known there was a reason for it. She'd touched him
deliberately, seeking to find out and yet she hadn't been
able to uncover his secrets.

Absinthe stopped abruptly, reached back and gently
took her wrist to remove her hand from his back pocket,
retaining possession as he pulled her up next to him, closer

than she'd ever been, right up under his shoulder. She found herself staring at the natural arrangement of the tall redwoods. They formed a circular towering wall, with a thick mossy carpet covering the interior. The small "doorway" was two larger trees that were really one that had spread out and looked to have split at some time perhaps a hundred years earlier.

"This is incredible." Scarlet stepped away from him, shocked. Trying to remember to keep her mouth from hanging open. She could see why he called it his cathedral. It was beautiful. There was even a kind of hushed silence around it, as if the wildlife respected the place. Once she thought that, then she heard the birds with their flitting wings and calls to one another—the chatter of the squirrels and the slide of lizards under the leaves.

"Isn't it?" He looked pleased. "I hike a lot. I hoped you'd like it. I haven't found evidence of other hikers around any of the times I've come." He stepped past her inside the circle of the trees, taking her hand to tug so she followed after him.

"Do you worry about anyone finding your motorcycle?"

"It's not that far from here and I've got it locked up."

He sounded very confident. He handed her the duffel bag while he spread the ground blanket. "If you get cold, you let me know. I've got another blanket as well as this jacket."

There was no wind in the trees. The top of the canopy swayed above them, and the trees creaked and groaned continuously, but where they were, the thick trunks were solid and unmoving. She found she liked the sounds. The notes were almost like music, a low symphony playing just for them. She sat on the blanket and pulled off the jacket, expecting to be cold. It was warmer in the forest than she thought it would be. The sun was out and had that same interesting strobing effect as it had on the road, the rays shining through the long branches of needles.

"It's almost hot, but not quite."

He nodded. "A perfect day." He handed her a bottle of water. "You've got to be thirsty by now. I should have gotten you something to drink at the grove."

Scarlet shook her head. "I wanted to be alone with you. I don't know what it was, but I just had this crazy feeling as if we have this one day together. This one perfect day and I didn't want to miss one second of it."

Absinthe frowned, his crystal-blue eyes drifting slowly over her face. "What do you mean, one day together? You planning on ditching me after this? I thought maybe we were building something here. I was hoping we were. I'm just laying it out there, lady. That's where I am. I'm thinking we might take a stab at a future together. Why the hell not?"

She took a breath. There were a million reasons why the hell not. "We don't really know one another, Absinthe."

"That's why we're here, isn't it?"

She wanted them to be there for wild sex. They were completely secluded. They could have any kind of sex they wanted, and no one was around to know what they did. She could walk away unscathed. Even as she thought it, she knew that wasn't the truth. She would never walk away unmarked from him. Already, he had gotten to her. Somehow, in the library, without even laying a hand on her, he'd managed to make his way inside of her.

She took the plates he handed to her. "Tell me about yourself then. Where are you from? Why did you say Aleksei died?"

Those eyes of his jumped to her face. She swore he saw too much. She had her own secrets and she had no right to ask him to reveal his and yet she wanted to know everything there was to know about him. He hadn't removed his gloves. His jacket had come off, just like hers, but not his gloves. Neither had hers, yet she longed to touch his skin and she wanted to feel his hands on her skin.

"I was born in Russia. I'm sure that isn't a big surprise."

He sent her a small smile. This one didn't reach his eyes and there was no humor in it at all. She waited, suddenly wishing she hadn't asked him.

"I had an older brother, Demyan. We lived well, I'm told, although to be honest, I don't remember. My parents were murdered. I do remember that. It's odd the things a toddler can recall. I see our former house perfectly. I can see my parents. I can remember the things they said, and I can remember the way they were murdered. Every word that was said to them before the gun was fired. I wasn't more than eighteen months, and my mother was holding me in her arms, but I can recall it verbatim. I wish I couldn't."

She closed her eyes. Sorrow hung in the air. She heard it in his voice. More, he said that he "had" an older brother. She didn't want to ask if those same people had killed his brother.

"I'm so sorry, Absinthe."

"My parents opposed a political candidate that a man by the name of Sorbacov supported. Sorbacov was very influential at the time. He had the backing of a secret and very violent small division of the military and he used it in order to get his candidate positioned for the presidency. He did that by murdering those who were opposed to and could damage his candidate. He took their children and placed them in one of his four schools to be trained as assets for the country."

He pulled silverware, napkins and then sandwiches and homemade chips from the duffel bag. "Alena kept it simple for us because I told her we were coming a very long way and we were riding on the Harley."

She had no idea what to say about his childhood. It was clear he had moved on from that revelation and she didn't blame him. He'd been honest and she needed to give him something just as honest back. She tried to think what she could say.

"My mother had me when she was very young; she'd just

turned eighteen. I never knew my birth father. He was never in the picture. She met my stepfather when I was three. He was awesome. They had my baby sister, Priscilla, a year later. She was the most beautiful girl ever born. I used to tell her all the time she was my fairy princess. She would demand that I read her all the fairy tales nightly and I always did. She never tired of them."

She drew her knees up and hugged herself tightly, unable to keep from rocking. She rarely let herself go there, but he'd given her that piece of himself, so she was willing to do that for him. She wanted to. It was something real. This was Scarlet Foley. The woman. This wasn't the bullshit outward shell she presented to the world. She wanted Absinthe to know who she was, at least as far as she dared let him see.

"God, she was so beautiful, Absinthe. I lost her when she was fourteen. My parents too." She couldn't tell him how. Not any of them. Or that it was her fault or that she did penance for that every single day of her life and would always. "It's strange how our lives are so weirdly similar." Even saying that gave away too much. She didn't dare look at him. Instead, she stared up at the canopy where the wind set the tops of the trees swaying.

"I'm sorry, *literaturnaya ledi*, we both have had a difficult time of it. I think we need to stop talking about our past. Let's just tell each other things about ourselves. I'll tell you something about me and you tell me something about you. Something easy and fun. My favorite color used to be green, like your eyes. Now it's scarlet, like your name or the red of your hair, which I'm obsessed with."

She found herself laughing in spite of the fact that she'd just wanted to cry her eyes out. How could he do that? Turn everything around? She liked that he was obsessed with her hair. She unwrapped the sandwich he handed to her. He looked delicious. She supposed the sandwich did as well.

"I tried to find out last night if you were allergic to anything, but you didn't answer."

There was no censure in his voice at all, but she found, for the first time in a long while, that she couldn't control the color sweeping into her face. She'd found his voicemail and his text, but it was too late to do anything about it.

"I'm sorry, I fell asleep so early. I think the bath made me so sleepy I just went out that fast. Fortunately, no allergies." She prayed she loved whatever Alena had made to eat. She was going to eat it no matter what it was.

"Good. You still owe me favorite color."

He'd taken her at her word. She hated that she felt so guilty. Worse, she hated that she'd lied to him. She wanted their relationship to be real. That was impossible when she was deceiving him. "I've found lately that I'm really enamored with blue, a particular shade of crystal blue." That was no lie.

He gave her that slow, melty smile. "Just how warm are you?"

She swallowed the bite of very delicious sandwich that she suddenly couldn't taste anymore and had no idea what she was eating because his voice had dropped low and sexy. His gaze had drifted over her body, that infinitely slow perusal that dropped the bottom right out of her stomach and made her heart beat right through her clit.

"Very." That was the truth as well.

He nodded. "I'm getting warm too. There's no breeze. Take off your T-shirt, baby, and see if that feels any better."

Absinthe pulled his shirt over his head one-handed and put it to one side. Her breath caught in her throat. Not only did he have more muscles than anyone she'd ever seen, but he had scars everywhere. Burn marks. What looked like whip marks. And tattoos covering them. Interesting ones. The work was incredible, clearly done by the same artist who had worked on his arms. He was incredibly beautiful.

She took a slow swallow of water and pulled off her own shirt, revealing her lacy mint-green bra. She had very few nice things, but she liked beautiful underwear. She'd been hopeful that she'd have a chance to have sex with Aleksei—Absinthe—and she'd worn one of her favorites. The bra framed her breasts, barely containing them. Already her nipples were hard. She had generous nipples and she always thought if she found the right partner, she would enjoy breast and nipple play, but so far that had never really happened. Just being with Absinthe, already she was aching just with his gaze on her.

His breath hissed out. "I don't know, Scarlet, now I'm just getting hotter. You're beautiful. When I come into the library, I'm going to know what you've got under your clothes." He lay back, his arms under his head, his gaze hot as he watched her through half-closed eyes.

She found herself smiling at him, feeling sexy. "You always looked at me like you knew what was under my clothes," she said. Her voice came out breathless. She felt that way.

She found it strange that with others, when she needed it, she had all the confidence in the world. Sexual attraction hadn't been real with the others, and she'd been totally in control. With him, it was all too real, and he had to be the one in control because for her, it had to be that way, or she didn't want it. It wouldn't be good for her. They would never be compatible. Still, that didn't mean she could make herself trust him, but they were alone, out in the middle of nowhere. She was nervous, excited, thrilled, and she'd never felt more sensual than she did at that moment.

"I spent hours mapping out your body under those skirts and blouses. I thought of all kinds of ways I could take you on that desk of yours, but before I did, I wanted to take my time, spend those same hours exploring with my hands and mouth so I know every single inch of you."

The way he said it so casually, so matter-of-factly, as if he meant every word, that it was his intention, sent flames licking over her skin and rushing through her veins. He didn't change his tone from that low voice he used. He didn't take his gaze from her.

"Eat your sandwich, baby. You're going to need your strength."

"I am?" She picked up the sandwich she'd abandoned when she'd stripped off her shirt.

"You are." He said that very decisively.

SIX

Scarlet Foley truly had a beautiful body, even more so than he first had thought—and he'd been obsessing over her for nearly two months now. Night and day. Absinthe had had no idea her breasts were as full as they were, or as high or as round. Her nipples jutted out, perfect for play. Her rib cage was narrow and her waist even more so. She was fit. Really physically fit. He could see the play of muscles beneath her soft skin with every movement of her body. She might have more than generous breasts and hips, but she was totally fit. He could spend all day looking at her.

She wanted him. He was Torpedo Ink, a man trained from childhood to know all the signs, but he didn't want to rush this. She was too important to him. He didn't want to turn what they had growing between them into something solely sexual. She was caught between the desire to make their relationship that, hoping they'd burn out fast, or, like him, wanting it to be the real thing but not quite believing it could be.

He was still trying to figure her out. She definitely wanted him. All the signs were there. Long before they'd even touched in the library, he had known she returned his interest. Their chemistry had grown, and they'd only looked at each other. It kept growing until he swore it was becoming a wildfire burning out of control. He couldn't imagine what it was going to be like when they actually fucked.

She was confident in herself as a rule, but her hands trembled, and sometimes her gaze shifted away from his, almost shyly, which didn't make sense. He'd waited, hoping she would make the first move because he didn't want to spook her. For all he knew, she might whip out the knife or gun he knew she was carrying in her boot and kill him, but she hadn't made even a small move toward him, even when he knew she wanted to. He hadn't asked her to remove her boots because he wanted her to continue to feel safe with him.

Absinthe had taken a chance, and because he was a man who took charge, he did so. She responded immediately, which not only surprised him, it shocked him. He had to think that over. He didn't mind looking at her while he contemplated whether he was going to take any more chances with her. He didn't want to blow the progress he'd made with her so far. The more time he spent with her, the more he was absolutely certain he was right that she was perfect for him. He had been careful not to use the advantage of his voice or his touch on her. He'd been more than careful. More than anything else, he needed to know that their relationship was real, and she wanted it as much as he did.

When she finished the sandwich and had taken a sip of water, he crooked his finger at her. "Come over here and let me kiss you. I've wanted to kiss you since the first time I laid eyes on you." He deliberately didn't ask. He didn't use his voice. He didn't make it a command. But he didn't ask.

Scarlet sat facing him, about three feet away, tailor fashion. She unfolded her legs and, to his astonishment and absolute excitement, put her hands on the blanket in front of her so she was on her hands and knees. Her breasts, framed in that amazing lace bra, swayed as she crawled toward him. He could see her nipples with every movement. They peaked even more, showing him that she was excited, liking what she was doing. Her breathing had turned ragged. His cock went to pure steel—maybe moved past steel to straight titanium. She was the sexiest thing he'd ever seen.

He reached down and unbuckled his belt and unzipped his jeans. "Sorry, baby, got no choice. Don't want to damage the important parts here." The monster could breathe a little and the relief was tremendous.

He half expected her to pull back, but she didn't. Instead, she shifted her angle of crawling so that she moved right up over the top of him, coming over his heavy erection, her breasts dragging over his cock and up his chest before she put her mouth on his. The moment her nipples and breasts made contact with his actual skin, images rushed into his brain—all erotic—moving from her head to his. In spite of her very real trepidation, she wanted him in every way. *Every* way. Fuck. He wasn't certain he could control himself with the way he had to handle both their desires. He knew she would be feeling his as well, feeding her own.

He licked at her lips, tasting her, his hands at the back of her bra. It was easy enough to release her breasts, and again, she didn't stop him, although he gave her the opportunity before he took her mouth. She tasted hotter than he expected. They both ignited the moment his tongue slid into her mouth. It was as if he'd touched flame to dynamite. There was no going back from it. Sensations rushed over him. He felt as if a blaze arced over his skin to hers and back again. He wanted her clothes gone. He wanted his gloves gone. He wanted to feel every single inch of her body. It was frustrating for her to wear gloves.

He pulled back. "Get them off."

Her eyes looked as dazed as he felt. "What? What? Tell me what."

"Everything. Boots. Jeans. The fucking gloves. I want your hands on me. I want your mouth on me. I want to do the same to you."

She blinked rapidly, and he could see awareness, fear, creeping back in. He caught the nape of her neck and kissed her again. And again. Deep. Hot. Over and over. So fucking hot they were both going to burn in hell.

"Get. Them. Off." He could barely growl the words.

Like a graceful cat she moved back and unzipped her boots and carefully placed them to one side. He caught a glimpse of the neatly built-in compartments for weapons he already knew were there. He lifted his gaze to the trees around him and then nodded, indicating the boots once. That was all the time he could spare, the only clue his mind was capable in that moment of giving to his brothers that her weapons were close.

She removed her jeans and panties as he dragged off his boots and jeans. His gloves were the last items he removed. She did the same, but when she did, her gaze was fastened on his face, as if that was the only thing that could keep her from bolting. They remained like that, staring into each other's eyes. He realized she was looking again for direction.

"We're good, Scarlet. Come here, *ledi*, and kiss me again. Let's see how this works for us when we're touching each other. We might really find ourselves burning down the fucking forest." Again, he was careful not to use the influence of his voice. He kept the tone low, velvet soft the way she liked, but not commanding and not the way he needed sometimes. He didn't need that now. He needed Scarlet's compliance. He needed this particular woman to want to be with him.

She crawled over the top of him, and again, he could see trepidation in her eyes as her gaze clung to his, but she didn't hesitate. She wanted him as much as he wanted her. He bunched all that red silk in one fist as her breasts slid over his bare chest, her nipples dragging over his scars and tattoos and he took her mouth. Immediately the flames erupted, even hotter than before. This time, he dared to slide his free hand down the curve of her spine, to take in the satin of her skin. He was immediately immersed in heat. In wild need. In desperate hope. In sensual anxieties.

As she moved over him, his cock grew even heavier, jerking with urgent demand, feeling the heat of her feminine build, that sweet mixture of soft skin and firm muscles sliding temptingly over it as she crawled over him. Her hands smoothed his shoulders as her mouth moved under his, spreading the flames, hotter than Hades, plunging them both deeper into a sinful mire of pure sensation. Her body slowly settled over his, and for the first time that he could ever remember, he wasn't receiving any images other than the overriding purely erotic ones burning through Scarlet's brain.

He was taller than she was by quite a lot and he had a reach on her. He could slide his hand all the way down her spine to the curve of her cheeks. He kneaded the exquisite flesh there. She had a beautiful ass. Perfect for him. For his needs. She had that sensual feline crawl that could make his cock so fucking hard he could barely breathe. She had beautiful breasts. She was so perfect for him in every way. Her mouth was hotter than sin and her body even hotter. That didn't even begin to describe what he loved about her.

He rolled her over, trapping her under him, his first aggressive move, but he made certain he rolled her toward her boots, so she would feel she could reach out and snag a weapon if she felt at all threatened. He framed her face between his hands and took her mouth, not giving her a chance to cool down. He loved that mouth of hers.

She was so receptive, following his lead, making her own demands, chasing after him when he started to pull back, her hands in his hair, tugging and then stroking long caresses down his back. Several times he felt the bite of her nails as she dug her fingers into his shoulders to hang on just from their wicked kisses spiraling out of control.

He reluctantly left that perfect mouth just so he could

take a bite out of her lower lip. He'd fixated on her pouty lip often in the library, thinking of the way he wanted to leave his mark there. He'd often sat right at the table, looking over the top of a book, fantasizing about sliding his cock over that pouty lip and imagining the way her lips would look stretched around his girth.

His teeth locked gently on her lower lip and he bit down and drew her lip toward him, his eyes looking directly into hers. Those green eyes of hers went wide, but she didn't look away. The green swirled with more heat, grew even darker with lust and excitement. His heart reacted, pounding right through his cock. He let go of her lip, and then licked at the mark he'd made.

"I sat at that table so many times watching you at your desk and all I could think about was your mouth and this lower lip. Just kissing you like this. Biting your lip. Walking right up to you, unzipping my jeans, bunching all that red silk in my hands and demanding you do something to relieve the ache you put in my fuckin' cock. Sometimes I was so hard I wasn't sure I could walk straight."

Her tongue touched her bottom lip right over his mark. "I wish you could have done that. I would have liked it. After hours, of course."

"Your desk is large and when you wear that one long skirt, the ruffle one that drops to the floor, I thought I should just crawl under there and pull your panties down and see how long it takes before you're screaming for mercy." He kissed his way down to her chin. He was very fond of her chin. "I'm not a merciful man."

Her eyes went wide, and her lips parted but no sound came out.

His teeth nipped before he continued kissing her throat, finding her pulse there and lingering for a few more heartbeats.

"Your skin is fucking amazing, Scarlet." It was. So damn soft. His cock stayed nestled in the cradle of her hips and felt

like he'd found a home there. His body wanted to stay
stretched over hers, that smooth satiny-silk bed he claimed
for his own.

To actually be with a woman and have his body react
naturally to her was a miracle. To *want* her with his brain,
to feel the way he did about her was even more than a miracle. He kissed his way over her pounding pulse, feeling the
answer in his heart, rushing through his veins, through his
blood, pooling in his cock.

"Love this feeling, *literaturnaya ledi*." He murmured it
against the top of the curve of her left breast. That lovely
curve. He kissed his way over it and then the right one.

"What feeling?" she whispered. Her arms slid around
him. Holding him to her.

"That you belong to me. That you're giving me you. I
want you to belong to me. Not just for now, Scarlet. I want
us to have a future together." He kissed her right nipple and
then her left, his tongue curling around the hard pebble.

Her body shuddered in response. He felt the answering
reaction in her mind to his statement. She wanted the same
thing. She wanted a future with him, but she feared it. She
didn't trust yet that he meant it, but she wanted to. Something in her especially reacted to belonging to him. She
didn't just want, but needed to feel as if she was his. He
picked that easily out of her head as he swept his hands
under her breasts, cupping them possessively.

"I want these breasts to be only for me." He took her
nipple in his mouth and sucked and then bit down gently,
pulled and tugged and then sucked her breast into the heat
of his mouth while he kneaded her other breast. "I like to
play, baby. A lot. And you have the perfect breasts for it.
Very responsive. But they're mine. For me." He tugged and
rolled her nipples, pinching and then using his tongue to
soothe her.

Scarlet gasped and arched her back, thrusting upward,
pressing herself into him with a little startled cry. Pleasure

burst through her mind, through his. She liked not only what he was doing, but what he was saying.

"I don't share well with others," he murmured, licking at her nipple again. "I'm demanding in bed, baby. I'm not going to lie about that, but I'd be damned pissed if you ran around on me." He wanted her to know the truth of who he was, but he was also feeling his way with her. He needed to know what was in her mind. "I don't cheat. I don't tolerate my woman cheating." He worded that one a little more harshly, punctuating each word with either his teeth or his tongue.

Scarlet by turns gasped, squirmed, bucked her hips or cried out. He switched his attention to her left breast.

"My mark looks so fucking sexy on you, *ledi*." He kissed his way around her breast and then under it, down her belly to her ribs, his hands on either side of her waist. God, she was small in comparison to him. His fingers, spread wide, could just about take in her entire belly.

He nipped the skin just below her belly button and then swirled his tongue over the sting. Lifting his head, he waited until her green eyes met his. She looked partially dazed, but he had her attention. "I need an answer before we keep going, baby. You with me so far? We on the same page? Looking toward a future? No cheating. Either one of us? Exclusive all the way."

His palms lay flat on her stomach, fingers spread wide to take her in, to feel everything she was feeling. Immediately chaos erupted in her mind, so many emotions. Most were sensual; desire and pleasure were uppermost. Scarlet wanted to please him. She would do whatever he demanded of her. They were alone and she didn't fear anything he would ask. She wanted it all with him now because she was afraid she wouldn't have this opportunity with him again. There was still the fear that he might turn out to be someone really bad. There was also a fear *for* him. Her emotions were very jumbled.

He pressed a kiss into her belly button, still holding her gaze. "I wish you could see into my mind, Scarlet," he murmured gently, allowing just a little of his mind to open to her so that she could see past the highly aroused feelings he had in that moment. "I'm not the nicest of men, not always. I'd hunt down whoever hurt you so much that you're afraid to trust me and I'd probably fuck him up pretty bad or worse, but I can promise you, I would never intentionally hurt you. You would see that. You would see that I mean everything I say to you. Say yes to trying with me, baby. Give us that much of a chance."

Again, he was careful not to push any influence into his voice, even though resisting the temptation was extremely difficult. He knew Scarlet Foley was made for him and he for her. He felt it with every breath he drew and every moment they were together. He did use persuasion with his gentle, velvet command he knew she had a hard time resisting, but he held back on using his talent, that gift that could take control even though she was the one. He knew it now more than ever, just glimpsing into her mind.

Her hands smoothed his shoulders and he saw the capitulation in the brilliant green of her eyes before she bit her lip and nodded. "Yes. I want those same things, Absinthe."

The smile might have started in his damn cock—hell, he didn't know, only that it spread through his body like a wildfire, culminating in an impossible-to-hold-back grin. He kissed her stomach, those very firm muscles already moving under his touch in eagerness, as he made his way to the very edge of those fiery red curls proclaiming her a natural redhead.

Very slowly, so she would feel the anticipation, he slid his hands over her hips, shaping that curve, the hollows, the sweet beauty of her feminine form. Absinthe took his time with her, paying attention to every little hitch of her breath. He was by turns gentle and then abruptly a little rough, watching her closely for signs of nervousness. Scarlet's hips bucked, her back arched, her breasts swayed and jolted as she squirmed and moaned, but she didn't ask him to stop or reach toward her weapons.

"Spread your legs wide for me, Scarlet, and put them over my shoulders."

Scarlet's green gaze jumped once more to his face, went so dark and vivid, she could have been born of the mythical fae right there in the redwood forest. Her ragged breathing turned up another notch as she slowly spread her thighs even farther apart, exposing her beautiful little pink pussy to him. Shit. She looked like a little flower, glistening with dew, just waiting for his attention.

She slowly lifted her legs and obediently draped them over his wide shoulders. His breath caught in his throat. She smelled like heaven. She looked like paradise. She did what he told her, exactly what he needed from his woman. Her red hair was slipping out of her braid with all the wind from the ride on the Harley and it spread out around her like a halo. She was gorgeous. She felt like his. She acted like his.

Absinthe rubbed his palms over her hips and then dipped his head to kiss his way up the inside of her left thigh from her knee to that sweet slick entrance just waiting for him. He found himself, for the first time that he could ever remember in his life, having to force control on himself. He desperately wanted to taste her. He liked to play. He liked to prolong and build anticipation. He derived pleasure from using his voice to command and control, to direct and watch reactions.

He could keep a partner on edge for hours sometimes until they were sobbing and begging him, willing to do anything for him. Those needs were now necessary for his own pleasure and were so deeply ingrained in him, he knew it would be impossible to ever be any different. He'd automatically used his voice to command those around him to do his bidding sexually in order to survive his childhood. Over the years, more and more, he had come to need every act of obedience. It was the only way to get his cock and senses to come together enough in a rush to explode in any kind of pleasure.

Now, inhaling Scarlet's fragrance, kissing his way up the inside of her satin thigh, running his tongue along her damp, swollen lip to collect the droplets of honey, he could barely maintain his own control. He desperately wanted to be inside her, to feel what she was like surrounding him, to move in her. She felt his completely. In that moment, he needed her to be completely his.

"Say it." His tongue swiped between her swollen lips, stabbed deep and she jerked so hard he pressed his hand on her belly, holding her in place.

Absinthe lifted his head and waited. Her green eyes bounced all over the place. He stayed calm, although he didn't feel that way inside. The way she looked added to his dark thrill. With an effort she focused on him again. His cock jerked at the deepening lust in her eyes. The wild excitement.

Watching her face, he licked at her clit and then flicked the inflamed nub with his finger and thumb. He made it a casual movement, when he felt anything but casual. She gasped and shuddered, her hips bucking.

"Say you belong to me." The command was issued in his soft voice—again, he didn't push influence into it and had to fight himself not to do it.

She swallowed hard and nodded several times. "I do, Aleksei. I do belong to you. I want to."

He narrowed his eyes. "I don't like that name, Scarlet, and my woman never calls me that. What do you call me?"

He lowered his head again to that perfect tight little pussy because there was no resisting her taste. Or her scent. He wanted her with every breath he drew. Where was all his control and discipline? Why was she driving him out of his mind? He should be the one driving her out of her mind. He should be spending time on her thighs. Kissing. Teasing. Nipping with his teeth. Instead, he devoured her, used his tongue to draw out as much of her nectar as he could possibly take over and over again. He was so damn greedy, driving her up, holding her on the edge, fluttering his tongue, stabbing wickedly, using the edge of his teeth and then pulling back.

He stroked her belly soothingly when he felt her body coil tight, blowing warm air over her hot lips and inflamed slit. She was so responsive. She was a little fucking miracle. "What do you call me, *moya literaturnaya ledi*?" he prompted softly, more to back her off from the edge of the precipice. She was so close.

He rubbed his face on her inner thighs. He didn't want this to be over. He wanted inside her, but he wanted more time. He knew that once he had her, she would start to retreat. She was very conflicted about what she wanted. And he was very certain about what he wanted.

"Absinthe." His name came out ragged. She caught his hair in two tight fists, trying to drag his head back between her legs.

"What is it you want, *miledi*? If you want it, you have to tell me."

"I'm so close. Please finish me off. Your mouth. Your cock. I need you."

He licked at the drops of sweetness, savoring them. So good. "I need you to be more specific, baby. My mouth? Is that what you want? Or my cock? I'm fairly large. I'm going to stretch this little pussy of yours. It might hurt if you're not ready for me."

He used his fingers, pushing into her, scissoring, deliberately finding her G-spot and stroking until her hips bucked and she cried out his name. He instantly backed off, once again using his hand on her belly, caressing her soft skin. He stroked her swollen lips and then between her cheeks, spreading her sweet-smelling honey all over her and then licking it off.

"Your cock, Absinthe. I want you inside of me. Please. God, I want your cock. I can hardly stand waiting another second."

He couldn't wait either. Not another second. He kissed that flower pulsing now with desperation and then either thigh before very gently lowering her legs to the ground blanket. "Since you asked so nicely, how can I possibly resist a lady's request when it's put so sweetly and with such enthusiasm?"

He came up on his knees between her legs, keeping her spread wide for him. Damn, she was beautiful. The more he looked at her, the more he thought he'd never seen a woman so absolutely gorgeous, especially in the throes of sexual need. She was definitely a true redhead with her pale skin. He decided he might want a little landing strip where all those curls were. Or the curls. They were sexy. But the landing strip would show more of her and give him more to explore and her more to feel.

He circled the thick girth of his cock with his hand, his heart pounding right through the thick vein, thundering through the blood filling that steel spike until he thought he might explode. He had to force calm into his voice. Force that low velvet command he knew she needed. Her eyes clung to his face and then dropped to his cock. She licked her lips, her eyes so darkly sensual a groan escaped him.

"Wrap your legs around my hips, Scarlet."

She did so immediately, without hesitation or question, her eyes remaining on his cock. He pumped his tight fist up and down, needing the shattering pleasure shooting through his body, and then without further preamble he lodged the broad head into the slick heat of her entrance. His breath hissed out of his lungs.

"That's good, baby. Now put your arms up over your head."

She licked her lips and did what he told her. Blood pounded through his veins and hammered through his cock. She was so perfect. The action took those perfect breasts and jutted them straight up, so her nipples rose toward the canopy and let him see how excited she was. He could see the flush over her entire body. More importantly, she obeyed him without question, something he needed from her.

He pushed steadily, watching her face. She was so fucking tight it shocked him. She was scorching hot. He didn't back off, not for a second, watching her the entire time, those green eyes, the shock on her face as he pressed into her slowly, letting the burn consume them both. She started to buck her hips, to press herself onto him, and he shook his head, stopping her. He wanted a slow invasion, inch by slow inch. Taking her over. Letting her feel him coming into her. Letting her know who he was.

"Don't move your arms, not until I tell you, that's so perfect. You're so beautiful." She was. In every way. He reached down and caught her right leg, wrapping his hand around her thigh and rubbing soothingly. "That's it, *miledi*. Do you feel me inside of you? That's where I belong. Right there. Sharing your body. Your skin. Tell me how it feels for me to be inside you."

Her breathing was so ragged at first, he didn't think she would be able to talk to him, but her gaze had jumped to his the moment he spoke. She was learning what he liked—what he demanded. "It burns. So hot. You're so big." Each word was punctuated by a gasping breath.

"Do you want me to stop?" He paused, watching her carefully.

"No." She wailed the denial and again tried to push her hips down on him, thrashing a little. Her breasts jolted and swayed, so beautiful. So sexy. But he couldn't let her take over.

He stopped her, digging fingers into one hip and her thigh. "We'll get there. Take a deep breath and relax for me.

I'm not going to tear you or do any damage. You're tight, Scarlet. You're ready for me, but damn tight. Let me do this right."

He kept his voice pitched low. The temptation to use his gift was so overwhelming he had to take several deep breaths of his own to back off from the lure of what he knew would be an additional turn-on for him.

He continued to rub her thigh soothingly and pressed steadily and very slowly forward. It felt like fucking heaven and burned like fucking hell. Little beads of sweat broke out on his forehead. He refused to give in to the need to slam into her and bury himself deep. Not yet. Soon, he consoled himself, just not yet.

"This little pussy is mine for a reason, baby. It feels so fucking perfect, doesn't it? It's never been this good, has it?"

She shook her head adamantly, more of her red hair spilling everywhere. "No, never."

The admission was the truth. He was touching her skin without gloves and he could hear lies, but more, when he touched any pulse point, he knew the truth, and she meant exactly what she said, sex had never been so good—not ever. More, he was in her mind, and she was in the same unfamiliar paradise he was in.

"You were born to be mine, Scarlet." He pushed that idea into her mind. That was being a bastard and maybe outside the rules he'd set for himself, but for him, it was the absolute truth. She had to hear that in his voice.

He was there. He angled his body again so she had to take more of him. Heard her gasp. She didn't think she could take more. He adjusted her again and then he was balls deep, his abs right against that wall of slick hot heat and snug in her tunnel of scorching silk. He could feel her heart pounding through his cock. He waited a heartbeat. Another. Giving her body a moment to adjust to him.

"Say it for me, so I know you're with me. I'm going to fuck you hard, baby, now that I know you can take me. Say you know you're mine and this is what you want. I need to hear it in your voice." He was giving her one more opportunity to back out because, God help them both, he wasn't going to be able to let her go if she was as perfect as he believed her to be for him.

"Please, Absinthe, fuck me as hard as you can. I totally was born to be yours. I know I was." Her breath might have hitched, but the truth was there, as raw as her begging.

He withdrew his cock to the very opening of her slit, feeling the cool air on his shaft, and then he slammed home, the tight grasp of her body making his blood sing. He set a brutal rhythm. Fast. Hard. Deep. Every surge and thrust as he pounded into her set her breasts rocking hard. He loved that. Loved to watch them dance to that vicious pace he set.

"Put your hands on your breasts, Scarlet. Cup them first, from underneath, and then knead them the way I did, hard. I want you to feel it all the way to your pussy. I'll know." And he would. She would get wetter, surrounding him with her hot liquid, adding to the scorching heat of her silken grip on his cock. "Pinch your nipples. Have you ever worn clamps?"

She shook her head, but when her gaze jumped to his there was curiosity there.

"Pinch them hard as if you were wearing clamps for me."

He hadn't meant to do it, but his voice had gone completely sensual, all command. Her hands immediately were on her breasts, squeezing and massaging. Her fingers went to nipples, a little hesitant at first as if she didn't know quite what to do, but then more aggressively. His cock swelled impossibly at the erotic sight and he pounded into her even harder, finding himself nearly out of control.

Her breathing changed. Her body coiled tighter and tighter. He knew if she went over, she would take him with her, but he couldn't stop himself. That had never once happened to him. Not one single time. Her mouth opened in a silent scream. Her eyes widened, stared into his in dazed confusion. He felt her body clamp down viciously. So fucking hot. A vise of pure ecstasy that felt like a cross between a thousand rasping tongues dragging over his cock and a thousand milking fingers grasping and pulling until his seed exploded out of him like a raging volcano, coating the walls of her channel, heating them even more.

He simply collapsed over the top of her, letting her take his weight, burying his face in her shoulder, her soft breasts pressing into his chest. The movement sent ripples through her body as another orgasm rushed through her. He got the benefits as her body clamped down on him again and they rode the wave out together.

He turned his head into her neck and nuzzled, then bit gently, suckled, deliberately leaving a light strawberry like some ridiculous schoolboy. Just that little action sent a rush of liquid heat surrounding his cock. She was that responsive to him. He could imagine the fun they would have together, the days and nights of play. The times they would be at the parties and he would be able to command her. Just thinking about it had his well-sated cock twitching in her.

Scarlet began to breathe very shallowly so he rolled over onto his back and trapped her before she could escape, simply by pulling her half onto him, positioning her body so she lay with her head on his shoulder and one leg over his thighs. He took her arm and wrapped it around his waist, threading his fingers through hers with one hand.

She ducked her head, clearly uncomfortable. "I should clean up and we should maybe get dressed. It's getting a little dark."

It was a little late, and dark fell faster in the forest, but it wasn't that late. "Don't hide from me, Scarlet. I just had the best fucking sex of my life. Tell me what you're feeling. No one can hear you but me. Just say what you want to say."

She didn't look at him, but her head stayed pillowed on his shoulder. She turned her head to stare up at the gently swaying canopy hundreds of feet above their heads. "I'm so fucked up, Absinthe. I'm really sorry. It's just that I prefer that the man takes the lead when we're having sex. It isn't because I'm not into you. I really am."

"Where the hell did that come from? Did I in any way imply or make you think that I wasn't happy with what just happened between us? Seriously, babe." With his free hand, he tangled his fingers in her silky hair. He loved the feel of her hair. "You can see I like to play, woman. Don't tell me you're fucked up because you like a man to take the lead. I want the lead. I *have* to be in control. I like to tell my woman what to do. More, that's something I need. Telling me you're fucked up because you want a man to take the lead when it comes to sex means you think I'm seriously fucked up." He was, but he wasn't admitting that to her—not yet. She'd find that out soon enough. He was hooking her all the way first.

She was still uncomfortable, he could tell. She shifted just a little away from him, although she didn't try to get away. He kept his hand in her hair, on the pretense of playing with the silky strands, but all the better to hang on to her if need be.

"You aren't understanding what I'm saying," Scarlet said. "I'm trying to be really honest with you, Absinthe, because you've indicated to me that you want me to be in a relationship with you, not just have a hookup every now and then . . ." She trailed off, and this time she did turn her head to look at him.

"No, damn it, not a hookup, so you can stop looking at me so fucking hopefully. You said you would try to have a relationship and I took you at your word."

She turned her face away again to stare up at the trees. "I thought maybe you said all that in the heat of the moment so you could . . . you know . . ." She swirled her finger in the air.

"Hmm, let me see. Fuck you once? Or claim the hottest little pussy in the world as my own? For myself? All to myself? Or just fuck you? Why once when it can be always? Just me. Exclusively. And on top of that, have *moya literaturnaya ledi* all to myself as well. Brains, beauty and a scorching-hot pussy. You tell me how stupid I'd be to pass all that up."

She sighed. "I've been told that men like a woman to be very eager and show how much they want to be all over a man, that it's important they make all the moves, or at least as equally as the man does. Otherwise, he doesn't feel wanted."

"Is that what you were told?" He had to work at keeping the amusement out of his voice.

"Yes," she said in a small voice.

"All men are different. I'm different. I'm the only man you need to please, Scarlet. I like to give my woman instructions; I get off on it. I use crude language, and I get off on that. I like to play, to take my time building anticipation, but always knowing that when we get there, she trusts me to know it's going to be spectacular. I don't do any of those things to degrade my woman, but some women find it that way. I worried that you might. I don't want you ever to find anything I do to you humiliating or degrading. I want you to find it all exciting and sexy. I hope you believe I'm the perfect partner for you, Scarlet, because I believe I'm that man for you. I know you're that woman for me. Each time we're together, that feeling grows stronger. I don't know what else to say to persuade you."

He didn't. He sat up, helping her to sit as well. Very gently, he handed her the wipes he'd brought with him. Normally, he would have cleaned her himself, just because he would want to do it for her. Instead, he gave her some privacy while he took care of his own business. He'd known she was going to retreat. He hadn't known she thought she should be all over him because otherwise it meant she wasn't into him. What a crock. Men and women had different needs. Didn't all adults know that?

Hell. He needed his brothers. He needed his colors. He was going to have to ride all the way home feeling naked and vulnerable after having the best sex of his life because he wasn't wearing his colors. After feeling absolutely certain that Scarlet was the woman for him. He could use his voice, but then he would spend the rest of his life knowing she wasn't there because she chose him. He wanted her to choose the man. He needed her to choose him. Then and only then, and with her consent, would he use his talent on her.

He packed up the picnic things, slung his arm around her neck and kissed the shit out of her before heading back to the bike. He was very grateful she responded, but he didn't like the feel of the tears in her mind.

SEVEN

—➤—

"Damn it, Absinthe, you fucking know better," Czar snapped, glaring at him. He stood behind the oblong-shaped table where the entire Torpedo Ink club had once again gathered.

Absinthe couldn't sit there. He paced the length of the room. He *detested* what was about to happen. He'd given Code the fork with Scarlet's prints and her photograph knowing Code could find anyone. With that kind of information, he'd have just about everything there was to know about her. It felt like a betrayal. It *was* a betrayal.

More, he'd taken a photograph of the teenager in the expensive frame sitting on the scratched nightstand beside Scarlet's bed and he'd turned that over to Code as well. There was nothing at all of Scarlet's past in that house but that one single photograph. That had been of a young girl, maybe fifteen or sixteen. She looked so much like Scarlet that for a moment Absinthe had thought it was a picture of her from high school. Looking closely, he could see small differences.

The girl didn't have as generous a mouth, or as full lips.

Her eyes weren't as large. She didn't look nearly as sexy nor was her hair quite as brilliantly red, not that Scarlet couldn't have grown into all of those things, but he was certain he would have recognized her.

Using his cell phone, he had taken a picture of the photograph, careful not to touch it, not to move it even a fraction of an inch. This was the one thing in the house that she clearly cared for. It was out, by her bed. Enclosed in an expensive frame. The photograph was turned toward the bed so that it would be the first thing she saw when she woke and the last thing she saw before she went to sleep. At the time he searched the house he knew that girl in the photograph meant the world to Scarlet. Now he knew it was her sister, Priscilla.

When Reaper had first met Anya, circumstances had made it appear as if she might be spying on them and Absinthe had been forced to interrogate her. Doing so had sickened him, but he'd done it for the safety of the club. He now knew what Reaper must have felt like. Scarlet wasn't there. She wasn't witnessing Absinthe's betrayal of her, but somehow, for him, that made it worse. He was going behind her back. He wanted her to tell him about her past. He didn't want everyone in the room to know her secrets even if they were his brothers.

"I took precautions," Absinthe said. "I'm not five fucking years old, Czar. She's one woman, no matter how trained she is. I'm more experienced than she is."

"But you knew she not only was experienced in some sort of martial arts and combat training, but she was carrying weapons on her."

"Of course I knew it. I was carrying weapons as well."

He refrained from putting his fist through the wall. That would shock the hell out of them all. He was Absinthe. Always calm. Always centered. Always the one who kept his voice low and matter-of-fact when he was jumping out of his fucking skull. Like now. Because they were about to take his woman apart. *His* woman. He didn't have the time to bind her to him, to get her to trust him enough to tell him on her own what or who she was afraid of. He wanted that from her.

"We were all over him." Master spoke up unexpectedly. "He told us where he was taking her, and we set up ahead of time and covered him. She didn't make one move against him. He indicated immediately where her weapons were so we would know if she made one movement toward them."

Absinthe loved that brother.

"I was with him at the library," Lana said. "Checking her out after he told us he was certain she was the one. She was wearing the cutest outfit, a blouse and skirt, but I could see they were concealed-carry clothing and told him so. He already knew and he pointed out her boots to me as well. He was on it. We watched her together that evening, and later, when he went into her home when she was out, I covered him."

The way Lana put it to everyone wasn't a lie at all. Every word was the truth. He had known Scarlet was carrying weapons and he knew about the ones in her boots. Lana acted as if they'd known Scarlet was away from her home, that it wasn't a mystery. She *had* covered him when he went in. He could have kissed her. Instead, he didn't look at her, but kept pacing.

"And this date you went on with her?" Czar asked. "At the restaurant?"

"We had him," Maestro said. "Keys and I were on the roof across the street. He took a table where we had the perfect shot." There was a ring of truth in Maestro's voice.

That hadn't been on purpose, but Maestro would have known if Absinthe took her to dinner, he would have chosen a table for two in a secluded spot. His brothers and sisters, standing for him. There was no wonder he loved them.

"Well, I feel a whole lot better about this then," Czar said. "Sometimes, Absinthe, you disappear, and you scare the shit out of me. I understand that you want to get to know this woman just by taking her out and talking with her, but you and I both know, for the safety of the members of this club, you included, it can't work that way. Especially when she's as lethal as she appears to be. This woman . . ."

"Scarlet. She has a name. Scarlet. Fucking use it, Czar. She isn't *this woman*. Her name is Scarlet, and she means something to me. I don't know if I mean shit to her, but she gives me something that I need. That I want. Her name is Scarlet." Absinthe felt like his chest was on fire, there was so much pressure.

Steele turned in his chair and regarded him with those dark, midnight-blue eyes of his, assessing his physical condition. Absinthe and Steele rarely interacted much. It wasn't because they didn't share the Torpedo Ink brotherhood, that unbreakable bond, it was the uneasy past between them that had never been resolved. Steele had been the last person with Demyan, Absinthe's older brother, when he had died. The two had been tortured together. Steele obviously survived. Demyan hadn't. He hadn't talked much about that day and Absinthe had been careful never to touch him, not ready for the details. Not wanting to see how his brother suffered on his behalf, because it had been on his behalf. There was more to it, things Steele didn't know and Absinthe should have told him, but could never manage to get out. Time just kept creeping by.

"Absinthe, what's wrong?" Steele asked quietly. "Your blood pressure is rising. Your heart is beating too fast. You're always calm. You aren't. I can feel rage in you. That's unlike you. Where's it coming from?"

That stopped his pacing cold. Steele was absolutely correct. He kept his emotions locked down tight. He was careful not to touch the others unless he was prepared for the assault on his senses. He forced air through his lungs and made every effort to not only get himself under control, but to quickly assess what was happening. He was pragmatic about the things Torpedo Ink had to do in order to survive. That included investigating their women. That included Scarlet Foley. He might want her to trust him enough to tell him her past, but he couldn't give her his, not without a true commitment from her. He never would disclose everything to her. He understood if she didn't. Also, even if he knew, it would still mean as much if she did tell him. So, what the hell was wrong?

"I'm sorry, Absinthe," Czar said softly. "You're absolutely right. Your woman does have a name. Scarlet then. Your librarian. I presume she's extremely intelligent or you wouldn't be attracted to her. You need a brainiac to keep up with you."

Absinthe took another deep breath, careful not to look around the room. Rage was present, a living, breathing entity. It was ugly. All consuming. Eating him alive. He knew Czar was giving him a chance to pull himself together and figure it out. Czar was president of Torpedo Ink for a reason. Steele was young, but he was VP for a reason. The two knew if Absinthe was acting out of character, and it wasn't his rage, it had to belong to someone else in the room.

"What do you have, Code?" Absinthe asked, needing something else to concentrate on.

It was difficult to breathe. He knew already exactly who was broadcasting that kind of rage. There was only one person who had the kinds of demons that ate him up from the inside out. None of them had found a way to help and all of them had tried. The room was large, the windows open, but still it didn't matter. At times, the rage inside of Savage built and built until there was no way to contain it. He was at a breaking point. Absinthe didn't have to touch him to feel the way the past haunted him.

Absinthe heard the screams in Savage's mind. Pleas. Smelled blood. The scent of sex. Heard whispered words of promises and then the whistle of whips or floggers. Not the kinds of whips found in adult toy stores. Whips that could cause permanent damage if not wielded by a master. He tried not to see the images pressing into his mind. He didn't want them there. He didn't want to see writhing bodies marked with red streaks and tears. He didn't want to smell burning flesh or hear the screams as a young child was encouraged to practice whipping, branding, piercing and eventually breath play.

It was all he could do not to put his hands over his ears and rush from the room. It was years of discipline that saved him. That was always what saved him. He'd been sharing the demons of the other Torpedo Ink members since he was a young boy.

"Her name really is Scarlet Foley," Code said. "She's twenty-seven years old."

Absinthe was relieved. He loved her name. *Scarlet* suited her with all that long red hair. He forced himself away from rage and hurt and the need for violence in order to crawl out from under the past and concentrated on breathing, needing to see his librarian, the woman who had the ability to save his sanity.

"When she was seventeen, she was convicted of attempted murder. Three men, college friends. Frat brothers. One, by the name of Holden—Robert Barnes-Holden the Third—apparently brought her to a party. She was already in her second year of college and he was dating her. I pulled up the trial itself," Code continued, "and it looks to me as though it was a clear case of self-defense, but Holden's family is very wealthy and her family not so much. Daddy Holden bought off the defense attorney. I know he did because I dug deeper and found the payoff."

Absinthe had to move around the table away from Savage to one of the windows so he could take a deep enough breath to fill his lungs with air. He made certain it looked natural, as if he had to pace, but his own rage, ever present, twisted with Savage's again, making it nearly impossible to control. She'd been seventeen.

"They tried her as an adult," Code added.

There was silence in the room. Absinthe stayed by the window, needing to know details, but afraid to ask, to hear. It was going to be bad. Code always read his reports in that same tone, but this one held a note of warning. Of underlying anger.

Or was Savage's rage feeding everyone's? That could happen. They were going to lose him if something wasn't done soon. Absinthe risked a look at him. Savage had his head down, one hand over his eyes, pressing his fingers deep, as if his head was pounding. Absinthe knew it was. He was angry on Scarlet's behalf as well as at the fuckers who had taken a little boy and shaped him into a monster.

"What happened?" Lana was the one who eventually asked.

Czar snagged a bottle of cold water and handed it to Absinthe, who was standing almost directly behind him. Absinthe was careful to avoid brushing fingers.

"Holden tried to get her drunk. He must have slipped her some kind of drug. During her testimony, she said she didn't remember how she got upstairs to the bedroom, but when she did, she didn't object to having sex with Holden. He was her boyfriend and she liked him. She was very honest and open about that. She agreed she would have sex with him. Unfortunately, here's where things get murky. Holden Jr. testified that Scarlet was freaky in bed. That she got off on him telling her what to do. She didn't like regular sex. On the stand, when his lawyer asked if that was the truth, she admitted it was."

Absinthe swore under his breath. That was private between two people, not something for a courtroom or newspapers. Naturally, Holden Sr. would make certain everyone heard that piece of information about a teenage girl. Now he understood why Scarlet was worried about his thinking she was weird for her wanting him to take the lead. It would also make it more difficult for him when he did explain more of what he needed from her. What fucking bastards they were.

"Holden claimed he was giving her what she wanted by bringing his friends, Beau Cabot and Arnold Harrison, in with them, and giving her orders. She freaked out when they were all over her. She began going crazy on them and when they tried to restrain her so she wouldn't hurt herself, she pulled a knife from where one of the boys had it on his belt and slashed and stabbed at them repeatedly," Code continued. "The doctor testified that she had defensive wounds all over her, severe bruises, that it looked as if they'd tried to tie her down, but she fought them off. She hadn't been raped and she didn't have sex with any of them, Holden included, because he'd been too eager to get his friends involved."

"The jury didn't believe him?" Alena asked.

"Holden's doctor refuted the testimony saying the bruising was from the boys trying to restrain her when she went crazy from the drugs she'd been using that night," Code said. "Her friends came forward and said she had never done drugs. Her teachers pointed out she was an honor student and well ahead of her grade. It became clear that Holden Sr. wanted her in prison, and he was going to get what he wanted."

"Prison?" Master hit the top of the table with the flat of his palms. "Are you fucking kidding me? Not even the county jail? They'd send a kid to prison for defending herself?"

"They made her look like a sick freak who enticed these college boys and then tried to slash them to pieces," Code said. "I think she'd still be there, but shortly after she was taken to prison, someone broke into her parents' home and her little sister was gang-raped."

Absinthe's eyes closed. The rage in the room increased tenfold. He didn't know if it was Savage or him or the combination, but it was lethal. He was lethal. This wasn't something Scarlet was just going to come out and tell him any more than he was going to tell her how Demyan had died. The ugliness in the world never failed to shock him. He'd been born to that shit, yet he couldn't seem to get over the shock of it.

"I wish I could say it all ended there, but it didn't," Code said, his voice heavy. "Priscilla, her little sister, hanged herself. Her parents came home, they'd been out for the night, and they found her. After cutting his daughter down, the father went into his bedroom, got a gun, shot his wife and then himself. The police found all three bodies together."

Again, silence hung like a pall over the room. Absinthe wanted to leave the room, get on his Harley and go to her. She'd been alone, behind bars, unable to do anything but blame herself. He knew how that felt. He glanced across the room at Steele. Steele knew exactly what that felt like. Maybe they all did. They'd been helpless, children really, but that didn't matter when it came to emotions.

"Fuck." Savage spit the ugly vulgarity out for all of them.

"Apparently, an advocacy group took up for Scarlet. They believed her testimony and tried to get a retrial. Another lawyer, a female, began going over the transcripts and took up her case. Holden made a big mistake trying to essentially bribe her. She recorded him. The lawyer was able to get Scarlet out of prison. She had already served three years. Everyone wanted it to just go quietly away. The judge retired, which was lucky," Code said. "I got into his bank accounts and found interesting documents between him and Holden's attorney. The judge took his money. Scarlet's defense attorney took his money. The doctor he hired to refute her doctor's testimony took his money."

"I'll need their names," Absinthe said. "And information."

"*We'll* need all information," Czar corrected, giving him a look that clearly said to back the hell off.

Absinthe rubbed his chest over his pounding heart. How the hell did Savage live with this? He nodded to Czar. "At least they got her out of prison."

"They did," Code said. "Holden tried to stop it. He and his son and the two frat boys, Beau and Arnold. I've got a couple of pictures taken of Robert grinning at Scarlet. He looks like he's taunting her. Now, he knows her family is dead. She was asked on the stand if she had any idea who might have broken into her house and savagely attacked her younger sister. She looked right at Holden Jr. and said, and I'm quoting, 'How could I possibly know who would be that evil of a person?' The photographs were actually taken by someone her new attorney had hired because she wanted to see what Holden's son was acting like at all times."

"How do you find these things out?" Keys asked.

"I dig deep," Code said. "I find a trail. Email, court documents. I get into files. I read correspondence. I can get into phones. The attorney was certain that Holden Jr. and his friends had attempted to gang-rape Scarlet, but she was able to fight them off. She thought, out of spite, they had then attacked her younger sister. There was no way to prove it. They didn't leave behind any evidence, they were smart enough not to do that, but she definitely speculated. If she thought that, you can bet Scarlet thought it."

"Did the city at least compensate Scarlet for her time in prison? Was she allowed to bring a civil suit against Holden?" Absinthe asked. He could do that on Scarlet's behalf.

Code nodded. "The city compensated her, but under the condition that she remain silent and not give any press conferences. She has done just that. She declined to bring a suit against Holden at that time, although her attorney offered to help her. Scarlet didn't want anything from that family, but said she would consider it."

"What about the boys?" Czar asked. "The frat boys and Holden Jr. Did you get anything off their phones or email that might lead you to believe that they had anything to do with Scarlet's sister's assault?"

"All three of those boys are dead."

There was a long silence. Absinthe, for the first time in a long while, was able to draw in a full breath. "I presume they didn't just die of natural causes." He kept his voice strictly neutral.

"No, they did not," Code said. "In each case, Robert Barnes-Holden Sr. accused Scarlet Foley of murdering the poor, helpless male. She was investigated, brought in for questioning and released. There are photographs of her looking directly at Robert Barnes-Holden Jr. I got the original digital from the newspaper file and enlarged it. Cops say she has an airtight alibi. She was a hundred miles away. Take a look at that girl's eyes."

Absinthe stepped close to the table and looked down at the eight-by-ten black-and-white glossy on the table. He found himself looking into Scarlet's eyes. She was looking back, deliberately taunting him. A little shiver went down his spine. This was a game of cat and mouse. Scarlet wasn't the mouse any longer. She'd spent three years in prison. She hadn't been idle in those three years.

"What did she do when she got out?"

"She applied for a passport and left the country. She was gone about five years and when she came back, she worked in a library about a hundred miles from her hometown," Code replied while the photograph was passed around and the Torpedo Ink club members studied Scarlet's eyes.

Absinthe walked around the table again, this time making a circuit of the entire room, needing to remove the pent-up energy that made him feel like a caged tiger. He knew that was coming from Savage, but his own demons had twisted up with Savage's now that he knew what his woman had gone through.

"Were you able to follow her trail out of the country, Code?" Czar persisted.

"Trail started getting murky," Code said. "Took some time to work it out. She got better and better at hiding it. She went to a series of instructors. The first couple seemed to be expecting her. I looked back at a couple of women she was in prison with. The really tough ones that might have befriended her, especially if she was a fighter and they believed her story. They would have told her who to go to if she wanted to learn how to take care of herself."

"True enough," Czar said. "Absinthe says Scarlet is very intelligent. She would know that if she kept going up that ladder, she would find people who would teach her the things she would need to learn if she wanted to know how to kill and get away with it. She would move from one person to the next, getting a name. Is that what you're thinking, Absinthe?"

That was exactly what he was thinking because it was what he would have done. He would have read books. He would have gone from place to place, person to person, seeking out the underbelly of society, the people who would know what they were doing. He was positive that was exactly what Scarlet had done. She'd been young, but she'd been driven. She would have been careful to compartmentalize so that only one person might know the next one she studied under. No one would ever guess her ultimate goal.

"Do you have the names of the people she trained under? Can we get an idea of her skills, Code?" Steele asked.

Code hesitated, always a bad sign.

Absinthe paused his pacing and turned back slowly to study the man who always got them any information they needed.

"You aren't going to like this. None of you are."

"I haven't liked a damn thing you've said so far," Absinthe admitted. "Why should I start now?"

"She spent her last year training under Adrik Orlov."

Code dropped the name like a bomb because it was one. Adrik Orlov had gone to one of the schools Sorbacov had created, the one Gavriil had attended, and he'd risen fast, just the way Gavriil had, as one of the top assassins for his country. He was used by Sorbacov to interrogate prisoners because he was very good at disassociating and, like all of them, knew the techniques that caused the most pain, prolonged life and consciousness.

Once free, he made his way to Thailand and lived far away from others. He didn't seek out company and anyone with any sense didn't seek him out. He was known to be hard on women. He never kept a woman for very long, making their life too miserable for them to want to stay with him. He did train fighters, but his students didn't always survive their training. Adrik had a very bad reputation. Torpedo Ink had come across him more than once in their travels when he was working or they were. They respected one another, but kept their distance.

"Gavriil?" Czar turned to his birth brother. "You spent the most time with him."

"A dangerous man," Gavriil confirmed. "But you all know that. He just wants to be left alone. I know what that's like. We all do. He isn't a bad man. He doesn't know how to operate within the rules of society, and he isn't a team player. You cross him and you're not going to live very long, but that's pretty much saying the same thing about any one of us here, me included."

That was Gavriil, short and to the point. Absinthe had the same opinion of Adrik both times he'd run across him. He just wanted to be left alone. He worked hard when he worked. He didn't talk much. He kept to himself. He took on the occasional student if they could pay or if they worked for him in some capacity. No one stayed around him long because he expected them to work the way he did, using the same brutal conditions he'd trained under.

"A year?" Transporter said. "She lasted an entire year training under him?"

Code nodded slowly. "It appears so. She returned to the States and took a job a hundred miles from her hometown as a librarian, and a few months later the first of the frat boys, Beau Cabot, died an ugly death."

"How?" Reaper asked.

"Someone went into his home, taped him to the bed, shoved sawdust down his throat, packed it in deep and taped his mouth closed and waited for him to suffocate. His parents were sound asleep in the other room. They never heard a sound. Found him the next morning."

"Classic," Maestro said. "An easy one. Where did the sawdust come from?"

"His father's a cabinetmaker. Right out of his very classy, high-end workshop. Not a single sign of a break-in. No tampering with cameras. Not at the shop. Not at the house and they live in a gated community and have security everywhere," Code said. "The cops looked hard at the father and his employees, especially because the son was a screw-up and constantly got good workers fired. Frat boy also made very costly mistakes. The father didn't want him working there, but the mother always made it the employees' fault and insisted her husband fire the workers."

"They found nothing that could connect Scarlet to the murder?" Lana asked.

Absinthe glanced at her sharply. He knew what she was thinking. Scarlet had managed to slip past them. Neither of them knew how she'd done it. He still hadn't figured it out.

"No. The cops assured both Cabot and Holden Sr. she couldn't have been involved. They're wrong," Code said.

Absinthe's heart dropped. If Code found some trail leading back to Scarlet, the police could find one.

"Your reasoning?" Czar snapped.

"Several." Code picked up the eight-by-ten photograph. "Her eyes when she looked at the Holden kid. She was taunting him right back. She believed absolutely those boys raped her little sister. She *knew* they did. Something they did. Something she saw that no one else did, but she knew, and she was telling him she was coming after him. He thought he was too out of her reach, but he didn't realize what he'd unleashed. He should have. There were three of them that night. Scarlet was drugged when they'd tried to rape her. She fought them off, managed to get a knife and nearly killed them. But no, the suffocation is one of the many ways we were taught. But both the other boys are dead too."

Absinthe thought those were all very good reasons. He was glad none of those were reasons the cops would be able to trace the killings to Scarlet. "How did the next one, I presume it was Arnold Harrison, die?"

"Two months later, Harrison was found in a bathtub. Again, very fancy mansion. Lots of security guards with dogs patrolling the very ritzy neighborhood. Mommy and Daddy were home entertaining their club friends including Robert Barnes-Holden Sr. Whoever killed him was in the house when they were all downstairs. The maid found him the next morning. He was hung upside down over a tub full of water on a pendulum-type device. He was hog-tied, hands and feet tied together behind his back. Again, his mouth was taped shut so he couldn't yell out. He controlled the pendulum. If he didn't hold the trigger balanced, his weight dropped his head toward the water. He was looking straight down the entire time."

"Total mindfuck," Gavriil said. "Adrik loved those."

"Eventually, the kid slipped up, and his nose went under. He struggled to right himself, but of course he couldn't. Every bit of the device was made from pieces from the art gallery the kids' family owns, right down to the pulleys and screws. Again, security all over that gallery. Paintings there are worth a fortune. Absolutely nothing on camera and no prints anywhere," Code said. "You have to admire this girl."

"Was Scarlet looked at for this murder as well?" Steele asked.

"Holden Sr. insisted. He threw his weight all over the place. Went to the press. Demanded the cops do their job. Demanded she be put back in prison. Told everyone she was a killer." Code placed the photograph carefully on the table in front of him, faceup, so he was looking down at her eyes. "Again, there was an investigation. She had an airtight alibi. Dozens of witnesses. She offered to take a lie detector test and she passed it no problem."

Any one of them could do that. Absinthe was damn proud of her. More and more he was certain his girl had undergone five years of learning from some of the best, always looking for the right person to instruct her on what she needed. Someone had finally told her about Adrik Orlov and she'd dared to seek him out. Somehow, she'd convinced him to take her on and she'd endured a year of training under him when most students didn't last six months. She had to have a will of iron.

"Holden Sr. ended up looking like he was a bully picking on this poor innocent girl who had lost her entire family. She cooperated with the police on both investigations. Her attorney showed up and made a point of telling the press that because Holden Sr. had money and her client didn't, he thought he could railroad her just the way he had done before. That resonated with a lot of people and public opinion turned very quickly against him."

Absinthe could see that. Scarlet was beautiful, small and at times, with her square-framed glasses and little pencil skirts, could look fragile in her librarian persona. He could imagine that Holden Sr. would appear the blustering bully shouting at her when she spoke so softly. She could play that role so beautifully, looking delicate while he shouted and raised his fist, demanding she go to prison.

"And the third death?" Czar prompted.

Code nodded. "That would Robert Barnes-Holden Jr. Just as Scarlet was getting into her car and leaving to go back to her sleepy little town, she turned and smirked at Holden Sr. At least that was what he told the chief of police. The chief took a report because Holden Sr. insisted, but by that time, all the cops thought he was a little crazy. No one believed a woman could have killed either of those men. They weren't boys anymore, no matter what Holden tried to say, they were men and they worked out all the time. They would have overpowered her easily. The cops believed a man had to have committed the murders."

Absinthe wanted to shake Scarlet. She deliberately wanted both Holden Jr. and Sr. to know she was coming after Robert Jr. Adrik had to have taught her better than that.

"Holden Sr. is extremely wealthy, and he's used to buying his way and his kid's way out of anything. He owns quite a few properties, but he lives in one that is very extravagant. He likes to show off and bring political friends there. The governor. A senator he knows. A few others he's backed. He runs in the fast lane. His wife is very decorative, and she was an heiress with a hell of a lot of money," Code said. "I'm telling you this because their son, Robert Jr, was the golden boy. He was raised to believe he was a prince and could do no wrong. The two other boys were always with him. Literally, they raced cars down the streets when they were old enough to drive. Robert hit an old man and killed him, and his father somehow got him off. He was seventeen when that happened."

"Shit," Ink said. "The little prick did whatever he wanted."

Code nodded. "I found so many cases against this boy. His father has a law firm employed that worked nearly full-time just to keep his son out of jail and out of the press.

There must be twenty women who brought rape and assault charges against him, all dropped and settled out of court. Most never got that far, they were too intimidated. The security firm employed by Holden doubles as his enforcement. Those men are, believe it or not, men from the Venomous club. They use scare tactics on anyone who won't accept his bribe money."

"The Venomous club? An MC? He employs them as his security force?" Transporter couldn't swallow that one.

"Not exactly," Code clarified. "The security firm hires the members of the Venomous club to use scare tactics on anyone who won't accept bribe money."

"Great," Absinthe said. "Is Scarlet aware that Holden Sr. uses clubs as enforcers and corrupts attorneys?"

"No doubt about it," Code said. "She's very informed."

Absinthe was so fucked. It was no wonder Scarlet was unhappy with him admitting to being an attorney. Now, when he had to tell her he was in a club, she was really going to hate it and with good reason.

"So Robert Jr. grew up believing he was untouchable," Alena mused. "Do you think he was even a little worried after what happened to his friends?"

"If he wasn't, his father was," Code said. "Robert Jr. lived in a guesthouse on the main property. It's a multimillion-dollar estate with tennis courts, swimming pools and stables. Seems like Robert Jr. was filled with remorse and had been punishing himself, using a very primitive device on his private parts."

A collective groan went up around the table. "A clapper," Mechanic guessed. "Adrik fucking taught that girl how to make a clapper and get a man to confess every sin he has. That's just not right."

The clapper could have been a medieval torture device, although it was too ingenuous for that. It simply slapped the penis or balls hard, no rhythm, an unexpected but highly anticipated blow that went through a man, the pain excruciating, jarring every organ and bone in his body. Sweat poured from every pore as agony burst through him, building and building as the torture caught up with his brain. Tears would come. There was no way to stop them. Then the pain would gradually recede, and the terrible anticipation would start. When would it happen again? That was almost worse than the actual blow of the wood striking.

The spring tightened by minute increments as the hours went by, causing the blow to become harder and harder. At first, it wasn't noticeable, because the initial strikes were so shocking, but as time passed and the torment continued, one had enough time between the blows to realize the slaps were much worse. The time in between was enough to recover so there was no way to become numb to the clapper.

The clapper was one of the worst kinds of torture to endure and it could be used for days. In the end, most men begged to do anything to get it to stop. A man like Robert Barnes-Holden Jr. would be sobbing and promising anything to Scarlet.

"That's what he used, all right," Code confirmed. "He wore a clapper on his penis and balls, and he wrote a letter confessing his sins to the press. It was very detailed, stating that his father had brought him his first whore when he was sixteen and demonstrated for him how to use her hard and share her with his friends. He chose Arnold and Beau of course for his birthday surprise. Daddy 'helped' him get it right. After that, Holden Sr. would bring him prostitutes all the time. That progressed to Robert Jr. and his friends finding their own girls at the college, using the drugs Daddy provided for them until they got their own sources. The letter detailed all sorts of crimes that Robert Jr. committed against dozens of women and men, including the rape of young Priscilla. Because she was one of many, it didn't seem as if he had singled her out for any special reason. He named his friends as accomplices in every crime and his father as knowing about all of them and laughing, saying he could easily get them off—and of course his father had."

Absinthe could picture Scarlet calmly instructing him to write out a confession of every crime he'd ever committed since early childhood. Apparently, he had done so quite happily to keep the clapper from pounding his bruised and terribly tender penis. "Did he write the letter in his own handwriting?" Absinthe asked.

"Yes, he did," Code said. "He made several copies on his own machine from the guesthouse and mailed them to various newspapers and to the police chief from the Holden estate almost a full six hours prior to his death. There were no signs of violence in his home. No signs of another person. After he tortured himself and wrote his confession, he hanged himself in the middle of his living room in the exact manner that Scarlet's little sister did."

By the time she was done with him, Robert Jr. had wanted to put his head in the noose. He couldn't think straight anymore. It wasn't uncommon for the recipient of that kind of torture, if prolonged over several hours or days, to be so disoriented they would do anything, including take their own lives. He was deprived of water and, in the end, he would have been babbling, and any suggestion from Scarlet's calm and reasoning voice would sound good to him.

"Holy shit." Czar looked at Absinthe. "You were alone with her. She had weapons on her, and you would have hesitated. Don't tell me you wouldn't have. I know you. You like her. You would have hesitated, and she wouldn't have."

That pissed Absinthe off. "Don't make her out to be any different than we are. She's not. She's trained to kill, the same as every person in this room. We all have backup, she doesn't. Even if she'd gotten to me, she wouldn't have lived through it. If I had killed her, no one would have known. She had every right to go after those men. They took years away from her and then her family, just the way our families were taken from us."

The others nodded. Absinthe could see even Czar agreed with him. How could he not when it was the truth?

"That isn't the point," Czar said calmly. "They deserved everything they got and more. I applaud her for her ingenuity and the fact that she planned so carefully step by step and carried out exactly what needed to be done. The point I'm making, Absinthe, is that you were not safe with her. My concern is that you behaved recklessly and out of character and it can't happen again. None of you can do that kind of thing, taking chances with your lives. We're responsible for one another. All of us. We're family and we're all needed even when it feels as if we're not. You get me, all of you?"

He looked around the table with his piercing eyes. Not singling out any one of them, but touching on Savage, Lana and Absinthe, on all of them. Absinthe felt the heat and weight of that gaze. He nodded, just as the others did. It was a fair assessment. He couldn't argue with Czar. In the end, he was right.

"What happened when Robert Jr.'s body was found?" Steele asked, diverting attention away from Czar's very real concerns.

"Robert Sr. found the body. He was beside himself and then the letters were made public. At first, he was told about the letter by the owner of one newspaper who was a friend of his. But two others published the letter on the front page of their newspapers. The chief of police showed him the letter sent to them. Holden Sr. claimed it was a forgery. Then he claimed it was written under duress, that someone held a gun on Junior. The investigation was very thorough. I went over the police files," Code said. "There was zero evidence that anyone had entered Robert Jr.'s home. He had a detailed diagram on his computer of how to make the clapper dating back two years earlier. It's not difficult to make and he had seemingly put together the device using his own tools."

Absinthe had to admire Scarlet. She had planned so carefully. Clearly she had planted evidence on Robert Jr.'s computer two years earlier and then taken the time to break into his home on more than one occasion to use his tools to construct the clapper.

"The materials were gathered from construction sites around the estate. Everything traced back to Robert Jr. Holden Sr. refused the findings and went to his friend the governor, insisting Scarlet Foley was involved. The governor had the Feds take a look into the case and they came to the same conclusion as the first investigators.

"This time, Scarlet took exception to once more being dragged through the mud at Holden Sr.'s whim. With her attorney by her side, she stated that while she felt terrible for the man, she was tired of him trying to ruin her life. She sued him and won a very large amount of money and he was court-ordered to stay away from her and stop harassing her. She moved to Sonoma and became the librarian there," Code continued.

Absinthe looked at him sharply. Code didn't sound like he was finished. The report should have been, but clearly it wasn't. A worried Code meant all of them should be worried and in this case, especially him.

"What is it?"

Code reached back and rubbed at the nape of his neck. "In my opinion, from everything I've read about him, Holden Sr. isn't the type of man to just fade away. One of the things his son wrote in the letter was that his father told him to do whatever he wanted with women now while he could and then marry as much money and advantage as possible. From that point on, you had to be careful, protect that, but it wouldn't be near as fun. It didn't much matter what the bitch you married looked like, you had money enough to pay for whatever you wanted, just make certain it never came to light, no matter how you had to do that. Holden's wife didn't like that much, and she initiated divorce proceedings."

Absinthe waited as did everyone else. There was more and none of them were going to like it.

Code sighed and continued rubbing his neck. "Holden Sr. couldn't talk his wife out of divorce, and it's turned really nasty. She's dug up all sorts of dirt on him in light of that letter. She was an heiress and there was a prenup, and naturally quite a bit of it had to do with cheating on her. If she can prove that he did, and her PI has turned up quite a few women his enforcers are having a difficult time intimidating, he isn't going to have quite such a cushy life. That being said, he'll still have millions. He also is planning on taking out a contract on his wife. He hasn't done so yet. He wants to make certain nothing can come back on him, but I've seen the exchanges with the head of his security company."

Absinthe continued to wait, feeling as if he was holding his breath. He felt as if the entire club was. Code's assessments were always right on point.

"Holden Sr. blames his entire world falling apart on Scarlet. He believes she's taken everything from him. I don't think for one moment that he's finished with her. He'll wait until the heat dies down, just the way she did, but he believes she killed his son. He doesn't know how, but he holds her responsible. Not only for the death of his son, but also his two friends. Now, for his divorce. I think he's going to come after her."

Absinthe was certain Scarlet thought the same thing. That was why she was always so careful. So, what was she doing in the restaurant the other night in front of the window? They had so many secrets between them. That had to stop if they were going to be a couple and work together toward any kind of a future. He wanted that. The big question was, did she?

She was skittish and after everything he'd learned, he didn't blame her. He was going to have to find a way to reel her in. That meant coming as clean as possible. He would have to do his best over the next few days to persuade her to come to him. If that didn't work, he would make another trip to the library. If that didn't work, he was damn well going to fall back on what he did know would work—with regret—his voice.

EIGHT

Scarlet was thankful the library was closed and she had time off—three days in a row. She needed to talk to Absinthe. She'd thought about nothing else over the last few days. He'd called her every night and texted her multiple times during the day. She looked forward to every call, every text, too much so. It was time to make up her mind. She either had to commit to a relationship with him and that meant coming clean—or as clean as she could without going to prison—and risking everything or telling him she didn't want to see him again.

She couldn't imagine not seeing Absinthe again. He was her one chance at happiness. She had been so certain her life was over. She would live within the walls of a library, inside of books, and be okay with that because she'd made that choice after Robert Barnes-Holden Jr. and his friends had destroyed her younger sister and all but taken her life. She knew she shouldn't blame them for what her stepfather and mother had done, but she still did. She'd lost her entire family because those men had thought they could savagely assault a young girl.

She would always feel guilt that she fought back. She couldn't help playing the "if" game. If she hadn't fought back and gotten the knife they claimed she'd taken from one of their belts—that had been a lie; she'd really knocked it out of Robert's hands when he'd threatened her with it— then most likely they never would have gone near her baby sister. They would have done what they always did, had Daddy's lawyers buy her off with money or, if that didn't work, Daddy would have sent his MC "security team" to intimidate her into shutting up. There were so many "what-ifs." So many regrets.

She would have to tell Absinthe about her family and about her time spent overseas and the threat Holden Sr. represented. She couldn't admit guilt because incriminating herself would be just plain stupid and she wasn't that. She'd worked hard to ensure she had airtight alibis for every death. She could live with what she had done. Absinthe shouldn't have to, but he had to know there was a possible threat and it could turn very ugly fast.

Still, just the idea that she might actually have a real chance of being with a man like Absinthe. That he'd just walked in out of the blue and found her. He was . . . everything. Perfect. Just thinking that way was exciting. She was really going to do it—commit to a relationship with him. It was scary to actually think she could jump off that cliff with both feet and trust a man enough to have the kind of a real connection she wanted and needed to have with a partner.

Scarlet had the type of personality to be all in or nothing and she knew it. With everyone else over the last years, since she'd been seventeen and her boyfriend—Robert Barnes-Holden Jr.—had betrayed her in such a terrible way, she had refused to allow herself to ever believe in a man. Absinthe changed all that.

She had become aware of the fact that not only was she very intelligent, but she had psychic gifts as well. Before, when she was very young, she thought she was just intuitive. She began reading about various talents and how to improve them, especially once she was in prison. She began trying to work on the talents she thought she had to make them stronger. It wasn't like she could find a mentor to help her, but she had a lot of time on her hands to work on herself. She did find references to different psychic gifts and how different countries had tried to utilize the gifts in various ways. She followed up on those references, tracking them from book to book, even learning languages so she could understand more.

Scarlet had a good, very fast motor in her little nondescript car, and several times she glanced in the rearview mirror, a little worried that someone was following her as she sped down the freeway toward the cutoff leading to Highway 20. It was more of a feeling than anything else. Sometimes her radar went off and usually it was good to act on it. She didn't spot anyone following her, and she slowed down to allow anyone to drop in behind her just in case, but no one did. She waited a length of time before speeding up again and moving into the fast lane. No one seemed to move with her. Still, she was careful, frequently watching her mirrors.

She could drive when she had to, she'd spent a great deal of money on instructors teaching her how to race around every kind of obstacle and through streets and alleyways. She had confidence in her skills. She had worked at learning to spot tails as well. There had been months of training with experts recommended to her by women she'd met in prison. She never stopped practicing and working at those crafts.

Occasionally she visited the four women who had helped her so much, just chatting, knowing everything they said was being recorded. She wanted them to know she was still alive and doing well and that she would always remember what they had done for her. They had no idea the fullness of the dark path she'd traveled down, and she would never tell them. They thought they had provided her with the ability to always protect herself from men like Holden Jr. and Sr. In return for their generosity in helping her, she always did her best to let them know they had a friend with money on the outside.

The plan was for Scarlet to meet Absinthe at a coffee shop near Fort Bragg, not in Caspar, where he said he lived. She was grateful that he was still seeking to make her feel comfortable with him. It was a public place, not his home. She had decided the fastest route would be to take the 101 freeway straight up to Willits and then cut over on 20 to Fort Bragg. She wasn't certain why Absinthe wanted to meet her at the coffee shop, but now that she was a little anxious, she thought it was just as well. She didn't want to lead Holden's people to him just in case she was being followed.

She had packed enough clothes for the weekend and brought the one thing that really mattered to her: her sister's photograph. She had a picture of her parents as well, but she had that in the go-bag in the wall back at the rental. She hadn't been able to make herself look at them. Maybe someday. They'd left her alone to face her sister's death. Perhaps they blamed her the same way she blamed herself.

There was a part of her that wanted to pull her car over and go through her phone to look at all the text messages Absinthe had sent to her. She'd done so a hundred times. Probably more. She lay in bed at night, unable to sleep, thinking about him, going over every word he'd said to her when they'd been in the redwoods together. Every expression on his face. He couldn't fake that. Not what was in his eyes.

Out in the redwood forest, she had deliberately touched him, bringing one of her strongest psychic abilities into play, almost hesitant to do so at first, moving her hands over his body, exploring the play of his muscles. But there was very little information she retrieved, other than that he was really, really into her. Intensely into her. That had added to the excitement of being with him. Everything about being with Absinthe was intense.

Whenever his blue eyes looked directly into hers, she felt her stomach drop away, and with it, walls inside her mind seemed to crumble to reveal the woman behind them—the real Scarlet. He was gentle. He didn't pound her defenses down, he just looked at her and the carefully constructed bricks and mortar just fell away.

He had talked to her in that voice, so low and soft, so commanding, and it resonated through her entire body. She loved being with him every single moment of that day in the redwoods. On the motorcycle. She'd felt safe to be herself the instant she had climbed up behind him and wrapped her arms around him. When the big Harley roared to life and they'd begun to move together through the streets with the cars so close, she hadn't cringed, she'd just held him tighter and moved with him.

The entire day with Absinthe felt surreal, a dream, a fantasy out of one of her romance novels. She told herself it was too perfect. Men like Absinthe really didn't exist and there had to be a terrible catch she wasn't seeing. She had proven already she didn't have good judgment when it came to choosing men, yet here she was, her small bag sitting next to her in the passenger seat, and her stomach in knots while a thousand butterflies flew around in a chaotic mess. The closer she got to the coffee shop, the more her heart accelerated out of control and her blood went hot and rushed through her veins straight to her sex.

She'd even gone shopping for more sexy lingerie. She couldn't help herself. She had a favorite boutique online and she'd had the bras and panties overnighted to her along with the sexiest transparent boyfriend shirt she could find. She hoped Absinthe liked green. She looked really good in green. Just the thought of his eyes moving over her body had her nipples getting hard and her breasts aching for his touch.

She really needed to get some perspective. The light turned green and she was on Highway 20, a twisting, turning road that was really only thirty-three miles to her destination but took an hour to drive due to the road conditions. Panic began to set in. What was she doing? She was crazy. She couldn't make a commitment. She needed to pull over on one of the turnouts and think. Get her head straight. She couldn't let the best sex in the world sway her. Or just knowing he might be the smartest man she'd ever met. Or the kindest.

Her heart really began to pound, but not in a good way. Her lungs burned for air. She had killed people. *Murdered* them. Most likely Holden was going to send his motorcycle maniacs after her. She would manage to kill a few of them, but eventually they would get her. She would go down fighting, because she wasn't going to let them rape her. Or sell her into trafficking as Holden Sr. would want to see happen to her. He wouldn't have her killed; he would want her to suffer in a big way.

She looked for a place to pull over, but if she did, she knew she would turn around, go back to Sonoma, pack her bags and make a run for it. Absinthe, with his brains, his gentleness, killer sex and sweet ways, was far too much of a temptation. And he wouldn't just leave her alone, he would show up at the library and try to persuade her. She would have to go. Run for it.

Her phone went off and she glanced at the wide radio screen. *Don't answer. Don't answer. Don't answer.* She couldn't stop herself.

"Absinthe." She breathed his name, knowing she sounded way too excited and he'd know she was thinking about him. Worse, he'd probably know she was thinking about having hot, amazing sex with him.

"Moya literaturnaya ledi."

Her heart skipped a beat and then began to pound. Her stomach did that slow roll and she found herself smiling. She loved the sound of his voice, even coming over her car speakers.

"I'm checking to make sure you're on the road. If you're not, I'm heading your way. It's been too long and I swear, *miledi*, I can't wait another day."

She loved that it was too long for him as well. Sonoma and Caspar were too far apart. Couldn't he practice in Sonoma? Did they have a library in Caspar? She'd have to find out where the closest one was. She didn't mind moving. She loved the coast. Was it too soon to think about that? Probably. She didn't want to be the one to suggest it. It had to come from him. She couldn't wait to see him.

"I'm on my way. I'm about just past Willits now and heading up 20."

"You were thinking of turning around and leaving me, weren't you?"

Her hands gripped the steering wheel. How did he know? He had crawled inside of her. That wasn't good. She wasn't a good person.

"Baby. You were, weren't you? What did I do or say wrong?"

That was worse. So much worse. His voice, that stroking velvet voice that moved over her skin like the touch of fingers, uncovering every one of her senses so that she was acutely aware of every nerve and cell in her body.

"Not you, Absinthe. It's me. You're so amazing. You're just . . ." She trailed off, her foot on the gas, her hands on the wheel, flying toward him, knowing she shouldn't. "I'm just not a good woman and I don't want anything bad ever to happen to you. Nothing can happen to you, not because of me."

There were tears on her face and she thought she'd cried them all out so many years ago. She'd forbidden herself to cry.

Absinthe had found that woman again, the one she'd hidden away. Now, just the sound of his voice brought her out.

"Scarlet, I have a friend who will drive me to you. We can leave now and meet you. He'll ride the Harley back and I'll drive your car. I don't like you driving when you're upset."

The genuine worry in his voice washed over her. When had someone in the last so many years ever worried about her? She certainly couldn't remember because the answer was no one.

"I'm very capable of driving and I didn't turn around. I'm coming to you. I shouldn't, but I am."

"Are you crazy about my cock or my brains?"

She knew he was teasing her, trying to get her to laugh when she'd been upset. He didn't want her crying and driving. She could love him so easily. "That's a fair question. Let me give it some thought. It might take me some time."

"Ledi."

There was a bite to his voice that sent blood pounding right through her clit. Right then, had he asked, she would have immediately said it was his cock she was crazy for. What was it about his voice that got to her the way it did?

"The proper answer is both."

She waited a couple of heartbeats on purpose, a smile curving her lips. Happiness blossoming. She didn't have any right to feel happy, but Absinthe made her that way in spite of everything. "Yes. Yes, of course. Why didn't I think of that?"

He laughed. "You're about an hour out."

"Thirty-three miles is not an hour."

"On that road it is." Now his voice sounded stern.

"Does it take you an hour to drive it?" She put snip into her tone. "Being a man and all?"

"Before you throw attitude, Miss Scarlet, it has nothing to do with you being a woman and me being a man. The Harley can take the curves at a higher rate of speed simply because I am used to the road and know it so well."

"It just so happens I'm a very good driver," she said. She was. She wasn't bragging. Well. Okay. Maybe a little. Just that fast he'd turned her entire mood around. She was happy all over again and very certain she was making the right decision.

"Scarlet." He went to serious, all teasing aside. "I don't want anything to happen to you. I absolutely believe you're a good driver and you can cut several minutes off that drive, but I'd rather you not chance it. Just get here safely. I'll drink a few extra cups of coffee and shoot the shit with a couple of the brothers while I'm waiting for you."

Everything in her stilled. Her mouth went dry. "A couple of the brothers?" she echoed.

He didn't hesitate. "I told you I was raised with a bunch of hell-raisers. A couple of sisters and fourteen brothers." He cleared his throat. "And Demyan. I told you. He didn't make it out."

She let out the breath she hadn't realized she'd been holding. "Yes, I remember, your brother." His birth brother, older than him. She would never forget that, any more than she would forget her own younger sister. It was another tie that bound them together. She had to stop looking for reasons not to trust him. "Are they really all hell-raisers?"

"Sadly, yes. I'm the nicest of the lot."

She found herself laughing again. "Do they all live close to you?"

"Yeah, we tend to stay very close. We look out for one another, watch each other's backs. We all lost too much and aren't willing to lose anyone else we love."

She didn't know what that would be like—to have someone watching her back. "I've been alone since I lost my family. I didn't realize how much I stay to myself until I met you." She could hear the lie in her own voice and hoped he couldn't. Maybe it just sounded loud to her because she felt guilty lying to him.

There was a long silence. Yeah. He heard it and he didn't like it.

She sighed. "I shouldn't have said that. I think I just retreated from the world after I lost them. You're the first person I've really let into my life at all."

The road climbed up the mountain in a long series of switchbacks. The drop-off was steep, trees rising from below trying to climb out of the valley, the tops swaying alongside the turnouts, providing a reality check of just how deep the drop actually was.

"I'm grateful you let me in, Scarlet," Absinthe told her. "Each day that I went to the library you brought me a sense of peace when I needed it the most. Some days I thought I was losing my mind."

"It was the library, not me, silly." She wanted it to be her.

She maneuvered the car around a particularly sharp curve. There was a large pond, very marshy, with reeds that protruded like a great jungle all around it. Vivid green plants grew on the surface of the water. A broken wooden fence added to the picturesque look of the landscape, and then she was sweeping around the next bend in the road, up into a grove of shady redwoods.

"It was definitely you, *moya literaturnaya ledi*. Do you have any idea how many libraries I've gone to over the years? There are libraries closer to where I live and none of them ever stilled the chaos that eats me alive sometimes. You do it. That's all you. Sometimes, I feel that I'm going crazy, that I can't get my brain to just be still, to be quiet, even when I go to the library, my one refuge, and there you were, my perfect *ledi*."

"Absinthe. I'm not a perfect lady."

"You're my perfect *ledi*. You don't have to be perfect for anyone else. Just me. You fit with me, Scarlet. Hopefully, you feel that I fit with you."

She loved that. She hadn't thought of it that way. She only had to fit with Absinthe. No one else. He definitely fit with her. She liked that he thought she was perfect for him. Maybe her imperfections were what drew him to her. Everything about him, so far, had drawn her to him. He had a way of thinking that made her believe she had a chance at life.

"These hell-raising brothers of yours . . ."

"I may as well tell you my sisters are a bit of hell-raisers too."

She laughed aloud at the mixture of mock exasperation and very real affection in his voice. "This *family* of hell-raisers you have, are they going to be around a lot?"

"They'll be in our back pockets," he admitted with another exaggerated sigh. "You'll learn to ignore them."

Her heart took a little plunge. "I'm not good with a lot of people," she confessed, genuinely worried again.

"They'll have your back too, Scarlet," Absinthe said, confidence in his voice. "They've suffered loss, just the way we have. Every single one of them. I wanted to meet with you at the coffee house, somewhere neutral where you would feel safe, because I want to tell you as much as I can about me, about my life and my family, so you know me, you know us, and you feel comfortable enough to make an informed choice. I want to be your choice all the way. I want you to give me your trust, and to do that, baby, you have to know me."

She took a deep breath. He was so amazing. He was everything she wasn't. Willing to make himself vulnerable, turn himself inside out in order to take a chance with her. She wanted to be like him, give herself to him so freely. Jump in with both feet. There was a time she could barely remember, when she was young, that she used to trust everyone. She couldn't remember her mother ever yelling at her. She believed in people and always told Scarlet that there was good in everyone. Her mother was wrong.

"I swear, Absinthe, I'm coming to you to do the same." She was. To the best of her ability, she was determined to give him what he'd asked of her. She was going to give him the woman she'd locked away—Scarlet Foley.

⌒

Absinthe glanced down at his phone. A message had come in from Code and there was an alert on it. "Gotta go, babe. See you in a few." He waited for her acknowledgment. Then he checked in with his team. "Transporter, you have her yet?"

"Your woman drives like a bat out of hell, Absinthe. She knows her way around a car and a road, that's for damn sure."

"Stay on her and pass her off as soon as possible. She has good instincts, and if she picks up that she's got a tail, she'll ghost out of here so fast we won't know what hit us."

Code's message was to call. It was urgent. Absinthe did so immediately.

"Patching you in on a conference call, Absinthe, with Czar and Steele as well," Code said. "I've got an alert on that bastard Holden any time he contacts his security company or his attorney, or Scarlet's name is mentioned. Basically, any time he moves. He rages against Scarlet more and more. At this point, he's obsessed with her."

Absinthe clenched his teeth, wanting Code to get on with it. He felt like reaching through the phone, grabbing him by the throat and shaking the information out of him. Instead, he calmly picked up his cup of coffee and took a sip, looking out at the street. The umbrella over his head was striped green and white, casting some shade over the table and chairs. No one but Torpedo Ink sat at the tables in the outside patio, but several cars lined the outside drive-thru to get drinks.

"Seems to be half the world is obsessed with Scarlet," he said.

"She's that kind of woman," Code conceded. "Holden's offered a reward to the Venomous club to bring her to him.

He wants her alive so he can make her suffer. He made that very clear, over and over. She is to be alive. He doesn't much care what shape she is brought in or how badly used—in fact, the worse the better—but she has to be alive."

Absinthe's gut knotted. He glanced at Savage and Lana and then across to Mechanic and Alena. They would be sent a report. He could imagine how they would all take it. They knew what it was like to receive the kind of treatment Holden was paying to have Scarlet get.

"Holden waited for time to go by, and he's done it carefully so law enforcement doesn't get wind of it. His attorneys represented members of the Venomous club and another little-known club called Twisted Steel. They were on the same run we were on not too long ago," Code reminded. "In any case, he made a very large offer to have the VCs pick her up, giving them first option before going to other clubs with his offer. He told them they had two weeks. I imagine they started out right away. He told them exactly where she was, her home address, her work address."

Absinthe's heart dropped. He actually started to rise as if he could outrun the order Holden had given. There were eyes on her, he consoled himself. She was a good driver and she was already very close to the coffee shop. Once she was there, Torpedo Ink would ensure she was safe.

"When was that offer made to the clubs?" Czar asked.

"The attorneys took it to the two clubs last night. I caught it because one of the attorneys always makes a point of recording anything Holden says because he's afraid Holden is going insane and will turn on all of them. The moment it appeared in his files, the alert was sent to me. If Holden knew about those files, he would lose his mind. There's some fairly damning evidence."

"All of which I'm certain you have now."

"That is correct," Code said.

"Send the others the reports," Absinthe ordered. "Thanks, Code. I really appreciate the heads-up. I hope she packed enough to stay with me for a while. She isn't going back until I can sort this out."

"We can get her things for her," Code said.

"Don't forget we have that job in Sacramento as well, Absinthe," Czar reminded. "This is all hitting at the same time."

"I'm in," Absinthe said. He was part of team one and wasn't about to let them down.

Absinthe didn't dare warn Scarlet. She would turn around the moment she knew he was in her business. As it was, he was going to have to be careful how he revealed everything to her. He would be as honest as possible, but he wasn't going to just let her leave and be killed because her feelings were hurt. Shit. He shook his head.

Savage looked down at his phone as the report came in and then up at him. He stood up and came straight to the table to drop into the chair across from Absinthe. He was a stocky, compact man, all muscle and steel, a scary, dangerous individual with the flattest, coldest blue eyes anyone might ever want to see. Absinthe was used to him, but being in close proximity with him, even outdoors, when his demons were riding him so hard, was difficult.

"I can take care of this for you," Savage offered. "Holden is a piece of shit. He'll keep coming at her."

It was that easy. It was always that easy. Savage was the club's go-to man. If not him then his brother, Reaper. Reaper had Anya now and Czar was doing his best to keep him from having to do so much of the dirty work. Absinthe could have told him; it was Savage who needed to be protected far more than Reaper did now that Reaper had Anya to anchor him. Savage had no one and he was being eaten alive.

Absinthe shook his head and leaned back a little in his chair, watching Savage with cool eyes, trying to find a way to help him. There was always a pathway, but in opening it, that connected them, and Absinthe had more than once spent months trying to get images from Savage's mind out of his head.

"Czar is working on a plan to take all of them down—the corrupt attorneys, the judges involved, any cops, all of them," Absinthe said. "Thanks, Savage. I appreciate the offer. Once she's sitting right here with me, I'll feel a whole hell of a lot better."

"Just understand the offer's always on the table. Send me the green light and I'm on it." Savage started to rise.

Absinthe leaned forward and he sank back down. "The Venomous club is really working to chip away at the Diamondback territory here in Northern California. Do you think they've really grown big enough to challenge them and no one has noticed?"

Savage shook his head. "Diamondbacks are the biggest club out there. They have chapters all over the world. They aren't the bloodiest by any means, but they have more chapters and more members than any other. The Venomous club is a gnat flying around."

"Czar said two of the three nightclubs were being negotiated for purchase by the attorneys for the Diamondbacks and the Venomous club attorneys swept in and made a deal that fast and took it out from under them. *Both* clubs, same time. Same seller owned them. He signed the deal and got out of town. Far more money for him too. That was on the Diamondbacks for trying to force the strip club owner to sell to them far below what the clubs were worth," Absinthe said.

"True," Savage agreed. "But the real question is, how did the Venomous club know to swoop in and take the deal?"

"That is a damn good question."

"I think so too," Savage said. "I don't know, Absinthe, but it seems to me, ever since we took that job and ran across the Ghosts and the Russian's assassins, we've run into more and more snitches. Not in our club, but I think other clubs have them planted in them."

Absinthe took a sip of his coffee. It had grown cold. He'd never liked cold coffee and he pushed the cup away. Shit. Savage was right. "You think the Russian has someone in each of the clubs feeding him information?"

Savage took his sunglasses out of his pocket and shoved them on his nose, hiding his glacier-cold eyes from the sun that was now permanently out. "No, he wouldn't waste his manpower that way. He would use his men to come at us, because he's a fucking pedophile and loves little kids. That means we aren't going to stop until we find him. He has to find a way to get someone in with us. No, someone else is looking to get an 'in' into the clubs."

"The Ghosts," Absinthe guessed. "They're just a bunch of dumb fucks looking to make money off the clubs. They have no idea who the Russian is or who the supposed hit men they use are. They're playing with fire and eventually, they're going to get burned. You can bet the Russian knows who they are. It's the Ghosts buying off snitches in the clubs."

"Has to be. They have money and they're paying the weak links in the clubs for information. Get the right intelligence on them, or use the right bribe." Savage shrugged. "The Diamondbacks are a big club. That big, you'd like to think all the brothers are solid, but it only takes one bad one and that one can bring a lot of good brothers down. Who owns the other strip club?" he added.

"The Venomous club rent it from a woman named Haley Joico. She has a very big insurance policy on the building and had a sit-down with the Diamondbacks recently. They wanted to buy it from her, and she refused to sell. She wouldn't sell to the Venomous club either. Both clubs got a little rough with her, but she didn't cave. According to Code, she inherited the club from her uncle and she's trying

to make it work for the women who work there. He had one
of the few places with a good reputation for his girls. Good
pay, safe work environment, that sort of thing."

"I take it we're not burning that one to the ground," Savage said. "Does Code know what the club manager is doing
with it? If the Venomous club is running the place, how did
they manage to wrest it out of her hands?"

"He's looking into that. It wouldn't make sense that she
refused to sell and then turned around and rented it out,
leaving her girls in the club's hands anyway," Absinthe
said. "Czar wants the information before we head out."

"Sucks that your woman is under threat and we've got
this hanging over our heads," Savage said. "Is Czar insisting you go with us?"

"I'll go. I'm part of the team. We don't break up the
team, you know that." Absinthe had the feeling Savage was
testing him.

"That's what I thought you'd say." There was a small
silence. Savage took off his glasses and looked Absinthe in
the eyes without blinking. "I need to find some action soon
or something bad is going to happen." He made the statement softly. There was no question. No asking for help.
Nothing whatsoever in that gently worded declaration, but
Absinthe knew what it meant.

His gut churned. He'd helped to cause this. It didn't matter that he'd been a child and didn't know better. He did
now what he'd done then—used his gift. It was so much
more powerful now. So strong. Few could resist his voice
when he wanted to influence them. They didn't use their
talents on one another, it was strictly forbidden—especially
his talent.

"You certain, Savage?" He had to ask. He hadn't asked
as a child. He'd done it to ease their pain. To make it easier
for them. He hadn't known what he was doing, what he was
helping to create. He still didn't know, if he had a choice, if

he knew the consequences, if he still would choose the same path.

"I'll kill someone, Absinthe. Or really hurt a woman. I don't want to do that, even if she gives me her consent. I couldn't live with myself if I did. You've managed to keep me going more than once. I don't know how you do it, but you do." He kept looking him in the eye. "I know it isn't easy for you, so thanks."

Hell no, it wasn't easy. Taking on those nightmares. Those images turned his stomach. He understood why Savage believed he was lost. Absinthe had spent a thousand hours, more even, looking up the making of a sadist in the library and the unmaking of one. How to cure one. How to make them "normal." There was no normal for Savage. There never would be. Absinthe accepted his part in creating that monster.

He couldn't actually label Savage a sadist. That was the closest thing he could come to calling him, yet Savage wasn't cruel to others. He didn't like to hurt people, rather he was the first to protect them. When it came to his sexual needs, that was a different story altogether. The things he'd endured and the things he'd been forced to do would never leave him and when the memories were too close and threatened to consume him, as clearly was happening now, rage welled up like a volcano in Savage, making him a very dangerous man.

Absinthe took a breath. "Just breathe for a minute, Savage."

He deliberately didn't share how he did this. He never touched his brother when he eased those demons. That way, Savage didn't realize he invaded his mind in the way he did when he interrogated their enemies. He was familiar with the pathways to every one of his brothers and sisters; he'd been working on strengthening them since his childhood.

With Savage, he always had to prepare himself for the blood and gore. The screams of pain. The scent of burning flesh. The way his stomach churned and the mixture of sexual need that all ran together. Dark and terrible cravings rushed at him like vicious tentacles ready to wrap around him, snakes of brutality struck at him with sharp teeth, biting deep. A little boy with a mop of blond ringlets all over his head curled naked in a corner, his body covered in bright red stripes.

Absinthe saw himself on one side, Demyan on the other, both trying to console that young Savage. There was no place to touch him, no place to keep from hurting him. Everywhere bled. Steele knelt, trying to find a way to make the bleeding stop. Reaper and Czar raged. Demyan and Absinthe both whispered to him: "Accept it. You like it. You like giving the pain. You like taking the pain. Accept the pain. It's your friend. You know you're alive."

Over time that mantra had changed. Savage had been the one expected to please their brutal captors by entertaining them with their whips and brands. If he didn't, so many would suffer or be killed. He was given little choice if he wanted his brother alive. He became very, very good at what he did, even as a young teen. It sickened him so much that Absinthe would whisper to him continually to help him, both before and after.

"You like this. You need it. You crave it. You have to have it."

Savage complied with their tormentors' demands, although it didn't stop them from beating him or treating him just as cruelly. Absinthe and his brother worked harder to make it as easy as possible on him.

Savage was so sick most of the time he couldn't keep down food. He cried. He stayed alone. He refused to talk to the others or look at them. Absinthe and Demyan both continued to try to help him accept what he couldn't change. None of them ever believed they would live through their time at the school. It didn't occur to them that what they were being trained to do sexually for their captors as children and then as teens, all the way to adulthood, they would continue to crave even after they escaped. Those practices would be ingrained in them.

"Accept who you are," he whispered to Savage under his breath straight into that pathway, his brain to his chosen brother's. "There is no monster. You do nothing wrong. You don't want to hurt anyone. Be at peace with yourself."

He did his best to try to take the worst of Savage's sins. He knew they weren't Savage's. Those were on the men who had so cruelly used a little child and then thought it would be great fun to teach that child to become one of them. They had never considered that the child would surpass the instructors. Not only had he learned from them dark sexual practices, but all of them had been trained to be assassins for their country.

If that hadn't been enough, in order to survive a school they weren't meant to survive, they had to crawl through vents as children and kill the worst of their instructors. While all of them had played their part gathering information, Reaper and Savage had been the two who had most excelled at the actual killings while the others kept watch.

Absinthe breathed deep, trying not to look or act sick in any way in front of Savage. If he failed, he knew his brother would never come to him for help again. He couldn't speak, so he waited in silence.

Savage sat for a few minutes and then slowly nodded his head. "I don't know how the hell you do it, but you fuckin' save my life every single time. Thanks, bro."

Absinthe shoved his cold coffee cup toward him and indicated it. Savage heaved a sigh. More than anything, he detested dealing with people. He stood up, looked over at Lana and Alena with such a pained look on his face that in spite of his churning stomach, Absinthe wanted to smile. Both women immediately rolled their eyes, stood up and took the coffee cups.

"You're such a coward, Savage," Lana hissed.

Savage looked completely unperturbed now that the women were doing what he wanted them to do. He sauntered back to his table, winking at Absinthe over his shoulder.

NINE

Scarlet's heart was beating far too fast as she watched Absinthe saunter over to the car through her rearview mirror. He took her breath away. He was tall with wide shoulders and wearing his jeans, motorcycle boots and that tight tee that stretched across his thick chest and incredible arms. He wore a thin leather vest over it. His hair tumbled wildly around his face and there was that ever-present blue shadow on his jaw. She could hardly breathe just looking at him.

Hand on the door, she managed to open it with shaky fingers and then she was in his arms and his mouth was on hers. She hadn't imagined the way he kissed, hotter than hell, consuming her, pouring fire down her throat until she went up in flames and there was only Absinthe with his rock-hard body and his amazing, most intelligent brain, those large, strong hands that could be by turns gentle and then rough, melting her.

She slid her arms around his neck and let herself surrender to him in a way she'd never given herself to anyone before. It felt good, and more, it felt right. Absinthe held her as if she were the only woman in his world, protectively, when she knew she wasn't the kind of woman who needed protection. Still, she wanted it.

She kissed him back, heat rising, blood rushing, feeling alive, that woman she kept hidden deep rejoicing in being set free. For him. She felt she could do anything for him. She might not have been with him for these past six weeks, but she'd connected with him. She'd noticed every little thing about him. She felt like she knew him whether they'd actually been physically together or not. She told herself a million times she was crazy, and yet she couldn't help herself. Being with Absinthe made sense, she fit with him. She didn't know why, she just knew she belonged with him.

He lifted his head and framed her face with his hands. Just the way he did that, his crystal-blue eyes staring down into hers, brought another rush of heat so that flames licked over her skin and settled in her stomach, burning brightly.

"You drive way too fast, *ledi*." That velvet voice was a low growl. A reprimand that slid over her, bringing more flames, this time fiery tongues that raged between her legs and stormed into her feminine channel, a blaze that wouldn't stop and only he could put out.

"I needed to get to you," she admitted simply. It was the truth.

"I told you I wanted you alive, Scarlet." He brushed a brief kiss across her lower lip and then caught that pouty curve between his teeth.

Her heart accelerated and blood thundered through her clit. Her breasts suddenly felt swollen and achy, too large for the sexy lacy bra she'd bought just for him.

He bit down gently, all the while looking into her eyes. It was so intense. She felt like she was drowning in all that strange light blue. No one had eyes like he did. He mesmerized her when he looked at her with that dark intensity that stole her will. She knew this man could command her to do anything. If he'd told her to take her clothes off right there in the parking lot, she would have for him.

"Alive is better than fast, isn't that what I said, baby? Alive is the most important to me. I'm grateful you wanted to get here, that means a lot to me, but that road can be dangerous, and your safety is what matters the most. I trust that the next time I say that to you, you're going to listen to me."

"Absinthe." She was a better-than-average driver. There hadn't been any danger.

His hand slipped to the nape of her neck. "Scarlet, I searched for years for the woman I could actually feel something for, let alone fall in love with. One I could have that kind of mind-blowing sex with. One I could talk to without wanting to lose my fucking mind. A woman who could bring my mind peace when it was so chaotic from feeling everyone's emotions. Years, babe. Fucking years. I never thought you existed. I walked into that library looking for a little peace. Just a little. And I found you. Do you think I want to risk you? I don't. Not for any reason. I don't want you taking risks when you don't need to. Not for a few extra minutes when I want a lifetime with you."

She blinked up at him, afraid she had stars in her eyes. He was . . . wonderful. "I'll be more careful."

"I want you to listen to me and do the things I ask you to do."

She had listened. She always listened. She loved his voice and went over and over every word he said. She couldn't help it. She nodded. "I will."

His smile was slow in coming. That one that started so slow it seemed to take forever so she found herself anticipating it. Watching that slow climb from the small quirk of his lips to the sheen in the crystal blue of his eyes. Her stomach dropped and did a slow roll and then the butterflies took wing. Did they really need to talk? Maybe they should just find a room somewhere. Talking wasn't as great as people made it out to be.

He bent his head again and kissed her. If he gave her kisses every time she did what he wanted her to do, then she was going to be so obedient he was going to be in heaven. He could have anything he wanted. She was addicted to his kisses and the best sex in the world. Her body turned pliant, boneless, melting into his. Little sparks of electricity snapped and sparked over her skin, bright and hot. Fire roared in the pit of her belly. She couldn't think straight. She clung to him when he lifted his head.

"We'd better stop before we get arrested."

"I suppose." She sounded pouty even to her own ears. "Although it would be worth it." She glanced down at the vest she was clutching with both hands. It took a moment to come down from the sexual rush his kisses produced to register what he was wearing.

Her mouth went dry. She tried to step back but he was holding her close, one hand still curled around the nape of her neck. She let her palm slide from his shoulder to one of the patches on the front of his vest. "You're in a club."

His blue eyes looked down at her, clear and innocent. "Yeah. All eighteen of us. Big club. I told you, we were all raised together. Now we ride together and look out for one another. I want you to meet them, but first, I want us to talk. This was one of the things I wanted to tell you about."

Scarlet hesitated, blinking up at him. She took her sunglasses off very slowly. "I'm not really fond of MCs, Absinthe. And before you think I'm judgy, I have reason to be."

"I'm striking out all over the place. You don't like that I'm an attorney and you don't like that I'm in a club."

He shrugged, that roll of his wide shoulders so casual she got that weird slow somersault in the pit of her stomach again. He could do that to her so easily.

"We both have pasts, Scarlet. That's what we're here for, to talk about them."

She lifted her gaze to look beyond him, sweeping the patio with the tables and brightly colored umbrellas. The rows of motorcycles and men seated, the two women. Immediately, she chose her targets. The big man, all muscle, seated at the middle table, with the shaved head and the dark, mirrored glasses would have to go first. She'd kill him and then the one seated to the left of him at the next table. The dark-haired woman who had come in the library . . .

"Stop it." Absinthe's voice was low. Commanding. Held a whip of fury. "Those people are my family. They protected you. They went out of their way to protect you. You don't get to even think about killing them."

She tilted her head to look at him. "What do you mean, they protected me?"

"I told you we had to talk. Let's sit down."

"I'll be surrounded by your club."

"You'll be surrounded by my family. I can ask them to leave if you're so damned worried. You aren't a coward, Scarlet. I wanted you to know as much about me as fast as I could let you in. That was important to me. These people know me. They lived through the nightmare with me. If I want to let you in, then I can't just give you a little part of me. I have to let you see who I am. Isn't that what we talked about over the last couple of days?"

He was right. They had. She just hadn't expected . . . this. But she should have. He rode a Harley like he'd been born on one. He'd referred to his "sisters" as women he'd been raised with. She'd thought they were in the foster care system with him. Now she knew he was from Russia and his family had been murdered. There was much more to his story, she realized. She did want to know all of it. She wanted to know every single detail because he was willing to tell her. He was right about her. She wasn't a coward.

She looked at those seated, drinking coffee, talking together at the various tables. She'd registered the occasional arrival of a motorcycle while kissing Absinthe somewhere in the distant background, but nothing had mattered to her but his kisses—then. This was his family. Eighteen of them, he'd said. It wasn't a big club. Not like the clubs Holden turned to when he wanted people to cooperate with him. When he wanted witnesses against his son to recant their testimony.

Scarlet took a deep breath and lifted her chin. "All right, Absinthe. Let's go talk." She had all her weapons on her. She would be closer to her targets.

He lifted his eyebrow but took her elbow and turned her toward the shaded tables on the patio. "I thought you'd feel better if we talked in a public place rather than at the club-house or my home."

"I can see why." She kept her voice low, trying not to sound sarcastic when she felt a little raw. She didn't know what to think and so she did her best to keep her mind blank. She didn't want to make a snap judgment. Absinthe had asked her to meet him in public. He had been open about his club first thing on her arrival. She couldn't fault him on that.

"What would you like to drink?"

She'd been looking forward to a latte, but her churning stomach warned her that she'd better be careful. "I think I'll stick with water for the moment."

He nodded his understanding and made some sign she couldn't really see to a man who had long hair swept back from his face and was unreasonably good-looking. Like Absinthe, he had more muscles than was good for him. He wore the jeans, tight tee and vest with motorcycle boots the rest of them did, but she could see why when he got up from his seat, several girls in cars waiting in the drive-thru hung out of their windows to watch him.

"Don't like you staring at Master, baby. Eyes on me."

"His name is *Master*? Really?"

"That's what we call him for a number of reasons."

He reached across the table and picked up her hand, the pad of his thumb sliding back and forth, mesmerizing her. She should have pulled away from him, just to keep her wits about her, but she couldn't resist him.

"Thank God you're not called that."

"You wouldn't call me Master?"

His voice dropped an octave. Turned sexual. Sensual lines were carved deep into his face. He brought the back of her hand up to his jaw and rubbed along the faint bluish bristles there. She tried not to breathe him into her lungs, but there was that faint scent of sandalwood she associated with him.

"I might, under the right circumstances." Unfortunately, that was strictly the truth.

He sucked the tips of her fingers into the heat of his mouth and then bit down gently on them. "That's the right answer. Thank you for looking past the club."

"I need to know what you meant when you said they were all protecting me."

"I'll tell you, Scarlet, but you're going to get pissed. Let me start at the beginning so things won't be out of context and then you'll understand. That way, we'll have a chance. More than anything, I want a chance with you."

She believed him. Over the last ten years she had worked very hard at developing the ability to learn how to listen to voices to discern the truth from lies. Maybe part of believing him was she desperately wanted him to be real. She glanced around them once more.

Absinthe had led her to the last table in the long row away from the street. The man she had pegged as the most dangerous sat at the table closest to them with the dark-haired woman and two other men. Now that she could see the men, they all looked dangerous. These men weren't just average everyday businessmen or simple hell-raisers as Absinthe portrayed them.

Scarlet assessed them now that she was closer. She was definitely in over her head. She had trained with a man that others who were threatening spoke of in whispers, yet she knew these men in the Torpedo Ink colors were equally as dangerous, or more so. She should have recognized it in Absinthe immediately, but she'd been too enamored by him. She'd first seen him in a library, the most non-threatening place in the world.

"Every one of the charter members of Torpedo Ink, our club, was born in Russia. Our parents were opposed to the same candidate, a man who had a powerful friend by the name of Sorbacov, who commanded a secret military branch. Mostly the families were feared because most of them not only had money and influence, but because they had some form of psychic gift or talent that ran strong in their family. At that time, the government was secretly acknowledging that there was truth to these gifts and were trying to utilize them for the military, something these families were against."

He had told her about Sorbacov when he disclosed the information about his murdered family. This was something that also rang true. She had looked up psychic gifts when she was trying to find ways to improve her own meager talents. She had traced the more detailed experiments back to Russia.

Master returned with two bottles of cold water. Up close he was daunting-looking. She could see tattoos running under his shirt and climbing down very muscular arms. He had faint scars on his face and neck.

"Scarlet, Master. Master, *miledi*, Scarlet."

Master had a killer smile. "Nice to meet the woman who conquered the unconquerable."

"Is that what I did?"

"Yes, ma'am. That's exactly what you did." Master saluted her and sauntered back to his seat.

Absinthe hadn't protested, but his eyes looked more

crystal than ever. His thumb slid over her inner wrist, landed directly on her pulse. "You seem very susceptible to him. Do you prefer him to me? Tell me the truth."

"No woman would prefer him to you," Scarlet blurted before she could stop herself. "All I can think about is you. I can't sleep or eat. I just want to be with you. Sometimes I think I'd do anything for you and then I remember I barely know you and that it's crazy to be so obsessed."

He brought her wrist to his mouth and pressed a kiss over her heartbeat. "Funny that I feel exactly the same way about you."

"Do you?" She was horrified that she'd told him the truth. What was wrong with her?

"Yes. I'm giving you things about myself I've never told anyone else. No one knows what I'm going to be telling you outside of those that are the charter members of Torpedo Ink. If you stay with me, you'll know things about me that even they don't know."

That was a lure right there. Absinthe wasn't the kind of man to just share everything about himself with everyone. He didn't have relationships. She looked around at the other tables. If she were to make an educated guess, she doubted if any of these men or women really did. Or if they did, like Absinthe, they didn't go into them easily or often.

"We weren't the only children that were ripped from their parents over the years. It became a very common practice of Sorbacov's. He established four schools. All were brutal. Three were legitimate schools training the children of the parents he had murdered to be assets for the country. The fourth school he set up for himself and his friends to use to play in. Although Sorbacov was married with children of his own and well-respected, although feared, he was a very sick man. He was a pedophile. He liked very young boys. More, he liked to torture the boys as he raped them. He especially enjoyed watching the torture and rape of young girls while he raped the boys. The fourth school he put in place was on the outskirts of the city, hidden away, and run by the criminally insane."

Scarlet heard the difference in his tone immediately. There was absolutely no question that he was telling the truth. He had gone from casual to disconnected. He could have been telling her about the weather. There was no expression in his voice at all. Her lungs began to burn for air, telling her she had to breathe, she needed to take a breath. He was holding on to her hand and she was afraid he might crush her fingers, but instead, he held her with infinite gentleness. She didn't understand how that was possible.

"I was taken to that school along with Demyan, when I was four and he just turning seven. We were taken there, more, I think, because Sorbacov liked our looks than because he understood our parents' psychic talents."

She wondered what those talents were, but she didn't want to interrupt him to ask. She glanced again around the patio at the other members of Torpedo Ink sitting there, talking low to one another as if they didn't have a care in the world. She couldn't imagine what had been done to all of them, only that it was so terrible, Absinthe couldn't speak with any inflection when his voice was always so expressive.

"There were two hundred and eighty-seven children taken to that school over the years and only eighteen survived. Those eighteen survivors are the charter members of Torpedo Ink."

Somewhere in the back of her mind she registered the fact that he had used the term *charter members* multiple times, but the number of children dying in that vile place that had *not* been a school was horrific.

"We were raped, beaten and tortured. We were taught to use sex as a weapon and multiple ways to assassinate for our country, although we weren't really expected to survive. We were thrown together in a freezing-cold environment without clothes or much in the way of food. Most of us continually had open wounds from whips and burns, the beatings and rapes. It never stopped. We were starving and hopeless. Often, if any of us fought back, they would chain a child up in front of all of us and beat them to near death and then leave them to die slow so we'd see what would happen to us if we resisted."

Scarlet had to turn away, her stomach threatening to heave. She pulled her hand away from his, vivid images finding their way into her mind. "Absinthe. How did *any* of you survive under those brutal conditions? My God."

She looked around her again at the various members of the Torpedo Ink club. Could any of them be sane? She wasn't entirely sane after what she'd been through. She knew Absinthe was telling her his history fast, whitewashing it to some degree, maybe to a huge degree. She heard the "assassinate for their country" part. They were every bit as lethal as she thought them.

"It took us years to get out. We were there until some of us were well into our twenties. One of us had to take an assignment to assassinate the international president of a motorcycle club. We discovered he was the brother of a billionaire and ran one of the biggest human trafficking rings worldwide. One by one, when we could, we joined the club he rode with in order to protect his back."

Absinthe handed Scarlet her water. "Drink something, baby. You're so pale. I want you to hear this, but if you need a break, just say so. We can go next door to the Botanical Gardens and walk around for a little bit."

He was so thoughtful, worried about her when he was the one having to relive his childhood for her. She shook her head. "Keep going. Get it over with so you don't have to think about it."

"Sorbacov tried to put out hits on all the students in the various schools he thought might reflect badly on him or his son, Uri, who wanted to be president. Eventually Sorbacov and his son, Uri, were killed and we were free to live the way we wanted to live. Czar, the one sent on the original assignment, rather than abandon it, after putting so much time in and working his way close, even putting his marriage on the line, decided to stay. He told us to go, but each of us made the decision to stay and take down the ring. Someone had to do it."

Scarlet closed her eyes briefly. Of course that would be something men like Absinthe and the others would do. After what they'd been through, they would detest anyone who trafficked in children or men or women. She took a slow drink of the cool water, letting it slide down her burning throat. She had never expected anything remotely close to what Absinthe was telling her. Not even remotely.

In Thailand, she'd lived with a Russian, Adrik Orlov, for a year. Rather, she trained with him, cleaned his home and cooked for him. She had her own tiny place on his property. She suspected he also had been from one of those schools, obviously not the same as the one Absinthe had been in, but one of the others. His brutal training methods made much more sense now. At first, he had been horrible, but she had persevered, determined to learn everything she could from him. Once he saw she would stick with him, he hadn't been quite so inhumane. She had bruises and he'd broken her arm once and on two occasions her ribs, but she'd turned up for training and he'd been the one to call it off, not her.

"Once we took that down, we came here to the coast to find Czar's wife, Blythe. It took a bit to set things right with her. They took in some children from the trafficking ring with no relatives and then another boy we found when we stopped another pedophile. So we ended up setting up the club here. All of us bought homes and started businesses here. We'd like to make this our permanent residence. We're very careful with all the locals including law enforcement to keep everything good. We want to raise our families here."

"You're serious?"

He picked up his water bottle, broke the seal on the cap and took a healthy swallow. "Very serious. I have a house I'd like you to take a look at. You don't like it, we can sell that one and look at others."

She sat back in the chair and regarded him with a small frown. "You're moving way too fast, Absinthe. We've had two dates. You don't know me. You don't know anything about me."

"Actually, I do. That's going to get us to the me-pissing-you-off part."

"Don't piss me off yet." Scarlet hated to admit it, but she had to use the bathroom. She'd driven all the way from Sonoma and now she was chugging water down so even though she wanted to hear everything he had to say, it had to wait. "I need to go inside and find the restroom."

"Small place, babe. I think you'll see it right away." Absinthe stood anyway and walked with her inside, his fingers tangling with hers.

He was right. It was a small coffee shop, but obviously popular. All the tables inside were taken as well, but not by Torpedo Ink members. That didn't surprise her. None of them seemed the indoor type to her, especially in close quarters. She went straight to the bathroom, grateful it wasn't in use.

The roar of pipes was very loud through the open window even over the sound of running water as she washed her hands. There hadn't been eighteen members of Torpedo Ink sitting at the tables, so maybe the rest of Absinthe's club had come to join them. Still, just the sound of the motorcycles made her tense up. She couldn't help herself and she needed to get over that if she was really going to make a real effort at a life with him—and she wanted to. This was her one chance with a man who would match her in everything she needed or wanted. Everything. They might have a million issues to work out, but every single one would be well worth the effort.

Before Absinthe got to the part where he pissed her off, she had to do some confessing of her own. He had definitely told her things about himself he wouldn't have told to just anyone. She had to learn trust all over again. The way her parents had died had shaken her belief in them and in their love for her. She'd lost faith that anyone could actually love her. That was really at the heart of her issues. Not only did she feel the guilt of her sister's death weighing her down, but she didn't believe anyone could ever really love her. If her own parents couldn't stay alive for her and see her through Priscilla's rape and death, if they blamed her, how could anyone else really love her? Wasn't a mother's love unconditional at least?

She looked at herself in the mirror. Her green eyes stared back at her. She'd come into the room believing she had a chance with Absinthe, and just that quickly she'd talked herself out of it. She had to stop and grab at life with both hands while she had the chance. If she didn't, if she was a coward, the chance wouldn't come around again.

The moment she stepped outside the restroom door; she knew something was wrong. The man named Savage was inside, one hip leaning lazily against the wall right next to the entrance. Absinthe waited for her beside the glass case of ice cream toppings.

"What is it?" Scarlet asked, looking up at him.

"Stay right in between Savage and me," Absinthe said. "Give us both room to maneuver just in case. We're going to walk to my motorcycle. We'll leave your car here. Savage will cover you while you get on and we'll head to the club-house."

He spoke very low, but there was something in his voice that told her not to argue and, more, made her want to obey every word. As he talked, he walked her straight toward the door. Savage opened it and then fell into step with the two of them.

Scarlet didn't ask questions because she saw the small group of bikers heading toward them. She could easily read the name of the club on the cuts. Venomous club. She'd been told by her new attorney how each of the witnesses had been visited by these club members and they were too scared to take the stand and tell the truth of what had happened that night. Her original defense attorney, and the judge, had known the witnesses had been intimidated and were too scared to testify on her behalf, although they'd written out sworn statements.

The men stopped the moment they saw Absinthe and Savage with Scarlet in between them. One stepped forward. A patch proclaimed him as the sergeant at arms.

"Absinthe."

"Iron."

"See you got to her first. We were supposed to have a few days' start. Since you found her first, we'll share the reward with you. And the fun. Holden wants her used hard, just brought to him alive. We can take her back to our club-house . . ."

"You fucking bastard," Scarlet hissed softly under her breath. The sense of betrayal made her sick. Her hand moved toward the gun concealed in her camisole.

Savage caught her wrist gently, but his fingers dug deep. "Don't be a fuckin' moron," he snapped, his voice equally as low. "Absinthe said you had a brain. You think he'd tell you all that shit about him—about us—if he was turning you over to Holden? You think you'd still have your fuckin' weapons? Choose your targets but don't tip them off. We don't want civilians hurt and they're all over the place. Be fuckin' cool."

"Iron, if you think I'm turning my woman over to you for any reason, you're wrong. She's mine. Your club makes a try for her for any reason, *any* reason, we'll consider that war."

Absinthe ignored the byplay between Savage and Scarlet as if he hadn't heard it. He didn't so much as look at her and she was glad. Savage was right. She just was so ready to always believe the worst, and it was really her lack of confidence in herself. Savage wasn't gentle in the way Absinthe was. She had the feeling if she was his woman, he would have delivered some kind of punishment, if not on the spot, then later. As it was, she felt the heat of his glare and was totally humiliated that she'd made such a mistake.

"War?" Iron smirked. "Last time I looked, you got shit members, Absinthe."

"Well I guess you'd better take another look."

Absinthe kept walking and Scarlet kept pace, although she wasn't certain if it was really her own choice. Something inside wouldn't allow her to stop. It was as if the moment Absinthe had given her that order in the coffee shop, she couldn't find it in her to disobey him. She did as Savage said and chose her targets.

She noticed that Lana was missing and did a subtle, quick look around, her gaze behind her dark glasses going to the rooftops. Lana was lying on a building behind a fence, rifle at her shoulder. She wasn't the only one. A good-looking man covered in tattoos sat alone in a chair at one of the tables, wearing the Torpedo Ink colors. Gathered around him, on the ground, were six big ravens. She glanced at the telephone line overhead. A dozen more ravens with thick, wicked-looking curved beaks sat on the line, making it sag with their heavy weight, while at least six others flew in a lazy circle in the air. She gave a delicate shudder. The scene was a little too reminiscent of an old scary movie she'd watched once.

Absinthe swung onto his bike while Savage faced the members of the Venomous club who had loosely trailed after them. Scarlet turned to face them as well.

"Put the helmet and jacket on," Absinthe commanded tersely.

Okay, maybe he was upset with her. She couldn't blame

him, but it had been a momentary lapse. Hopefully, once she explained herself, he would be his usual understanding self. She vowed that whatever he had done that he said would "piss her off" she would be very understanding about.

She caught up the Torpedo Ink jacket he all but shoved into her hands and slipped it on without a word. The helmet was next. She tucked in her hair and then put her foot on the peg and was behind him, wrapping her arms around him. She heard several bikes start up.

"What about Savage?" She had to yell in his ear to have him hear over the loud pipes.

Absinthe glanced at her over his shoulder with a look that asked her if she was crazy. She looked at the man who just stepped right into Iron, backing him and the other six men he was with away from Absinthe's Harley, making room so he could turn onto the road and drive onto the main highway leading back to Caspar. Several bikes dropped into formation behind them.

Scarlet wished she could be in two places at one time. She wanted to see how many had stayed behind to make certain Savage was safe. He hadn't seemed in the least worried facing the seven members of the Venomous club. In fact, they'd looked more scared than he had. She knew the reputation of the Venomous club because she made it her business to find out. They were working hard to make a name for themselves. To do that, they were getting as dirty as possible, which meant running drugs, guns and girls and getting bloody when they had to.

They always looked for new allies. Only the smaller clubs who had no one else were aligning themselves with the Venomous club, yet all of a sudden they were gaining numbers in their ranks and picking off the edges of other clubs' territories. They seemed to have money to purchase real estate. She couldn't figure out where they were getting their money. Holden gave them work, but not the kind of money needed for the purchase of clubs and fronting the types of deals they were making.

She pressed her hands tighter into Absinthe's abs, moving with him as he took a long curve in the road. She loved riding with him on the Harley. She suddenly was very glad he was in a club. His hand moved over hers just for a moment and then they were speeding up a slight grade and slowing for a turn off the main highway into Caspar, the other bikes close behind. He went considerably slower as he maneuvered the narrower streets of the small town going toward the ocean.

She could feel the cool breeze and smell the salt air. Looking over his shoulder, straight ahead, the ocean was a deep blue with white waves rushing toward rocks and then folding over the top of them. The sight was beautiful. They drove through an open, wide rolling gate surrounded by an extremely high fence that could turn a large lovely piece of property overlooking the sea into a fortress in seconds.

There was an enormous building looming up just ahead and Absinthe rode straight to it. The parking lot was paved. There was a narrow sidewalk in front of the building, but on the side was a long, wide field of flowers with several fire pits, large outdoor barbecues, benches and picnic tables. She could see it would be easy to have outdoor parties there for a sizable crowd.

Absinthe put her hand on his shoulder and she climbed off the bike. This time her legs weren't shaky. They hadn't ridden hundreds of miles as they had the first time. She removed the helmet and started to take off the jacket, but he was already off the Harley and he took her hand before she could. Two men came out of the building to greet them.

"Fatei, Hitch, keep a good lookout. If anyone from any other club gets close, warn us and shut everything down. The bar's already been warned. Preacher's closing early for the night." Absinthe switched his grip from her hand to the nape of her neck. "Scarlet's been threatened by the Venom-ous club and it looks as if that club won't be the only one."

Fatei nodded and Hitch looked grim. Both men avoided looking too long at her. She caught their quick glance and then they were moving away.

"Fatei is about to become a full member and he's earned it. He went to the same school Gavriil attended. Most of the others were moved from one school to the other. A few were even brought briefly to our school, but it was more of a threat than anything else. Fatei's tough and he's loyal. Our club is really for those of us that have nowhere to go. We don't fit anywhere and we never are going to. That's the bot-tom line with me, Scarlet."

Absinthe stopped at the door to the clubhouse, turning to face her, one hand on the doorknob, the other on the nape of her neck. "I'm fucked up. I always will be. There aren't any cures for us. When I ask you to trust me, that's exactly what I need from you. I'll give you everything I am, but I'll expect everything from you. I won't accept less. Before you make your decision, you need to know things about me and determine whether or not you can live with them. I want honesty between us. I'm doing my best here, but I'm not getting anything back from you."

He was right. She was protecting herself, feeling like the woman who'd retreated behind the mask she'd created for herself. She was hiding there again, terrified, afraid of be-lieving anyone could really love her. The moment her faith in him had been tested, she'd failed. She knew it would happen again and again.

"Before you open that door and we go any further, Ab-sinthe, you have to know that I want to be with you more than anything in the world. I came to you with that inten-tion. You think you're fucked up, but you don't hold the corner on that market. I am too. I have issues as well and, sadly, I'm not certain I'll get over them no matter how much I want to. And I do, for you, for me, so we can be together."

"No matter what, whether you accept me or not, our club is going to protect you, Scarlet. We're not letting you face Holden or any of the MCs he sends after you."

Scarlet's heart skipped a beat. "Just how much do you know about Holden and me?"

TEN

Absinthe pushed the door open and waved Scarlet inside.
Someone had already turned on the gas fireplace and the
logs were burning low, sending heat through the cavernous
room. At one time, the building had originally been a pay-
master's building. Turning it into their clubhouse had been
a labor of love. Master, Keys, Player and Maestro were all
woodworkers in their way, builders and craftsmen. Aside
from loving instruments and all things music, they had an
affinity for building things.

The four members of Torpedo Ink had taken on the older,
run-down properties the club had acquired and, one by
one, began to rebuild them, most from the ground up. Together they formed a construction company, although they
rarely took a job outside of the club because they were busy
restoring Caspar into the beautiful little village it once was.

The common room was a favorite of Absinthe's not only
because was there a tremendous amount of space, even
when they were throwing parties, but because the design fit
with the actual layout of the outside landscape. The long

sweeping bar was curved, the top made of a gleaming oak. Bar stools were comfortable and inviting, but not as comfortable as the furniture Lana had chosen for the room.

Lana had asked him what, if anything, she had a talent for. She might think she wasn't good at anything, but it wasn't so. Anya could look at the bar and immediately notice all the things that would help Preacher improve it. She could shave steps off the work areas, make the drinks faster and more efficiently, just by the placement of the alcohol. She did the same with the tables and chairs and where the dance floor was located in relation to where customers purchased drinks, but she didn't know the first thing about seating.

Lana knew how to make everyone comfortable seated in those chairs. She knew the exact tables and chairs that would look perfect in the bar. Or the clubhouse. Or Alena's restaurant. Between Anya's eye for the details of making things work easier for Alena and Lana's eye for comfort and beauty, and Alena's for food, the restaurant was a huge success, the bar as well, and all of them felt right at home in the clubhouse.

He indicated one of the armchairs across from the fireplace for Scarlet to sit and glanced up at the camera before tapping his finger on the table next to it. Just walking through the entrance they'd been scanned for any recording devices. It was imperative that they were always careful. Scarlet had weapons on her, but hopefully she hadn't come prepared to record any conversation between them.

Soft music flooded the room in answer. She was clean. Absinthe took the chair at an angle from her, very close. He wanted to see her face, but if necessary, be able to run his fingers over her pulse.

"I told you about how we lived in those harsh conditions as children and what those fuckers did to us every damn day. We had to find a way to survive, Scarlet. You may as well know one of the worst things I've done. We began to target them. First the worst of them. The ones that liked to kill and do it especially painfully. Some of us would crawl through the vents together. One or two would be on lookout. I would make the suggestion to look the other way or not to see. Either Demyan or I would sacrifice ourselves, whoever was in the best shape, and let the fucker have us until the others were in place. Then we'd make the suggestion to look the other way, to not see, and either Reaper, Savage, Maestro or Keys would come out of the vent and slit their throat. At the same time, Mechanic would disrupt the security cameras, looping them, so no one would ever see any of us with our chosen victim."

Silence stretched between them. He didn't speak again. He knew she had killed on behalf of her family. She'd taken her revenge, or what she may have considered justice for her sister, yet she just stared at him with her vivid green eyes. There was no judgment in them, no shock, just a strange kind of disbelief.

Scarlet eventually shook her head, frowning. "Absinthe. You were just little kids. Children. All of you, right?"

He nodded. "I was barely five years old the first time I went with them. It was scary, but we all did our part. It was the only way. We knew they were going to kill us. So many were already dead. Not everyone could know. They would tell. Sorbacov would bribe some of the kids with good food and candy, pretend he would let them out or tell them he would let their younger sisters or brothers go home. He wouldn't, but he'd lie, and you'd want it so desperately that some believed him."

"You didn't?"

"Even then, I could hear lies."

"Who planned these attacks out?"

He shrugged. "It wasn't me. I have brothers who are brilliant strategists. I can do things, but I wouldn't have thought of that particular solution, not in time anyway. At least I don't think so."

He wasn't about to incriminate anyone else any further. Even if she told someone a preposterous tale about his fellow club members murdering their pedophile captors, who would believe her? He'd given her enough truth about who he was. Either she was going to give him something of herself back, or she wasn't.

Scarlet sighed. "I'm not a saint no matter what you might think. There's a reason Holden wants the Venomous club to bring me to him alive. He has a reason to hate me. I dated his son, Robert Jr., in college. I was very young, only seventeen and in my second year. Emotionally, I may have been even younger, I don't know. I certainly looked at the world through rose-colored glasses."

He reached out and took her hand, rubbing it between his to give her courage.

"I don't know why I have this weird thing about sex, but I just don't get aroused unless a man is telling me what to do."

Her gaze jumped to his face. He felt the leap in her pulse. Her heart accelerated. Color rose under her skin.

"I mean I *really* like it."

There was more to it, even more than Code had gotten from the testimony from the court trial, but then her idiot college boyfriend probably didn't really know the first thing about what she'd tried to tell him she needed. She'd been brave to ask him for what she wanted, but the little pissant, privileged Holden Jr., had been too immature to realize he'd been looking at a treasure. Absinthe remained silent when he wanted to reassure her there was nothing wrong with asking for what you wanted in the bedroom.

She bit her lip hard and then looked down at his hand on hers. "We went to this party. It was very crowded and he seemed off, so I was very nervous and uncomfortable. I kept waiting for him to reassure me, but he didn't."

She had good instincts, he noted. She would have been fine with the party and the crowded conditions if her man had taken care of her, but he had been too busy thinking about what he was about to do. Absinthe wished the fucker was still alive so he could have his own "talk" with him.

"Robert gave me a drink and kept kissing me, but it didn't do anything for me. I just couldn't relax, and I wanted to go home."

"Did you tell him that?"

"Yes. That made him angry. He took me upstairs and told me to get undressed and lay on the bed. He was going to tie me up. I didn't like the way I felt. I was half-in and half-out of it. I told him that. The next thing I knew his friends had come into the room. I'd made it clear I didn't want anyone else to touch me. He had other ideas and so did they. At that point I realized he must have given me some kind of drug."

There was a note in her voice that alerted him to something more, something he didn't like. Guilt? Shame? The emotions were twisted together, difficult to pull apart and look at. There was something else he couldn't put his finger on yet. He could "see" the images if he chose, but he wasn't going to rip them out of her mind.

He stroked her inner wrist over her wild pulse. "Breathe with me, Scarlet." He kept his voice low, soft, pushing the command gently into the path between them. "You're safe with me. Just breathe with me."

He caught glimpses of men's faces coming at her. A man with a knife, his face ugly that she dared to defy him.

"I shouldn't have fought them. I shouldn't have. It was wrong of me. I never should have done it."

Unexpectedly she pulled her wrist away from him and began rubbing her hands up and down over the faint white scars where the defensive wounds were.

"Scarlet, their intention was to rape you."

"I should have just let them. If I let them, my sister would still be alive. So would my parents. They all blamed me for what happened. I blame me. I just should have let them do it. If I hadn't told Robert what I was like in the first place . . ." There was loathing in her voice, as if she thought her need to have a man lead her in the bedroom was to blame for Robert Jr. bringing in his friends. "He wouldn't have thought he could get away with it."

"Scarlet." Absinthe kept his voice gentle. She was slipping away from him, moving back in time, flashing back to that moment when someone had told her about her family. The emotions pouring off her were all too raw and real. "People aren't thinking clearly those first few terrible moments of grief. Your parents just saw their daughter, that was all they could see, nothing else could come into their minds. Sorrow has a way of narrowing vision. You know that. You're allowing that child, that seventeen-year-old devastated girl, to think for you with those same intense *grieving* emotions. I can hear the sorrow in your voice. That grief isn't ten years old. It's today. This moment."

He took her wrists and she resisted him, pulling back. He released her instantly.

"Scarlet. Look at me." He used his voice again, but only a whisper of command, threading it through the natural velvet brush of his tone she was already susceptible to. He waited, knowing the order would push and push until she couldn't stop herself from obeying him.

She raised her eyes to his and blinked several times, clearing her vision. He reached for her arms again, taking his time, letting her see he was going to take both wrists. He did so, turning her arms over to inspect the damage the knife had done when she defended herself. Any doctor, any law enforcement officer would have been able to see that she had been attacked. The scars were from classic defense wounds and some of them had been deep. She'd needed stitches.

"Scarlet, every person has the right to defend themselves."

"I'm strong. Priscilla wasn't. She was always so gentle and kind. She didn't understand meanness or why or how

people could be ugly. She wouldn't have known what someone like Robert and his friends wanted from her. They were
getting back at me. Robert would never have considered
going after her if I had just cooperated with him. But I took
the knife away and that humiliated him. Then I wouldn't be
afraid when his father wanted me to. The moment I saw
Robert's smirk in court, I knew it wasn't over, but I never
thought, for one moment, that he would go after Priscilla."

Her gaze started to shift from his. Absinthe shook his
head. "Baby, keep looking at me. You were seventeen years
old. You had no way of knowing those little fuckers were
going to go after your sister. They didn't even know about
her. At that time, there was only you and them and he was
threatening you with a knife, he'd drugged you and you'd
made it clear you didn't want any part of any of them at that
point. Believe me, every member in this club understands
what it is like to say no and say it clearly. To fight back and
mean it."

He brushed at the hair sliding over her face with gentle
fingers. "You aren't alone in fighting this battle anymore."

"You don't understand how powerful Holden Sr. is, Absinthe. He'll kill you. He'll put out a contract on you and
every single person you love. Your brothers and sisters.
Your club. He'll do it. He'll do it because he hates me that
much." She lowered her voice to a thread of sound and
leaned into him. "I killed them. He knows I did. He can't
prove it, but he knows I did. I'm not going to let him kill
you or people you love to get to me. I can disappear. I know
how. I've got people I can go to."

A hot flame licked at his gut. "Like Adrik Orlov? Because you're not going to him. You're staying with me."

She went very still, and he didn't care that the anger and
suspicion began to build in her eyes.

"That's right, now we're at the you're-going-to-be-pissed
part. I told you that you would be. You were scared. In the
library, you were always careful to check the exits and the

windows all the time. I watched you, the same way you watched me. You were afraid someone was looking for you. I thought maybe an ex-husband or ex-boyfriend was hunting you. A stalker. That would fit. I kept thinking you'd tell me yourself, but you didn't. You carried weapons, you were trained in self-defense and I could see you knew what you were doing. Things didn't add up."

She remained silent, just watching him; the suspicion was still there and that kept the flames burning low in his belly. She should have just a little faith in him after all he'd told her about himself and his brothers. He'd put a lot of trust in her.

"The other night when I asked you out, you lied to me. I couldn't tell what you were lying about, but something was wrong, and I was afraid for you. I hung around and followed you, thinking you might be making a run for it, or that you were trying to deal with whoever it was that was looking for you on your own."

Scarlet started to speak, swallowed what she was going to say and then shook her head. Her eyes lost some of their misgiving. She shook her head a second time. "I haven't had that, Absinthe. I don't know what to do with you. I should be upset that I didn't know you were following me. My survival depends on spotting a tail. But the fact that you cared enough to actually follow after me is rather wonderful."

That wasn't what he expected her to say and it sent the flames in his belly rolling into something else altogether. He glanced around the clubhouse. While they were talking, a few others had drifted in, knowing a threat was hanging over Scarlet's head. The members of the Venomous club had made that clear. They wouldn't attempt to take her from the clubhouse, not with only half a dozen members, and certainly not when they knew they were intruding on Diamondback territory. They wouldn't want to start an all-out war. It was going to be interesting to see what move they would make next.

"I hope you keep thinking I'm wonderful when I tell you that I followed you back to your house and Lana and I sat up on the hillside overlooking the property just to make certain no one disturbed you. She's damn good with a sniper rifle."

Scarlet looked up, her lashes fluttering, making his body react as she looked around the room until she was flashing a small smile at Lana.

"It took me a while before I realized you weren't in your house," he continued. "Damn, woman, you are good at what you do. Really good. I can't remember the last person, if any, that's gotten past me. And Lana was with me. We were both watching, and you still got away."

He poured praise and pride into his voice. He felt it and he wanted her to know that he did. He'd rather she focused on that than everything that came next, because if she thought too much about it, she wasn't going to like his behavior.

"I don't know what tipped me off, but I realized you weren't in the house. I had no idea how you slipped by us, but you did. That doesn't happen with Torpedo Ink. You're the first that's ever gotten by us. I went down to the house to be certain and went in. Immediately I knew something was wrong. I saw that you were ready to leave at a moment's notice and knew someone was after you. I gave you every opportunity to tell me the next day. Lana, naturally, told our president she was worried about you and the possibility that someone could hurt you and, through you, me as well. I turned over your information to Code, our resident computer genius."

Absinthe continued brushing the pads of his fingers back and forth over the pulse pounding so wildly in her wrist, assessing her reaction—soothing her while he spoke. "It was so important to me to make certain you were safe. It was more important even than losing you, and I knew you'd be royally pissed with me for prying into your business."

Her face softened and his heart clenched hard in his chest. He wanted to lean over and kiss the hell out of her, but they had to finish this. He had to make certain she understood that once this was out in the open, there was no taking it back.

"Look at me, Scarlet." He had to see her eyes, read her expression, not just her pulse.

Her gaze jumped to his.

"Your trial and subsequent history were easy enough for Code to discover, but then after you left the country, the trail became a little murky. The longer you were overseas, the more difficult it was for him to follow you. You clearly had an itinerary, and when you came back and the men who had raped your sister died one by one, that agenda became very clear." He didn't take his gaze from hers.

She didn't so much as wince. "Your point?"

"You killed those men just as I killed the men who raped and tortured me and mine."

"They deserved to die, and no one was going to stop them from continuing to hurt other women. Or in your case, women and children."

"Exactly," he agreed. "Where were you the other night? Who was the woman who provided your alibi?"

She lifted her chin. "Josefa Diaz. I helped her escape from a human trafficking ring. They were holding her in a hotel in San Francisco. I freed her and kept her safe here while I had her documents forged and set up a life for her in Chile. She needed money in the bank and people I trust on the other end to help her get started in a good job there. When I had everything ready, I waited until I needed her and then I called on her. She did exactly as I asked her in return."

It was brilliant. She had a woman indebted to her who would be richly rewarded for helping her. The woman would never have to testify, never have to lift a finger to do anything other than sit in a restaurant or movie theater, someplace public where cameras could pick up Scarlet. She would go back to her country with money and someone on the other end to help her with a new life. By that time, she'd learned to trust Scarlet's word. The plan was beyond brilliant. Clearly, she'd used the same type of alibi every time she'd killed successfully.

"What happened the other night that you needed to use Josefa? It was the teenager, wasn't it? The girl in the library."

She nodded. "Her name is Joan. Her mother, Brenda, really loves money and the lifestyle it gives her. She was married to a wealthy man at one point, but in her divorce, because she cheated multiple times, she lost everything but child support for her two children. That support is not enough to keep her in the lifestyle Brenda wants or thinks she needs."

Absinthe sighed. He'd met more than a few greedy women who would do just about anything for money.

"Giles McCarthy is a very well-known philanthropist in the area. Very generous."

"Yes." Absinthe nodded. "He died in an accident at his home. A gas leak, I believe." He watched her the entire time. "It's still being investigated, but from everything I've read, it looks as if it really was an accident."

"McCarthy paid Brenda ten thousand a month to make Joan available to him when Brenda took Luke out of town. She would get bonuses the more cooperative Joan was. Brenda wasn't the only woman he made arrangements with. He was a straight-up pedophile and he managed to get the cooperation of a few of the greedier women in town willing to sell their daughters to him."

"You have proof of this?"

She gave him a look that should have withered him on the spot. "I do my homework. Of course I have proof. I went to Joan's house and was there when she was supposed to meet him. First, I went to his home, to ensure everything was in place for his little accident. It would be easy enough to undo it all. I checked his computer. Thousands of pictures of pornography, all young girls. Lots of Joan and other girls in our area. I wiped the ones of Joan. He had thousands of dollars in cash in his safe. I removed most of it but left enough so that no one would notice missing cash. He had videos of the girls and him. I took the ones of Joan."

"They can get those off the hard drive."

"I'm not an amateur. I went back to Joan's house and typed a note from her saying she was sick and had to get help, that she'd meet him in a couple of days. I left it on the bed for him to see. He was so angry. He jacked off, leaving her a 'present' and a note saying she'd better be there or he'd inform her mother she wasn't cooperative and he wasn't paying that month. He left and went back home."

"Pleasant fellow."

"Right? I just sat in the car Josefa had gotten for me, just down from his estate, waited for the house to go up and then checked to make certain he didn't make it out. He lived in the hills, so it was easy enough to get closer to home. I drove the car to a ravine, pushed it over and made my way home." She shrugged.

Absinthe slid the pad of his thumb over her inner wrist and the pulse beating there. Every word she'd said was the truth. She'd killed a pedophile. Managed to bankroll a human trafficking victim and recouped cash. Saved a young teen. Had an airtight alibi. She'd been smart enough to make McCarthy's death look like an accident.

"*Moya literaturnaya ledi*, I didn't think it was possible to admire you any more than I already did. Holy mother but you get the job done."

"Someone has to." For the first time, real tears swam in her eyes. "The cops knew they raped my sister. They left behind evidence, but as usual, Robert's father bought his way out of it. He bought the cops, he bought the attorneys and he bought the judges."

"What evidence?"

"There were photographs of my sister's body and the scene where my parents were in the living room. Robert's necklace was wrapped around Priscilla's wrist. How do you miss that? It was wrapped around her wrist and the medallion was clasped in her fingers. She was smart and she'd torn it off his neck and when she decided to hang herself, she wrapped that around her hand to make certain they knew who had raped her. It was very distinct. Thick chain links. Real gold. The medallion was flat and had the words *Rule the World* engraved on it."

"How did you see the photographs?"

She shook her head and pressed her lips together. "I can't tell you that, but I did get screen captures of them and gave them to my attorney. It was part of the reason I was able to get out of prison and the state made a very lucrative deal with me."

He knew immediately that someone on the inside of the prison, someone with skills like Code's, had gotten to those photographs, and Scarlet would never break her silence and compromise them. It shocked him that the pictures hadn't been destroyed. Someone was either thinking in terms of protecting themselves or blackmailing Holden down the road.

"Fair enough, *ledi*, you had the proof, and that was the big thing. We don't hunt unless we know those we're after are guilty."

He eased back in his chair to let her know he was switching gears. He wanted to take her to his house and see if she was willing to make the coast her home, to commit to him and his club permanently. He knew it was fast for her, but in order for both of them to disclose the things they needed to each other, they had to count on the connection, that pathway their brains had made—and the truth they shared. They had to jump in with both feet. That meant Scarlet was the one stepping off the cliff, and he knew it was much harder for her—more of a matter of trust than for him. He would have his club to make him comfortable. She would only have him. She'd been let down and she would be afraid.

"I want you to come home with me. I own a house here

in Caspar. I'd like you to see if you like it. If you don't, I'm telling you up front, I'm willing to find another one, anything at all you prefer. Czar wanted us to put down roots here and each of us to find a home. All of us more or less chose one that suited us best, depending on needs. This one appealed to me because it has space and I like that. I need it. I like to see what's coming at me. I think all of us do. But I want you to see it and make up your own mind about it. I haven't really lived there. I stay here at the clubhouse as a rule until I can't take the noise around me and need solitude."

"Why would it matter if I don't like the house?"

She was going to make him lay it out for her. He glanced at Savage and then over at Mechanic. Both men got up from the bar stools without a word. Savage drifted over toward the front door and draped his muscular frame casually against the wall, pulling out his phone to look over text messages. He rarely texted anyone, so it was probably a ruse, although he looked thoroughly engaged. Mechanic leaned on the bar right beside the door leading to the back rooms where all the bedrooms and the back exits were. His solid body was between Scarlet and any doors just in case she got it in her head to make a break for it.

"I want you to stay with me. Give the library your notice and live with me. The Venomous club isn't going to back down. Holden made it clear that he's putting the word out to other clubs as well, so it won't be safe to go back to work. You already know that. You only have two choices. You can run, hit that go-bag you have hidden in the wall back at your house."

It wasn't there anymore. Already, Steele and Maestro were cleaning out her house of everything she'd left behind and bringing it to the clubhouse. They'd sweep for anything she might have hidden carefully. She wasn't going back there either, not for money, not for passports, not for anything that might get her killed.

"Or you can stay here and make a try with me."

Scarlet's gaze clung to his. He could see the longing there, but then fear crept in. Rejection. She was used to running. Hiding. She believed Holden was a powerful man.

"We're assassins, Scarlet. Eighteen of us, the original Torpedo Ink members, trained from the time we were children. We have an additional two members: Czar's brothers both trained in other schools, also from the time they were children. That brings us to twenty. We recently patched over twenty-five members of a club, all trained in a school one step down from ours. Trained assassins, all experienced. All lethal. They could wipe up the floor with a club like the Venomous club. With our prospects and theirs, we're at fifty. All trained assassins. We aren't talking men who might have some military training or think they're badasses because they grew up on the streets."

"I don't want any of you to get hurt. He's very vindictive and he'll never stop."

Absinthe shrugged. "He's going to die. We're already locked on to him. I want you to come home with me, look at the house and decide if you want that one or if you want to go house hunting. I need to talk with you alone. We have to decide one way or another if you can live with me. I know I can live with you. I want you to stay with me permanently. For me, it's a done deal. You have to be as certain. Either way, whatever decision you make, I swear, we'll protect you until Holden's dead, then you can go your way if I'm not what you want."

Scarlet's gaze moved over his face and then jumped back to his eyes. "Any woman in her right mind would want to be with you, Absinthe. I'm not a great bet."

"*Ledi*, did I not tell you that I've already taken the leap? My brothers know it. My sisters as well. I want you to say yes to me. That's all I need from you. One fuckin' word. Come to the house. Look it over. Hear me out and tell me yes or no." He didn't wait. He stood up and held out his hand, giving her no option. "A couple of the brothers will come with us just to make certain none of the Venomous club members lose their minds and try to follow us."

She put her hand in his without hesitation. He closed his fingers around hers. Her hand was so much smaller and felt delicate. He had to remember at all times what she was capable of. Czar had been right; he might have hesitated had she attacked him. The more he was with her, the more he could feel the connection to her growing stronger.

The ride to the house was smooth. She was a good passenger, moving with him and the Harley as if born to do so. He slowed as they approached the drive, wanting her to see the way the slow-curving road opened up to the beautiful sprawling explosion of plants. The former owners had been master gardeners and they'd spent a great deal of years putting together so many amazing areas, each with colorful flowers or bushes that were indigenous to the coast. Pathways of blue and gray stone rambled through various gardens, matching the fence surrounding the property and the house itself. The house was a single story, with high, vaulted ceilings, gables and rambling verandahs. It was shaped like a U with a courtyard of stunning gardens to enjoy.

He parked the bike close to the front stairs and sat for a minute, taking his time, watching her as she wandered around near the back porch looking toward the ocean. The views were spectacular. He'd paid for those views. He loved the house, but he'd paid for the way his home sat on the bluff perfectly overlooking the ocean on three sides. He could sit anywhere on his verandah from those three sides and see the waves crashing. When he was on the front of the house, he was surrounded by the garden.

"This is incredible. You own this? I love it and I haven't even seen inside."

He slid off the Harley and walked up the stairs to her. She had her head tilted back and the sun hit the red in her hair so that it blazed with fire. "Take your hair down, baby."

He leaned down and brushed a kiss along her cheek. "I love when it tumbles down your back like a waterfall. It's so fuckin' sexy I can barely breathe."

She followed him to the front door, her hands in her hair as he inserted the key and stepped back to allow her to walk in first. The floors were hardwood. He hadn't yet gotten the throw rugs he wanted to make it warmer. Anya told him he needed a few, especially in front of his fireplaces. He had two. One in the living room and one in the master bedroom.

"I like that you were honest when you said you preferred a man to take the lead in the bedroom, Scarlet," Absinthe ventured.

The door opened immediately into the enormous expanse that was the living room. The vaulted ceilings added to the feeling of space. The room was turned so the windows on one side showed the garden and the other the views of the ocean. The third side was open to flow into the next room, so there was little to designate between the living room and den, where the pool table and floor-to-ceiling bookshelves made up two walls. Lana had chosen the chairs and short table between the chairs for comfortable reading in the evenings.

That room flowed into a dining room with a long table for guests. There was a chandelier he planned on replacing. Lissa, a famous glassblower, the wife of one of the brothers, was making him a custom one. The dining room flowed into the kitchen. All the rooms had a view of the ocean or gardens. The sprawling house looped around to form a long U shape with a protected courtyard in the center. The house protected the center from the winds coming off the ocean. The garden was stunning, surrounding the courtyard, protecting those inside from anyone coming up on them from seeing in.

The master bedroom, guest bedrooms, offices and bathrooms were all built along the U shape's arms. Absinthe walked slowly through the house, letting her see it while he talked to her.

"I wasn't completely honest," Scarlet denied.

He glanced over his shoulder at her. She had her gaze fixed on the bed. He was a big man. The bed had a large gray-blue frame and the quilt matched. One side of the wall was made of sheer glass, an enormous framed sliding door that went out onto the verandah or into the courtyard. It was the only room that had access to the verandah. The carpet was a soft dove gray with a bluish cast to it. The wall behind the bed was a dark gray painted with geometric designs in light blues and grays. Two lamps hung from the ceiling to either side of the bed, leaving the space open on the two small black end tables. He found the entire effect soothing.

He had guessed she hadn't been, but she didn't need to be. He already knew. "Let me tell you what I need, Scarlet. That way, if we're not compatible, you don't have to say anything more. If we are, you can tell me what you need."

He gestured toward one of the two chairs in front of the fireplace. "Sit over there for a moment." The master bathroom was just off the bedroom through one door, the enormous closets through another door.

Scarlet sat immediately, her long red hair falling around her face and down her back.

"What I didn't make clear to you when I told you I was pretty fucked up is that when I was a child, I was taught to like certain things in the bedroom. Not just like them. I need them to get off. I need to tell my woman what to do and have her obey me. I have the ability to use my voice to make her do things, and I have done so in the past when I was forced to. I swore I wouldn't again, and I never have."

He stole a look at her to see how she was taking what he said. It was difficult to tell. Her fingers stroked her throat, but she didn't so much as blink.

He forced himself to continue. "I find myself wanting to be able to use my ability with you, but I want your consent. I want you to know what I'm doing at all times and still consent to it. So, in other words, I want your full cooperation. I need you to want to do these things for me. Are you understanding what I'm saying to you? You would hear my commands and have no choice other than to obey them, but you would have consented ahead of time although you won't know what I'm going to ask of you."

Absinthe didn't take his eyes from Scarlet. He could tell by her heightened breathing that she was sexually aroused just by the suggestion, but she was also very afraid. He couldn't blame her. She was connected to him, but she didn't really know him.

"What kinds of things?"

"Anything I ask of you."

"Other men?"

"Absolutely not. I don't share. You're my woman. I'm not going to lie or mislead you in any way. We were brought up together in a situation where we relied on one another to watch each other's backs. That means we breathe easier having sex when we're around one another. When we party, we feel safer close together. Having said that, we don't share our women. Blythe is Czar's. Anya is Reaper's. Breezy, Steel's. Soleil belongs to Ice. If any man touched any of them or you, the club would kill them. You have not only my protection, but also the club's. I give you my word of honor on that, Scarlet, but you have to decide whether you can trust me on it or not. That's obviously a huge one because this is something I need."

"We had sex and you enjoyed it."

"You did everything I said."

"You didn't compel me."

"No, but I find myself thinking about it all the time. Sooner or later it's going to be an issue. I won't be able to stop myself. I don't want that to happen without your full consent."

"If you betrayed me, Absinthe, I would kill you."

"I would expect nothing less, Scarlet, because if you betrayed me or this club, I would do the same."

"I don't want to be humiliated. Ever."

"That would never happen. I have nothing but respect for you. I will always give you the option to say no to me. Or if we agree ahead of time to make it better for me, then the option will be for you to shake your head and I'll bring you out to talk it over. We can come up with something that will work for us both."

"I can agree on that."

"You say yes to me, Scarlet, you're agreeing to staying with me. It's a permanent yes. We don't walk away. We agree to work things out. If things get bad, we go to Czar and Blythe. If they don't help and we can't find a book that helps, we talk to a fuckin' marriage counselor. I'm not going to lose you because I don't know anything about relationships."

"Why are you assuming you're the one that's going to fuck it up?"

"I barely remember having parents. We raised ourselves. Czar was our moral compass and I'm not positive he was that good. Now I'm counting on you."

Scarlet burst out laughing. "I don't know that I'm going to be that good of a positive effect on you. I've got to go back to the house and get the rest of my things."

He smiled at her. Maybe it was a smirk. "Don't worry about that, babe. The club did it for you to save you the trouble. You might want to give the library the song and dance about how you've been called away unexpectedly and very permanently."

"I have to give a proper notice or I'll never get another library job, and I love working in the library."

"We'll make it right when this blows over," he promised. "Let me give you a real tour of the house and then we'll go grocery shopping, out to dinner and come home." He liked saying the word *home*. "You okay with that?"

"Very okay with it."

ELEVEN

Scarlet found herself trying not to look for trouble in Caspar at the grocery store. Women gawked at Absinthe. It wasn't his fault. He was unbelievably good-looking. In spite of several times risking looking up at him from behind her dark glasses in an effort to catch him looking at the other women, he never seemed to look back at them when they stared at him. He held her hand and seemed completely focused on her.

"We're trying to find a decent manager so none of us have to do the job," Absinthe said.

She blinked at him, trying to catch up with what he was saying. "I'm sorry. I was trying to decide on whether or not to be bad and get pastries."

"Pastries aren't bad. They're a staple, but we don't get them here," he corrected. "We get them from Alena. She's a goddess when it comes to pastries. We'll get them tonight at the restaurant. We own the grocery store. Right now, Inez Nelson is running it for us, but she owns the one in Sea Haven. We're looking for a manager. We thought one of us could manage it, but we're not the actual work-on-a-schedule type of people. You have to be nice to customers and employees, it turns out."

Scarlet burst out laughing. "Imagine that. As opposed to taking out a gun and shooting them when you're annoyed?"

"Much too subtle. And closing down the store when we want to ride." He brought her hand to his chest. "We found Inez frowned on that as well. Who would have thought? She had all kinds of rules. For such a little woman she can really throw all kinds of attitude."

They had come up to the counter and Scarlet got her first good look at the "little" woman Absinthe was talking about. She was older and fragile looking, very small and thin.

Inez put both hands on her hips and glared at the biker, not in the least intimidated. "I heard that."

Absinthe leaned over the counter and brushed a kiss on Inez's paper-thin cheek. "You do have more rules than hell does, woman. I can't even remember them all. This is Scarlet, *moya literaturnaya ledi.* I am going to marry her very soon. She's amazing, beautiful and brilliant. Scarlet, Inez Nelson, our guardian angel. Inez helps us out as best she can when we're trying to figure out how to get through all the business labyrinths."

Inez beamed at her. "It's wonderful to meet you. Absinthe is one of the sweetest boys. I'm so glad he's found you."

Her gaze dropped to their joined hands, specifically looking at her finger. She was clearly old-fashioned enough to think there should be a ring there with his declaration. For some reason that made Scarlet blush, the color moving up her body into her cheeks. She felt like pulling her hand away and hiding it, but that was silly, especially when Absinthe was clasping her palm firmly against his chest.

"Ice is making our set of rings. He started the minute I told him I found my woman. He's the best jeweler I know."

Inez touched the little tanzanite tears surrounded by tiny diamonds dropping from her ears. "He made these for me.

I told him he shouldn't give them to an old lady, but he insisted he made them just for me. No one ever did that for me before. I treasure them."

Scarlet looked up at Absinthe. He was telling the truth to Inez. He was having a set of wedding rings made. When he said he moved fast, he wasn't joking. That should have frightened her, but somehow it reassured her that he meant what he said. She was always afraid no one really wanted her, but Absinthe seemed hell-bent on making her truly his no matter what baggage she brought with her. Things were moving a little fast, and she would have to talk to him about that, but she liked that he was that sure.

"Savage came in the store the other day, at Sea Haven," Inez informed them, chattering on, clearly embarrassed to having shown so much emotion over her earrings. "He was so sweet. I needed some help with Donny."

Scarlet was shocked to hear anyone call Savage sweet. She couldn't imagine the man having a sweet bone in his body. He looked like he might kill you and eat you for lunch.

Inez began checking their grocery items as she talked. She was fast and didn't seem to need to look. She just kept talking. "Donny Ruttermyer is a sweet boy born with Down syndrome. He lives on his own and works at the store for me. My friend Donna owns the store across from my grocery and has a studio apartment over her store that she rents to him. Her home is behind the store. It's quite lovely behind the little white picket fence." She rattled off the details in a friendly voice almost without taking a breath.

Scarlet wanted her to get to the part where Savage was sweet. Inez had almost gotten to the last item and Absinthe was busy putting everything in a burlap bag he'd brought with them.

"Jackson was out of town and Donny got into some trouble . . ."

Absinthe's head went up and he paused in the act of putting fresh fruit into the bag. "What kind of trouble, Inez? What does that mean?"

"Oh, nothing big. He made a mistake with his checkbook. He's usually very careful. Jackson helps him. He got one of the columns mixed up, or at least I think it was something of that nature—he wouldn't let Donna or me look. He was so upset he was hurting himself. I couldn't stop him."

Absinthe's gaze dropped to her arm and the long sleeves she wore. He reached across the counter and very gently pushed her light sweater back to reveal the dark bruises on her arm. "Savage see these?"

Inez sighed and pulled her sleeve down. "He did. He wasn't happy. Donny didn't try to hurt me. He's strong and he was agitated, hitting his head on the wall and throwing himself around. I got in his way. The minute he banged into me and I hit the wall, it was awful. I called Savage. He's one of the few that can stop Donny when he's that upset. Czar can too, but Savage seems to really reach him faster. I don't know why, and I was terribly afraid he was going to harm himself, especially after I fell."

Scarlet could tell by Absinthe's stillness that hearing that Inez had fallen made the situation worse.

"Was Savage aware that you fell?"

"Donny told him. He stuttered and cried. He was rocking back and forth. Savage didn't try to touch him or comfort him like I expected, he just let him talk. When Donny told him about me falling into the wall and then onto the floor, he called Libby Drake. I didn't know he knew the Drakes that well or even that she was a doctor. She wasn't home so he called Steele. He insisted Steele come immediately to see me."

"As he should have," Absinthe said. "I hope you were cooperative."

"I don't go to the doctor often. I find they seem to like to prescribe drugs and I don't take pills, but Jackson and Savage are the two men I can't seem to say no to when they insist on bringing a doctor around." She heaved a sigh. "It's ridiculous how bossy they can be." She patted Scarlet's hand. "Be careful, honey, these men tend to be difficult to say no to."

Scarlet laughed. "I'm finding that out. Was Savage able to help Donny straighten out his checkbook?"

"Yes. I think he had to deposit quite a bit of money into his account, but if he did, he wouldn't tell me. Jackson will look into it when he gets back." There was an underlying note of worry in her voice for the absent Jackson. Scarlet didn't know who he was, but it was clear Inez loved the man.

"If Savage wanted to bail Donny out, Inez, you have to let him," Absinthe said and caught up the two burlap sacks by the handles, dragging them off the counter.

A low whistle slid through the store. The sound seemed to vibrate right through Absinthe. His body didn't exactly react, more like he turned slowly, and as he did, he swept Scarlet behind him.

"Inez, stay behind the counter and if there's shooting you get down and stay there until the cops come or I tell you it's safe." His voice was very low, holding a soft, compelling note that seemed to push into the mind of the older woman.

Scarlet watched her nod. She didn't seem as if she was in any way hypnotized or under a spell. Her eyes weren't glazed; in fact, they appeared clear, but she shifted deeper behind the counter and kept her eyes glued to Absinthe as if waiting for any signal or word from him.

"What is it?" Scarlet asked. She didn't reach for a weapon. She knew where they were and how fast she could get to each of them when needed.

"Why don't you stay here with Inez and protect her. I'll head outside," Absinthe said. "And see what's up."

"Not a chance," Scarlet said. She had the feeling he knew exactly what was up. "And don't use your voice on me. I agreed to the bedroom, not to anything else."

"Sex," he corrected, glancing down at her, "not necessarily in the bedroom. Most definitely not just in the bedroom. Inez, keep away from the windows." He didn't argue with Scarlet, he just dropped the money for the groceries on the counter, put both bags into one hand and walked boldly out the door, Scarlet right behind him.

Savage lounged just to the right of the door as if he didn't have a care in the world. Across the street, up on the roof, Scarlet thought she caught a glimpse of someone, but when she looked again, there was no one there. Still, she was certain they were covered. Absinthe kept walking. Scarlet went with him to the Harley. Savage dropped into position on the other side of her, matching pace as if they'd been doing it for a lifetime.

At the motorcycle, Absinthe stored the groceries in the compartments, all the while looking down the street. Scarlet could see the truck he was inspecting. It was a newer model. Two of the Torpedo Ink members were on the opposite side of it, seemingly disinterested, talking to each other just inside a doorway of a closed shop. There were several closed businesses on the street, but others that were very new. Clearly, the little village was being brought back to life again.

Absinthe's fingers slid into Scarlet's hair. Tapped gently. Rhythmically. Slid into the thickness and massaged. She wouldn't have thought anything about it but she noticed that Savage's hand came up to his chest and his fingers tapped over his heart, just for a few seconds, and dropped away. It was just an odd coincidence.

She flicked a gaze over to where another man stood. She had never seen him before but he had long, dark hair streaked with silver pulled back in a ponytail that went down his back and was dissected by bands every few inches, dark facial hair also streaked with silver, gray-blue eyes and tattoos on his neck and over his very muscular arms. His tattoos hadn't been done in the same artist's distinctive work as the others in Torpedo Ink. His tattoos looked much more like prison art.

"Who is he?" Scarlet indicated him with her chin.

"That's *Razrushitel*. At least we call him that. I suppose the outsiders call him Destroyer. He patched in with the other chapter, but Czar put out a call and essentially, he's a loner, so he came. He seems to fit better with us."

She didn't know what any of that meant. Why would a man be in one chapter and then go to another? Then the door to the small hardware store two doors down from the grocery store swung open and a man emerged. He was stocky, shaggy but very distinctive and there was no mistaking him. Her breath caught in her throat and she stepped back away from Absinthe, or tried to—Savage was in the way, crowding her.

"Don't," Absinthe ordered, his voice a thread of sound. "Don't you fuckin' move, Scarlet. You're with me and you show that to him."

She stopped immediately. When was this nightmare ever going to end? "I've put you all in so much danger." She had. It was the last thing she wanted to do.

Savage made a sound under his breath that sounded a lot like "Bullshit." Worse, it sounded like he, what? Laughed? She couldn't imagine Savage laughing.

"Adrik," Absinthe greeted. "You're a long way from home."

Adrik nodded, but his gaze was on Scarlet. Something dark and uneasy crawled down her spine. Adrik was unpredictable. He had explosions of temper that could be horrifying. It was impossible to know what he might do in any given moment or circumstance. She had no idea how he would react or why he was there. His dark eyes seemed to be drinking her in, swallowing her whole, and she didn't like what she saw there.

"A man contacted me a couple months back. Said some

bitch killed his son and he wanted her picked up and brought to him quietly. Didn't want anyone to know. Said I was recommended to him. Gave a name."

Another chill went down her spine. Scarlet knew whoever had given Adrik's name to Holden Sr.—and she was certain the man who had contacted Adrik had been Holden—was already dead. Adrik would never have stood for anyone recommending him as a hit man.

"I don't do that kind of work anymore. I live quietly. Imagine my surprise, Scarlet, when your name came up. I knew you were in trouble, so I came to bring you home. You can't stay here or sooner or later you're going to get killed." He looked around at the Torpedo Ink members spread out around him, boxing him in. "For all I know, these men have taken the contract to turn you over to him. It was a big one."

Her heart slammed hard in her chest and then began to pound. Adrik lied easily. He might very well have taken the contract with Holden and was saying what he thought would get Torpedo Ink to turn her over to him. She just didn't know. It sounded like Holden to contact someone out of the country first in order to try to acquire her and when that didn't work, turn to his local biker clubs. Holden didn't want to risk the publicity.

"She's safe with us, Adrik," Absinthe said. "It was nice you came all this way to try to protect her, but we've got this."

Adrik began shaking his head before Absinthe even finished speaking. "That doesn't work for me. I can see you're already gone on her. She's like that. She crawls inside you and takes you apart. She'll use you until she uses you up and then she moves on, leaving you an empty shell. You can't eat or sleep. You just think about her. It isn't worth it, Absinthe. Don't make that mistake. Step aside and I'll just take her out of here."

Scarlet was shocked. More than shocked. The things Adrik was saying didn't make any sense. She tried to step around Absinthe and when that didn't work, she pushed aggressively against his side in order to be seen.

"We had a contract. It was *your* contract, Adrik. You were the one who made it very, very clear to me what the terms were from the moment I arrived at your compound. I was very careful to abide by the rules you set. You said there were to be no emotions between us. It was strictly business at all times. I was not to get sentimental."

"You were to pay for your lessons with your body."

She tried not to wince. He stated that overly loud, wanting Absinthe and everyone else to hear what she'd done and condemn her. She lifted her chin. "Those were your terms, Adrik. You laid it all out. I also had to clean your house and cook for you. I did those things all without sentiment. All without emotion. And at the end of the year, I left, just like you told me was required of me. I packed and I left without a word, because you said you didn't want to see me ever again and I wasn't to come back or contact you or give your name to anyone else. I've kept my end of the bargain."

"Is that true, Adrik?" Absinthe asked, his tone mild in that way he had.

Scarlet wished he would touch her, but he faced Adrik, both hands free, his body relaxed, acting as if he wasn't in any way worried about Adrik and his strange accusations. She wanted to warn him, but there was no way to make him understand that this didn't make sense, at least not to her. Adrik very well could have taken Holden's money and now be looking for a way to get her away from Absinthe and the others.

"Adrik, did the two of you have a contract? Did you set the terms, and did she fulfill those terms?"

Adrik shrugged. "It doesn't matter."

"Adrik, you want to give me a truthful answer. Did Scarlet fulfill the requirements of the contract you set for her?" Absinthe's tone was lower than ever, but his voice carried across the sidewalk to the other man easily.

"Yes," Adrik answered grudgingly.

"Are you working for Holden? You want to tell me the truth, Adrik."

That velvet-soft voice could wrap a person up so easily. Scarlet felt the power and she found it irresistible. More, she found it darkly sensual. There was something about the combination of softness and power that stroked at her insides and her sex, making her want to do anything he said.

"I told you no. I want to take Scarlet back with me. She won't love you, Absinthe, any more than she did me. She'll tear you up and leave you a shell. She's some kind of a curse. You won't be able to get her out of your head." He pushed his hand against his head as if it physically hurt.

"Adrik, have you been having headaches?"

"Since she's been gone, all the time."

"He had them while I was there. I used to massage his temples and his head for him. He would have these terrible fits of violence and then blinding headaches," Scarlet whispered. "He wasn't able to have sex most of the time and it made him so angry."

"You want to go with Savage to see Steele and then you'll do whatever Steele says is necessary. You know Destroyer. You knew him as Rurik Volkov. He will go with you and Savage. Gavriil will be at the clubhouse as well."

Adrik rubbed his temples several times and shook his head. "You have to be careful, Absinthe. I came to tell you to be careful."

Absinthe's voice dropped another octave. He moved several steps closer to Adrik, reminding Scarlet of a wolf homing in on prey. She went to follow him, matching his footsteps, but Savage caught her wrist, preventing her. He ignored her glare, just giving his head a quick shake, barely sparing her a glance, his gaze fixed on Adrik and Absinthe. Not knowing how Absinthe's talent worked, she remained still, watching as well, her hand dropping to a weapon, just in case Adrik became hostile.

Absinthe was very close to Adrik now. "I appreciate the warning. You came to tell Scarlet she was in danger. You wanted to warn both of us that we were in danger. You wanted to help us stop Holden from hurting her."

Adrik nodded several times and rubbed his head. Absinthe very gently reached out and brushed his fingers over Adrik's inner wrist. Scarlet stiffened, her breath hissing out in warning. Adrik *hated* to be touched unless he initiated the contact. He didn't seem to notice, or Absinthe's ability to exert mind control was so strong it was just plain scary. She knew Adrik was a strong man. What kind of power did Absinthe actually wield?

Her heart went wild, a crazy, almost out-of-control response to his abilities. What was wrong with her that seeing and hearing, just knowing what he could do made her weak for him? She watched him walk Adrik to his truck, open the door and help him into the passenger side, all the while talking in a low tone to him. The tattooed man he'd identified as Destroyer slid into the driver's seat and started up the truck. Absinthe stayed on the sidewalk until the vehicle had disappeared down the street, Savage's Harley following behind it.

Absinthe came straight to her, caught her hand and pulled her into his arms, tight against his chest. "Are you all right?"

"Yes. What was that? Why did you have him go to the clubhouse? He can be very violent, Absinthe."

"Destroyer indicated something was very off with him. I thought it best before passing judgment to have Steele check him out, especially once you said he'd had headaches and violent outbursts and had problems having sex. It's very possible he has a tumor, or some kind of medical condition."

She would be thoroughly ashamed of herself if Absinthe had figured out that Adrik had a tumor in five minutes when she'd been with the man for a year. "Is Inez going to be all right?" She glanced back at the grocery store. "I liked her."

"Everyone likes her. You can't help it. Yeah, she'll be fine."

He straddled the Harley and placed her hand on his shoulder. Scarlet stepped on the foot peg, feeling like she was getting the hang of riding with him. The moment the bike roared to life, so did the fire between her legs that had started when Absinthe had spoken, showing his power so casually.

She hugged him tighter, pressing her body closer to his. She had questions for him, all kinds of questions about what he would want from her sexually, but part of her didn't want to ask them. She wanted to be alone with him and just find out what he would demand of her. She found the idea of him demanding something from her exciting, even thrilling.

If he really partied around his friends, and initially, when he'd first told her that his friends might be around them when they were having sex, she had rejected the idea of it out of hand. Absolutely not. It wouldn't happen. Never. She wasn't going to take that chance. Now, knowing about the members of Torpedo Ink and their past together, she wasn't certain what she thought. The idea of being completely safe and having Absinthe commanding her to do things for him was shockingly sexy, so much so that her body grew slick with heat just thinking about what he might demand or do.

Scarlet found the drive up to the house just as breathtaking as she had the first time they'd driven up that winding road, even knowing what to expect. The house was an incredible find. She couldn't imagine anyone not loving it. She also knew it must have to cost an impossible amount of money. Absinthe didn't volunteer where he'd gotten his money, but she stole hers, plain and simple, and she always had plenty to live on.

She made a mental note to herself to make certain that Joan was taken care of. She'd set it in motion already, putting money in a trust for the teen that would pay out only if

Brenda cooperated. If Brenda rehired Alison as a house-keeper and treated Joan right, under Scarlet's watchful eye she would receive money to live on. Scarlet had plenty of cameras installed in the house to make certain she could see if Brenda complied. The evidence that Brenda had sold her teenage daughter to a pedophile would be turned over to the DA immediately if she didn't. She would be receiving that good news any day now along with the news that her benefactor had died in a house explosion.

Scarlet helped Absinthe put the groceries away, familiarizing herself with the kitchen. She'd always wanted a home of her own. She wasn't the best cook in the world, but she was willing to learn for him. He didn't seem to care that she couldn't cook, and he'd told her it didn't matter. She was big on reading and there were thousands of cookbooks. He said his sister Alena was a dynamite chef.

Since they'd entered the house, he hadn't said much at all, only to indicate where he wanted things to be put. He was very precise about where each item belonged. She found herself looking around. She noticed his bedroom had been very neat. Every room had been. She'd put it down to the fact that he'd told her he didn't really stay there often, but now she thought it was because he couldn't take chaos.

"You really do pick up other people's emotions and feel their demons, for want of a better word, don't you?" She needed to understand him.

"Don't you?"

She frowned, following him from the kitchen down the open space to the door leading to the U-shaped area of the house where the bedrooms were. Did she feel other people's emotions? "Not really. Yours to some extent because we have an unusual connection, but I don't have that with anyone else."

He glanced at her over his shoulder. "I like that it's only me you have that connection with. I wish I only had it with you. I can't be in the same room sometimes with too many people and I really don't like touching people. There are times when I think my head is going to come apart. You take all that craziness away for me. I didn't think it was possible."

Scarlet felt an explosion of happiness blossoming up from her deepest core. It happened very fast and was so strong it shook her. She loved that she did that for him. She wanted to do so much more for him.

As if he could read her mind, and she was fairly certain he could, he kept talking as he walked. "I didn't think there was a woman alive who could make my cock so fucking hard without me commanding it to become that way until I walked into that library."

She loved that too. Absinthe stated it so casually and that made his declaration all the more real. He walked to the master bedroom and opened the door, stepping back to allow her to precede him. The moment she walked in, her heart began to beat overtime again in anticipation. She had no idea that just the thought of what Absinthe might say or do would be so exciting to her. She spotted her bags on the floor just inside the door and leaned down to pick them up.

"Run us a bath, baby," he said, removing the bags from her hands.

She nodded and started to turn toward the master bath.

"Strip first. You don't need clothes in here. I have clothes I like you to wear in the bedroom, or nothing at all. You have the most beautiful body I've ever fuckin' seen."

He hadn't pushed her into obeying him, but she wanted to. She had that weird proclivity she couldn't quite overcome. She found it strange that she didn't have the same thing in other areas of her life, only when it came to sex, and especially when it came to Absinthe, a thousand times stronger when it came to him.

"You have a problem with what I just asked of you?" The question came low, no judgment, no animosity or anger, just a simple query.

She shook her head. She didn't. She stood uncertainly in

the middle of the room, waiting, but he just walked to the door that he'd told her earlier led to the closet. He leaned one hip against it and folded his arms across his chest, his eyes on her. Her mouth went dry. Her heart did that strange acceleration she found promoted a thundering through her body that led straight to her sex.

Her hands shook as she shimmied out of her jeans and underwear. His eyes drifted over her body as she removed her top and bra. She looked around a little helplessly as if she didn't know what to do with her clothes.

"There's a hamper in the other room. I like the bathwater very hot, *miledi*."

She lifted her gaze to his and her entire body flushed with heat. The lines in his face were carved with pure carnal desire, all for her. He was completely focused on her. He had a way of looking at her she'd never experienced with any other man and she couldn't quite explain. It was as if when his crystal eyes moved over her body, dwelling on her breasts and drifting farther down, brushing her skin with those strange blue wicked flames, she felt them licking at her skin. He seemed to see right through her, branding her bones, claiming her, until she felt so completely his, she didn't know how she could explain it to herself let alone to someone else. He was in her mind, moving there, stroking and caressing, whispering even, until she wanted to please him and do anything he asked of her.

Absinthe had power in him. So much it shocked her. She'd witnessed that power when he spoke to Adrik and yet she'd put herself in his hands. She should be afraid of him. She was intimidated. She was standing in the middle of the room naked, without a single weapon, knowing he was a trained assassin and had a voice that could command someone to do his bidding, yet she was putting herself in his hands. She began trembling, her entire body shaking almost to the point she could barely stand. What was wrong with her?

Absinthe straightened slowly, walked over to her with

his easy, measured step and stopped right in front of her. He leaned down, framed her face in both hands and took her mouth. Instantly there was an explosion low and wicked. Flames leapt. Fire rushed through her veins like some terrible drug. She wound her arms around his neck, needing to hang on to something solid when he was transporting her to a place she hadn't known existed.

He lifted his head. "You're safe with me, Scarlet. You're always safe with me. We're going to make good partners."

She could get lost in his eyes. They were so strange, really, like two crystals that could see inward, not outward. She liked that he used the word *partner*. She wanted to be considered a partner. She was more than a plaything in a bedroom. If she gave herself to him of her own free will and did as he asked sexually, that was one kind of partnership. Outside of that, she wanted to be considered on equal footing at all times, otherwise they would never work.

"Keep giving me your trust."

"You haven't said what you need from me sexually other than you want to be able to tell me what to do and that sometimes your club might be around us when you do that." She felt the breath he took and that gave her pause. He was worried she wouldn't like what he would ask of her.

He took another deep breath. "I know, baby. Some things, in our bedroom, might be difficult for you, and I'll understand if you can't do them for me."

But he would still need them. That was unspoken between them. She got that. He dropped his arms and turned away from her, but she caught the expression on his face and for the first time, the real concern in his mind. He was definitely worried that she would leave him over his sexual needs, whatever they were. Absinthe was reluctant to disclose them to her until he had pulled her in deeper.

She contemplated that while she ran the bathwater. His hesitancy gave her more confidence than ever. That glimpse into his mind actually let her see just how much he really wanted her. All along she had been certain a man like him couldn't possibly really want her or fall in love with her because—well—she wasn't that lovable. In spite of what he'd told her about grief, she still was that seventeen-year-old in an adult prison hearing that her beloved sister had committed suicide and her mother and stepfather had followed suit, leaving her alone. She'd been grief stricken, horrified, terrified of being alone. And she'd wondered why she hadn't been enough for her mother to live for. Now, it seemed, she was enough for Absinthe. More than enough. For him, she was everything.

The door to the closet was open when she had the bath ready. She walked through and stopped dead in her tracks. The closet was nearly the size of her former house. It was that enormous. Really it was two separate closets. Absinthe sat on a long low bench, his shirt off and his jeans open, working on the cords of his motorcycle boots.

"Kneel down, Scarlet," he said immediately and leaned back, indicating she take over.

That little thrill went through her. Her stomach did a slow roll and her sex fluttered, heat rushing through her veins to pool low. She dropped to her knees in front of him, deftly loosening the laces.

"Pull them off."

That was much more difficult, and she couldn't do it from the position she was in. She looked up at him after struggling for a moment or two with the first boot. "I'm going to have to stand."

He smiled at her. His smiles were never completely genuine. She was beginning to know him, mostly through the connection that was getting stronger. She realized the more they touched, the stronger they established a bridge between them. Her brain had always worked fast, but she had thought of it in terms of speed in learning academics. She had quick reflexes, which allowed for physical capabilities as well. This was something else altogether.

She wanted to be able to make him really smile. To find a way. She hadn't seen him smile at any of his fellow club members either. She knew if she could have a genuine laugh, one completely real, it would be a gift. "I don't know what you want me to do," she admitted.

"You didn't ask, baby."

That voice, so gentle, played over her skin so gently it felt like the touch of fingers. She wondered if that was part of his gift. Could he do that? Make a sound feel like an actual physical stroke? She stood up, graceful because she had good balance and for him, she wanted to be as sensual as possible.

She tugged and removed first one boot and then the other. Before she could strip away his socks, he reached out and slipped his fingers through the tight red curls adorning her mound.

"Love the fire in these curls, *ledi*. You're my little sexy *kiska*. We're going to trim them down, but never get rid of them. I like them far too much."

Absinthe stroked caresses through the red hair, and each time the pads of his fingers moved confidently over her curls, they dipped lower to her lips and clit as if he owned that part of her. Every word he spoke sent flames licking at her sensitive skin right along with his touch, as if his tongue held fire and he could turn her body into an inferno anytime he wanted.

"You make me feel sexy, Absinthe," she blurted out without thinking and then shook her head and removed his socks.

"You are sexy, Scarlet. I've never found another woman more sensual." He put one hand on her belly and eased her back a step so he could stand up, stripping his jeans off as he did. "Everything about you is sexy. Go get in the tub, babe. I'm right behind you."

She was very conscious that he meant it. Absinthe simply tossed his clothes at a hamper and followed her to the bathtub. She could feel his eyes on her the entire way. She stepped into the bathtub and slid into the hot water. The tub was deeper than she expected, the color, teal, turning the water an incredible shade of blue.

Absinthe got into the steaming water directly behind her, his legs wide, pulling her body back into his so she was sitting between his legs. Immediately he cupped the weight of her breasts in his large hands, his thumbs gently strumming over her nipples. She let her head fall back against his chest and closed her eyes, enjoying the feeling of him playing with her nipples.

She loved being with him, skin to skin, close to him, the heat of the water rising around them, melting her body into his so she felt like she was sharing the same body with him. She let herself drift off for the first time in so long she couldn't remember. She always had to be so hyperaware of everything. So vigilant. Here, with Absinthe, she felt safe. Peace settled into her as his hands moved over her body, claiming her.

Ordinarily, she didn't like anyone touching her. She had tried using money to exchange for the needed lessons in survival training, and most of the time it had worked, until Adrik. He'd been merciless. Daunting. She'd nearly given up until she realized he was the real deal. An assassin, and he could really teach her the things she needed to know in order to get to the man who had taken his friends to her little sister's home and beaten and raped her. This was the man who would show her what to do.

"Shh, baby, you're safe with me," Absinthe whispered, his fingers moving over her ear gently, his mouth brushing kisses into the messy topknot she'd made of her hair to prevent it from getting wet. "Anything either of us has done in the past stays there. The past shaped us into being who we are, why we need one another. I need you. I swear to you, Scarlet, I want you just the way you are. I hope like hell you want me the same way."

She realized she had tears running down her face and knew just sitting in the water with Absinthe was some kind of catharsis, a purification, a cleansing. She knew Absinthe meant every word. They had a connection, a path that lay open between them, and she felt his loneliness. She'd always been alone, and she'd accepted her path. Absinthe was different. He'd been with his family, those seventeen people who still surrounded him and yet he was desperately lonely. Why?

He thought himself unlovable. That she could never love him if she knew the truth about him and what he wanted from her. His deepest need. His darkest craving. Her stomach did a slow roll as she tried to puzzle it out. Absinthe was such a gorgeous, handsome man. Intelligent. More than intelligent. He had amazing gifts. What could he possibly need from her that he would think would make her want to run from him? That was in his mind. What made him think the others didn't know him? And if they did, that they would turn their backs on him? Detest him, even kill him. That made no sense. What was it that he needed? Why was he so lonely?

She knew he said he could command with his voice, but she still wasn't certain he could do that to her, or that she was willing to give her consent.

What was it he didn't think she would do for him that he wanted the most? Scarlet waited. They were skin to skin. Her mind was open to his. He knew all of her secrets. She wanted him to just open up and tell her his. She realized he was considering just using his voice on her, forcing his will on her without her consent, but that went against everything he'd ever promised himself once he'd left the hellhole he'd been raised in. He was struggling with his decision: tell her, let her go or do what he always had done—force his will.

The moment he considered forcing his will on her, his

mind turned into a world of horror. It became a kind of jumble of torture and rape, with men slamming little boys and girls into walls and hitting them with fists or even whips, laughing and forcing them to their knees. She caught glimpses of Absinthe as a child. She recognized him by his eyes, or was it his brother? She only knew there was blood, rape and twisted things that should never have been experienced by anyone, let alone a child.

She caught glimpses of so many horrendous images crowding into his mind that she couldn't stand it. She had to do something to stop it. She reached behind her with one arm, caught his head to bring it down to hers as she turned her own and initiated a kiss for the first time in her life.

For Scarlet, it was daring, terrifying and desperate. For her, at that moment, more than anything else, more than her own fears, her own needs, she had to stop those memories from eating him alive. She could see the demons devouring him. Ugly. Real. These weren't from a book, a horror story he'd read, a movie he'd seen or a nightmare that needed waking from. Absinthe had lived through torture and rape. He had seen things she never wanted to see again. A boy huddled in a corner with blood all over him, whispering, naked and cold, tears running down his face, trying to comfort other children, some dying, some already dead.

She initiated the kiss and knew it was tentative and awkward, but she stroked her tongue along his and poured what she felt for him into it. Her need to give him everything. Her promise of submission to him. The very unexpected and growing affection she had for him. Emotion spread through her like a tidal wave, consuming her with astonishing and unforeseen passion that built until she recognized it as being too close to love. She barely knew him and yet she was already feeling that strong of a craving toward him. That outpouring of a promise that she would be the one person to love him unconditionally. She could give him that. She knew she could.

Deliberately, Scarlet concentrated on the fire between them, pouring the flames over the images in his mind, building that terrible burn slowly because she had no real idea what she was doing, only that she had to take the horror away and give her man the knowledge that she could love him no matter what they had done to him. No matter what he demanded, wanted or needed from her. As long as he gave her the same back, she was willing.

TWELVE

❧

Absinthe pulled back, shocked that Scarlet was reading his mind. She was. He knew she was inside of his mind; he could feel her there. He had forgotten how quickly her brain adjusted to every possible puzzle presented. She was often unaware of how fast her mind solved enigmas for her, because once done, it would likely dismiss the mystery as solved and go on to the next new problem. But this would be different because this was all about him and why he was so fucked up.

He slammed down every hard shield he had and stood up fast, the water pouring off of his body as panic set in. "Stay right there." His voice was low, a soft command that pushed its way into the brain and lodged there, forcing obedience even against will.

Her face registered distress and hurt, but she didn't move, her green eyes on his face, still looking up at him over her shoulder.

He was tall and had long legs, so stepping out of the tub was easy in spite of the high sides. Catching up the towel, he glared down at her, daring her to move, all the while monitoring her brain activity through their connection. His order had failed to take hold in her brain. She obeyed, but not because she *had* to obey. She was *choosing*.

He could barely breathe, his lungs raw and burning. He knew she couldn't possibly get at him even through that same pathway. He was too strong. Too experienced. Her brain might seek a way to do that for her, but he had shut down every conceivable entry. Now it was a matter of whether or not she actually responded to his voice in the way every other person he had ever encountered did, and she hadn't. She just fucking hadn't.

He backed away from the tub, toweling the water from his body, not paying attention because the only thing that mattered to him was whether or not she was lost to him. Why hadn't he remembered how her mind worked so quickly to solve puzzles? That had intrigued him, drawn him to her. The mystery of her, the way she was so like him and yet not at all. She was soft where he was hard. She was submissive where he was dominant.

On the other hand, she was lethal as hell and he fucking loved that. *Loved it.* He loved that she was so intelligent, and he could discuss any topic with her, and she actually knew what he was talking about. Looking at her, touching her, thinking about her, made him as hard as a steel rod. He was already completely gone on her. She was the one for him. He knew it with absolute certainty and yet . . . she was thinking too much. *Thinking.* Her brain shouldn't have been assessing his command. She should have been obeying blindly.

He turned away from her, pacing across the room because his body was restless, the panic of knowing he couldn't control her, the most important person in his world, choking him. The bathroom was spacious, the steam from the hot water still curling through the air in places. Scarlet stayed very still, her green eyes following his every movement. She didn't speak and she looked stricken. He processed that even as he rapidly went through every possibility he had to choose from.

He could cut her loose. Have the club watch over her, keep her safe and he could get the hell out of there and go as far from her as possible until this was over, and she was gone. He didn't trust himself to be around her and not want to be with her. Adrik was right about one thing, she got into a man and wouldn't let go. He already thought about her day and night.

"Damn it." He swore out loud, furious with himself for being so careless. He'd been so eager to have her that he hadn't guarded against her getting into his head. No one had ever been able to do anything remotely close to that. Demyan, his brother, was the only other human being he'd known with the same kind of psychic gift. While Scarlet didn't have his abilities, she had some kind of talent that enabled her to build a resistance to his voice, to his commands, but more, to connect to his mind when he was open to her.

He stopped a few feet from her, standing over the bathtub, staring down at her. He couldn't let her go. It was that simple. He'd found her after all this time of thinking there would never be a woman for him, and he couldn't let her go. He just didn't know if this would work between them. He needed to find out. To know for certain.

Without another word, he left the room, leaving the door open between them. The carpet in the bedroom was thick and warm on his bare feet. He used the remote to turn on the fireplace. Donning a pair of loose drawstring pants, he made coffee right there in the bedroom using the setup he had installed in the corner next to the bar. It might be a long few hours. They weren't going to make it to the restaurant after all tonight.

Absinthe ran his fingers through his hair several times, agitated, worried, afraid that even if Scarlet stayed with him he would still lose because he wouldn't ever have the courage to tell her what he needed from her. Role-playing out of their house was one thing. She played the librarian very well. She hid the real woman behind those glasses and skirts, so role-playing would come easily to her, but that wasn't what he needed. He wished it was that simple.

Pushing open the sliding glass door, he stepped outside onto the verandah. The sun was still high, but already a few wisps of fog had begun to drift in, looking like gray fingers. He set the mug on the railing and watched the waves crashing onto the bluffs and the rocks out in the midst of the blue of the sea.

Sometimes the sight of the waves would bring him peace, but now, all he saw in his mind was Scarlet sitting in the bathtub, her red hair piled on her head and her green eyes looking up at him. Just the thought of her like that, doing what he asked of her, waiting without moving, brought up a million different erotic images.

He caught up the coffee cup and went back inside, closing the sliding glass door carefully and setting the cup near the fireplace. He paced back and forth on the thick carpet, making certain he had the discipline not to look into the bathroom to see if Scarlet was doing as he told her.

He hadn't used his full ability on her, but he never would. Not even with her consent. She would never know and that would make her a robot. Had she been susceptible like he thought she would be, she would have known but would have been helpless to do anything but obey. That way, she would have been able to signal to him if she didn't like something.

"Damn it," he whispered again. He would have taken a chance had he been able to command her. Now what was he going to do? He would never be satisfied. Over time it would become a problem, but he couldn't live without her now that he knew she existed.

He continued to pace, letting the time pass, minutes turning to an hour. The water would cool and then grow cold. What would she do? This was the easiest way to find out whether or not Scarlet had the resolve to obey his command on her own. She would be uncomfortable. There was no reasonable explanation that she would be able to give to herself. He told himself she would never stay there. The thought that she would sent heat rushing through his veins. He forced himself to stop pacing and sit in the chair in front of the fireplace with a fresh cup of coffee and drink it slowly.

He spent another hour reading. Most of the time, he couldn't see the words on the page. He didn't hear the sound of the water splashing. Not a single sound. The sun began to sink. He got up and stretched and left the room before he gave in to the need to check on her. Thirty more minutes. If she could really last thirty more minutes, if she could choose to obey his command on her own, making it her choice without the reinforcement of his voice, they would have a chance together.

He paced through the entire length of the house for the next quarter of an hour, the energy building until all he could think about was slamming her up against the wall and burying himself in her. The erotic images wouldn't stop flooding his mind. She still hadn't made a sound. He stalked back to the bedroom and warmed towels and made hot chocolate before making his way into the master bath. The temperature had dropped by several degrees.

Scarlet sat in the bathtub exactly as he had left her. There was no attempt to cover up. No attempt to pull her knees up or make herself warmer. She was shivering and there were goose bumps on her skin. Her head was still turned looking over her shoulder, her eyes on the doorway. She focused on him immediately. Utterly. Completely.

His cock leapt to attention, became hardened steel. He continued straight to the tub, bent down and twisted the stopper to drain the water. It was extremely cold. He held out his hand to her. "You did good, Scarlet. I'm proud of you." He kept his voice soft, stroking praise over her like soft feathers brushing her skin.

She put her hand in his and let him pull her to her feet, her eyes lighting up at the admiration in his tone. He wrapped a towel around her. She was shivering nearly uncontrollably.

"Stay still and let me take care of you." He had warmed the towel and he used it slowly, rubbing it over her body, taking away the droplets of cold water. He wrapped her in a second warm towel and led her from the room into the warmth of the bedroom.

He pointed to the thick rug on top of the carpet in front of the fireplace. It was between the two chairs. "Sit there, *moya malen'kiy kotenok*." The rug would be sensuous on her bare bottom while adding extra warmth. "Drink this." He handed her a mug of hot chocolate he'd prepared in advance for her. Sinking down onto the chair, so she was virtually sitting between his legs, he poured warm lotion into his hands and began to massage her stiff shoulders. "You did as you were told to do without any influence. Why? You didn't have to."

"I told you I would do whatever you asked of me." Her voice was very low. She was still shivering.

He dug his fingers deeper into her muscles and followed the line of her spine. She had a beautiful back. "That isn't answering the question, Scarlet. Why did you choose to obey me?"

She didn't answer immediately, and he respected that she took her time and was thoughtful in her reply. He wanted her to be. He wanted to know if she could really be his partner in every way, both outside of and in the bedroom.

"I want to please you, Absinthe. I want to give you everything you need or want, no matter how difficult it is. You've indicated to me that it might be very difficult. I want you to know that I will be willing to follow your commands always as long as you stay within those boundaries I've asked of you, and I trust that you will. Pleasing you is what makes me happy, and also, following your orders makes my body very, very responsive."

"You mean when I tell you to do something it makes your fiery little pussy very wet," he corrected. "You're my *kiska*. That means pussy. Or pussycat. That's what I want you to be for me here in this room quite a lot of the time."

He watched her closely. Her face was turned away from him, but he watched her body and he was more than adept at reading body language. Little goose bumps rose on her skin and a little shiver went through her. He swept his hand down her back and then back up to her nape, using his fingers to caress her before removing the towel.

"I think you're warm enough. The fireplace will warm you up fast." She didn't understand yet what he was telling her, but so far, she wasn't opposed to anything he had said or done. "Turn around and kneel so I can see your face while we talk, *kiska*." He used his commanding voice, ensuring she would know he meant business.

She didn't hesitate. She placed the mug of chocolate on the table and turned to face him, shifting to her knees, looking up at him, her green eyes meeting his.

He dropped his hand to the top of her head and began a slow massage of her scalp. Gentle. Loving. He felt that way toward her. He used his other hand to play with her nipple. Her left one. He teased it idly on purpose, as if he wasn't thinking. As if he wasn't even fully aware of what he was doing. Tugging and then flicking. Rubbing. Using the pad of his thumb and then pinching down, a slow soft burn that got steadily tighter as if he didn't notice while he spoke.

"I like to play. I haven't been able to satisfy my urges or cravings in years, Scarlet, and I thought I would never be able to again. You've come into my life and now all I think about is telling you what to do and watching you do it for me. Taking you right to the edge over and over and making you beg me to let you go over. I also find a sense of peace when I have my little pet in my bedroom with me. In this room I would very much like you to agree to be my little *kiska* until I say otherwise."

He kept his eyes on hers, refusing to look away from her. His hand slid from her nipple down her belly to her fiery red curls. He fed one finger into her hot, slick entrance. There were several ways to tell if a woman was seriously into whatever suggestion a dominant gave her. Testing her reaction was a very good one.

"I mean that literally. When you are my *kiska*, you will be naked, on your hands and knees. You will serve me, doing anything I ask of you." His finger was treated to a flood of hot liquid. "You will wear a collar of my choosing and it may change depending on my mood for the day. It won't be every night, because I want my sensuous woman and my sexy little librarian as well, but I am in desperate need of my pet. So, most of the time, I will want her with me. I will decide when my pet will have the night off."

He kept his voice low, penetrating, just the way she liked, that soft command, but firm, the one that meant there was no arguing or negotiating. Her feminine channel clamped down like a vise around his finger, scorching hot, slick wet silk, pulsing with life. Her breathing changed, turned ragged. Her bare breasts rose and fell. He removed his finger and held it to her mouth. "Lick, *malen'kiy kiska*. Clean my finger."

Keeping her eyes on his, she leaned forward and licked at his finger just like a little kitten might. Her tongue curled around his finger, and his cock, already hard, swelled to bursting proportions. He reached down with his other hand and pulled the drawstring to open the pants. "Open your mouth and suck."

She parted her lips and he pushed his finger into the warmth of her mouth. She sucked and his cock went diamond hard. He needed to be able to have stamina. So far, she was accepting everything he'd demanded of her. He lifted his hips.

"Pull them off, fold them and put them to one side."

Scarlet did so. The relief to have the material off his straining cock and balls was wonderful. "While you are my pet, you will always be on your hands and knees, crawling in this room, never walking until I say you can. Why, *kiska*? Why won't you be walking on two feet?"

Her gaze dropped from his face to his fist, where he pumped his cock lazily, and then jumped back to his face. There was hunger in her eyes. Desire. "Because pussycats don't walk upright, Absinthe, they crawl on all fours."

He nodded. "Very good. That is correct. And that is what you are in this room unless I tell you differently. You will be my beautiful, fiery, sizzling-hot pussy, won't you?" He dropped his hand to her right nipple and tugged and rolled gently. "So red, when I do this to you. If I pinch harder, it's bright like your hair. So much for me to play with. Put your knees apart for me. I like to see your pussy so I can see if you like what I'm doing to you."

Scarlet complied immediately.

"You will wear whatever I choose to lay out for you that day and whatever leash I put on the bed. I will feed you myself. I am responsible for your care in this room. You will not touch any food unless it is from my hand. I will decide if you drink from a glass or a bowl."

He watched her carefully when he gave her that instruction. Her lashes fluttered but she didn't object, not even with her body language. That was one major hurdle. There was one more. The most difficult for her. He was going to have to ease into it. So far, Scarlet had been perfect for him just as if she'd been born for him. And more importantly, as if he'd been born for her.

"Turn around, lie down on your belly facing the fireplace. I want you to be very comfortable." He waited until she did as he instructed and then he took the large, firm pillow he had set by the chair and lifted her hips to slide it under her, pushing her ass into air. "Spread your legs wide for me."

Scarlet did so, again without hesitation. Absinthe went to his knees in between her legs, poured warm oil into his hands and began to massage it into her thighs, first the left one and then the right. He worked until she was very relaxed and then moved his attention to the firm globes of her bottom. She was very fit, and he dug his fingers into the muscles, kneading and rubbing.

"Have you had anal sex before?"

She started to turn her head.

"It's an easy enough question to answer, *kiska*. When I ask you a question, my little pussycat is expected to answer immediately, without hesitation."

"I'm sorry. I was embarrassed."

"It doesn't matter if you're embarrassed. In this room, you are to please me. If I ask you something, I want an answer, and to answer is to please me."

"Yes."

"Often?"

"No. Only once."

Absinthe could tell by her voice Scarlet hadn't been impressed by her experience. That would raise the stakes between them. In a way, it would make what he required of her even more exciting. If she would really do what he asked of her of her own volition, just because she wanted to please him, because it turned her on to do so, they definitely had a perfect partnership. If she couldn't, he would know he would have to find a way to live with her without fulfilling his most basic craving.

He continued rubbing the oil into her cheeks, his thumbs sliding into the seam between them, finding that forbidden little star and deliberately sweeping over it again and again. Claiming that territory as his own. "Scarlet. What do red-hot little pussycats have right here?"

He pushed his thumb into that star between her cheeks and fucked her slowly. Gently. At the same time, he flicked her clit and strummed and circled it. He was rewarded with another flood of scorching-hot liquid, little droplets collecting on her curls and the inviting entrance to her sex.

"A tail?" For the first time her voice trembled.

He pressed a kiss into the base of her spine. Working her clit. Working her ass. His cock was so hard he thought he might explode. "That's right, baby. Smoking-hot pussycats have a tail, and when they crawl around, that tail shows off their beautiful ass and the way they can work it. The way they tempt their man. The way they say without words, 'Come and fuck me. Use me. Use my lovely mouth and give me my treat straight from your cock.' That sassy tail says, 'My cute little pussy needs filling up.' It says, 'My gorgeous ass is empty and is desperate for your cock.'"

All the while he talked in his low voice, he kept working her body, using that oil on her, pushing his finger, first one then two, into her, fucking her with his fingers while still fucking her ass with his thumb. She was pushing back into him now, trying to find a rhythm, her hips lifting. He leaned down and scraped his teeth over her left cheek, raising more goose bumps. She was very receptive. More than receptive.

He pulled his hands away to replace his fingers with his mouth. She cried out and he stopped, lifting his head. "Pussycats purr. They don't scream. They can dig their claws into me, or the carpet, but they never scream. They don't use their voice like that. It's my fault for not reminding you, so I won't stop, but you will have to remember, *kiska*."

Absinthe couldn't help but smile as he bent his head again. She tasted like fucking heaven and he was going to feast on her. She wasn't going to get the relief she thought she would because he was too damned good at what he did. She didn't have a chance, but that was the fun of playing. That was what he loved. Scarlet had entered into the game with him willingly and she hadn't looked at him as if he were the most perverted, fucked-up man in the world. Someday, he would tell her why he was the way he was and how he got that way, but not tonight. Tonight, he would see if they were really compatible and if they could fulfill each other's deepest cravings in the bedroom.

He sucked on her pussy lips, knowing he was going to shave them bare so she would feel everything he did to them. He used his tongue creatively, drawing out her honey, stabbing and fucking and then stroking caresses, hard, using the flat of his tongue, then soft, licking again, changing the rhythm so she couldn't get used to it, always putting a steady pressure on that very sensitive little magic button of hers.

Her purrs changed to growls. The nails curled into the carpet. Her hips bucked. She was so close. He flicked and stabbed. She gave a guttural cry and then another little scream escaped.

With a little grin, Absinthe lifted his head, wiped his gleaming jaws on her thighs and then swatted her ass lightly. "Naughty, naughty, *kiska*. What did I say about screaming? Now you have to wait a very long time before your little pussy is satisfied. Still, you were so good for me, staying in that cold water all that time. You do deserve a reward." Once again, he rubbed her firm cheeks, feeling the lovely shape of them, tracing the seam between them.

"Stay very still, *kiska*, and relax for me."

He pulled the large jeweled chest he had out from under the coffee table and flipped it open. His heart accelerated. He couldn't believe he was actually going to do this—that Scarlet was letting him and he was daring to take the chance. He lifted the tail from the box with great care. It was beautiful. Jeweled. Fiery red, to match her hair. The moment he'd laid eyes on Scarlet, he'd gone to Ice and together they'd drawn his visions out on paper. Ice was a genius when it came to jewelry. Every tail was different and the plug was progressively larger in size. The silky fur had glittering rubies strewn throughout, so whenever it moved, if the light hit it, the gems would gleam. The glass plug the tail was attached to was the same red as the actual rubies. He hadn't told Ice about Scarlet at the time, but Ice had still worked tirelessly on the tails and collars for him because that was what brothers did when you asked them for favors.

This plug was on the thinner side and shaped carefully, so as to not hurt her in any way. She could wear this one for long periods of time, and it should remain comfortable. He was using their specially made oil that was the best lubricant and stayed longer and was also made to enhance the sex drive. He'd had several tails made for her with various-size plugs. She didn't need to see those or think about them yet, but the thought of them waiting for her sent his cock into a frenzy.

"Look at this, baby, I had it made just for you. It's beautiful, just the way you are."

From behind her, so she couldn't see his face, heart pounding, he held the tail in front of her, letting the flames from the fireplace catch the rubies and light them up from every angle. She let out a little gasp, but before he could reprimand her, she made a little purring noise in her throat. He rubbed her bottom to reward her.

"Such a good little pussy. You like your tail, don't you?"

She nodded and purred again, this time the sound stronger and much more like the vibration of a kitten. He used the lube on the glass plug and then once again poured more between her cheeks, rubbing gently and then pushing his thumb into the little star to prepare her.

"Relax, *kiska.*" He used his most commanding voice, dropping it several octaves. "I want to see how your tail looks, and if you're a good little pussycat I'll give you a reward. If not, there will be no treats and you will have cold milk from a bowl before bed and your little pussy will be hot and swollen with need all night, but you won't have any relief."

Instantly, her body flushed a wild rose and he could see

little droplets of needy liquid once again on her lips. She liked the kitten play with him much more than he'd thought she would. He pushed his thumb deeper and then inserted his finger to his knuckle.

"Breathe for me. I'm being gentle. I told you, I'm never going to hurt you."

He pushed a second finger into her. Two fingers were wider than the plug. His cock was becoming a problem. Aching. Painful even. He desperately needed relief. If he wanted to lead her around the room with a collar and watch her crawl with the sexy little tail, he was going to have to have her milk him dry before he did anything else.

His heart pounded in time to the heartbeat in his cock as he began to push the red glass plug into the tiny little star between her cheeks. He watched his red plug slowly disappear into her ass, making every part of her belong to him. There was some resistance and that just added to the sexiness of the act. It was hot. Dirty. So fucking carnal and erotic he could barely contain himself.

She made little mewling noises just like a little kitten. That added to the sexual excitement for him. He didn't care that he'd been programmed to crave this. To be addicted to the need for dominance, to love watching a woman with a tail in her ass crawling on her hands and knees for him. He needed his pet, and to have Scarlet, a woman he felt emotion for—actual love already—willingly giving herself to him like this gave him more of a sexual rush than he'd ever had in his life. His body was nearly undone by the sight of her as she shuddered, the plug finally seating fully, the base lodging tight and the tail lifting high, just the way it was made to do. He rubbed and massaged her cheeks until she purred for him.

"You look so beautiful, *moya kiska*, I'm so proud of you. You're being so good." He reached into the jeweled box and took out the thin collar adorned with small rubies embedded in the leather and buckled it around her neck, checking to ensure it wasn't too tight. It had three gold rings on it, and he attached the matching leash to one of them.

"Come up onto your knees but be very mindful of your tail. You definitely deserve a treat and you have to be thirsty. This is all for you."

He towered over her, loving the way she looked, his collar around her neck, the silky tail blazing with the flames from the fire shining through it between her ass cheeks, her breasts thrust toward him, nipples hard and those green eyes on his, awaiting his orders. He had so many other toys for his kitten now that he knew she would play with him.

She remembered to keep her knees apart and he could see her little pink pussy wet for him. It was going to be that way for a while before he would give her satisfaction. When she did come, it would be spectacular, and she would deserve it. She was so perfect. Better than he'd ever imagined any woman could ever be.

"Open your mouth for me, *kiska*."

He saw the way his voice took her, and it was beautiful to him. She willingly gave herself to him, and that was even more beautiful. She *gave* herself to him. The collar. The leash. The tail. Kneeling in front of him. Her eyes on his. Parting those lush lips. This woman was lethal when she wanted to be, but for him, she was submitting completely to his demands of her own accord, through her own desire. He gently pushed the crown of his cock around those soft lips, leaving smears of his seed behind. When her lips were coated as if his come were lipstick, he pulled back.

"Start with my balls and work your way up just the way a kitten would do. Swallow me down and suck every drop out of me. I don't want anything left. You earned your treat, pussycat." Once again, he emphasized that his cock was her reward for her cooperation.

He waited until she leaned into him and began lapping at his balls with her tongue, and he put his hand on the back of her head and held her to him. The feeling of her attention was exquisite. He'd had women go down on him a million times, but he'd always had to command his body to cooperate.

He'd never felt anything like this, her tongue on his sac, her breasts brushing his thighs, her hands on the seam between his thighs and ass. Sometimes her nails dug deep and other times she stroked little caresses. No matter what she did with her hands, it was always in counterpoint to her amazing mouth as she worked his balls, sucking, jiggling, laving and licking her way up the wide girth of his cock.

His entire body shuddered with pleasure as her tongue curled and danced along his shaft to the crown of his cock. She licked him like he was an ice cream cone, and then engulfed the entire wide head, purring as she did so, the vibration sending such an amazing sensation rolling in waves through his groin and belly. His fist tightened in the thick red hair she'd knotted on top of her head. He couldn't quite decide what to keep his eyes on, the way her lips were stretched around his thick cock or the tail bobbing wildly as she tried to take more of him.

"That's it, *kiska*. That's what I like." The words came out a groan. She was better than any mouth he'd ever had. She was killing him. Taking him to paradise.

She lashed him with her tongue. She did something that felt like she twirled circles around his shaft with it, which would have been impossible. She was wet. Wild. She kept a tight suction. She purred, the vibration sending those waves through him again, this time stronger. She tightened her fingers in a ring around his shaft, putting pressure on his penis while she fed him deeper into her mouth. It was so damn sexy watching her lips stretch, watching himself disappear another inch. There was no way she could take all of him, but it added to his excitement to watch her try.

Then she purred a third time, the pulsation and shuddering of the waves so powerful that his balls were tight and hot. She did the ring with her fingers, trying to feed herself more of him, another inch deeper, and her mouth was so tight around him she nearly choked. He felt the head of his cock hit her throat. She tried to cough. Her eyes swam with tears. He fucking couldn't pull back.

"Swallow. Fucking swallow right now." He growled the command, his voice low and shockingly velvet, that voice that he used when no one could disobey but Scarlet. No one but his woman. His kitten. And shockingly, Scarlet, his personal kitten, was the one woman who chose of her own free will to obey him, and that was hotter than forcing his will on anyone. He erupted like a fucking volcano, his seed rocketing out of him like a never-ending fountain, and she valiantly did her best to do exactly what he'd ordered her to do. She swallowed. Over and over.

Absinthe had the presence of mind, even in the most blissful state of ecstasy he'd ever been in, to pull his cock out of her mouth so she could breathe. He wrapped his arms around her and pulled her into him, holding her close while he tried to find a way to come back to earth. She'd taken him somewhere else, somewhere close to paradise and far, far from the hell he lived in. Emotions threatened to swallow him. He found he was nearly crushing her, and he had to pull back from doing that as well.

"Are you all right, *kiska*?" He brushed kisses on top of her head when she nodded and then indicated for her to move back enough for him to stand. "Let's get you some water." Heart beating fast, he picked up the leash and stepped around the chair. It took a minute for his legs to work. She'd drained him. Wrecked him. She'd made him feel loved in a way he'd never felt before. He didn't know how to process the jumbled, never-before-felt emotions he was feeling, but he didn't want them to ever stop. He wanted this bond, this closeness she was giving him, to continue for as long as possible.

Scarlet dropped to her hands and knees and began to crawl after him, her tail high and swaying just as he knew it would. It was gorgeous, the rubies throwing unexpected sparkles across the walls as her ass swayed with every forward movement of her knees on the carpet. The way the last of the sunlight caught the gems through the glass was so perfect, he led her in a slow circle around the room just to watch the way the rubies blazed red streaks across the walls.

He stopped her in front of the bar and took a cold bottle of water from the refrigerator there. The bottle was glass with a long, narrow neck, and ice-cold, the way he preferred his drinking water. He kept the temperature in that small fridge low enough to produce small ice chips in the water. The shape and coldness of the bottle fueled his already carnal imagination.

"Did drinking your milk get you hot, little pussycat?" He walked behind her and dropped his hand to her bottom, ruffling the tail and then massaging her perfect firm little cheeks. He slid his finger between her cheeks and rubbed. That specialty oil had a hint of ginger in it, just enough to fire up all the nerve endings, bringing them alive with need. "I asked a question, *kiska*."

She purred and pushed back against his hand.

Absinthe smiled. He was already in love with her. So much more now than he had been before, and that had been over the top and beyond what he'd thought possible in the short amount of time he'd known her. He didn't know what love was. He just thought of the emotion he felt for her as their connection, but she had wrapped herself so deeply around his heart with her acceptance of his peculiar needs, his craving for owning his hot little pussycat.

He rubbed the seam between her thighs and cheeks and then dipped his finger into her hot, tight, silken tunnel. He had that oil coated on his finger and rolled it around, making certain to introduce the mixture to her already burning nerves.

Even after she'd drained him dry so he could take his time playing with his kitten, his cock reacted to her heat, jerking, straining to attention. He flicked her clit and then tugged. She hissed and then purred loudly, pushing back, seeking his fingers. He gave her two, fucking her with them, curling them to find her most sensitive spot, stroking over and over, getting her close. He pulled his fingers free just before she could find release and pushed the cold bottle into the scorching heat, rolling it and plunging it gently in and out as if it were a dildo.

"Do you like your toy, *kiska*? I thought it might help cool you down."

She panted, her breathing ragged again. He pulled the bottle free and licked her juice from it before uncapping it. She tasted great and he wasn't wasting anything belonging to him. "Drink up, kitten. You're going to need it. This is going to be a very long night for you. You're a very lucky little pussycat. Some kittens are kept in cages. I like mine curled up next to me. Close. I like my hot little *kiska* always ready for me."

While she drank, he turned on the dim lights that sprayed beams from all around the corners of the room. It was as if he could spotlight his kitten from every angle. He rubbed his cock along her cheeks and then began to play with her tail again, watching the way the light lit the rubies every time he moved the fur. It was a dazzling display. When she was finished drinking, he took the bottle from her, capped it and led her back to the bar so he could put it in the fridge to keep it cold.

"We want to make certain that tail stays lubed, baby. If you're ever uncomfortable, you need to let me know immediately." He removed it and added more oil, generously pouring more between her cheeks and massaging it in. He enjoyed watching it disappear and helping it with his finger. She pushed back against him, appearing to love his administrations, even purring when he inserted the tail again.

"You like your tail now, don't you?"

She nodded her head, purring louder. She had a beautiful purr. He rubbed her cheeks, wanting to fuck her there, but she wasn't nearly ready. He used the glass plug to fuck her with instead, being gentle, while at the same time his fingers were on her clit. He kept his manipulation slow, wanting to show her how it could burn so good. Once again, he brought her right to the edge and then he stopped, withdrew his fingers, caught her hair to pull back her head so he could look at the dazed desperation in her beautiful green eyes and then he licked at his fingers.

"You taste so incredibly good, *kiska*." He put his fingers in front of her mouth. "You're a good little kitty, so I'll share sometimes."

He watched as she licked at his fingers. It was so sensual to watch her little tongue darting out to take his offering. When she was finished, he led her around the room once again, pointing out the streaks of fire glittering on the walls from her fancy tail and collar. All the while his cock grew harder and harder.

He walked her to the bed, where he urged her to bend over the side, half on and half off. Her tail was very much on display, a high arc, sprouting a beautiful red between her trembling cheeks. He used his hands and voice to soothe her, once again nuzzling her with his mouth, feeding on her, licking and sucking to bring her close until she was trembling and purring, nearly frantic. Once again, he backed off, rubbing her back and the base of her spine, fucking her gently with the plug.

"You're going to feel very full, *kiska*, when my cock is in you. It will feel so good. You're going to be used to that feeling. No matter what, there will always be such a fullness stretching you, but it will always feel good."

He remembered how tight she'd been that first time he'd entered her. He'd barely managed to push his cock into that constricting, scorching tunnel. Now, with her plug so solidly in her ass, even as slender as it was, there would be even less room. She was slick though, and so ready for him. Desperate for him. Her breath sounded like ragged little counterpoints to the small thrusts of his hips as he pushed the crown of his cock into her hot entrance.

Her body didn't know what it wanted to do. He felt her muscles frantically grab for him, surround him and squeeze down, fearful that he might escape, and yet he was so large, at the same time there was that need to push him back out. He found himself needing to watch the urgent fight and at the same time throw his head back and howl at the exquisite torture. He was on fire. He was in paradise. He was in hell. It was the best fucking moment of his life and he hadn't even entered her fully.

He caught hold of her hips, stilling her motion, refusing to allow her to move forward or back. She was trapped between him and the bed, mewling softly, a small agonized plea for his cock, the need building in her to a frenzied state, just the way he knew would happen. He wanted that for her. A spectacular orgasm, a series of them. Something different only he could give her.

He surged into her, driving through her silken tunnel, that tight, scorching-hot place that took him out of the world of sin and hell that he was mired in. She lifted him, short-circuited his brain, driving everything out of it until there was only his woman, his red-hot, sizzling sex kitten squeezing the life out of his cock, determined to milk him dry. He buried himself deep over and over, listening to her soft cries, the breath hissing out of her lungs, watching the way her fingers found the quilt on the bed and her nails buried deep to try to hang on when there was no way to stay anchored. He was going to send his woman flying as high as he could.

That silken channel pulsed around him with her frantic heartbeat, a frenzied symphony of urgent need. He slammed his cock home over and over, streaks of fire racing up his spine, spreading like wild flames through him, dancing over her, taking her by surprise.

She screamed as her body clamped down on his like a vise. The orgasm swept through her, a formidable surge racing like a tidal wave. The waves kept coming, sweeping through her body, each more powerful than the last. He reached up and caught the beautiful furry tail, and in time with his thrusting hips, began to fuck her with that thin plug, over and over, creating a new sensation, adding to the overwhelming contractions in her body.

He felt those waves rolling through her thighs, the cheeks of her ass, all the while he kept hammering into her, fucking her with the plug, feeling the power of those orgasms, one after another progressively growing stronger as they raced through her. Fiery living silk, hot as hell, gripped his cock from every angle, squeezed and massaged with a thousand fingers, licked with a thousand tongues, burned with as many flames, killing him with a beauty he'd never experienced before.

He moved in her with brutal strokes, hard and fast, but with each fierce stroke he knew he was loving her. He was giving her something extraordinary, his gift in exchange for the beauty and wonder of hers. He wasn't going to last much longer, but he held out as long as humanly possible. "Scarlet, *moya literaturnaya ledi, ya tebya lyublyu.*" He couldn't tell her in English. But it was the fucking truth. He loved Scarlet Foley more than life itself.

Her body surrounded his with that scorching fire, so tight now, gripping and milking, working his cock over and over. Her ragged breathing was music. Her mewling cries and little accompanying hitches filled his mind, adding to the amazing sexual tango rushing through his system, every nerve ending alive.

Then his vision was blurring, the edges of reality fading further until there was only the two of them in a world of bright hot colors and pure feeling. He felt like they were spinning together, winding tighter and tighter until they were bound so close in that web of pleasure it was impossible to separate them. Sharing the same skin, the same body and mind, they'd been thrown into a vortex, a mind-blowing world he wanted to stay in—with her. She'd given him back life. A way to live. A sanctuary.

He collapsed over her, his head on the mattress beside her, one hand at the base of her spine, fingers spread wide as he rubbed soothingly, whispering softly to her to help bring her back. Her body continually shuddered, still rippling with aftershocks. He could feel every one of them, the clamping around his spent cock, desperate for more, still trying to milk more seed from him. Each squeeze on his sensitive cock sent streaks of fire like lightning jolts up his spine.

Ordinarily, his kitten would curl up all night with him in the bed, and he'd take care of her, gently petting and loving on her, waking her when he woke and needed or just wanted to play, but Scarlet was new at this and she'd given so much. She was exhausted. He forced himself to breathe, to rouse his body when all he wanted to do was drag himself on the bed with her and sleep. Gently he pressed a kiss onto the base of her spine and removed the tail. Another spasm ran through her body. He rubbed her cheeks.

"Stay still, baby, don't try to move. Let me take care of you."

It took a few minutes to find his strength before he could make his way into the bathroom to clean the tail properly and then himself before getting her a hot washcloth and warm towel. He cleaned her as gently as possible, taking his time, making certain he was thorough before drying her off. Gathering her in his arms, he shifted her into the middle of the bed and drew up the covers. She watched him with sleepy eyes as he returned the tail to the jeweled box and the towels to the hampers in the bathroom.

Absinthe returned to the bed and gathered her into his

arms. "You were amazing, Scarlet. Thank you for playing with me tonight. You gave me a gift beyond any price."

She pressed her lips to his throat. "I was surprised that I liked it so much. At first, I wanted to be a kitten for you. I thought if it made you happy, why not? I found I felt safe. You made me feel cherished and beautiful."

"You are cherished and beautiful."

She rubbed her face against his chest, the action making him think of a little kitten. She had those tendencies naturally whether she thought so or not.

"Strutting around the room for you really made me feel sexy. I was so turned on all I could do was think about sex. I could barely breathe I wanted you so much." The confession came out in a little rush. "That tail is the most sensual thing I've ever seen. It never occurred to me I'd think that way."

He smiled. She really was a natural. "I want to try so many things with you, Scarlet. I like that you respond to my voice and my commands." He drew his finger down her arm and felt goose bumps rise immediately on her skin. That was a good sign. She was still very responsive. He wanted her to always think of their bedroom as a place where she immediately went into her submissive kitten role. Or her librarian role. Or his loving, beautiful wife. He had it all with her.

"I didn't know what I was doing so I'm sure I didn't please you as much as I could have the first time out. I'll do some research on behaviors and mannerisms."

His heart clenched hard in his chest. For a moment he couldn't respond. She was doing so much for him. He had been going to suggest she do a little research, but she was already one step ahead of him. His fingers settled in her hair and he massaged her scalp gently. "Don't think you didn't please me, Scarlet. You were magnificent."

She turned her face up and kissed him again. "I'm so tired, Absinthe, I can barely move."

"You're going to be sore as well. I would have gone out

to the hot tub, but you aren't used to any of this yet. You'll build stamina."

"I want to. I was surprised when you used my name and I realized we weren't going to continue all night."

"You needed to rest and relax. Were you disappointed?"

She was silent for a moment, thinking it over in that way she had, a deliberate pondering. "I think so, a little, yes. I've never been that sexually aroused before, or had that feeling of safety and care. But I did want to ask questions and I was exhausted."

He loved her answer. "That's good that you were so aroused. I had Ice make the tails for you the moment I laid eyes on you. I haven't had kitten play with anyone since I left Russia. I haven't wanted to until I saw you. He's very talented and he makes all kinds of toys. I gave him a large order and he's busy completing it for us." Deliberately he referenced his Torpedo Ink brother. Scarlet needed to know that she was safe not only with him, but with all of them. That would take time, but the feeling had to start somewhere.

There was a small silence again. "He knows about this kind of play?"

He rubbed his hand over her breast, cupped the fullness and rubbed her nipple. "Of course. We were all together at all times even during sex. We watched out for one another in order to keep from being killed. Ice is the only one I would trust to make me toys that wouldn't hurt you." He rubbed her nipple gently. "Jewels for you everywhere, but nothing that's going to hurt you. He does incredible work. Don't you think so?"

"The tail is beautiful," she conceded. Her voice was reluctant.

"What's wrong, *miledi*? You always need to tell me when something concerns you."

"Will they see me like that?"

"Not unless you're comfortable with it. You're *my kiska*.

This is our special place. If we're here in our home and someone comes to visit and you want to go out and be shown off,
then I'll take you out of the room, but if not, then no. That will
be your choice."

Her entire body relaxed. She wrapped her arms around
him. "That's good then."

"Do you think that you might ever get that comfortable
as my *kiska*?"

Again, Scarlet didn't just answer immediately, she thought
it over for a long time. "I don't know. Maybe. It's pretty damn
hot thinking about you leading me around with that tail.
Would it make you hot?"

"As hell." Just talking about it had his cock reacting,
which was insane after the wild sex they'd shared. He put
her hand over his growing erection. Fortunately, it was a
pleasant feeling instead of an urgent demand. "Showing my
sizzling little pussycat is part of the fun and is sexy and hot,
especially if I have her all decked out in her finest jewels,
but what matters to me most is that my kitten is happy and
feels safe and secure, so having you here in the bedroom is
enough. Also, it's nice to have you sit quietly beside me
while I'm talking with the others, my little kitten at my
feet. You have to remember, we don't respond the way others do to nudity or sexual stimulation. None of us do."

"You never know, I might work up to that kind of confidence," she said.

Under her hand, his cock jerked hard. He felt her lips
curve against his chest. "Go to sleep, Scarlet. I've got club
business to take care of tomorrow and then we're sorting
out Holden."

"Do some people really put their kittens in cages, Absinthe?" Scarlett asked, her voice sleepy. She sounded curious, not judgmental.

He shut down instantly, slamming his mind closed, not
wanting one image to chance escaping from his mind to
hers.

"I said go to sleep." He didn't push at her, but his voice had naturally dropped into command octave. He even removed her hand from his cock, bringing it to his chest. His heart accelerated and his mouth went dry. He couldn't think about those kittens locked in those cages, not before he closed his eyes. In desperation, he caught her chin and turned her face up to his, finding her lips and kissing her until he couldn't think straight, until she took everything away.

THIRTEEN

"Team one will be moving on Sacramento tomorrow night. We want to be finished with everything by three A.M. That's when the security changes in the buildings we're burning down. We want them completely in flames and impossible to save but with no loss of life. We're not touching the building Haley Joico owns. The more Code looked into it, the more it seems as if she took out a huge insurance policy after talking with the Diamondbacks. She expects to profit from a fire."

Czar looked around the table at the Torpedo Ink members sitting in the large room. The windows, as usual, were open to let in the ocean breeze. "She threw her girls under the bus, allowing the Venomous club to manage them because it gave her a larger paycheck than the Diamondbacks, and now she wants to get out from under them because they aren't paying her the money they said they would."

"You dance with the devil . . ." Ice said.

"Exactly," Maestro agreed. "She can reap what she sowed."

"Her building stays standing. We'll do the managers because the Venomous bikers are pieces of shit and they're willing to gang-rape one of ours and then turn her over to Holden for a price. Code, we have to have up-to-date information on where those three managers are at all times. We know when the clubs shut down in the early morning hours and who is on."

"There's actually six of them: the three main ones and their relief managers, the day ones," Code pointed out.

"The Diamondbacks did include them in the contract, so we'll take all six," Czar said. "They won't get a pass even if they work days. We need to know everything about all six of the managers: What are their names? Are they married? Any of them have long-term partners?"

Absinthe knew Czar would hate taking out a family man, even if that man was an asshole, unless he beat his woman and children, or worse, was into really ugly criminal behavior such as rape or that of a pedophile, something they hunted on a regular basis.

"None of the six are married. Good thing too, they think they've hit the jackpot with their new smorgasbord of women at their clubs. The women have tried to quit, but the Venomous club like to fall back on old habits and they use intimidation to get their way. No one has dared to cross them after they made examples out of the first girls that tried to leave."

"What did they do to them?" Savage asked quietly.

Absinthe threw him a quick glance. That particular tone didn't bode well for the six managers.

"Beat the holy hell out of them, raped them, and one was chosen to be a prime example for all of them. She was strung up on the pole in the middle of the stage and whipped to death. They had a lot of fun doing it," Code said grimly. "I found photographs and video on their phones."

"Send whatever you found to my phone," Savage said, his tone mild as always.

Absinthe wanted to say that wasn't a good idea, but he

knew better. Whenever Savage got that tone, and he'd already been close to the edge, there was no holding back.

"We know what we have to do," Czar said. "Code will give all of team one the necessary information. Team two will take care of everyone on the home front. Transporter and Mechanic, you two pull our vehicles for us, match plates and give them to Code to make certain if a cop runs them everything is on the up-and-up. Same thing with licenses. Alena, you ride with Code. I want you looking completely different. Contacts, hair color, nothing the same. I don't want Ice and Storm to be able to identify you. We'll make certain the buildings are empty before you take them down."

Alena nodded. "No problem, Czar."

"Mechanic, you make absolutely certain no camera is working. I want them all disrupted. Even if you think Code has shut them down, you disrupt everything for blocks around. Alena can't be seen. None of us can be identified, but I'm not taking chances if this is in any way an attempt to get at her."

"You got it, Czar," Mechanic agreed.

"We leave first thing in the afternoon, each of us going at different times, starting around two. We can't be seen together. Transporter or Mechanic will have your assigned vehicle and your partner. I'll send the assigned schedule of departures. Use the phones Code provides. You know the drill. Keep texting to a minimum. Dump the phones as soon as we're on the road home and use the second ones until we're back and only in an emergency."

They nodded. They knew the drill. They'd run far too many of these operations together.

"Any last-minute questions?"

They all shook their heads.

"Good. The other very important thing we have to discuss this morning, Absinthe, is your lady. Code's been monitoring Holden and he got word from the Venomous club that Torpedo Ink is harboring Scarlet. Holden is trying to reach out to the Diamondbacks, looking to get them on board," Czar continued. "He hasn't managed to make contact yet, but he has money and connection in the MC world. He will soon. How serious are you about this woman?"

"She's my woman, one hundred percent," Absinthe said without hesitation. "I've only had this last week alone with her, but it's been good. Great. We've spent the time getting to know one another as best we could. I knew this was coming up fast and was lucky it got delayed as long as it did."

"I suggest we have a wedding between now and tomorrow when we have to leave. The Diamondbacks won't give up one of our old ladies. Family is family. Code, get the papers done so they can be married today. License, all of it. I presume you're good with that?" Czar challenged.

Absinthe nodded. "I have no problem. Scarlet might freak, but only because she likes time to process. I've already been railroading her fairly fast."

"She doesn't have time," Czar said. "I'll get Blythe on an afternoon reception. Alena, can you handle a cake and the rest of it?"

"Of course, if we're not here too long."

"We've only got a couple of things to discuss." Czar glanced at his watch and then picked up his cell to text Blythe. "We can have the ceremony at the house. It's beautiful there and private, easily protected. Lana, can you help Scarlet with finding a dress?"

"I'll try. It isn't like there's much here, Czar, in the way of wedding attire, but I'm sure all the women will help me. Blythe probably has the best connections. She knows the Drakes and they know everyone. Inez Nelson knows everyone as well. I'll start reaching out as soon as the meeting's over."

Absinthe glanced at Transporter and Mechanic, a small half grin on his face. He could well imagine Scarlet's face when he told her they were getting married in a matter of hours, that they'd have one night together and then he'd be leaving her with the other team to protect her, men and women she barely knew, while he went somewhere doing things he couldn't tell her. That was all going to go over really well with a woman like Scarlet.

"We can pull some really great gifts together for her," Ice said. "Women like to have gifts on their wedding day, right, Alena?"

Alena glared at him. "That depends. What are you up to?"

Ice winked at her. "We're all just wanting to help Absinthe out with his lady and their wedding. You just make the cake. We'll see to the gifts."

Alena and Lana looked at each other and groaned, shaking their heads.

Czar tapped the table, getting everyone's attention. "I've got one more item for today that's very important. I'm proposing bringing in a new member. Rurik Volkov is a member of Torpedo Ink already. He belongs to the Trinity chapter, but he doesn't really fit in with them. He's had a difficult time there and the president has reached out to me and feels that he would do better here with us, and I agree with him. I've discussed this with a few of you already."

"Why wouldn't he fit with them?" Lana asked curiously. "Don't they know him?"

Czar shook his head. "Rurik is not a man easily known to very many people. He's much like Reaper or Savage. I think he makes the others uncomfortable."

Alena made a rude noise under her breath, drawing a sharp glance from Czar, but she kept her head down and didn't say anything.

"Gavriil, you went to school with him. What do you know about him?" Transporter asked.

Gavriil shook his head. "I didn't go to school with him. He was there briefly, just for a short time, maybe four years, but even as a kid he was quiet and kept to himself. He had a younger sister, quite beautiful. Calina, I think was her name. They were pulled out of the school when he was thirteen or fourteen. I never saw him again."

"Great," Alena said. "He's probably the plant the Russian sent to spy on us. Or assassinate us all. And you want to bring him right in and let him join, Czar."

"Do you have something you want to share with us about Rurik, Alena? What do you know about him that the rest of us don't?" Czar asked.

Absinthe put a restraining hand on Alena's wrist beneath the table. He recognized the little bite that could barely be heard in Czar's voice. For some reason, Czar was championing the unknown biker. It was clear that Czar knew something about him, something very important, and that somewhere earlier in Czar's history, the two men had crossed paths. Alena needed to listen before she drew her own conclusions.

"I don't like him," Alena said, ignoring Absinthe's silent instructions not to voice her objections yet. "He's a total asshole."

"Has he done something to you we should know about?" Czar challenged softly when the others sat up straight. Ice and Storm leaned toward their sister, shaking their heads.

Alena tossed her wild, naturally platinum hair back over her shoulder a little defiantly. "No, of course not. If he had, he'd be a dead man. I'm like the others in his chapter, I guess. He makes me uncomfortable."

"That's total bullshit." Czar glared at her. "We aren't anything like those in that chapter. If you were like them, you wouldn't be alive right now. Savage is your brother. Reaper is your brother. If either of those men walk into that chapter on my orders, you better believe they're going to make them uncomfortable. He's called *Razrushitel* for a reason. They know it and they fear him. He belongs with us."

Alena rolled her eyes. "Destroyer? Ruiner? What the fuck, Czar? He calls himself a name and builds himself a rep and joins them. They believe him because he stands around looking like a hard-ass. I'm telling you right now, the man is a spy for the Russian. If he didn't go to school at the same one Gavriil attended, for more than a couple of years, then he either was a golden boy and was cut loose because he sold someone down the river, or he attended one of the easier schools and skated by."

Absinthe winced at the real venom in her voice. This was personal. She carried a real personal grudge against the man and every single member of Torpedo Ink had to hear it in her voice, just the way he did.

"Ice? Storm? Since your sister refuses to tell the truth and I don't want Absinthe to have to use his skills on her on his wedding day, I'm asking you both a direct question. There is no way you aren't aware why your sister is holding a grudge against Rurik."

Alena went white. "That is so wrong, Czar. I have the right to vote not to admit a new member into our chapter and I just did."

"You have every right to vote no. I haven't called for a vote. We need information and that's what we're doing, gathering information. Actual facts, not that you don't like him because you think he's an asshole. Or your bullshit lie, that you're uncomfortable around him."

Czar's fury nearly shook the room. For the first time, Alena seemed to be aware of it. Whatever grudge she was carrying against Rurik Volkov paled in comparison.

"Ice?" Czar prompted relentlessly.

Ice was the eldest of the twins by only a few minutes, but he was still the acknowledged older brother. Ice sighed. When Czar demanded answers, when he, as president of Torpedo Ink, demanded anything, he was given a response out of sheer respect.

"When we were teens, Rurik would sometimes show up at some of the same events where we were working. Clearly there was more than one target, so we ended up knowing one another by sight. Once in a while, he would have his sister with him."

He looked at Alena, who shook her head and then looked down at the table, both hands in her lap, twisting her fingers together. Absinthe put his hand over hers, trying to ignore the images pushing into his head as her distress level rose with her brother's telling of the past.

"Sorbacov held a huge dinner for his political friends, a fund-raiser, but he brought along several men and women as well as Storm, Rurik, Calina, Alena and me to the event. The men and women he brought were clearly to be used by his political friends who wanted to play. We were barely into our teens, the girls not quite there, but Sorbacov was selling us to the highest bidder. Not everyone knew it, of course. He was in his element, acting the wonderful states-man while brokering the sale of children for his perverted friends."

Alena looked up at Czar. "Do you really need to hear this?"

Czar just nodded. "It isn't like we all didn't suffer rape and torture, Alena. It was a daily occurrence. Continue, Ice."

"Once everyone else was gone and the winners of the bidding had thoroughly used us all, Sorbacov proposed a new game to be held, a challenge between Rurik and my brother and me. We were a year or so younger and he was, well, colder and a little deadlier. So Sorbacov thought it would be fair to pit two against one. While we met the chal-lenges, the two girls would be passed around to the men and women to be used any way they liked. They could use them together, beat them, hurt them, whatever they wanted. And we'd know. The money had to equal the raised stakes. We would be shown what was happening to our sisters be-tween each of the challenges to spur us on. The winner would be allowed to leave the schools permanently. Go live with other relatives."

"I see," Czar said. "And the challenges?"

Ice shrugged. "Those betting were allowed to help choose. Clearly, they wanted time with the girls, so they made each of the challenges difficult and as long as possible, involving running and climbing, physical fighting, that sort of thing. Rurik was extremely fast, but there were two of us and we had Alena to protect as he had Calina. It was . . . ugly. In the end, he won."

Czar turned his cool, piercing gaze on Alena. Absinthe knew what it was like to have those eyes on him. Czar had a way of seeing too much. "You are holding a grudge against a man because he won a fight as a teen against your two brothers? He was fighting for his sister as your brothers were fighting for you. Is this your reason for disliking this man?"

Alena looked down at her hands, refusing to meet Czar's eyes.

"Answer me." Czar's roar nearly shook the table. When she still didn't respond, he flicked his gaze to Absinthe and then back to Alena. "Are you truly that fucking petty?"

Swearing, clenching his teeth, Absinthe wrapped his hand all the way around her wrist and, just for a moment, let his mind open to hers fully. He saw the young girl giving herself, opening her heart and soul fully, for the first time trusting a male with her bruised and battered body and emotions. Rurik was so loving toward her, tender even, kissing her, showing her that the things the men were doing to her were wrong, that it could be good, could be beautiful with trust, with someone worthy. The betrayal had been visceral, tearing her apart, shattering her soul, making her realize that she was only worth something to those brothers and the one sister who claimed her in Torpedo Ink. No one else.

Absinthe let go of her wrist. "She is not that petty. Rurik didn't do anything to her that one of us wouldn't have done for our flesh and blood. It is just something difficult to over-

come, a childhood trauma. She was left behind to see her
brothers raped and tortured, as she was over the next de-
cade or more while his sister and he went free."

Nothing he said was a lie. Alena's business was her own.
No one else needed to know any of the details of her deal-
ings with the man called the Destroyer. He had destroyed a
young girl's dream, shattered all hope of a future and con-
demned her to living in a dungeon, growing up with the
ugliness of depraved humans.

"They didn't go free," Czar said. "Rurik and Calina were
never set free. Sorbacov didn't allow them to leave. I suspected as much the moment I got wind that such an event
had taken place. I crawled through the vents and eventually
found them. It took me weeks. Months. They were in an
older part of the building."

Alena looked up quickly. Ice and Storm turned their
heads toward Czar. Savage shifted in his chair. The others
all came to attention.

"Calina was in bad shape and there was no way to save
her. I could see that. I was aware that Rurik knew it too. He
whispered to her night and day. He hung in the loom, and
they raped him. Sorbacov's buddies—the ones that liked to
smell blood and bathe in it when they fucked—they'd hurt
him and then hurt her. He was a mess, so woven up tight in
that torture device. I snuck him food and water as often as
I dared. One night I got there too late. There were two men
there, two of the worst ones that were always training
Savage."

Absinthe glanced at Savage, but he didn't flinch. He
never did. He owned who he was and made no apologies
anymore. He couldn't change it, and if he raged against his
nature, he did it where the others couldn't see it—only Absinthe.

"They used an actual whip on Calina until she was dead.
They did so in front of Rurik, which was a big mistake. He
went berserk, something they should have known would

happen. Anyone would have seen he was a fighter. He was like us. He tore himself off the loom, destroying it, mangling his body. He killed both men and the loom master. That's why the punishments with the loom stopped for so long. Rurik stopped them. He earned the name the Destroyer."

"If he did all that," Alena challenged, still not ready to believe, "why didn't Sorbacov have him killed?"

"What do you mean, *if*?" Czar challenged. "Didn't I just say I saw Calina die and Rurik woven into the loom? That he tore himself free and killed the men who murdered her? Sorbacov didn't kill Rurik because he's a first-class bastard and he thought he'd make it far, far worse than death for him. He sent Rurik to Black Dolphin Prison."

There was a collective gasp. "He was a minor," Code said. "That's a prison made of serial killers, cannibals, pedophiles, all the worst possible criminals with life sentences. Minors don't go there."

"Sorbacov knew everyone at that time. His candidate by that time was president. Sorbacov ran the secret police. He could do anything he wanted, including throw a fourteen-year-old boy into the worst prison he could think of."

"How did he get out?" Alena whispered; her voice slightly hoarse.

"He was trained as an assassin and inside the prison he'd made a name for himself. He was too tough to kill. Inmates left him alone. Guards were leery of him. Sorbacov checked on him, and in the end, wanted him back. He decided he could use him if he could find a way to control him."

"How did Sorbacov do that?" Ice asked.

"He found someone else Rurik was willing to trade his soul to protect. He left the prison and continued to work for Sorbacov running high-risk operations. We crossed paths a couple of times, but Rurik is difficult to spot if he doesn't want to be seen. The bottom line is, he needs a home, and this is it or he's on his own. He needs an anchor. He's willing to accept me as his president and abide by the rules. He insists on a unanimous vote. So, Alena, if you can't give a yes, then you can shut him out."

There was no doubt in Absinthe's mind why Czar was president of Torpedo Ink, why he had taken charge of all of them at such a young age and managed to get them out of that hellhole alive. Had Czar not revealed to all of them that Rurik wanted a clean vote, then Alena would have cast a no. She couldn't now. None of them could, not with what he'd endured. Not with him winning the contest fairly, losing his sister and then going to a worse hellhole than what they'd all been put through. None of them could be that petty.

The vote, of course, was unanimous, just as Absinthe knew it would be. Alena was the first one out of the room, muttering that she had a cake to bake. The rest of them scattered to get the gifts together or find decorations under Lana's directions. Lana was busy texting everyone about where she might go to find dresses. Czar headed home to Blythe to help her get their place together for the wedding.

Absinthe made his way to the back part of the clubhouse where all the bedrooms were. Scarlet waited for him in his assigned room. She was on a laptop, the sounds of kitten noises playing while she mimicked them, making his cock jerk the moment he walked in. He grinned at her when she hastily closed the lid. They had been playing pet every other day so she would get used to it slowly. He wanted to make certain she was comfortable in the role. Evidently she enjoyed it enough to want to try to perfect her role.

"What are you doing, *ledi*?" He brushed a kiss on top of her head. All that silky hair fell like a red waterfall, tumbling down her back. She looked so beautiful she made his heart ache.

"Passing the time. Did you get everything worked out that you needed to?"

Her lashes were long, curled up on the edges, tipped that

same bright red as her hair. He picked up her left hand. "This hand is a little bare, babe. I had a little talk with Ice. You do know he's a famous jeweler, right? I told you that. He makes one-of-a-kind jewelry for various stores. Not just things for us, but high-end jewelry stores. In any case, Scarlet, I'm very much in love with you and I'm formally asking you to marry me."

She blinked. Her lashes fluttered. "We talked about marriage, Absinthe. I said, yes, of course, but . . ." She hesitated, watching him carefully.

He really loved her all the more for her quick intelligence. "I mean now. I want to marry you now. Today. Be my wife today." He brought her hand up to his mouth and nibbled on her knuckles.

Suspicion crept into her eyes. "What happened? What did you find out at your happy little meeting that you haven't told me?"

"I want you to say you'll marry me today because you love me enough to throw caution to the wind, not because you're afraid, or you have to, or for any other reason. I want to be wanted for myself, Scarlet. Be *moya literaturnaya ledi*. My wife. My *kiska*. Be all those things for me because you want me. Because you need me as much as I need you."

He didn't take his eyes from hers but transferred her fingers to his mouth, scraping his teeth along the pads, so gently, back and forth, willing her to choose him.

"I don't know how you do that, Absinthe," Scarlet said, her eyes darkening with desire. "You get to me every single time. I must be out of my mind, because I don't just jump off cliffs, I have to think things through, but with you I seem to just go for it. You want to get married today, I don't know how we're going to do it legally, but I'm all for it."

His smile started somewhere in his gut and just kept moving up. He tackled her, throwing her down to the mattress, barely managing to sweep the laptop out of harm's way as he kissed her, pinning her under him. His hands went to the sweet pearl buttons of her prim blouse, opening them to reveal the sexy fire-engine-red bra surrounding her glorious round breasts. He had that bra unhooked and both breasts out, while he kissed her over and over, using his hands to pinch and tug at her perfect nipples.

He dropped his hands to the waistband of her jeans while she was fumbling with his, trying to free his cock. He got hers open first. "Lift up, baby," he mumbled, his mouth still over hers, desperate for her. She obeyed him and he shoved the jeans as far down as he could over her rounded ass. He knew those cheeks so well now. The size and shape of them. He'd shaved her little curls and left a landing strip. He left her mouth to kiss his way to her breasts, tugging with his teeth on her nipples, back and forth, then sucking.

She was barefoot, so he just shoved her jeans as far down as he could and then dragged them off of her, one leg at a time. He just needed his cock out enough to get to her. The sight of her laid out naked, sprawled under him, her skin red from his teeth, excited him. The door behind them opened and Ice waltzed in.

"Sorry, Scarlet," Ice said, sounding more distracted than sorry. "I'm making you a present and I need to see your nipples really quick. Nice timing, if I do say so myself." Ice came right up to the side of the bed and peered down at them, his eyes on Scarlet's breasts. "Nice tits, woman. You have really great nipples."

"Worst timing ever, get the fuck out of here," Absinthe objected. Scarlet tensed under him, but he draped his body over hers and glared at his Torpedo Ink brother. "She isn't a fuckin' exhibitionist, Ice."

"Yeah, I get that. I just needed some sizing. Sorry, honey, I'm really not into touching." Ice lifted his hand and sauntered out.

Scarlet put her hand over her eyes. "I don't know whether to laugh or cry. I might not be able to ever look at him again."

"When he's naked and fucking his woman at the parties

right in front of you it won't matter," Absinthe said gruffly, kissing his way down to her fiery curls. He licked his tongue across her clit and then her bare lips before dipping it deep. She was hot and slick. Evidently, Ice's visit hadn't cooled her need of him.

Before she could object, he caught first one leg and then the other and wrapped them around his waist, opening her body to his fully. Pressing the head of his cock into that wet heat, he looked into her green eyes and grinned. "Today's our fuckin' wedding day, *ledi*. You've made me the happiest man on the planet."

Behind him the door opened again. Scarlet groaned. "Hurry. Just hurry."

Absinthe rammed home. A tight fist of scorching-hot, wet silk closed around his cock. He ignored Preacher, who had walked in and was standing close to them. He just kept driving into her. With every hard thrust, her breasts jolted and swayed. She looked like a feast laid out in front of him.

"Absinthe, you drink the pineapple juice every morning I recommended to you? And take the special blend of powder I make up for you?"

Scarlet kept her eyes glued to his. Absinthe grunted his assent, never looking away from his woman's eyes. So far, she hadn't run screaming from him. His brothers weren't helping. He knew what they were doing. It didn't occur to them they were doing anything wrong. They didn't view sex as anything private; in fact, they preferred to watch one another's backs so they knew no one could hurt them or the ones they cared about.

"You allergic to anything, Scarlet?"

Scarlet moved with him, her body growing hotter and tighter, a fresh wash of liquid scorching his cock. She shook her head, her gaze never leaving Absinthe's.

"Good, good." Preacher wandered out.

Her breathing turned ragged. His turned labored. He caught her hands and slammed them to the mattress, rising above her for a better angle. Then she was crying out, her body clamping down around his, her orgasm taking him with her, his release blasting through him like a rocket.

"Oh, for God's sake, Absinthe, you couldn't wait a couple of hours? I need to get her ready for her wedding. You know, the entire spa treatment. Get out of here," Lana snapped.

Absinthe groaned, collapsing over his woman, looking over his shoulder. Lana was draped artfully against the door, speedily texting on her phone.

"You'd better not be taking pictures of my ass," he warned.

"I should be. That's blackmail material right there," she quipped. "Get off that girl, you lunatic. I've got to get her ready for her bridegroom. He used to be a gentleman."

"He's a gentleman." Absinthe glared at her. He was still carefully shielding his woman, but mostly trying to recover enough to move.

"Not when he's wearing out the bride on the day of her wedding and I presume he plans on wearing her out all night tonight as well."

That much was true. He leaned down and bit Scarlet's ear gently. "Hell," he whispered. "I do plan on keeping you up all night. She's right."

"I'm all for that," she whispered back.

❧

Scarlet looked so beautiful dressed in the gown Lana had somehow managed to find for her, no doubt with the help of the famous Drake sisters of Sea Haven. The dress was classy and very elegant yet so sexy that as she walked toward him, he could barely breathe. The entire bodice and long sleeves of the dress were lace. The lace continued in rounded panels, draping down the skirt of the dress. Each panel was separated with a rounded sculpted accent of cutout stitching woven just like the lace. Beneath the lace was a sheath of darker emerald.

She wore white lace stockings on her legs and emerald heels on her feet. At her ears were emeralds surrounded by diamonds. The neckline was almost square, from shoulder to shoulder, all lace, and around her neck was a choker of emeralds with a golden ring every few links. Absinthe knew instantly Ice had given a shout-out to his need for control in the bedroom. He knew his brother had made a similar collar of rubies for his *kiska* as well. Her hair was up on top of her head, and down the back in a complicated twist with tendrils falling around her face.

She stood beside him, smelling like a dream, and he knew Preacher had been at work again. Besides being the one who would officiate, he was a chemist and could somehow manufacture perfect scents that enhanced natural attraction. Preacher smirked, holding a worn book open while they stood beneath the arbor. Absinthe would have liked to have gotten a good look at what that book actually was.

Behind them, all of Torpedo Ink was present, even Steele, Breezy and their son, which meant Adrik was in a hospital somewhere. To get him to go, Steele had performed some kind of miracle. Blythe's children were seated between Czar and Blythe, taking up one row of chairs. Destroyer, the newest member, stayed all the way at the back, probably grateful, like Savage and Reaper, that the ceremony and reception were outdoors, but he didn't show it. Destroyer had no expression on his face at all.

Absinthe, after that first sweep of his eyes he couldn't help, taking in his surroundings, making certain everything was safe for his woman, kept every one of his heightened senses alert for every tiny nuance of the moments as they went by. He didn't want to forget one single detail. He fixed his gaze on her. Walking toward him. Standing beside him. Shivering slightly. The way she looked. Smelled. The way the breeze moved in her hair and ruffled those stray pieces of hair around her face. The way the sun hit the emeralds at her throat and ears, dazzling his eyes, but nowhere near as beautiful as his bride.

Her fingers trembled slightly when he took her hands and turned her to face him. Preacher began to speak. He was short and to the point, asking them to repeat their vows, asking Absinthe if he took Scarlet to be his wife. *"Hell* yes, I do."

Blythe cleared her throat.

Preacher glanced at her over his book. "Sorry. Aleksei Solokov, we have to be official here, or it isn't legal, and we want your woman tied up good and tight so she doesn't run the first time she realizes you're totally fucked up."

"Preacher." Blythe glared at him.

Torpedo Ink roared with laughter. Even Scarlet tried not to laugh. Absinthe was grateful for the humor. She stopped being so nervous.

"Sorry, Blythe. Aleksei Solokov, do you take Scarlet Foley to be your wife for better or worse, in sickness or in health, for richer or poorer, to love and cherish until death do you part?"

"I do."

"Scarlet Foley, do you take Aleksei Solokov to be your husband for better or worse, in sickness or in health, for richer or poorer, to love and cherish and obey in the bedroom— wait, where did that come from? Absinthe? Until death do you part?"

In the middle of the laughter, no one noticed that Preacher didn't correct the mistake. No one noticed but Scarlet. She looked directly into Absinthe's eyes. "I do."

"Do you have rings?"

"Ice hasn't finished them yet, but we have substitutes," Absinthe said. "He made me a laminated one for Scarlet." He pushed it onto Scarlet's finger. "Your ring will be beautiful, I promise, baby. Ice is the best."

"Just fuckin' kiss her and let's eat," Reaper said.

"You owe me *lots* of money for that bad word, especially during a wedding," a little voice called out.

"That's little Emily," Absinthe whispered to Scarlet, "Czar and Blythe's youngest daughter. I'm pretty sure she has enough college money collected from Torpedo Ink swearing to go all the way through her master's program at any school she chooses."

Scarlet laughed softly. "Your family is a little nutty."

"They're your family now too."

"I pronounce you man and wife, kiss your bride and hurry up before we get mobbed," Preacher said, waving his hand at them.

Absinthe took his time, stepping close to Scarlet, cupping her face with gentle hands and turning it up toward him. His heart felt as if it stood still, or maybe it was time. Her bone structure was so perfect. Those high cheekbones. He turned her face slightly, so the curve of her cheek and the pout of her lower lip were spotlighted by the rays of the sun. Her hair blazed that brilliant red that made his heart flutter and his soul ache.

"I'm so in love with you." He murmured the truth softly against her lips, that generous curve that took him to paradise every time he kissed her. It didn't matter how gentle or rough he was, it was every time. This time was no different in spite of their audience.

He touched his lips to hers and, just like always, it was as if he'd touched a match to dynamite. To an explosive. Flames leapt between them. Fire roared in his belly. Licked at his skin. Rushed through his veins. She was raw fuel for survival when he thought there was nothing left for him.

Her arms slid around his neck. She kissed him back, adding to the thunder in his ears and the lightning whipping through him. Her body melted into his, pressing close. Emotion welled up to blend with the genuine physical reaction. She was a fucking miracle.

"May I present Mr. and Mrs. Solokov. That's it," Preacher declared, "we're good. Time to party."

Torpedo Ink let out a roar of congratulations and the party was on. The music started up and the barbecue was lit. For the next couple of hours, they danced together, Absinthe holding her as close to him as possible. The children danced around them, laughing and holding hands, happy for them, their faces beaming.

He tried to keep Scarlet on his lap while they ate, but she insisted on sitting beside him, paying attention to the introductions so she'd remember everyone's names and put them together with how they looked. They cut the cake and fed each other a piece. He was much more erotic about it than she was, having her suck the frosting off his finger. She obligingly did it for him, making his cock as hard as a rock.

He was quite happy to abandon the party and take his bride home early, long before the setting sun. His family had given them gifts, laying them all out on their marriage bed at home. His brothers and sisters tended to be a little on the kinky side, so he was looking forward to seeing what they'd been gifted.

FOURTEEN

"Scarlet, it's your wedding night, you tell me what you want to do. We can celebrate any way you'd like. I'm up for anything." Absinthe was being truthful; she heard it in his voice.

She looked at the presents laid out over their bed. Each was so Torpedo Ink. She was beginning to understand Absinthe's brothers and sisters. A large fiery-red pillow trimmed in white piping was made of crushed velvet and had been pressed down like crowns with covered buttons of darker red. It was gorgeous. On the front of the pillow was beautifully embroidered, *Absinthe's kiska*.

"That's for you to sit on when you're not resting on the rug by the fire. You can sit on your pillow while I'm reading or when I have other things to do in the evening, but I want you waiting in here for me."

Scarlet ran her hand over the pillow. "Who made this for me?"

"Lana did. She actually made your dress as well. Not the lace, but the sheath beneath it. She has this little thing with materials. She didn't like the sheath and said it wouldn't suit you, so she found material at one of the shops and put it together for you. She's quite good, isn't she?"

"Where did she learn?" She wasn't certain whether to be embarrassed that all of Torpedo Ink seemed to know about the kitten play between them.

Absinthe shrugged. "You'll have to ask her."

She nodded and continued to look at the display of gifts strewn across their bed. "All of them know I'm your kitten in the bedroom, don't they?"

"They know what I need. If you're my woman, no doubt you give me what I need. Why? Does it bother you?"

She considered that. Did it? She supposed it should. She pranced around the bedroom on her hands and knees with a collar and a leash and a tail. For him. For Absinthe. Everyone in his family apparently knew. She sighed, looked at him and shook her head. "I must really be in love with you."

"I think you're in love with my cock."

"That too," she agreed, because there was some truth in that.

The presents that intrigued her the most were the ones Ice had given them. Those sparkling jewels sitting in long velvet boxes. They were rubies to add to the collection he'd started for them. Just looking at them made her so wet and needy. She wasn't certain how best to ask for what she wanted.

She'd spent time during the last week and again during the short couple of hours while Absinthe had been in his meeting looking up kitten play online and on YouTube. She wanted to extend her ability to communicate with him and also to move like a cat with her body, slink, be more feline and sensuous for him. She practiced sounds. She read and also listened to other women talking about how much they loved playing the part of a kitten for their "master." Just reading and practicing made her want Absinthe. She found she wanted to try out the things she'd learned. And she wanted to please him all the more.

Now, looking at the wedding gifts laid out on their bed, her gaze couldn't help straying to the sparkling ruby jewels. There were earrings, two pair, both chandelier, one much longer and heavier than the other, with screws on them. A complicated harness that wrapped around both breasts and clearly somehow buckled around her bottom cheeks, and framed her pussy lips. Little rubies were embedded throughout the leather, but the best part was, the harness had a matching collar that said *Property of Absinthe*. She *loved* that.

She licked her lips, her breath causing her breasts to rise and fall. Helplessly, she looked at Absinthe, willing him to understand. He stood her up and turned her around to unzip the dress. "Leave on your stockings. I'll put the harness on you and attach them to that. I'm going to take you through the house tonight, so the stockings will get ruined, but I want to see the tail with the ocean light shining on it from every conceivable angle."

Her heart felt as if it skipped a beat. "I'd like to give you a wedding present, Absinthe, since you're giving this to me," she said shyly, feeling very daring.

His hands stilled on her shoulders. His mouth moved in her hair and then touched her earlobe. She felt his warm breath. "What would that be, *miledi*? You've given me yourself as my wife. There is nothing I want more."

"I want to remain your kitten all night, even if it's difficult. I'd like to do that for you." They hadn't tried that once yet. She didn't know why that was important to Absinthe. Why he craved obedience from his woman, especially when he knew she complied with his every demand of her own free will and loved him unconditionally. She caught, over and over in his mind, how important it really was to him, and she was determined to be his everything, to fulfill whatever he needed until he believed in her. In them.

"Are you certain? Having a tail in you all night when you aren't used to it might be difficult. I will wake you often and lube you so you stay as comfortable as possible, but you won't get much sleep. I'll use you often."

That excited her. She hoped he would. "I want to stay your kitten all night tonight."

"It's our wedding night, *kiska*, so expect it to be long and sometimes uncomfortable. If it's too difficult, you are to let me know. But remember, pussycats give their masters what they desire, and they get their rewards. If they don't, there are no rewards, not even on wedding nights."

That was so much a part of what made playing that role so hot for her. Scarlet nodded and allowed the dress to slide from her arms. She carefully hung it in her closet along with the high heels, but she left the white lace thigh-high stockings on her legs. Starting back into the bedroom, she remembered at the last moment to drop to her hands and knees. She crawled, utilizing her new skill set as best she could.

Absinthe waited for her, already out of his wedding attire, once again dressed only in his silken drawstring pants. He held the harness in his hand and beckoned to her. "Come here, *malen'kiy kiska*, you're going to love your harness. Ice made this for you. I gave him your measurements. I wanted him to see you in it just in case he needed to make changes but knew you would be too shy."

She was beginning to find the idea of him showing her off to one or two of his friends hot. She knew Absinthe liked the idea of showing her off all decked out in her tail and rubies with him safely on the other end of the leash making certain no one else touched her or petted her. Only him. Ice had walked in on them and he'd already seen her naked. Preacher had as well. It wasn't as if either of them acted like they wanted to touch her. She was getting used to the idea that Torpedo Ink members thought very differently about sex and nudity.

Absinthe drew the halter up over her hanging breasts. She

had very generous breasts, high and firm and very round. The top two pieces curved over the tops of her breasts and then the leather stretched in a circle around each breast, lifting and dividing them. The harness ran along the sides of her hips down to her front to frame her pussy with jeweled leather, framing her bare lips and the fiery curls of her mound, then ran back up along her hips to her back where the harness buckle was. He tightened it and then snapped her stockings into the garters at her thighs.

The harness was very snug around her sex and breasts. That brought heightened awareness to her body instantly. Absinthe stroked her skin, her nipples and her sex, touching her all the time, whispering to her how proud of her he was. What a lucky man he was. How beautiful she was. How extraordinary. How he couldn't believe she'd married him. He made her feel so sexy and wanted.

He went to the chair by the fireplace and sank down into it. "You remember the special oil, don't you, *kiska*? How it made your little ass and pussy burn for me? It does the same for your nipples. When it's rubbed all over your body, it can make you mad for sex. It starts with a slow burn and then just gets hotter and hotter. I used a mild version on you the first time. Do you see that bottle on the bed right next to your special gift from Ice? The bottle Savage gave us? I want you to bring that to me. Use your little kitten mouth."

Scarlet remembered the oil. It had made her a little crazy. Although she wasn't certain if it was the oil or Absinthe or a combination. She was already so wet and needy she didn't see how oil could possibly make a difference. Using her newly learned feline, kitty strut, she made her way to the bed, hoping Absinthe noticed she'd been practicing at least a little. She managed after two tries to get the long, narrow bottle into her mouth without using her hands. She brought it to him.

He took it from her and stroked a caress through her hair.

"Very good, *kiska*. Now, go back and get the heavier chandelier rubies that Ice gave us. Use your mouth, no little paws."

Her heart was tripping a million miles an hour. This was the best wedding night ever. The chandelier rubies were in a velvet box that was open and on display on the bed. It was long and narrow. It took even more tries to find a way to get the box in her mouth, but she managed. She was very proud of herself. She strutted back to Absinthe.

He bent to brush a kiss across her lips. "You are perfect."

She purred. A long, drawn-out, rolling purr. He looked happy and rubbed his fingers in her scalp.

"I see you've been working, *kiska*. That's very good. I'm lucky to have a kitten caring enough to pay attention to the things that matter to me. Kneel up between my legs." He widened his thighs so she could crawl between his legs.

Scarlet eagerly crawled between his thighs, hoping she could undo his pants. He had a thick bulge and she wanted to taste him. He petted her hair, but he didn't let her get to his cock. He indicated for her to kneel all the way up. When she did, he cupped her breasts and leaned his head down slowly. So slowly. The anticipation made her nipples hard pebbles. Made them ache. Stand up for him. Little drops of liquid heat teased the entrance of her sex.

She felt his breath, hot, like her empty channel, and then he drew her breast deep, pressing her nipple to the roof of his mouth while his fingers tugged and rolled the nipple of her left breast. She mewled and purred alternately, even when his teeth elongated the nipple and he sucked especially hard before switching sides. She daringly put her nails into his thighs and kneaded the way a kitten might. He increased the stimulation and then smiled down at her.

"Beautiful, baby. Look how red and gorgeous you are."

Obediently, she looked down at her nipples. They were very red from the marks of his teeth and his ministrations. She wanted more and pushed her breasts, framed so beautifully by the harness, toward him. He opened the bottle of oil and poured a little into his hands.

"You'll love this so much, *kiska*. My little pussycat is going to be feeling so good. I love to make you feel good."

Absinthe covered both breasts with his palms, her nipples right in the center where a pool of the oil coated his skin. He just held his hands there for a moment, letting it soak into her and then he began a slow, deliberately erotic massage. "Feel good, my sizzling little red-hot *kiska*?"

Her breath caught in her throat. At first it felt amazing. His mouth. The massage. The warm oil. A slow burn growing heated, then hot, now it was a fierce fire. He took the chandelier rubies from where they were nestled in the velvet box and held them up as her breath hissed out.

"Is something wrong, *kiska*? You're made for fire." He reached down with his oil-coated finger and rubbed her bare pussy lips. "That's why I had to leave some of your curls. That's why every jewel is a high-quality ruby, especially the one that will be on your finger."

Every jewel in the harness was real? On the collars? The leash? Was he crazy? That nearly distracted her from the burning on her bare lips and her nipples. Almost. The burning in her nipples seemed to streak through her body to leave her sex arousing her all the more. It made no sense, and yet still, it burned through her, straight to her most private core. Her gaze was on his hands as he put one of the chandelier rubies back and opened the screw of the other one.

"This is an alligator clamp. See the rubber tip? That keeps it from hurting. I'm going to put it on and apply the amount of pressure you just felt and enjoyed when I pinched with my teeth and fingers."

While he talked to her, he deftly applied the first clamp, adjusting the screw, watching her face as he tightened it. When her breath caught, he added another twist and then slowly lowered the golden chain of three large rubies each surrounded by small diamonds. She felt that bite instantly and the additional flare of scorching heat rushing through her left nipple and breast, streaking straight to her sex. Absinthe flicked the chain and set it swinging, turning his head to watch the light play through the rubies, displaying the exquisite fire onto the wall.

"Beautiful," he breathed and bent to press a kiss onto the top of her head. "You're so beautiful, my little *kiska*. In a room filled with other kittens and their masters, I would always be the envy of everyone."

That made her wonder how often he'd taken other women into rooms filled with other men and their kittens.

He tugged and rolled her right nipple, the oil on his fingers spreading the heat easily so that it roared through her body as he applied the second clamp and flicked that chain as well. He sat back for a moment, playing with the chandeliers as if she were an object, his plaything, and that fed the fire building between her legs.

"Such a good little pussy. So patient. Get down and turn around for me."

Scarlet did so, putting both hands on the carpet. The moment she did, her breasts shifted in the harness and the chandeliers dropped, the weight of the gold, diamonds and rubies tugging at her nipples and renewing the fire of the oil.

Absinthe began to knead and massage the cheeks of her bottom, rubbing the oil all over her skin, along the seam meeting her thighs and then pouring a liberal amount into the crack between her cheeks. She gasped and fisted her hands into the thick carpet. He continued massaging and rubbing the oil into her skin, casually sweeping the thick lubricant down that seam, over her inflamed clit and pussy lips, flicking and circling with that heat and then pressing a coated finger deep inside her.

"You're already slick, and so tight, little pussycat."

She couldn't help rocking her hips back. The burn had already started. The oil was fierce, much hotter than the other one. With every movement, the chandelier rubies on their golden chains rocked so that the clamps pinched down onto her nipples, sending more darts of fire straight to her sex.

Absinthe didn't pick up the pace like she needed him to. He kept that slow massage and then found her little star and began to push his thumb deep over and over. He poured oil into her and used his finger, pushing all the way to his knuckle while he rubbed her clit and pinched it so hard it felt like the fire in her nipples. She undulated her hips, pushed back onto his thumb and then his finger, helpless between the two sensations.

"This is another tail Ice made for you. I designed it. I love this one in particular. It's a little longer and fluffier, rides higher. The plug is larger, longer and thicker, and goes a little deeper, but it should be comfortable and fit the contour of your body. If it doesn't, you have to tell me, especially if you're going to stay my pussy all night."

When they had played "pet" throughout the week, he'd kept to the smallest plug, making certain she was comfortable at all times. She turned her head to look at him when he said the plug was bigger. That scared her a little. He lifted the tail to show her. It was gorgeous. Much fluffier than the other one. Blazing red, scattered with even more gems. This one had diamonds and rubies twisted among the red fur of the tail. The plug *was* thicker and longer. The glass was a brilliant red like the rubies, with a wide base.

"Open my pants, *kiska*, and take out my cock. I want you to compare the length and girth with that plug."

She turned back to him and did as he said, her fingers trembling. His cock was beautiful, even more so than she remembered. He had a wonderful taste, addictive. She didn't know how he managed to taste so good when most men didn't. He kept himself groomed so he didn't have hair to get in her mouth. She loved his cock, but he was right, it was a great deal longer and thicker than the glass plug anchoring the gorgeous tail. She purred over his cock and bent to lick the soft, velvety head and the little drops leaking just for her.

He shook his head. "Naughty little kitten." He flicked the ruby chandeliers, setting them swinging, sending fire racing straight to her sex. "Turn around and put your paws on the floor right now."

She obeyed, excitement coursing through her. She loved that particular voice.

He rubbed her cheeks again with the oil, poured more and massaged her little star before he began to push the plug deep, a steady pressure that was much fuller and more uncomfortable than the first one had been. Then his thumb was working her clit and two fingers were curling inside her, stroking her sensitive nerve endings, and that sense of fullness mingled with the fiery oil became something altogether different.

"You like that, don't you, *kiska*? You're going to like my cock when I take your ass."

She did like it. She was burning up. Right then, if he had wanted to, she would have let him take her in the ass, or her pussy, either one, she was that desperate. Every part of her body seemed to be on fire for him. Even her mouth. Her brain raged for him.

He kept massaging her cheeks and around to her breasts with more oil, before showing her the new collar. This one was thicker and stiffer. It said *Absinthe's kiska* in fiery letters. He buckled it around her neck and attached the leash. The leash was thicker too but had the same sparkling gems.

He led her over to the bed, where the gifts were laid out. "There is a variety here. That particular tail is unique for a reason. Ice is an exhibitionist. I'm certain you know what that is. Storm, however, is a voyeur. He gets off on watching. Ice made the tail, so he gave me a remote to go with it. Feel what this can do to you on low."

He switched it on and instantly the plug began to vibrate, sending little waves of delight right through that fiery wall of nerves. Scarlet thought she might die of insanity as her body coiled tight, but there was no relief. She hissed and rocked her hips. The tail switched madly in the air, throwing streaks of fiery red all over the walls. Absinthe laughed and ruffled her hair.

"We haven't even gotten started. Look at all these wonderful gifts." He opened the long box. "This is from Storm. He calls it the stormy weather. He had Mechanic make a few of them because he's crazy, but they're very cool. It's his design."

He lifted it out of the box and Scarlet gasped when she saw the dildo. It seemed large and thick and colored like a dark storm with streaks of lightning. When Absinthe turned it on, white streaks burst across it and with each one the thing jolted hard right through the vibrations. Absinthe smiled at her as he coated it with oil.

"Storm, of course, was hoping I'd bring my little *kiska* to one of the parties, stuffed full of his stormy weather and her beautiful tail so he could watch her as she strutted around or sat on her cushion with her little pussy and ass all ready to be fucked. Unfortunately for him, I get that privilege tonight all by myself." He pushed two fingers into her and then began to slide the toy into her. "It isn't as large as I am, so you can take it. It will hook to your harness so you won't have to work too hard this time to keep it in, although it will be good for you to work those muscles."

As the stormy weather intruded, her sensitive folds giving way, he turned it on low and it countered the vibration of the tail. There must have been a shuffle program on the remotes because the next thing she knew, the vibrations began to vary. She wanted to cry out. She could barely purr and then she'd mewl or hiss, digging her claws into the carpet.

"Just one more thing and then we'll take a walk through the house. We can't leave your beautiful ruby chandeliers on for too long. Preacher is our chemist. He makes the various lubes, which, by the way, are edible, although if you try too soon it can burn your mouth. He sent you a very, very special catnip." He opened another box slowly. "If we ever go to a party and you're sitting on your cushion and need reassurance, you'll have this. Open your mouth."

Scarlet complied. Absinthe put a very realistic-looking cock in her mouth. "Suck."

Her green eyes jumped to his face, but she did as he said. When she did, to her shock, the contents spilling into her mouth tasted exactly like his cock. Hot, musky, a hint of something she could never quite put her finger on, but she loved it. Absinthe pulled the cock away from her and put it carefully back in the box. "That is yours for special occasions."

He picked up the leash and began to lead her out of the bedroom. Every move she made she was aware of the tail swishing high in the air, the plug vibrating deep between her cheeks and the vibrator creating waves that wouldn't stop in her deepest core. She could barely breathe, but she'd never been so excited. She passed the long window and saw herself, her body oiled, tail high, breasts hanging down with the rubies swinging, the harness framing her body, white stockings covering her thighs, and she loved the way she looked.

Absinthe clearly loved the way she looked too. She could see his reflection, his cock so hard it looked delicious, making her mouth water. His hand casually pumped up and down as he walked her, watching her slink like the sensuous feline she was—a feline in heat. She lifted her hips over and over, seeking to entice him, and made little mewling noises. Frantic ones.

He stopped near the front door, shaking his head. "You are such a bad little kitty. I shouldn't reward you, but you did give me such a gift. Is this what you want? Are you so thirsty for your milk?"

She purred over and over, trying to tell him she was desperate for his cock. At least she could get that. She wanted him so much. She crawled to him and knelt in front of him, staying in position on her hands and knees, waiting to see what he wanted her to do. Her heart pounded. He couldn't deny her now. He just couldn't.

"My cock is yours then, little naughty *kiska*." He rubbed her lips with his cock.

Scarlet didn't want to give him a chance to change his mind. She licked up the underside of his sac and then over it, lapping at it and then sucking gently. She continued up his shaft and all around it, flicking and stabbing her tongue under the crown of his cock. She loved his cock and she lavished attention on it before she finally began to take it in her mouth. The weight felt perfect on her tongue. The heat, the girth stretching her lips was sexy to her. She loved looking into his strange, crystal-blue eyes.

This was when he allowed her to use her hands and she did so, forming a tight ring and squeezing and then letting go to pump slow, casual pumps while she took more of him into the heat of her mouth. She was good with her tongue, curling it around him, flicking and dancing her way up his shaft. She reached under his sac to softly and gently jiggle and then moved her hand up his shaft in that ring before pumping more of him into her mouth.

He suddenly caught the back of her head by her hair. "Relax for me, little *kiska*, I'm going to take over and control this for a few minutes. You keep using your tongue and suck hard. Breathe for me and relax. Do you understand? You're going to take more of me. A little more, that's all. Just a little. You're safe with me. When I come, you swallow every single drop. You're not to waste any of it. To you, it's very precious. Do you understand?"

She already knew it was. Everything about him was precious to her. Every single thing. His voice seemed to rumble through her, but still, to give up all control was very frightening. She blinked rapidly, keeping eye contact. As long as she was looking into those crystal-blue eyes, she felt as if she had an anchor and she would be able to see if he would watch out for her, keep her safe no matter what, even if he was in the deepest throes of pleasure—and she wanted him there.

His voice softened. Dropped another octave. "*Malysh kotenok*, you are always safe with me. This is something you have to learn. To always know deep in your soul so that no matter the circumstances, like what happened when the others walked in on us, you have to know I would protect you. That when I give you my word, it is always the truth."

She tried not to remember what had happened to her when she had been young and inexperienced, with a man who didn't care, but the thought sometimes edged into her mind. She knew Absinthe was there with her, on that path they forged together there in the library, because he reassured her.

"We will attend parties and all around us there will be others having sex openly. If it is at our clubhouse, we control what goes on. You will be safe. No one will ever touch you. Not only will I look after you, but every one of my brothers and sisters will as well. What happened to you as a young teen was traumatic and will be difficult to overcome, but we can do it together."

While he spoke in that soft, velvet voice, he rubbed the top of her head gently, petting her, soothing her.

"If we are on a run, that is a more difficult environment and our rules are tighter for a reason. Always, you have to know I will keep you safe. Here, in our home, is where you learn my word is good."

He waited, never forcing her. She could end their play. She knew that. One word. One gesture and it would stop. She nodded, keeping her gaze fixed on his. Excitement had built with every word he said. She wanted that kind of trust with him. That kind of bond. He was difficult to read, his mind nearly closed to her, other than allowing her to read his intense pleasure and the fact that he was telling her the truth, but now she felt his pride in her, and that stoked the fire between her legs.

The vibrators kicked up a notch, making her breath hitch in her throat. When she gasped, he thrust his cock into her mouth deeper than she thought she could take him. He did so fast, abruptly, his hand holding her head still so she couldn't move or pull away from him. The girth of him stretched her lips impossibly, almost to the point of hurting, so that for a moment panic set in.

Scarlet kept looking into his eyes and forced air through her nose. He smiled gently at her. His eyes changed, going nearly smoky, approval making her almost giddy. She almost forgot what she was doing she was so mesmerized by him. Then she felt the familiar weight of him on her tongue, the heat and taste of him. Everything vanished but the need to give him as much pleasure as possible.

She used her skills, tongue curling, lashing, sliding over him and up him, and then the vibrations rocked her body and she gasped again. He jerked her head back at the same time and aggressively thrust deeper. She felt him invading, pressing into her throat. Automatically, her throat tried to close, to cough, to gag, her body telling her she couldn't breathe and she might die.

For a moment she couldn't see him through the liquid swimming in her eyes, but then she managed to blink rapidly, and she found herself reassured by that gentle, steady look, so blue, so completely loving. At this moment, so filled with calm and pride in her. He wouldn't let anything happen to her and in any case, he wasn't in her throat. He was just sitting there, deeper than he'd ever been. She could still touch him with her tongue, still suck when she got over being alarmed. Still breathe through her nose. She did all those things, stroking and caressing, and he pulled back and gave her air immediately.

Her body was so close to orgasm she was undulating, rocking back and forth, the chandelier rubies on the nipple clamps swaying as if an earthquake was occurring. Absinthe pulled his cock from her mouth and moved around her body, one hand sliding down her back and over her hips and bottom. The vibrator in her pussy stopped abruptly and he pulled it out.

Scarlet tried desperately to still the little mewl of protest, but she didn't have time to even get it out before his hands were at her hips and he slammed his cock into her hard. Fire streaked through her from her deepest core to the very tips of her nipples, to short-circuit her brain.

A strange rolling thunder started in her ears, drowning out all other sound. The vibration between her cheeks increased and the plug began to pump of its own volition. She knew, because Absinthe's fingers bit deep into her hips as he jerked her back into him with every thrust forward. His cock felt so thick, almost too big, taking up too much room, driving through her folds with deep hard strokes that sent roaring flames spreading through her like a wildfire out of control.

Her breath turned so ragged, her lungs burned. There was no air, no way to breathe, but it didn't matter. Only that delicious burn that seemed to be growing hotter and hotter, consuming her. She knew she was going to go completely insane unless her body let go but that coiling inside her just kept building and building like some great tidal wave, higher and higher in the deepest part of the unseen ocean, a wall waiting to overtake her and drown her.

Absinthe was a machine, a piston driving into her, hammering his body into hers. Every time he withdrew, her silken muscles tried to drag at him, hold him to her, and when he drove back inside of her, her nerve endings went into a frenzy of shocked lust and carnal need, the pleasure so intense she wasn't certain she could bear it.

The furry tail was swishing madly against her sensitized

skin, adding to the sensations coursing through her body. Her nipples were sending fiery messages to her swollen clit. The plug pulsed and vibrated, making her fuller, the thousands of nerve endings shockingly desperate for more, heightening that building wave inside of her. Absinthe's pistoning cock, so thick and long, driving into her as if he owned her and then dragging over her inflamed clit, hitting her G-spot, was too much.

She couldn't process. Her body was too far gone. There was no controlling anything, least of all herself or her orgasm. She felt an overwhelming tidal wave start somewhere inside, welling up, traveling through her, raging like a storm out of control, the force so strong she was afraid but couldn't stop it, no matter how hard she tried to hold back. It just swept through her, taking everything in its path.

Her body clamped down like a vise on his. Through the roaring in her ears she heard him swear in his native language, a velvet curse, and then his hot seed splashed into her, coating the walls of her spasming channel, triggering a larger, even more powerful crashing wave so that she screamed, and went down to her elbows, unable to support herself.

Absinthe wrapped his arms around her waist, his cock still jerking and pulsing deep inside her, so hot she thought she was burning from the inside out. Was that possible? To die from too many orgasms? To implode? To burn from the two of them being so hot together they went up in flames? Her body continued to orgasm, rippling and rippling until she could no longer, even with his help, hold herself up.

Scarlet collapsed forward right onto the floor, the hardwood crushing the clamps into her nipples painfully, but she barely felt it she was so exhausted. The swells kept coming, undulating powerfully through her body, again and again, rocking her, squeezing down on Absinthe's cock. He stopped the movement and vibration of the plug, and that helped to ease the power of the surges but didn't stop them. She felt tears on her face.

His arms were around her and he rocked her body gently, his breath warm in her ear. "You did so good, *kiska*.
You were perfect. You're all right. Are you are hurt? You're
crying. You need to talk to me with your human voice."

She didn't want to. She'd told him she wanted to give him
the wedding gift of being his kitten all night. She shook her
head but did as he commanded. "It was so good. You made
me feel things I've never felt before. Thank you." Her voice
was a hoarse whisper. "I love being your wife. And your
kiska. I want to continue." Although she wasn't certain how
she was going to make it back to their bedroom.

He solved the problem for her. After a few minutes of
breathing hard, he simply stood up and lifted her, carrying
her back through the house. She curled into him, her head
on his chest, eyes closed, so exhausted she just wanted to
sleep. He held her while he ran a hot bath, removed her tail
and stockings and then laid her on the rug in front of the
fireplace.

"I have to take off the clamps, *kiska*." He did so, un-
twisting the right one and pulling it off, replacing it immediately with the warmth of his mouth, sucking gently as the
blood returned.

She wrapped her arms around his head in a fierce grip
as pain rushed for just a brief moment and then subsided.
He didn't wait but proceeded to do the same on the other
side. When he had them off, he kissed both nipples.

"I'm proud of you, *moya malen'kiy kiska*. You didn't
make a sound." Once again, he lifted her and put her in the
bathtub so the hot water soothed her tired body. "Just rest."
He put a small pillow behind her head. "I'll clean your toys
and tail and move our gifts from the bed."

Scarlet jerked awake when Absinthe returned to her,
washing her gently, soothing her when she tried to sit up.

"Stay still, baby. Let me take care of you."

She lay back and he washed her breasts, being very gentle with her nipples. He had her stand and lean on him so

he could wash her intimately front and back and then he lifted her out and dried her off. Carrying her to the bed as if she were an infant, he laid her down and applied soothing ointment to her nipples and breasts and then worked more into her mound, pussy lips, clit and pussy. It was cooling and felt good.

"Are you certain you want to spend the rest of the night as *moya krasivaya malen'kiy kiska*?"

She mewed softly, raising her eyebrow, needing an interpretation. She knew some Russian words, but not that many.

"My beautiful little pussycat," he explained.

She had no idea why those words, as dirty as they sounded, as possessive, gave her such a thrill, but they did. "Yes, please," she murmured, lifting her lashes to look into his strangely colored eyes. Immediately she was rewarded with that softness, the look of love and pride she needed to see on his face.

Absinthe bent down and brushed her lips very gently with his. He slipped her thin, ruby-studded collar around her neck and buckled it. She found it strange that when he put on that collar, just that simple act made her feel safe and even more cherished.

"Turn over, *kiska*, I need to put your tail in. You've made me feel so loved tonight."

She obediently rolled over and tried to relax. The thought of that heating oil was a little terrifying. Preacher, the mad chemist, was a little diabolical. Absinthe rubbed the soothing lotion into her cheeks and then poured lube into the seam between her cheeks, pushing into her star gently, and added quite a bit. The lube was just as soothing as the lotion had been on her nipples and she was grateful. He coated his finger and once again pushed deep before coating the plug and inserting it slowly. She knew immediately it was the same, wider plug.

"Is that comfortable, *kiska*?"

She managed to purr sleepily. He laughed softly, pulled back the covers and once again lifted her in his arms. "Sleepy little kitten. It's not even close to bedtime, but you earned a nap."

Scarlet curled up next to him on her side, pulling her legs into her chest, her tail feeling strange, but not uncomfortable. She was too tired to care about it. Absinthe petted her hair and down her back, his hands feeling good on her body, reassuring her. She'd never been so tired or so satisfied in her life.

"I love you," he whispered in her ear.

As she drifted off, she realized she'd fallen in love with him too. She wasn't just falling, she was already there.

FIFTEEN

Scarlet had a weird dream that Absinthe woke her once asking her some silly nonsense about whether she wanted him to leave her alone there in the room while he spoke with the others or whether she wanted him to talk to them there in the room. She murmured to him not to go. It was their wedding night. She was his *kiska*, wasn't she? He petted her head and leaned down and kissed her, murmuring to her that his sleepy little kitten should go back to sleep. She was warm and exhausted after so many orgasms and that was exactly what she did.

Scarlet woke to the sound of men talking in low voices in a foreign language. A woman laughed softly. She was so tired, at first she thought she was dreaming, but then she realized there were others in the room with her and Absinthe was no longer in bed beside her. Her heart began to pound. There was no hiding the change in her breathing from those in the room, and at once there was silence. She lifted her head slightly.

The scent of cinnamon and spice mixed with oranges

and the oil Absinthe had used on her. The combination was potent in the very warm room. The flames in the fireplace leapt high, the only light casting eerie glowing shadows on the wall. Alena stood up, put her hand on Absinthe's shoulder and leaned down to brush his cheek lightly.

"I'm sorry we had to disturb your night, Absinthe. Scarlet is a treasure. Give her my love. I'm going to bed. You three carry on without me. You're almost finished and I'm so tired I can't think straight. Enjoy the rest of the orange-spice cookies."

With a little wave, Alena sauntered out the open bedroom door and disappeared down the hall, leaving the men she knew to be Steele and Savage behind with Absinthe. The two sat facing Absinthe and the fireplace. Absinthe was on the outside and her red cushion was next to him, his chair solidly between her cushion and the men. His chair was the only one turned slightly toward the bed, so he could see her at all times. The master bedroom was large so there was plenty of room between her and the men. The door was far closer to her so she could conceivably escape.

"Sit on your cushion right here beside me and wait for me silently by the fire, *kiska*, or stay there in bed. Your master has important business. If you're in need of comfort, you can play with your catnip. I left it out for you beside your cushion."

Absinthe didn't turn his head directly toward her, as if she was a real kitten and not a human being at all. "If that is not enough, I give you permission to use my cock." His hand dropped idly to the ever-present bulge between his legs and stroked just once. He was wearing his silk drawstring pants and nothing else.

For some reason, giving her options and not even looking at her or making her feel like a human made it easier to stay curled naked, her tail protruding, listening to the men once again speaking in low tones in Russian. She knew that the pets she'd read about often used their master's cocks for comfort in times of stress. He offered not for himself, but for her.

Night had fallen, although it wasn't that late. The sun hadn't been down very long because outside the glass wall the sky was more a darker gray than black. She yawned and stretched, needing to work the kinks out of her stiff body. Her fingers brushed a gun. She turned her head to look at the weapon lying beside her. It hadn't been there before. Why had Absinthe put it there? She realized that no blankets covered her, and her naked body was completely exposed to the men in the room.

She hadn't been dreaming. Absinthe had woken her and asked if they should come into the room with her or take the meeting away from her. She'd told him she wanted him to stay. He had stayed, but he'd given her a weapon. She had no idea how long they'd been there, but Absinthe had made certain no one had touched her. She would have woken instantly had they tried. That was why he had given her a weapon, so if his word wasn't good enough, she would feel she could protect herself. She loved him all the more for asking her permission and then giving her a weapon just to reassure her that she was safe.

She let herself breathe again, realizing that she'd gone from holding her breath to ragged breathing to slowing her breathing deliberately to normal again. No one seemed to be paying the least bit of attention to her, so to test that theory, she moved to her knees. With a tail, there was no sitting. No one turned around, but Absinthe's gaze flicked to her, and for a moment, she felt approval in his gaze and that warmed her. She had no idea how he could do that. She looked down at her body, and her nipples had peaked just at the thought that she'd pleased him by kneeling up on the bed. She stayed that way for a few minutes while their conversation continued. She could tell whatever they were talking about was important. No one looked her way and her heart settled down even more.

If she wanted to go to the bathroom—and it was becoming imperative she go—she would have to crawl on her hands and knees across the room to the bathroom door, which was thankfully open. She eyed the distance and then looked at Absinthe a little desperately. He hadn't given her permission. She wasn't certain what to do. The YouTube videos hadn't covered that kind of mundane, not-so-sexy task.

"Excuse me for a moment," Absinthe said and reached down to pick up her leash. He stood up in that easy way he had, all power and grace, looking dangerous and sexy as hell. He came right toward her without hesitation, the leash running through his hands.

Immediately her heart began to race all over again, her gaze shifting toward the men sitting in those chairs.

"Eyes on me," he commanded, his voice a low whip of velvet, impossible to resist.

Her gaze jumped to his. He snapped the leash to one of the golden rings and turned and began to walk toward the bathroom, so she had no choice but to slide off the bed after him. She didn't know if the others watched as he led her across the room. She crawled automatically, her tail waving sensuously, her hips feeling slinky and provocative, her hands and knees positioning themselves like she'd practiced over and over for him.

Once in the bathroom, he reached out and closed the door behind her. She hadn't even considered how she would remove the tail or reinsert it after.

"I'll show you how and you can practice," he said, clearly reading her mind. "But that will come much later. You're doing fine."

She could see he wasn't leaving the room, but he did go to the sink and rinse her plug while she did her business.

"You can crawl to the bed or be led to your cushion. This meeting is extremely important but we're almost finished. There has been a change in plans for tomorrow, so I couldn't get out of it and I didn't want you to wake alone and frightened. I also wanted you to realize you can trust me and the others, but I know this is a huge leap of faith for you and way too soon, *kiska*."

Again, there was a ring of truth in his voice and he took his time, not hurrying her or telling her the others were waiting. He didn't seem to care that they waited for him. Once she was ready, on her hands and knees in front of him, Absinthe pressed the flat of his hand between her shoulder blades to push her down to her elbows, leaving her bottom high for him. He was careful, taking his time to prepare her for her tail before inserting it.

Scarlet's breathing went ragged. She began trembling. It felt like a momentous decision. The gun was on the bed. If she went with him to the cushion, she would be kneeling stark naked as a pussycat, his plaything, in front of his friends. Would that be an invitation to join in?

Absinthe's hand dropped to her head and began to stroke caresses down her hair and back, and then over the cheeks of her buttocks. "You are my beloved wife. My very cherished *kiska*. I do not *ever* share. I don't let others touch or play. I take care of you always and I take pride in you. Do I like to display you because I find you beautiful, both as my wife and as my *kiska*? Yes, but it is not necessary. It will never be necessary. Do I want you to reach a point where you trust me that much? Yes, but again, I expect that will take time. This meeting is necessary and unexpected. You can curl up on the bed and go back to sleep. If you prefer, now that you know where I am, I can take them into the other room."

Again, Absinthe didn't hurry her, allowing her to think it over.

She took a breath and leapt off the proverbial cliff. She nudged the leash in his hand. His eyes went that strange opaque that could turn her inside out.

"Be certain, my beautiful little pussycat. Once there, I will expect you to remain on your cushion without fidgeting or interrupting the meeting. If you do, you will be expected to use your catnip or my cock. As it is, just thinking of you doing this for me, trusting me this soon, makes me so fucking hard, I don't know if I can possibly concentrate on the details my brothers are giving to me."

That made her sex contract and begin to pulse. At once she grew damp and needy. She almost wished she had the hot inflammatory oil that demon Preacher had devised coating the plug in her bottom and maybe painted on her lips and clit. She nodded her head and purred, rubbing her body against his leg, deliberately rubbing her cheek against the hard bulge between his legs.

He snapped on the leash. "You are the naughtiest *kiska*, and at the same time, the sexiest. I can barely resist you. I have to keep reminding myself you haven't been trained properly." He opened the door and led her out.

Scarlet concentrated on a sensuous feline crawl, letting her body do the work, keeping the image of a cat in her mind, the way it moved across the floor, enticing male cats to come close, showing off her attributes to Absinthe as best she could. Her breasts. Round, firm, high, hard nice-sized nipples he could clamp and have fun with. They swayed with every movement of her body. Her hips were generous, her cheeks rounded firm globes, smooth, and she knew he was particularly fond of that part of her anatomy. Even now, as he walked her to her cushion, he stroked her cheeks.

Her tail was beautiful. The fur was gorgeous. The gems, both diamonds and rubies, caught in the firelight and threw a blazing light on the walls. She hadn't expected that, and as soon as it happened, she heard shifting in the chairs. Her heart accelerated and she faltered. What had she been thinking? She glanced toward the door leading to the hall. To the bed where the gun was. To the chairs were the two men had turned to look at her tail and the glittering diamonds and rubies.

"Eyes on me." Absinthe's voice was low, a caress sweeping over her.

The pressure was slight on her collar and she went with him to her cushion and knelt up onto it, facing away from the men, toward him. Her profile was toward them. They could see her bushy, gem-filled tail, now really set ablaze by the flames. Suddenly, she became the kitten in her mind, safe, far away from everyone but Absinthe. She didn't look at either of them. She was his and only his.

It was strange to feel safe in the persona of a cat, especially when a gun was only a few feet away and having guns and knives had always made her feel safe these past few years. She was proficient with weapons and had become very skilled in hand-to-hand combat. Still, she doubted if she was anywhere near the expertise of those in the room with Absinthe, judging by the way Adrik had been so cautious with them. Still, deep within the cat's body, she felt very safe.

She found she liked assuming the persona of a cat for Absinthe. She would never, not in a million years, do so for anyone else, but she loved the feeling of belonging to him. She had plenty of time to analyze her feelings as she knelt beside him. She was comfortable, the fire warm on her skin. Being a kitten was a role for her, not something she needed to be. She enjoyed playing the role, but mostly she just liked being whatever Absinthe wanted from her—and the sex was spectacular.

She knew she could take the kitten thing or leave it. What was most important to her, what made her happiest, was that Absinthe was dominant in the bedroom, leaving her to follow his lead. That was what made her hot. Slinking around as a hot little sex kitten was fun, and she loved being what he wanted, but it was all for him. She loved providing for him. She *needed* to provide what she knew he needed. She stayed very still, wanting to be the perfect kitten for him, hoping that was what he would want.

As time went by she became aware, as she tuned herself

more and more to him, that although on the outside Absinthe seemed absolutely calm, something was wrong. The two men were talking to him, but he no longer seemed to be listening. There was a fine sheen of sweat building on his body. She could see little beads of sweat on his forehead. One trickled down the side of his face. He made no move to stop it. That was so unlike Absinthe.

Steele rose, murmured his good-bye, but Absinthe didn't look up. Savage was the one who answered, walking with him to the bedroom door while Absinthe absently stared into the fireplace. The flames seemed to roll over his face and burn in his nearly transparent eyes. He was looking inward, not outward, and she realized he was far away from her. Far away from the room, trapped back in time in the hell he'd been raised in.

Her heart began to accelerate. His skin looked off. His eyes vacant. She glanced toward the door. Savage was nowhere in sight. He must have followed Steele down the hall. The men moved so silently she couldn't hear them. Breathing deep, she concentrated on Absinthe, trying to connect with him, follow that path they'd forged between them.

His brain was complete chaos. Horrific images were back, crowding into his mind, real demons eating him alive, consuming him. She made every effort not to change her breathing, afraid the moment he was aware that she shared those images with him, that she was too close to him, he would shut down. At least she thought he would. As she continued to share his mind and his past, she feared he had been pulled into the past. He wasn't just going down memory lane. He was in it. Living it.

The first time she'd seen those horrific vignettes playing through his mind, she thought she was looking into hell and she'd just wanted to stop it, but now she felt it was important to see what he faced. She needed to assess the images, the ones Absinthe dwelt on, seemingly was caught in, as if he was trapped there and couldn't escape.

There he was, Absinthe as a teenager. Already gorgeous, breathtakingly so, even then. He was tall and already filled out. Naked, he moved through a room filled with girls, some on their hands and knees with fluffy cat tails, others on two legs but with bits in their mouths and horse tails. Grown men directed the various girls, using whips on their legs or buttocks when they didn't move fast enough or comply with orders.

Clearly exasperated, the men directed Absinthe to train their "pets." Absinthe would go to a girl and whisper to her and she would instantly do so much better, looking happy to do whatever her master wished of her. She could see Absinthe cuddling with one particular girl, very young, trying to soothe her when the man "owning" her clearly scared her.

The girl's master, a huge brute, roared at Absinthe, grabbed him by his throat and slammed him into the wall, face-first. An eerie silence fell over the room and everyone turned to watch. The grown men began grinning, looking evil, their pets looking terrified. Absinthe didn't fight back as he was punched in the ribs repeatedly. The brute pulled out his cock and rammed it into the teen, slamming him into the wall, crushing him deliberately as he assaulted him. Several of the men moved closer, pulling out their cocks, one directing the brute to turn his victim so he could use his mouth. The other men turned to the girls, choosing the nearest ones to use, uncaring that they were terrified or crying.

Chaos erupted. The girls, all pets of the grown men, suddenly came to life, ignoring every command, rushing under the outstretched arms of their masters, some even striking out as they flew by, flinging themselves at the brute, kicking, biting, pulling hair, attempting to drag him backward and down under the sheer weight of their little bodies as they tried to protect Absinthe.

The mutiny was over in minutes. The brute swung his massive fists at the little girls, kicking with his boots, knocking their bodies around, clearly breaking bones. Absinthe, broken and bloody, tried to stop him, but the other men quickly pulled him away. He was more valuable to them than the girls. He could train others. They couldn't get another trainer, but they could get more pets.

The brute wasn't satisfied, not even when he had all the girls on the ground, bloody and barely moving. He stomped on them, spit and kicked. He stalked out and returned, splashing a liquid on the walls of the room and then over the girls. When one tried to rise, he casually kicked her in the face and poured more of the liquid over her.

Absinthe began to yell. Scarlet had never seen or heard him raise his voice. He tried to use the power of his voice to stop the brute, but one of the men clapped his hand over his mouth, to keep the brute from turning his attention to the teenager. Absinthe struggled wildly. He was strong, but it was impossible when there were so many grown men muscling him from the building.

The brute stalked to the doorway, casually turned, an evil smirk on his face. He tossed a match inside and shut the door, immediately barricading it so no one could get out. Within seconds flames roared, climbing up the walls, raging toward the ceiling, breaking out the glass so that air fueled the hungry blaze, turning it into an inferno.

Outside, the men released Absinthe, who rushed the building completely nude, stripping away the barricade with his bare hands. The brute laughed and pointed to him, nudging the others, making bets that he wouldn't enter with the entire room engulfed in flames when he was naked.

Scarlet knew better. She held her breath as he ripped the door open, threw his arm over his face and started inside. Before he could take another step, two others caught him from behind and dragged him back outside. She recognized Savage and Steele. Absinthe turned on them viciously, fighting, punching with his fists, head-butting, kicking with precise, beautifully executed kicks. Savage blocked, but didn't fight back, keeping his attention while Steele circled behind him. Another boy, one who looked like an older version of Absinthe, came up behind him as well and wrapped him up in hard arms, taking him to the ground, holding him down.

The screams of the trapped girls and the smell of burning flesh were horrific. The night turned orange and red as the roof collapsed and the pitiful cries ceased abruptly. Absinthe let out a wail, the sound like that of a wounded animal. Then, abruptly, he went silent. His brother got off of him slowly and reached down to help him up.

Absinthe didn't take his hand. He didn't look at any of the other boys. He stood in silence as he was directed by one of the men to go to the long building in the distance. He did so, stumbling like a zombie, his expression blank, looking like he was in shock. The three other boys followed behind him.

Next, Scarlet saw Alena bending over Absinthe while his brother and Savage held him, Steele examining him, Alena trying to coax him to eat. The scent of cinnamon and orange was heavy in the air. Clearly, Absinthe was willing himself to die, refusing to eat.

The bedroom door swung closed, the sound loud in the silence, startling Scarlet, bringing her back to the present. She turned around, pulling out of his mind, shocked and very happy to see Savage was back.

"Thank God. Something's wrong with Absinthe. He's having a flashback. He's so far in his mind, he's gone, Savage. I can't reach him." She couldn't. Not through their connection. Not shouting his name. Not pinching him. She felt like the four helpless teens desperately trying to save him when Absinthe was starving himself, willing himself to die.

Savage's ice-cold gaze jumped to Absinthe's face and he let out a groan. "No. Damn it, Absinthe. Don't fuckin' do this." He swung around and took two steps toward the door. Both heard the truck leaving the drive. Steele was gone.

"He clearly has done this before. How did you get him

back?" Scarlet might feel desperate inside, but she was cool on the outside. She wasn't going to lose her husband to his past. He had every right to suffer post-traumatic stress syndrome, but his demons weren't going to swallow him whole.

"We had a club girl be his fucking little pussycat and suck his cock until he knew what was going on in real time. He wasn't this far gone. I had to scare the crap out of her so he'd come back and protect her."

"Then that's what we'll have to do. I'm his pet and you scare me."

Savage studied her face for a long moment and then shook his head. "You aren't the type that scares so easy, Scarlet. You took a knife away from a rapist and his friends. You fought them off with it. You went by yourself to a man whose reputation would put off most very scary men and you stayed with him a year in order to learn how to kill the men who raped your sister. You don't scare easy, honey. You're a fighter. You already know what I'd have to do and you're prepared for it."

Savage looked as if he might shake Absinthe—or her. He paced across the room. "This is bullshit. We fuckin' set this up, the perfect storm. Steele. The fire. Alena. Her cookies. Me. You. What the hell were we thinking?"

"Tell me what I have to do to get him back." Scarlet poured conviction into her voice. "You're the scariest man I've ever seen. I have no doubt you'll figure it out. Tell me what to do. What he needs. I can play any role. I'm good. I can get into his mind. We have a connection. We have to try. We have to do this." She made it a demand. Savage had his back to her but she saw him stiffen. His shoulders went straight.

Savage took a deep breath and turned to face her. When he did, he looked different. The change was subtle, but the man that was raging with so much worry for his brother had been taken over by something that reminded her of the Grim Reaper. His eyes were flat and cold and carried death.

"You only think you know me, Scarlet. I'm not like the rest of them. You don't want my demons in this room with only the two of us here. So you bring him back. Be his little pet. Make him think you can't live without him, that if you don't do what you're told I'm going to end your life. That's what's going to make him come to you. Your fear. Your need. He has to feel his little kitten's fear. Get your mouth on his cock and get busy."

She turned her attention to Absinthe, stroking his thighs, but she knew it wasn't going to work. He was so far away. She reached for him. Tried to connect and there were only . . . nightmares. Ugly nightmares. No matter what she tried, mind-to-mind contact, she couldn't reach Absinthe. He just wasn't there.

Savage began to pace back and forth behind her. A shirt fluttered to the floor beside her knees. She caught another quick glimpse of Savage, thick chest bare, his muscles rippling, a belt in is hands, folded in two. His chest was covered in scars and whip marks. Branded into his flesh were the words *Whip Master*. Up close, the sight of him was terrifying. She wanted to run for the bed and the gun Absinthe had left her for protection.

Savage suddenly towered over the top of her, caught her by her hair and yanked her head back, setting her heart pounding madly.

"What the fuck are you waiting for? I can't reach him. You can see he's too far gone. Bring him back. He's trapped there again. He's in his mind. It happens and he can't get out. You have to bring him the fuck out."

She tried to knock his hand away from her scalp, her reaction to being touched by him almost visceral, but his arm was so hard it actually hurt to hit him with her forearm. She felt the jolt all the way up to her shoulder. Savage didn't seem to notice. His eyes were so cold and dead she shivered with fear. She knew death when she saw it, and she was looking straight into the eyes of the Grim Reaper.

Still, it was going to take a lot more to really get beyond her need to fight back. She pushed down the urge to slam her fist right between Savage's legs.

"You're hurting me."

"Then get to work." But he let her go.

She shifted her gaze to the bed. "Let me get my gun."

He glanced toward the bed speculatively and then at her face. Very slowly he shook his head and a chill went down her spine.

"I don't think so. You have a great deal more incentive to save his life knowing yours might be on the line."

She stared into those flat, cold eyes and then, without another word, she crawled off the red cushion, pushed past Savage, and deliberately wound around Absinthe's legs to create the feeling in him of his pet—his live pet—the one who gave him a semblance of comfort so he could sleep and keep the nightmares at bay. Why he had a fireplace in his bedroom, she had no idea, but they weren't going to light the damn thing before he went to sleep, not ever again.

She purred and rubbed her cheek on the inside of Absinthe's thighs as she deftly opened the drawstring of his pants. She nudged his hand with the top of her hair, still acting the part of the kitten. He had told her she could come to him for reassurance if she needed it. A part of her wondered how he would choose a woman like her—one who didn't need his protection the way someone much more fragile might.

She concentrated on making the opening in the drawstring trousers as wide as possible in order to get full access to Absinthe's cock and balls. Even soft, his cock was long and thick, the promise of it making her mouth water. She licked his balls and then up his shaft. There was no response.

"You get five minutes, you fucking little pussycat, and then I'm going to think you aren't putting any effort into saving my brother," Savage snarled, leaning over her shoulder so fast her heart jerked hard and then began to pound in growing fear.

Behind her, he began to pace again up and down the length of the room. She tried to concentrate on Absinthe's cock, but she couldn't keep Savage in sight other than for a brief glimpse every few moments when he moved into her peripheral vision. Scarlet tried to ignore him, to feel the weight and texture of Absinthe's cock on her tongue, to stroke it lovingly, but Savage was so silent and so menacing that it felt as if she was in the room with a caged tiger, ready to leap on her any moment and rip her to shreds.

She found herself actually pulling Absinthe's cock deep and sucking a little desperately, almost for comfort, her heart pounding so frantically she feared that pounding beat could be heard throughout the room. Certainly, it thundered in her ears. She found the energy in the room was dark and menacing, a strange combination when she'd been feeling Savage's deep concern for Absinthe. Now there was none of that, only this terrible need to strike at her.

She used everything she'd learned that Absinthe loved, pouring attention and care on him, trying not to let the pacing that was coming closer and closer behind her get to her. Savage was like an animal. A terrible predator waiting for her to screw up.

"Fuckin' get to work. Don't you know the first thing about suckin' cock? I can text one of the little club girls, get them to go down on him and do a better job than you're doin'," he hissed, contempt in his voice.

Fear beat at her, but anger mixed with that fear. As long as she felt anger toward Savage, as long as she thought about coming to her feet and driving her fist into his mouth to smash his ugly words right back down his throat, she was never going to convince Absinthe she was that frightened little kitten who desperately needed him to come save her. She was too busy formulating plans to save herself.

She understood flashbacks. She did. She'd had a few of her

own. What was wrong with her that she was never enough for anyone to stick around? All while a part of her tried not to think of herself or why she couldn't reach Absinthe, she worked her skills on him, doing her best to ignore the growing threat of the predator prowling behind her. She kept trying to find Absinthe, to connect with him. To reach him. Even with their pathway forged so solidly between them, nothing got through to him. Nothing at all.

Savage crowded behind her aggressively, his fist once more in her hair. "You don't seem to believe I'm serious, little pet. I think you need a little persuasion."

Her eyes met his, those cold, dead blue ones, and at once her vision changed and she was in the past again. There were girls, not women, but girls. She couldn't begin to guess their age, late teens maybe. Several were tied in twisted torture positions to various racks or benches, much like she imagined a modern-day bondage room might have, only this looked as if it might be the real thing. No velvet whips. No soft floggers. A loud whistle cut through the air and a stripe of red lit up one of the girls. She screamed. Immediately, the crack of other whips followed as a dozen men followed suit, whipping other girls.

One man stepped forward and a hush fell over the room. Even the girls went quiet. He was completely naked, his body all raw muscle, scarred, burned, with the words *Whip Master* branded into his chest. His hair was a mass of blond curls. He walked up to a girl crying and squirming on the rack in the center of the room. On his back, he had the words *Master of Pain* branded into his skin. He had scars all over him, both front and back, chest, buttocks, thighs. He was covered in scars and burn marks.

He leaned into the sobbing girl and licked at her tears, cupping her face gently and whispering to her. She nodded over and over. He kissed her and then backed off, walking away, muscles rippling as he coiled the whip. Abruptly he turned back to her, lashing out, striking repeatedly, turning her body into a series of red stripes forming patterns over her breasts, belly, sex and thighs. She didn't scream, but tears continued to run silently down her face.

The whip master turned his head and Scarlet's heart stuttered. He was no man. He was a teen, already with a man's body, all muscle, his cock large and powerful, his eyes as ice-cold as the densest glacier. She recognized Savage staring at her before he walked back to the girl and once again licked at her tears, his hands roaming over her body, his cock sliding into her slick pussy as he took her hard and fast, uncaring of the blood running down her body.

Scarlet was staring into those same blank eyes right at that moment. She had no idea how she connected with his past so clearly, that terrible vignette of his life, but those images of his teenage training sent chills down her spine.

"You see me," he said, his voice completely devoid of emotion. "Now we understand each other." Once again, he moved out of her sight. "You fuckin' bring him back."

The sound of the belt snapping was so loud she jumped, her body flinching under the crack of leather. Real fear skittered down her spine. Absinthe's hand moved into her hair and stroked down the back of her head. His cock jerked, the first sign of life. She closed her eyes and let herself envision him sitting in the chair by the fire, concentrating on his kitten. Stroking her hair, murmuring praise and reassurance.

She felt rather than heard movement, as Savage passed very close to her, the belt sliding over her back, just a whisper of leather. Another shiver crept down her spine. The danger felt all too real. Savage liked to see marks on pristine skin, and she was showing far too much skin. A chill seized her. Absinthe's fingers in her hair curled, dug into her scalp. Massaged. His other hand curled around the nape of her neck, his thumb sliding along her jaw, encouraging her to use her mouth.

"Suck, *kiska*. You're safe. No one can hurt you." His

hand dropped away from her neck, but the one remained unmoving in her hair, keeping that connection.

Triumph burst through her. He still *felt* far away, but his voice was that soft, reassuring blend of gentle and command that only he seemed capable of producing. She did as he said, sucking harder, feeling him growing in her mouth, the weight of him heavier, his girth stretching her lips. She needed him to come closer, to acknowledge that she was his kitten, not some vague girl in his past. That he knew who was in the room with him. His wife. His woman. His partner. She would find his trigger and be so careful that this didn't happen again to him.

She ran her tongue up under the broad, velvety crown and flicked that sensitive spot, then rubbed, feeling his cock grow even harder. Now he was beginning to feel more like Absinthe, but he was still far away, not present, and Savage seemed to know, stalking back and forth like that horrible prowling jungle cat, moving closer and closer until he suddenly reached around her with the belt, looping it around her collar before she was even aware he was going to strike.

The leather tightened. She gasped. The weight of Absinthe's hand pushed her head down onto his cock so she took him deeper.

"It's all right, *kiska*. I'm here."

But he wasn't. He was close. So close. She could almost reach him, but he wasn't quite there. She knew it. Savage knew it.

Savage bent down so that his breath was hot in her ear. "Did you know that when a woman is deprived of oxygen when she's orgasming, it can be very addictive because it's such a fuckin' rush? It's also damn dangerous because she can die. So that's a rush as well. What do you think, pussy-cat? Do you want to play? Or do you want to swallow him down and get him off?"

The belt tightened a second time for just a split second,

making her gasp again, and this time she deliberately took more of Absinthe down, her heart going crazy. Savage might really kill her. He was that crazy. She didn't know anything about him, but even the scent of him was real. He smelled dangerous. Feral.

She had to think like a frightened kitten. She moved closer to Absinthe, using her throat to make distressed-like sounds to vibrate through his cock to both call to him and massage him. The images in his mind receded more, bringing him closer to her. She turned her eyes to his face, her gaze clinging to his. She didn't realize tears were falling until he was blurry. Those crystal eyes filled with rolling red and orange flames. She wanted those flames gone. She wanted them to turn at least to blue flames.

She poured her heart and soul into her administrations, trying to please him, trying to get him to recognize her, now as lost as he was. She didn't belong here with him. She didn't belong anywhere. She fit better in Thailand with Adrik. At least she understood his rules. He didn't let emotion into his world. He said it fucked things up. This was about as fucked up as it got.

"Shh, *kiska*." Absinthe's thumbs wiped at the tears on her face. "You're here with me right where you belong. No one is going to hurt you."

His voice. That voice. Always so gentle, pouring over her like love should sound, when this was anything but. His hands in her hair, cupping her face, thumbs sliding over her skin, brushing at her cheeks, then back up to her hair while his hips thrust into her mouth. She locked eyes with him. Was he there with her? Was he really there?

She didn't understand the world of Torpedo Ink. These men and women had been born into violence, they had banded together for survival, becoming much like a wolf pack learning to kill at a young age, using sex and a kind of feral ferocity to endure and outlast the predators they ended up hunting. She thought she knew violence after being ex-

posed to the Holdens, but they were nothing in comparison.
Even when she'd deliberately sought out those who could
train her, none of them could compare to these men and
women—not even Adrik. She had to go. She had to get
away before she lost herself.

Absinthe gripped her hair unexpectedly, his body moving, his cock full and hard, suddenly aggressive, filling her
mouth, sliding deeper, retreating. She was no longer the
one in control, it was all him. His eyes flared down at her,
going from red-orange rolling flames to a blue blaze as he
fed her his cock. She could tell he was close, tasting that
unique taste that was all his, the one that was addicting, and
she knew, long after she left, she would never forget.

Then he was pouring into her mouth, one hand stroking
her throat while he murmured to her to swallow him down.
She couldn't stop crying. The moment she could, she pulled
away from him, wiping at her mouth, letting fury rise. At
him. At Savage. At herself. Fear had a lot to do with it. She
was a fighter and she never should have put herself in such
a vulnerable position.

The belt was gone from around her neck, slithering
away as if it had never been. It had never actually touched
her throat. It had locked down on her collar, but that didn't
matter. What mattered was how Savage had made her feel.
Small. Helpless. Insignificant. Hopeless even. She had
vowed she would never feel those things again. She knew
exactly how her sister had felt in those last moments of her
life, just as Robert Holden Jr. and his friends had made
Scarlet feel. She wanted to vomit. She wanted to smash her
fist in both their faces. She wanted to claw at her own.

Savage was all the way across the room, lounging
against the wall as if he was innocent in the entire drama.
She had no idea how or when he got there and she didn't
care. She rose fast, stumbling away from Absinthe when he
reached out a hand to her.

Reaching behind her, she ripped the tail from her and

flung it toward his face and then turned to walk toward the bathroom. At the last second, she raced for the bed. Absinthe was on her as she flung her hand out for the gun and turned at the same time, the grip in her fist, heart beating wildly. He pinned her to the mattress, straddling her, hands controlling her wrists so she couldn't turn the gun on him.

"Drop it, now, Scarlet. I don't want to hurt you, but you don't know what you're doing."

His voice was calm. Steady. All Absinthe. His fingers dug into her pressure points. She wasn't certain what she planned to do anyway. She let the weapon fall from her palm onto the mattress. He immediately picked it up and handed it off behind him. Savage took it. She refused to look at him.

"Who did you plan on shooting, *miledi*? Savage? Or me?"

Absinthe brushed at her face again and she realized she was still crying.

"Get off me now." She poured venom into her voice to make certain he knew she wasn't playing games with him. Hell. She would have shot both of them. She might not have killed them, but she would have shot them. She had fully participated and even asked Savage for his help, but the results had shaken her beyond her ability to cope. She knew she didn't belong with Absinthe or Torpedo Ink. She could never, *ever* go through that again.

Absinthe immediately slid off of her and she rolled, was off the bed, on her feet and made her way to the bathroom to scrub herself clean. She left the door open so she could hear every word they said to each other and/or so she could see an attack coming.

"What happened?" Absinthe asked calmly.

"What the fuck do you think happened? The same as last time and the time before," Savage snarled. "You have to get a fuckin' lock on this, brother. It can't keep happening."

He stalked across the room and snagged his shirt, dragging it over his head and chest. "I scared the shit out of your wife in order to bring your ass out of it. Do you know what that cost her? Do you have any idea what that cost me? I was already in the downward spiral. I could have resolved the issue with the fuckin' job we're pullin' tomorrow but now I've got this craving and I've got nowhere to put that shit. Not to mention, she knows what a fuckin' psycho I am."

"Savage," Absinthe cautioned. "What do you mean, you scared the shit out of her?"

"You're not listening to me because you don't want to face this. You're still trying to blame yourself for every damn thing that happened to all of us. It happened. We can't change it. They fucked us up and we're the way we are. We can do our best to live with it, not hurt anyone who is innocent and keep to the code. You do that, brother. You're the best of us. You can't keep traveling down this path of guilt. It's got to stop."

"What do you mean, you scared the shit out of her?" Absinthe repeated, his voice dropping another octave. He stood, coming off the bed, sudden aggression in his body.

Savage shook his head. "You don't want to go there with me right now, bro. I'm pissed as hell with what I had to do here tonight to bring your ass back to her. She's worth it. You're so fuckin' lucky and you don't have the brains to know it. Some of us don't have a chance to have a good woman who would do what she did for you. She could take the kitten role or leave it. She does it for you, of her own free will. The woman is like, what? One in a million. You've got her and yet you're risking her going down that same path of guilt. All for what, Absinthe? Tell me for fuckin' what? Sorbacov and his fucked-up friends? You're going to let them ruin your life forever? You're going to let them take a woman like that away from you? If you do, you sure as hell don't deserve her and not because of what happened to us, but because somewhere along the line you stopped fighting back."

"What the fuck did you do to Scarlet?"

"What do you think I did to her, Absinthe?" Savage countered. "What's the strongest trait you possess when it comes to women? You fuckin' ran into a burning building naked, barefoot, to save them."

Absinthe winced visibly. Scarlet gripped the sink until her knuckles turned white, studying his face. He rarely showed emotion, but with her out of the room, he was showing it to Savage. His expression was a mixture of anger, guilt and, shockingly, fear. Not fear of Savage; fear of discussing a topic he didn't want to talk about.

"I'm not talking about that."

"No, you never want to talk about that. You'd much rather take the chance of going somewhere we can't reach you. You were damn lucky Scarlet was here with you. What happens someday when you get triggered and no one's around to pull you back? What happens then, Absinthe?"

"What did you do to scare her?"

Despair hit and, inside, that last bit of hope she'd clung to faded. Savage was right. If Absinthe wouldn't talk about his past and the things that were triggering his flashbacks, they would continue to repeat, and he would be caught in a deadly cycle. This was her wedding night and she'd given him a gift she thought he would love, and he'd still fallen into that trap of the past. He refused to work through it, even for her, even when Savage was pointing out how problematic the episodes were.

"What the fuck do you think I did? I let her see who I am inside. Just let the monster slip a little bit, just enough that she couldn't tell if he was in the room with her or not. And, bro, you better believe that fuckin' monster was in the room with her. He's slipped the leash and he's had a taste and he wants more. But in the end, it was worth it because the hero came charging up like the white knight he is. You came back to save her, just the way you always do."

Savage walked toward the door shaking his head.

"You're so damn intelligent, but you don't seem to have one single grain of common sense. Don't let her leave you, because that's in her head right now. I guarantee it."

Scarlet wound a towel around her body, knowing Savage was absolutely right. Leaving was in her mind whether she wanted to or not. It was a matter of saving herself.

SIXTEEN

~◆~

Absinthe stared at the bedroom door for several long moments after Savage had closed it with his controlled anger. Swearing under his breath, he rubbed at his pounding temples. He had a vicious headache, the aftermath of a flashback. They were becoming more frequent, much more intense and more difficult to come back from. His mind wouldn't let go. Savage was often a trigger, as was Steele or Alena.

"Shit," he whispered and turned to look at the fireplace. He'd lit it for Scarlet. She'd become his little pet, one he needed to keep the nightmares at bay, but to keep her warm, he'd activated the fireplace, another trigger. Savage had come with Steele to talk to him about changes they had to make the following day due to a big blowout barbecue Code had discovered the Venomous club was putting on down by the river. Alena had come with them, bearing gifts of her orange-and-cinnamon-spice cookies she knew he loved to make up for the late-night visit. He should have known, with the flames rolling and the three of them close, he would snap. "Damn it," he whispered again.

It was his fucking wedding night. Scarlet deserved one night before the universe dragged her completely down into the mire with him and showed her she hadn't gotten such a bargain. She'd already accepted his strange needs in the bedroom and yet, clearly, she was expected to accept more. She still hadn't emerged from the bathroom, giving him a bit of a reprieve, and he was grateful. He had no idea what he was going to say or do when she decided to join him.

He picked up the bushy tail Scarlet had thrown at him and ran his hands lovingly over the fur and jewels. Ice was a master at designing beautiful jewelry and accessories. He'd outdone himself when it came to these tails. He needed to clean this one and put it away. He just needed to act calm and in control. Scarlet responded to his voice and authority in the bedroom.

Absinthe sauntered into the master bath as if everything was all right and found Scarlet sitting on the edge of the tub wrapped in a towel. He crossed to the sink and began to clean the plug meticulously using the soaps he had. Very casually he raised his eyes to meet hers in the mirror. His heart stuttered. She'd been crying. She still was, although she'd dashed at the tears the moment he entered the room. Worse, she was shaking visibly.

Laying the tail on a towel on the sink, he turned to her immediately, taking several steps toward her. She stood and backed away from him, shaking her head, one hand up defensively. He stopped. She looked scared. Confused. Angry.

"Baby, don't cry. Did Savage scare you? He wouldn't hurt you." He kept his voice low, gentle, his eyes meeting hers in the mirror.

She had the most expressive eyes, and right now, they were a vivid green, almost pure emerald, the tears making them look as if she was drowning in emotion, and maybe she was, maybe they both were. He reached out on their connective path, needing to touch her mind, to know what she was feeling, but she had completely shut him out. Completely. She folded both arms over her breasts, holding herself away from him. Making herself small. Tears still ran down her cheeks but she cried silently. It was the shivering that got to him, that continual shaking that wouldn't stop.

"Don't defend him. You have no idea what happened and yet you're immediately defending him." Her voice shook with both fear and fury and her hand crept up to her neck, fingers touching the collar that was still there, declaring her his. The pads of her fingers slipped above the thin leather and rubbed as if her neck hurt.

Absinthe's gut clenched hard. "Scarlet, Savage didn't touch you. He wouldn't do that." He poured conviction into his voice, wanting her to believe it. "He wouldn't hurt you."

"Why the hell are you defending that monster?"

"He isn't a monster." He reached behind his neck and tried to rub the knots that formed there. Scarlet had done that for him. He despised this conversation. "Let's go into the bedroom and calm down. There's no point in talking about Savage. He is what he is . . ."

"No point? You don't even want to know what he did? He's psycho. For God's sake, Absinthe, that man you're defending could be a serial killer."

"That's fuckin' bullshit, Scarlet. If you say that about him, you might as well be talking about any or all of us including about yourself. We're done discussing this. We're both tired and need to sleep."

Scarlet stood for a long time regarding him from under her lashes and something in her expression told Absinthe he was really in trouble. He didn't know the first thing about relationships. Not one damn thing. His first instinct was to always protect his brothers. His club. Torpedo Ink. Scarlet was his wife, his woman. He wanted her as his partner. He wanted her to be a life partner and he was already blowing it. He should have kept his strange needs to himself. He should have been more careful about triggers that could cause flashbacks. None of this was Savage's fault. It was his.

Scarlet shook her head. "Fuck you, Absinthe. You aren't asking me what he did or didn't do, you're defending him. I'm supposed to be your wife, but clearly you're all about protecting your insane brother, not me. Now you're not even willing to discuss it. This is going to be the shortest marriage on record. If you think I was going to put up with your scary, mean bastard of a brother while I was on my knees sucking your cock just for the hell of it, you're out of your mind."

She lifted her chin. "I might have willingly done a lot for you because I thought it was a mutual respect-and-love fest going on, but clearly I was wrong."

She stalked past him, straight out of the room, toward the closets. When she moved, he could see the predator coming alive in her. She was shaking off every last bit of his *kiska*. By the time she had taken the first step into the closet she had removed most of his last name. She was Scarlet Foley and not the librarian. She was the woman trained in survival and steeling herself to go to war.

Absinthe closed his eyes briefly. He was losing her. Little beads of sweat broke out on his forehead and trickled down his chest. She was really going to leave him.

Scarlet yanked open the drawer and pulled out a pair of lace panties, sliding them up her legs, uncaring that he was standing directly behind her, leaning against the door frame, arms folded across his chest. He could block the doorway. That was uppermost in his mind. He had to find a way to persuade her.

"Go away, Absinthe. I need to pack, and I don't want you staring at me while I do it. I don't need your crap. Making a fool out of myself twice is a bit much."

"A fool out of yourself?" he echoed. Hell, he had an IQ off the fuckin' charts and he couldn't think of a damn thing to do or say to make this right between them. Her body language screamed at him not to touch her. There was no physical way to persuade her. He'd always been able to fall back on his voice when he needed it, but she was the one person he couldn't use it on effectively.

"Yeah, babe, I'd say I made a royal fool of myself with you, believing you cared about me. I fucking crawled around on my hands and knees playing the sex kitten for you, happy to do so, thinking we were partners, believing your crap, and when it came time for you to take my side and stand for me, the way I took yours, well, you chose the other way, didn't you? Then I gave you a second chance. I told you everything, but you weren't so willing to bare your soul to me, were you? So, fuck you, Absinthe. Fuck you and your lies. I'm *so* gone."

"You aren't leaving me." He made that a statement, hoping she would hear the conviction in his voice. She *had* to hear that he would fight for her, fight for them. He tried to find a way to appeal to her that would give them both a way to calm down and then start over to figure it all out. If they could move the conversation away from Savage and put their attention somewhere else even for a few minutes, he was confident they could get past this.

"For one thing, you're in trouble. Holden has sent word to all the clubs and they're looking for you. Marrying me gives you that protection."

She didn't bother to turn around. She donned the matching bra to her panties. She had the sexiest underwear and he loved the idea of her librarian clothes, knowing what was underneath. There was something deeply sensual about Scarlet, the way she moved, the way she thought, just that little detail, the prim and proper clothing over the sexiest lingerie. He fucking loved that about her.

"I know places I can go out of the country they won't find me, even with their chapters there. I have go-bags stashed with plenty of money and a couple of very good passports. You don't have to worry about me."

Scarlet dragged a T-shirt over her head and fished around for her favorite pair of jeans. She kept her face averted as she dragged a small bag from the closet and began to throw clothes into it, but he could see tears still tracking down her face and she was still shaking. He couldn't decide whether she had gone from fear to fury or if it was a combination of the two.

"Do you really think you're going to get past me? It's too dangerous for you to leave, Scarlet, and you know it. You're acting crazy. Just because I don't want to talk about something that happened a long time ago, you're going to walk out on me? You're going to put your life in jeopardy? Does that even make sense to you? It isn't logical."

Deliberately, he lowered his voice another octave, desperation putting temptation in his mind. He had vowed, *sworn*, that he would never use his ability on someone he loved without their consent, and he loved Scarlet Foley. No, Scarlet Solokov. She was his wife. What the hell was she thinking leaving him? And what was he thinking that he might consider using his voice on her to force her to stay?

He rubbed his pounding temples and breathed. "Scarlet, I don't want you to go. I know I'm screwing up all over the place here, but I don't know how to make this right. I want to make this right. Tell me what the fuck to do and I'll do it."

She swung around to face him, and the pain etched into her face gutted him. It added to what he was already feeling, nearly taking him to his knees. He'd done that to her, put that look there. Betrayal. Shredding her. She'd believed in him and he'd torn her apart. He didn't know how to make it right between them, he wasn't lying. He might be one of the smartest men on the planet, but he didn't know how to fix things between them.

"Baby." He wasn't even trying to soften his voice. The plea was real. "I'm begging here. I don't want to lose you. You're the best thing that ever happened to me. Tell me what to do to fix this. I swear to you, I want this to work." He held out his hand to her. "We don't have to stay in the bedroom. We can go anywhere you want and just talk. Just talk. Talk to me."

She didn't take his hand. She just looked at him. "No, Absinthe, *you* have to talk to *me*. That's the only way this is going to work. I told you everything about me. All of it. You have to do the same. It's the only way I can understand you and your family. Why you champion them in the worst of circumstances. I need to know why you need to have a kitten in the bedroom at night . . ."

"I don't. We can stop . . ." His heart started with a slow acceleration and then began tripping overtime at the thought of talking about his past. The pounding in his temples increased. His mouth went dry.

If she knew the things he'd done. What all of them had done. The killings were the least of it. She could accept those things, but there was so much more. The shame. The guilt. He was responsible for the majority of it. He just couldn't let her see that. He could barely look at himself in the mirror. Most of the time he couldn't. The demons in his head roared, threatening to swallow him.

She shook her head. "You're deluding yourself. You do need a kitten. If you can't be honest with yourself then you can't be honest with me. I've shown you that I'm willing to be a partner for you in every way, but I need respect from you. I have to be able to trust you. You have to be able to trust me. You don't. You only trust them. Savage and the rest of Torpedo Ink. I don't know why you put Savage before me in the situation tonight, but hopefully you had good reason because it cost you more than you'll ever know."

Scarlet gave him a very sad half smile. He heard the absolute conviction in her voice. She was really going to leave him. She meant every word. She believed he'd betrayed her and their marriage vows, and he had. She'd been frightened by Savage. He might know in his heart that Savage wouldn't hurt her but she didn't. He should have listened to her, heard her out, let her rage, cry, waited until she said her piece and after she was calm and he was holding her in his arms in their bed, talked to her about Savage and reassured her gently that his brother would never really hurt her. He hadn't done that.

Absinthe glided forward, closing the gap between them before she could move, before she was aware, and caught her hand, opening her fingers and placing her palm over his heart. "You're going to leave me after I tell you the terrible things I did, what I'm responsible for, but if that will stop you even for a few minutes, enough to give me the slightest chance, I'll take the chance."

He didn't know what the hell he was saying. He really didn't. He was out of his mind to think he could reveal to her what he'd never told another soul. So much guilt and shame, so many sins weighing down his soul. He was ashamed that Savage thought he was "the best of them." He was the worst. He was the monster, not Savage. He despised when others thought that of his brother. Savage bore the brunt of Absinthe's sins, because outwardly, Savage appeared to be the "monster." Absinthe knew who the real one was.

Scarlet's green eyes moved over his face, assessing the risk in that way she had. Processing. It wasn't in her nature just to take that leap off the cliff as she'd done with him when she'd come to him and then married him. Now, he could see, she was going to be much more careful. He'd done that—pushed her back to her wary nature. Broken the trust he'd built between them. He'd put Savage before her. He'd put Savage in the position of having to frighten her and clearly things had gone terribly wrong. He needed to find out what, but first he had to talk to her and hope she listened to him and cared enough to stick around.

She turned her hand around and threaded her fingers through his so she was holding his hand, but when he tried to touch her mind on that connection between them, her mind was closed to his. She had already figured out a way to shut him out. He knew he could find another pathway, but that would be intrusive and also, in a way, another form of betrayal. He wouldn't do that unless he had no choice. He wanted a relationship with her, a real one. If they were going to survive, she had to know the real Absinthe and accept him, just as she accepted his need of a pet kitten in his bedroom. He couldn't imagine anyone, let alone a woman as strong as Scarlet, accepting him and the things he'd done, but he had to try. He'd already lost her. He refused to be a coward, and that was what it would amount to if he didn't just come clean. In a way, it would be a relief that someone knew the real truth.

They walked together down the hall and back to the main part of the house, to the living room. When he went to the fireplace to warm the room for her, she took the remote from his hand.

"I don't need that on right now. I'd rather sit with just the light coming in from the moon and the sea. I like the way it appears silver."

Absinthe liked that effect as well. The moonlight reflected off the surface of the water and poured through the wall of floor-to-ceiling glass. Scarlet curled up in the wide armchair Lana had chosen for him. There was always a feeling of comfort in Lana's furniture the moment one settled into it, and he could see that once Scarlet tucked her bare feet under her, she was much more relaxed in spite of herself and the seriousness of the situation.

He went to the bar and pulled out two icy glass bottles of water, trying not to notice how the shape and feel of those bottles reminded him of how sexy it felt when he pressed one into his little kitten's heat. He opened a bottle for her first and set it on the table between the chairs before opening his and taking a long drink. He hadn't donned a shirt and he pressed the icy bottle first to his forehead and then to his chest, trying to relieve the feeling of feverish heat sweeping through him.

It took a few minutes before he could force himself to

sink into the chair beside Scarlet, and immediately there was a lightening of his heart, an easing of his burden, and he recognized Lana's gift. She had said she had no gift, but there it was, and no one, including him, had ever managed to put their finger on it, when it was right there in plain sight. She eased that heavy load they all carried. She put herself into the furniture she chose, into the clothes she mended for them, the patches she stitched on their vests or jackets. He would have to tell her so she knew what a miracle she was. When he needed her the most, she'd come through for him.

"Start with Savage," Scarlet said. "He scared me to death even when I asked him to help and I knew what he was going to do."

"Did he touch you?" Absinthe countered. "Actually put his hands on you? You were naked, completely naked and vulnerable. He could have done anything to you. Did he?"

Scarlet thought about it. "He grabbed my hair and pulled it, that was scary, and it hurt a little bit. He threatened me mostly, just pacing behind me where I couldn't see him and then when you didn't respond, he took off his belt and cracked it. That was terrifying. He wrapped it around my neck, but after, I realized he put it over my collar."

She raised her hand to her throat and rubbed her fingers along her skin. "I was having a difficult time really being afraid until that moment. I connected with his past somehow, when he was a teen. He had his shirt off and I saw the burn on his chest. *Whip Master*. I saw him whipping a girl. And then he fucked her. She seemed to want him to, but his eyes . . . He was so remote, as if he wasn't really there."

"Reaper was being tortured and assaulted to keep Savage in line," Absinthe offered. "I'll tell you more but I want to know what happened. Did he hurt you?"

"Not like you think." She touched her hand to her throat again. "After he put the belt around my throat and threatened me, I was scared. I went back to being seventeen, that place where I was half-drugged and Robert and his friends attacked me. I felt helpless and so afraid." She shivered and wrapped her arms around herself.

He tried to touch her and she jerked away from him, shaking her head. "I swore I would never feel that way again. No one would ever do that to me. I knew how Priscilla felt. How so many other young girls feel. I was so angry with him. With you. But mostly at myself. I can't be that person you need, Absinthe. I can't save you when you refuse to save yourself. When you won't even try. I can't. I'm not sacrificing myself. I can't do that. Not even for you."

She was crying and that turned him inside out. "Scarlet. I wouldn't want you to sacrifice yourself for me. You're exactly who I need."

She shook her head. "I'll never let him do that to me again. Never. I thought he might really kill me. Even knowing ahead of time, I still thought that of him. He's that dangerous and you know it, Absinthe."

Scarlet took a sip of water, her eyes on his face. Steady. Expectant. When he didn't respond and his gaze shifted from hers, she was the one who sighed. "You're going to have to tell me why you so adamantly defend him. You touch people and you see what's inside them. I don't have one quarter of your talent and I'm in the room with him and I know he's not a man you ever want to piss off. He could cut you into little pieces and not bat an eye. Tell me I'm wrong. What I saw of his past was very real, wasn't it?"

Absinthe pressed the icy bottle to his pounding forehead, his gut churning. "Yes," he admitted, his voice a whisper. "It's true. For a long time, when he was just little, they used him. They'd take him from us and whip him, laying his flesh open, raping him repeatedly. He'd come back so bloody and nearly dead that we didn't think he would make it an hour let alone through the night."

He felt those green eyes of hers jump to his face, but he couldn't look at her. He forced himself to look at the ocean, that beautiful sea with the sprays breaking against the rocks and bluffs. He felt like the rocks; slowing being worn down by the ever-present waves crashing against him.

"I wasn't much older. None of us were. Demyan was alive at the time. Reaper, Savage's older brother, would hold him and rock him, but Savage would try to push him away because it hurt so bad to be touched. Steele would try to heal him. We were all little kids with no real food, no medical aid, the conditions were unsanitary, it was freezing."

He shook his head and shoved one hand through his hair. "I don't know, Scarlet. We tried everything we could to make things better. Demyan and I would get on either side of Savage and just talk to him. We did it to all the kids that were beat the hell up. Girls and boys. We were beat up and raped and we'd do it for each other. We told one another that we were strong, stronger than the instructors were. We could be so much better at what they did than they could because we were so much stronger and more disciplined. They couldn't defeat us. We would always be the best."

She didn't make a sound, just watched him with that same intensity she got sometimes, never blinking, never taking her eyes from his face. She looked as if she could see right into his soul. Maybe she could, and if it was possible, she'd see only darkness. There was nothing left in him.

He shook his head again and pressed his fingertips hard into his pounding temples. "We were just trying to get each other through the next minute. The next hour. We had no idea we had any real talents or gifts. We just tried to encourage one another. We continued doing it day after day, week after week, month after month and year after year."

Scarlet nodded and shifted a little closer to him. That settled his churning stomach just a little. Her presence always seemed to help.

"From the time we were little, Czar began training us. At first, most of us didn't realize what we were doing. He had us throwing pebbles through holes. Acorns, tiny objects through very small holes. We did push-ups and he wanted us to become stronger and stronger. He was a little kid too, but he started us working on how to hold various weapons even when we didn't have them. Master, Maestro, Player and Keys were so good with wood and they could make these incredible darts. He taught us to use them like blow darts. It wasn't a game anymore, but we couldn't be careless and ever leave them where anyone could find them."

Absinthe knew he was putting off the inevitable. He had to circle back to his sins and get it over with. "We were all growing and with our age and bulk and training as assassins, the instructors in the schools were far more brutal. Sorbacov had really given them a buffet and they embraced it, becoming more and more depraved and vile in what they chose to do to kids. So many had died, and they got away with it. The more that happened, the more children became disposable to them, the more brutal they became toward us. Czar insisted we work on developing our psychic skills and we all did, whether we thought it would work or not."

He pressed his fingers into his temples, wishing he was lying on the bed with her and she was massaging his neck and shoulders. His Scarlet. He couldn't lose her now that he'd found her. He could hear the blood roaring in his ears as loud as the pounding waves outside breaking against the rocks.

"Savage was forced to be with sadists all the time. The ones who loved to flay the skin off the boys or girls or carve their names into them. Some liked to brand them. Or pierce them. He was a favorite because he was so strong and he never made a sound. No one could break him. He caught the whip one day, pulled it out of the wielder's hand and he took over. No one stopped him. He became the whip master and the top trainer."

Again Absinthe paused. He forced himself to meet those green eyes, needing to see how deep the condemnation would go. "I had been talking to him for months, years really. Repeating the same things to him. You're a better trainer. You like what you do. You like seeing the red lines on their bodies. It makes you so hard. You want them. You can make them enjoy it. You have to be the best, better than any of them, better than all of them so they admire you and want you to train theirs for them."

He saw the comprehension dawning on her face. His voice. That velvet tone, the one that persuaded others, influenced them. Years and years of influence, from a child to an adult. He had created that sadist, that insatiable need for pain in others. That craving and addiction that would never go away.

"It wasn't just Savage. I persuaded all of them to like what they did. To need it. I didn't realize what I was doing at first. I don't think I really ever did until it was too late. We were all such a mess, bloody and broken all the time. Hating ourselves and what was happening to us. Feeling out of control. Czar set rules for us to remain human. He was our moral compass in a way. I mean, we were learning to kill and having sex in every way possible from the time we were little kids, but he made it clear that what they were doing to us was wrong, even if they made us feel good, and we were never to do that to children. Never. That was abhorrent to us and we had to repeat that daily, hundreds of times a day. We should always have one another's backs and watch over one another to make certain we never became the predators they were. We also had to grow strong enough to strike back at them and to watch out for one another and protect one another."

Scarlet set the bottle of water on the table between them and continued to regard him steadily. He couldn't see judgment in her eyes, only that comprehension of what he was telling her. He had to keep going. Why did his life have to be so damn fucked up?

"You'd think it would have gotten better when we were

older, but it didn't. It got steadily worse. Maybe we just knew more. Or the newer instructors were more brutal. Sorbacov reveled in finding really fucked-up men and women to come in to teach us how to perform under any circumstances. We had to be in control of our bodies no matter what was happening to us. I went overboard with the others, trying to help them stay in control so they weren't brutalized. God, it was so ugly. Those days. The nights. They were so vicious, Scarlet. Not human. There was no real way to fight back."

He was sweating again, and he rolled the cold bottle over his forehead, grateful for the ice chips he always made certain he had floating in the glass. Sometimes, at night especially, he couldn't get those days and nights out of his mind.

"No matter how much I talked to them, planting suggestions, or Demyan did, or sometimes the both of us working together, it never seemed enough, it was never strong enough. They came back broken and bloody. Sometimes so shattered it took everyone to put them back together. Sometimes I was in bad shape, or Demyan, and we couldn't help them. It was a bad time, so I practiced harder, studied longer, was more determined than ever to be able to use my voice to help them."

Absinthe dropped his forehead into his palm. "I had no idea what harm I was doing to them, Scarlet. None of us really thought we were going to make it out of there. So many were dying all around us. Demyan and I wanted to make what they had to do easier on them. They had no choice. None of them did. I'm not making excuses for what I did. I really didn't realize in the beginning. But there did come a time when I was aware of it."

He made that admission hastily so he couldn't take it back or leave it out. He would have to tell her no matter what. Her long lashes fluttered. There was so much pressure in his chest. His heart hurt and he rubbed over it, hoping to ease the ache.

"I tried using my voice to influence one of the girls being trained as a pony girl for a very harsh master. He had put painful shoes on her, a plug too big, and scared her so bad she could barely function. She responded to my voice and tried very hard to please him. He saw that after I spoke to her she really did whatever he asked of her and he liked that, mostly so he could humiliate her more, but still, both won a little. She didn't seem to realize it was as awful as it was or as harsh, and he got to do so much more."

Scarlet rested her chin in her palm, her green eyes never leaving his face. Again, he couldn't see condemnation, only interest.

"After that, I was asked to help train the girls in various roles for those wanting 'pets.' I tried to influence the 'masters' to be a little kinder. Some were more susceptible to my voice than others. I had to be cautious in how I worded the suggestions. The girls and boys were easier. They were younger and desperate for kindness and guidance. I found that the more I was around the kittens, the more it felt like I had a pet, someone to take care of, to cuddle and play with. I needed that. I needed that control and in return for my help, they gave me my own kitten. I knew I was saving her from a horrid master. Some of them were brutal."

He took a deep breath. "At least, that was how I justified it. In the meantime, I was still persuading the others that they liked what they did, and they were the best, stronger than any other pitted against them. I made Steele believe he could be the best surgeon no matter what they were doing to him. That Alena could cook a seven-course meal and assassinate Sorbacov's enemies right under the noses of their guards while her dessert was served to them. She wouldn't get caught; her meals were so good no one would notice if anyone was dead because they were too busy enjoying the food. It goes on and on. The worst that I am responsible for is Savage. What I did to him, what I shaped him into, is unconscionable."

He didn't wait for her to respond. "There is more. Far

more. Just let me get it out before you say anything, or I won't be able to. In that world, if you loved anyone, Sorbacov had the perfect hostage to hold over your head. You had to endure every kind of brutality or the one you loved was raped, beaten and tortured in front of you. My brother, Demyan, was taken with Steele to entertain some of Sorbacov's 'special' friends while I was held there with Sorbacov and some others. Sorbacov wanted his 'special' friends compromised, so he gave them the word that they could do whatever they wanted. He was videotaping everything. He told Demyan that as long as he cooperated, I wouldn't be hurt. He lied, of course."

Scarlet sat up straight. He saw her swallow. She shook her head, but her gaze didn't waver from his.

"I had a deal with Demyan. I had practiced holding a bridge with him—a connection between us over a distance. We were both very strong. He was older and much stronger than I was, so he usually could hold longer, but I was growing in strength. That way, we knew what was happening, even if it was ugly and brutal. At least we knew the other was alive. They didn't take him very far, just to another building a distance away on the same property, which was often the case. Sorbacov didn't want to take the chance that any of his more disturbing proclivities could leak out into the world. Suffice it to say, it got very ugly for Steele and Demyan. I was being used pretty brutally, but nothing like the two of them."

He paused, unable to breathe for a moment. His hands shook and he had to place the water bottle carefully on the table. Scarlet was very observant. She noticed, but she didn't interrupt him.

"There were whips, chains, branding irons. They carved their initials into their bodies and wrapped barbed wire around them. The worst was, they separated them. They weren't supposed to do that. No matter what was being done to me, I kept that path to Demyan. We'd been taught such control; I was able to separate myself from what was happening to me. Then, all of sudden, I don't know what happened, one of the men beating me hit me so hard I think I blacked out for a second and couldn't hold the bridge. It was gone and I couldn't get it back."

There was no holding back the despair. He wiped at his face, shocked at the feeling of the wetness on the end of his lashes and the bristles along his jaw. He forced himself to continue doggedly on. "Steele believes it was his fault that Demyan died. I couldn't bring myself to tell him the truth. I let my brother down that day, not Steele. It was my responsibility to keep him alive. We had a pact. I didn't hold him to me. I didn't keep him safe. All these years, Steele has believed he was at fault and I let him. I tried to tell him, but the words just wouldn't come. I can't man up enough to tell him because I'm so fuckin' pissed at him. At him. At Savage. At Demyan. At Alena for forcing me to stay alive and eat when I wanted to die." He shoved both hands through his hair. "Hell. Maybe at all of them. I just can't let it go."

He caught up the water bottle and took a healthy drink of the icy water because his throat was burning raw. He could barely breathe, his lungs squeezing down, refusing to work properly. His brothers were royally fucked up. Sisters too. His fault. Demyan dead. His fault. And the biggest crime of all.

"All those innocents, Scarlet. Those girls the true monsters collected. Their prizes I trained for them to put on display. I helped them. I even helped train the masters." He capped the bottle again, frowning, rubbing the ice-cold glass back and forth over his forehead. "It doesn't matter that I want my motivations to be altruistic. They weren't. I needed something. One decent thing for myself. I was going fucking crazy. I had everyone's demons in my head. Not just the others, the children's, but the instructors. Sometimes I thought I was going insane. I needed that little kitten to cuddle and take care of. To totally concentrate on. I saw to her happiness. I could make her purr all the time. I needed her to keep me sane."

His head hurt so fucking bad he was afraid it would explode. "The kittens were content when they sucked their master's cock. To them it was like getting a reward, cream from their master, their favorite treat. It calmed them. It felt good. I wasn't getting beaten or raped. I was her master and she was always happy and content. As long as the masters of the kittens and pony girls were happy, I could have my kitten. I made certain the girls were very well trained and did whatever was required of them and were happy to do so. I did what Savage did. He trained the girls and boys to like pain. I trained them to be pets."

He couldn't keep the self-loathing out of his voice. "There was one brute of a man. He chose the youngest girl. She was so scared, and he liked to hurt her. He liked to scare her. He didn't want me to train her. He didn't like me going near her. He wanted to do all of her training himself. It was an ego thing. I hated that she was so frightened all the time and one day, when I didn't think he was watching and she was sobbing, I whispered to her, pushing obedience into her mind. He went ballistic. He raged at me. I could have taken the beating. Gladly would have taken it. I was used to it. I was used to rape. It had been going on practically since I was a toddler."

Memories were close. Too close. He rolled the bottle over his pounding temple, first one side and then the other, trying to find a way to breathe. "Those girls, they just wouldn't leave it. When the other men wanted to join in— and it often happened that way, I could take that too—the girls lost their minds. They attacked. Brutus, that's what we all called him, had a huge ego and temper to match it. He was so furious. He beat them back, beat me, kicked them. They were like little rag dolls. I tried to protect them, but

he was huge and the other masters overpowered me and
dragged me out of the training hall we had."

His breath was coming too fast and he was close to hyperventilating. Getting dizzy. He forced himself to slow
down, drink another swallow of water. Get back in control.
Own up to his fuckin' sins. He was laying out his blackened
soul to his wife. Condemning Savage as a monster, a serial
killer, was naming the wrong man. She'd tied herself to the
real one.

"They all knew Brutus and they probably realized before I did what he was capable of and what he planned to
do. I couldn't conceive of that kind of evil, even after all I'd
seen. He stomped those girls, those beautiful little innocent
girls, and then doused them with an accelerant. He lit the
hall on fire and barricaded the doors, leaving them inside
to burn alive. I tried to get them out. I fucking tried with
everything I had. I couldn't stop him using my voice because the other men had their hands over my mouth. They
didn't want him killing me. Then when I ran back to try to
get them out of the burning building, Savage and Steele
stopped me."

He took another swallow of water. "I fought them off.
Demyan came. I fought them all. The building collapsed
and they were all dead. All of them including my little kitten. I hadn't saved any of them. I hadn't protected a single
one of them. They were all dead. I wanted to die too. I
made up my mind to die. I went back down to our dungeon,
that sickening place where so many others had died, and I
refused to speak or eat. I didn't care who threatened me,
raped me or beat me. I didn't respond when they threatened
anyone else. I was going to die. They'd finally broken me. I
welcomed death. Nothing Czar said, or Demyan, or Savage
or Steele mattered. Demyan's voice didn't work on me. I
just waited to die. They couldn't force me to eat."

He fell silent, raising his gaze to Scarlet's. Her green

eyes were that brilliant emerald. Tears swam in her eyes. He knew they were in his.

"Alena has a gift with food. She can make you taste anything. She can do this thing where she transfers food into you somehow when it's really nothing. I hated her. I fought her for so long. She wouldn't stop and Demyan sat with me in his lap just whispering to open my mouth, that I wanted what she was giving me. That it was the best there was and I craved it. To this day, that dish is always my favorite. Savage and Steele stayed close to make certain I didn't harm myself. One of them always guarded me. When they couldn't, it was Reaper and Czar, but it was always Savage, Steele, Demyan and Alena I blamed for keeping me alive."

Scarlet pressed her lips together tightly as if to keep from speaking. "You hunted Brutus down and killed him, didn't you?" she finally asked softly.

He nodded slowly. "All of them. Each of the masters. It took me years to find them. We didn't get out of there for a long time. We were in our twenties, still running missions for Sorbacov. I looked for them every time I was on the outside. Savage sometimes got one. Or Steele or Alena. Sometimes Reaper or Czar. I knew by the way they were killed which one of us it was. In the end, all of the masters were dead. Brutus went first and he was the one I took satisfaction in killing slow. The rest I just wanted dead. Savage never kills any of the pedophiles slow or easy and, honestly, I don't mind that in the least."

If he expected her to protest, she didn't.

"I can't sleep at night. I can't get the smell out of my head. Or the sight. I have everyone's demons running around in my head all the time and I have enough of my own demons to carry. I don't have natural erections. None of us do. We have to order our cocks to cooperate if we want relief. Our lives aren't normal. We're never going to be like other people. We're predators and we always will be no matter how hard we try to fit in. We watch each other's backs at all times to keep one another safe. That includes when we have sex. We don't think too much about it. It's just normal for us."

He shoved his hands through his hair again. "I've been a fucked-up mess all my life, Scarlet, far worse than anything you've ever imagined you've been. Anything you've ever thought you've done, you're a saint in comparison. When I told you I walked into that library and fell like a ton of bricks, I wasn't lying to you. Everything you are appealed to me. You took my breath away. More, you stilled every one of my demons. Little by little, when I was around you, you took that chaos in my mind and brought me peace. I sat at that table surrounded by books, and my cock was so hard just looking at you that half the time I was afraid I would shatter if I moved."

He sat back in the chair and looked at her. Took her in. Devoured her. It was probably going to be the last time he really got a good look at her. He could hear the ocean crashing against the rocks outside the house in the distance. His heart and soul felt battered like those rocks.

"I knew if I asked you to share my life, what I'd be asking of you. You are such an innocent in comparison to all of us. Don't get me wrong, you would be an asset to the club, you're a badass and we could count on you and build on your training. But for me, you're just a plain fucking miracle. *Moya literaturnaya ledi*, and you always will be. You're perfect. The sun rises and sets with you."

Absinthe watched her lips part. He reached casually across the table and very loosely circled her wrist with his fingers, forming a bracelet, his fingers over her pulse. She wasn't letting him into her mind, giving him back their connection, so he wanted to know every word she said was the absolute truth.

"Why do you believe you are so responsible for everything the others have become?"

"Weren't you listening to me?" He dropped his voice low so he wouldn't make the mistake of reacting negatively.

"I listened to every word. You were a child when you were taken to that place. It sounds as if most of the others were toddlers or barely above that age group as well. All of you were being abused in every way possible and just trying to stay alive. You used every means possible to keep each other alive. Those are survival instincts, right? That includes fighting back if we're fighters as well as honing psychic gifts if we have them. Am I not correct, Absinthe?"

Her voice was sweet, like a fresh breeze blowing through his mind. He'd felt that before from her. Clearing out the demons, sending them scurrying before her as if just by that simple innocent tone, so logical and sweet, the demonic images ripping him apart were dispersed. His woman carried a gun and hunted dangerous men, just as Torpedo Ink did. They were from the fires of hell. Could she be sent from heaven? An angel? Was there even such a thing? He didn't know. He'd never allowed his mind to go in that direction.

"Absinthe?" Her voice had gone gentler than ever. "Am I not correct in saying you were all just using survival instincts? We're born with those, right? You're an intelligent man. You must have read all the studies, the same as I did."

He had. Of course he had. He rubbed the pads of his fingers over her pulse. That heartbeat that connected the two of them.

"Yes, *literaturnaya ledi*, I read them. You are correct. We ran on our instincts. But later . . ."

"As teens? Trying to survive impossible circumstances? You said worse and they sounded worse. Sorbacov brought in brutal men and women. You and your brother did what each of the others did. You banded together in order to find a way to survive, your instincts kicked in. You were older, so they were more sophisticated and more developed. None of you knew if you would live. You got by minute by minute, hour by hour. Isn't that true?"

That was certainly the truth. Sometimes it felt as if it was seconds. He nodded.

"When you were beaten and raped and barely alive, the others rallied around to save you. You became a single unit to survive. You're an intelligent man, Absinthe. Step outside your emotions and think about what those teenagers were doing together. They formed a pack. A tight pack. A unit where they each played a part in order for all of them to live. They needed one another. If one went down, they all were going down. They *needed* each other. If you didn't know it at that point, the leaders certainly did. They needed your talent and your brother's talent in order for each of them to survive what was being done to them. What they were forced to do. Do you really think Savage would have stomached what he was doing if you hadn't helped him? He's strong. A fighter. He would have forced them to kill him."

"Maybe it would have been more merciful," he said, stating aloud what he'd thought so many times. "He lives in hell. He fights his inclinations every day. Sometimes I can help him, but most of the time he doesn't come to me."

"He's alive and that means he has hope."

"For what? What chance does he have?"

"You found me."

His heart jerked hard in his chest. He couldn't seem to comprehend what she said. "Scarlet . . ." He didn't know what he was going to say. Hadn't she understood him? "All those girls? Demyan? I let them down when they needed me the most. They counted on me and they died. Savage was here in our home and you were terrified. You had your own flashback because of me. I was somewhere else, taking a trip down memory lane, and I couldn't come back. That could happen anytime, anywhere, when you need me the most."

"First of all, Demyan's death was definitely not on you. Had you been connected to him, he still would have died and you know it. He disconnected, not you. You're holding a grudge against Steele because you can't face that loss. You already know this, I don't have to tell it to you. You're too intelligent not to know. At some point you had to have put your emotions aside and studied this horrid event from every angle. You know those men killed him. I assume you hunted them down as well."

"Steele killed them. Every one of them. He returned broken, a mess, but he killed them all himself," Absinthe admitted.

"That doesn't surprise me in the least."

"You're right. I did look at Demyan's death from every possible angle. I knew the highest probability was that my brother had been the one to disconnect and I had changed the way things had happened on my end in my mind because I couldn't face my brother's death. Someone was to blame. Steele or me. I wanted to condemn both of us, but you're putting the blame squarely on the shoulders of the monsters attacking the two of them. Even while you're doing it, my mind is screaming no, we were to blame. It was my responsibility. It was Steele's."

"You blame the two of you because you had already formed your pack, that tight unit, and all of you were taught to watch out for one another. Steele has to feel as guilty as you do. It's ingrained in you to watch each other's backs. In this case, neither of you were able to do so, it was an impossibility. You both have to let that go."

On some level he knew Scarlet was right, he'd always known she was right, but he couldn't accept it.

"Have a conversation with Steele, Absinthe. You both need to talk about this or you're never going to put it to rest." Scarlet kept the arm he held so loosely—but that was his lifeline—very still, but she raised the water bottle with her other hand. She took a deep breath. "You know what happened to those girls wasn't your fault. You were as much a prisoner as they were. You tried to make their lives easier. That was all you were doing, Absinthe. You know I'm not lying to you and I wouldn't. If for one minute I thought you were to blame, I'd tell you, but you weren't."

He shook his head and started to take his hand away. She turned hers up and caught his, her fingers threading through his. "Absinthe."

There it was. That voice. The one that took away the worst demons a man like him could have. Sweeping them out of his mind.

"I'm with you because I love you. I want to be with you. You have to believe in me, but even more than that, you have to believe in yourself. I really can't save you if you're not willing to save yourself. It won't be easy to change the way you think about all of this, but you're smart. Use your mind, not your emotions. Think with your brain when these things creep into your head. Come to me and we'll talk about it. And you have to find a way to forgive the others. They were doing exactly what they were taught to do. What they needed to do to survive. You're part of their pack, their unit, and they can't lose one member or they all go down."

She was right. His woman was right. He'd hit the jackpot when he'd walked into that library. He brought her hand up to his mouth, kissing her knuckles.

"I'm so tired, Scarlet. My head is killing me. I need to lay it down tonight. I know I owe you so many more explanations and apologies. But I have to sleep. I just want to hold you."

"Fireplace is off."

"I want you warm."

"I can be warm with you next to me and a ton of blankets. We'll figure things out together, Absinthe, but I'm protecting you until we do."

He framed her face with both hands. More and more he

was finding love was an overwhelming emotion. "You really are the most intelligent woman on the planet."

"I know. Just kiss me. I think that's the only thing that's going to get you out of the trouble you're always going to be getting into."

He kissed her.

SEVENTEEN

—➤✦◄—

"They're going to dry that chicken out," Mechanic observed, frowning. "Why the hell do they have someone on the barbecue that doesn't know what he's doing?"

Alena bumped him with her hip. "Did you try the potato salad? I tried to rescue it for you, but I was a little afraid that even I couldn't make it better."

"You can make rat poison palatable," Transporter said, his eyes on the large group of bikers enjoying the sun setting over the river.

The members of the Venomous club wore their colors openly as they partied right in the middle of Diamondback territory on the banks of the river. It was either very foolhardy or they were deliberately taunting the larger club in a defiant gesture to come after them.

"If the Diamondbacks start a war with them, the Feds will blame the larger club," Czar observed. "The Venomous club can plead innocence. They weren't doing anything to provoke the Diamondbacks. They're clearly willing to sacrifice a few of their members to achieve larger gains. Those higher up know what they're doing, but the ones here don't have a clue they're in harm's way. They think their brothers are looking out for them."

"They joined the wrong fuckin' club," Reaper said.

Savage shrugged. "Goes to show, men like that find one another. There's the one they call Jacko. He's the manager of the day shift at the Gypsy Club. He's in the bright red tee with his vest open. Has some woman doing him while he's eating. Nice guy, just shoved her on her ass and laughed when she fell." His voice dripped with ice.

Beside him, Destroyer was utterly still, but the temperature around him seemed to drop by several degrees.

"It's going to be dark in the club when you go in with Savage, Destroyer," Czar said. "How's your night vision?"

There was instant silence. The Torpedo Ink team had been working together since they were children. Bringing in another individual, no matter how skilled he was, could be dangerous to all of them. Savage had agreed to work with him as his partner.

"Used to keep us blindfolded," Destroyer murmured. His voice was slightly hoarse, as if somewhere along the line his throat had been damaged. "I spent a great deal of time alone so had time to practice listening for sounds. Became very accurate at finding rats scurrying in the cages with me. Could hit them precisely every time by my second year there. By my third year, I didn't need eyesight."

There was no bragging. He didn't look at any of them. He wore dark glasses most of the time. Absinthe had rarely seen him without those glasses. Up close, he was all muscle, but the kind of man that could move fast and strike hard. There was no wasted movement. When he was still, he was absolutely still. Like a mesmerizing cobra. Absinthe had the feeling that if he took off those glasses, his eyes could hypnotize his prey. He had scars everywhere. Far more numerous than those of the Torpedo Ink members— and that was saying a lot.

"You aren't eating," Alena pointed out.

Absinthe knew it cost her to even talk to the man. She didn't want any part of him but when it came to food, she didn't like anyone going hungry.

"I can make it taste better. I know it's pretty nasty," she offered reluctantly. Destroyer was the only one who hadn't handed his plate over to have her doctor it.

Storm had stolen a large bowl of potato salad right out from under the noses of the Venomous club. He'd taken it off the back of one of the trucks when they were unloading. Ice had scored the plates and silverware while Alena had somehow gotten a few spices, pickles, olives and condiments.

Destroyer shrugged. "No need. I'm used to crap food."

"Don't be an asshole martyr," Alena snapped and yanked the plate out of his hands.

Absinthe had to turn away, hiding a smile. He noticed her brothers did the same. Destroyer might tower over her, but she didn't back down from anyone. Not ever.

"The other two daytime managers for the other clubs down there as well?" Czar asked, ignoring the byplay between his newest team member and Alena.

Absinthe knew Czar never missed anything. He was well aware of the tension between them. Alena wasn't happy Destroyer was a member of their chapter and Destroyer was well aware of it. He simply didn't care. No one could survive the prison he'd been in for the years he had without becoming one tough, brutal being. He was an enigma.

Absinthe had faith in the president of Torpedo Ink. Czar had never steered them wrong or misjudged anyone. He had personally vouched for Destroyer. That meant he knew more than the rest of them. He might not feel it was his right to share everything with them, but he believed in the man. That was enough for Absinthe. Clearly, it wasn't for Alena and it might not be for some of the others. Destroyer would have to prove himself, although it looked as if he wasn't in a hurry to make that happen.

"Wings is there, just to the left of Jacko. He's daytime manager for the Felix Club," Savage identified.

"Wings is reputed to have been the one to decide the fate of the woman they chose as their example for the other women to cooperate," Absinthe said. "He came up with the punishment and wrote it all down step by step and sent it to the other managers so they'd all know exactly what to do when they took her. Code sent the emails to us. I read them and you know once I get that shit in my head, I can't get it out."

He rubbed at his neck, wishing Scarlet was there. He'd left her with Steele's team. He knew they'd guard her, but he didn't like the separation, especially on the heels of their traumatic wedding night. They didn't have the best start to their marriage, but she was sticking with him. He didn't know how much sleep she'd actually gotten the night before. He'd been so exhausted after his flashback and confessing everything to her that he'd fallen asleep almost immediately.

Scarlet was dozing when he'd woken in the middle of the night and kissed his way down her body, burying his mouth between her legs, waking her fully, devouring her until she was screaming for mercy. He'd buried himself in her again and again, looking into her green eyes, watching her face when she came apart, seeing the love there. It undid him. Overwhelmed him. It was almost unbelievable to think that she could feel that much for him when he'd told her the truth about his past, but it was there on her face and he was holding her hands, his cock buried deep, and there was no way for her to lie to him.

She had been the one to come to him close to dawn when he was sitting on the edge of the bed, nightmares close. She crawled off the bed, her body feline, sensual, her body movements so perfectly like a cat that he couldn't stop looking at the way her muscles moved beneath her skin as she crawled up to him. He parted his thighs, beckoning his kitten to him. Immediately she responded, purring, crawling sensuously, rubbing along his inner thigh with her body, her hair, her cheek. She licked with her tongue, sending fire racing up his groin. His cock responded. Then she lapped at his sac so his balls tightened at the exquisite feeling. Her nails kneaded his muscle and her teeth nipped along his inner thigh then her tongue worked him, sliding up his balls to curl and tease along the base of his shaft.

He had dropped his hand in her hair and sighed contentedly, demons dispersing under her ministrations. He had been remembering how he had tried so hard to die. To just slip away after he had lost all those he had trained. Demyan had held him while Lana sang to comfort him. Steele healed his vicious wounds. The others had watched over him. All the while Demyan had whispered to him day and night about the kittens and how he needed them. How he loved them and wanted them to comfort him. How he had to care for them.

Demyan told him repeatedly that there was a kitten somewhere out in the world, one in desperate need of him, to take care of her, to provide for her, give her food and water. Give her special treats, the warmth of his cock. She wanted to snuggle with him. Show off for him with his brothers only so she was always safe. She couldn't have any of those things without him. It was the only way they had gotten him to come back.

Scarlet had a mouth on her to rival the best of the best and she used it to give him paradise. She didn't have her tail in and he missed seeing it, the way it rose up in between her gorgeous cheeks, a furry declaration of pride and sass, but it didn't matter, she didn't take her green eyes from his. There was love in her eyes and he needed that more than he needed a tail. She was his kitten, his *kiska*. She was his wife. His everything, because she *chose* to be. He hadn't ordered her. He hadn't used his voice.

Absinthe closed his eyes, reliving those few moments

after with her, holding her in his arms, wanting her to know she was his world and he would spend his life making her happy. He tried to tell her, but she just kissed his throat and snuggled back into his arms, sliding right back into sleep. She was naked and warm, and he had gone to sleep as well, this time undisturbed by the demons in his past.

Something white came at the side of his head and he picked a wadded-up napkin out of the air. Storm grinned at him. "You're looking goofy. Ice gets that look when Soleil is under the table on the balcony in the morning giving him head while we're trying to have a discussion about the price of gold going up."

"Bullshit," Ice said. "You're jacking off, not talking."

"I was *trying* to talk. It's a little difficult when you two go at it. She gets very enthusiastic. And you're always pointing to your feet and then taking off her top when we're having breakfast. What the hell do you expect?" Storm defended. "I like watching. It's a fuckin' turn-on."

Absinthe wasn't certain how to feel about that. He'd had a hand in that as well. Exhibitionism and voyeurism. The twins had been beautiful children and had been forced to perform continually for Sorbacov and his friends. Demyan and Absinthe had tried to help them overcome their reluctance and disgust. Now it was ingrained in them to want, even need, the sexual gratification of both traits. He sighed. Scarlet would tell him to let it go. Maybe she was right.

He glanced at Destroyer. He hadn't been raised with them. He'd been in a prison, a completely different environment. There was no way to know what he was thinking. No expression crossed his face and those dark glasses were very dark, hiding his eyes. He might not have heard any of the exchange, although Absinthe knew better.

Alena handed him the plate of potato salad. Destroyer murmured a polite and succinct "Thanks" before she could turn away. She nodded abruptly without looking at him. Absinthe didn't think they were going to be friends any time soon. He couldn't tell with Ice and Storm. Her brothers hadn't given any indication of where they were leaning as far as Destroyer was concerned. Savage and Reaper were the kind of men who were black or white. If he made one wrong move, they'd kill him. If he worked with the team, he was part of Torpedo Ink and welcome.

"Coming up the embankment is Holler, the last one of the day managers. He manages the Devil's Palace. That's the most hedonistic club. They have quite a back room set up and a basement with a bullshit dungeon," Savage informed them. "Guess they don't want trouble with the cops because nothing in that dungeon is the real deal."

"Too bad," Reaper commented. "You would have some fun with these boys. They'd find out they don't know shit about what they were doing with that woman."

"They'll find out," Savage said. "I'll re-create their work and critique it for them."

He stood up and stretched, a lazy ripple of muscle, much like a panther. "You about done with that salad, Destroyer? Thought we'd take Holler since he's so set on givin' us the opportunity."

Destroyer nodded and handed Alena his empty plate. "Big difference," he admitted. "You've got a rare talent."

She'd opened her mouth to protest that he'd given her the dirty paper plate to dispose of but pressed her lips together at the compliment. Destroyer sauntered off, not a whisper of movement or sound even in the grass following in his wake.

Ice and Storm were all business, both retrieving sniper rifles to cover the two men as they crossed the asphalt-covered parking area to intercept Holler as he came toward the upper parking lot where the vehicles, mostly motor-cycles, had been left. A couple of bored prospects guarded the bikes but paid no attention to the trucks and two cars the women had brought to carry chairs and food. The prospects had their backs to the stairs carved into the side of the embankment Holler climbed.

Destroyer casually wrapped the Venomous club member up as he swaggered past, one hand over his mouth, muffling any sound, while Savage injected him directly in the neck, putting him to sleep almost immediately. The two carried him back to the other end of the lot where Torpedo Ink's trucks and cars were parked along with several others enjoying the sunset. It took all of five seconds to finish stowing him under a tarp.

Savage glanced at his watch. "Wings and Jacko have a little rendezvous planned in a few minutes with an underage girl they've been corresponding with online. They'll be coming up those stairs any moment. We'll have to be their welcoming committee. She's very young. Black hair. Hot as hell. Sent them her picture and everything. Wearing a string bikini to show them her smokin'-hot bod."

Destroyer glanced at Alena, who patted the short black wig she wore. She opened the little button-up shirt she had on, showing her generous breasts nearly falling out of the triangles held up by two strings. She had flawless skin dotted by tiny freckles that made her look even younger than usual. She batted her eyelashes at Mechanic and Transporter as she closed the shirt she wore.

Absinthe noticed she avoided looking at Destroyer. It was impossible to tell if he was looking at her, although who wouldn't look at her? She was beautiful, even in a black wig. She was a true platinum blond, just as Ice and Storm were, but somehow, she still managed to pull off the black hair.

"They'll definitely be looking at you and not anywhere around them," Transporter said, grinning. "You're on, babe. Don't draw the attention of the prospects by walking like a model."

Alena rolled her eyes. "Since when am I an amateur?"

She swung a thick coat around her, making her look shorter and much blockier. When she walked, she hunched, shuffled her feet and kept her head down, hands in her pockets. Absinthe noted one of the prospects glanced toward Alena as she made her way toward the two restrooms at the end of the parking lot. Her steps were slow and measured, almost plodding. He looked away immediately. Absinthe wasn't worried about her anyway. Ice and Storm had rifles trained on the two prospects at all times.

Savage and Destroyer waited until the prospects were once again staring down at their phones, uncaring what any of the civilians were doing in the lot as long as they didn't approach the bikes. The two loosely followed Alena, spread out so they took up residence on either side of the stairway leading to the river below. Hidden in the dense brush, they disappeared completely.

Alena shrugged off the bulky coat, laid it on top of the stairs, opened her top to reveal her breasts in the little bikini and waited until she caught sight of the two Venomous club members coming toward her. She stood and, like an impatient and nervous teen, began to hop from one foot to the other and bite on one fingernail. The movement sent her breasts bouncing, drawing the eyes of both men. They approached her, grinning, their leering gazes trained on the tiny triangles that couldn't quite contain her full, rounded flesh.

Savage was on Jacko while Destroyer pushed the needle easily into Wings's neck. Transporter drove the truck right to the edge of the lot, allowing the two men to dump the bodies into the bed of the truck and cover them with the tarp. Savage tied the tarp down tightly, leapt into the back with Destroyer and signaled Transporter they were good to go.

Alena caught up the coat, wrapped it around her and assumed the same shuffling walk back to the second truck, where she climbed into the back of the cab. Ice appeared carrying a case and slid into the front passenger seat beside Mechanic, who was driving. They pulled away. Czar, Code and Reaper followed in an Audi.

Absinthe and Storm fell in behind them, bringing up the

rear in an older-model Dodge Viper that had a powerful racing engine Mechanic and Transporter had designed. It performed like a miracle and could outrun just about anything on the road. Absinthe had to admit, he loved driving the very deceptive-looking car. Each of the other vehicles had a performance engine designed by the two men so the vehicle could handle and make a run if necessary.

Transporter drove to the location they had already scoped out and deposited the three Venomous club members inside the stuffy, dilapidated barn. It was out in the middle of an abandoned property Code had found that had been put up for sale several years earlier that no one had wanted because there was no water available to it. For Savage and Destroyer, it was perfect for their needs—away from everyone with zero chance of anyone overhearing screams.

Savage dragged Wings out of the truck by his boots, not paying attention as the man grunted and thrashed, starting to come around as he hit the dirt and bounced over the rocks and debris leading to the barn. "We've got plenty of time before we have to pick up the night managers. Torch will do her thing to the two clubs after hours. These assholes will be left at the Gypsy Club on the stage."

Destroyer caught Holler by his neck, flung him over the side of the truck onto the ground with more ease than one might expect and reached for Jacko. The Venomous club member had come out from under the drug enough to try to pull a weapon out from under his jacket. Destroyer casually slapped it away and drove his gloved fist into Jacko's mouth. His fist was wide, and his knuckles shattered the man's teeth as if they were glass. Just as if he weighed no more than a doll, Destroyer picked Jacko up and threw him into the rocky dirt beside his moaning friend.

Savage leaned down and began to strip Holler of weapons. Destroyer did the same for Jacko. They tossed the guns, knives and brass knuckles into the back of the truck. Later, they'd leave them on the stage at the Gypsy Club with the bodies of the Venomous club managers. When Holler tried to rise up and fight, Destroyer casually kicked him squarely in the face, his motorcycle boot striking him hard in the jaw. Holler fell to the ground, his eyes rolling in his head. Destroyer picked him up, slung him over his shoulder and carried him inside the barn, where he threw him down beside Wings. Savage followed with Jacko.

"They brought plenty of condoms with them. Guess they planned to use them on the underage girl they lured to them," Savage commented.

The three men were stripped naked and tied to the rickety supports holding up the tilted loft above their heads. Facing them was a screen brought in and set up ahead of time. Code had meticulously prepared the presentation for Savage. Their tools were laid out on the floor on a tarp. They didn't much care about blood getting on the floor, but they were bringing the tools back with them and didn't want them ruined.

Destroyer doused the three men with buckets of icy water, making certain they were awake. Savage smiled at them. "Good of you to finally join us. I have a little surprise for you, kind of a walk down memory lane." He put the first slide up, a picture of a beautiful, smiling, very vivacious woman. "I'm sure you all remember her."

The three men exchanged worried looks. Jacko moaned, blood dribbling down his chin, and he spit several times.

"What do you want?" Holler mumbled, his jaw already swollen on one side.

"Her name was Diane. Diane Miller. She was a single mother and had two kids. She worked at the Felix Club stripping. When she went to work, the policy was she didn't have to do more than strip. If she wanted to do lap dances in the back room, that was her prerogative and she got the tip money and was paid extra for that. If she wanted to make arrangements beyond that, she was protected and, again, it was all up to her. Your club made it mandatory to do it all and she got nothing for it. She protested that shit along with the other girls, so you decided to make an example out of one of them. Wings, you chose her."

Before any of them could protest, Savage put the next slide up, the email that had gone out to all the managers with the step-by-step details of exactly what they were going to do to Diane Miller. Her picture was on the email. She was in her stripper costume.

"Just so there's no mistakes, I had the steps written in very large letters with bullet points," Savage explained when he changed slides to show the step-by-step instructions in much larger print. "Destroyer wears those dark glasses of his and I don't want to take chances that he might miss a step. Now, I know we're only two here, not six of you, and I don't like to brag, but your pussy floggers were shit. I brought the real thing and I'm damn good with a bullwhip. Destroyer claims he's no slouch, so I want to see what he's got. That might make up for the lack of manpower. I think we can pull it off, and we do have a pole waiting at the Gypsy Club to hang you off of later tonight," he assured.

Holler struggled in the ropes. "You're crazy. Do you have any idea who we are?"

Savage went forward several slides until he found the one of Diane Miller's bloody body, hanging upside down on the pole of the stage at the Felix Club. "You're the ones who did that to a single mother trying to make a living for her children."

He put the slide back up of the step-by-step instructions and glanced at Destroyer. "Which one you want to start with?"

"Don't much care. They all look like dead meat to me," Destroyer said.

"I think we should leave Wings for last. He seems to be the brains behind all this. Holler is the idiot who believes no one can touch him because he's part of a pussy club challenging the Diamondbacks. Too stupid to live." Savage shook his head. "Those running your club sent you here as sacrifices. They knew the Diamondbacks would eat you alive."

He slashed through the ropes binding Holler to the support beam and dragged him by his hair into the middle of the room, where he bent him over a sawhorse, anchoring his hands to the ground by a ring in the floor on one side and both ankles to rings they'd drilled into the flooring on the other, leaving his legs spread wide.

Savage indicated the array of tools to Destroyer. Destroyer took his time. There were several types of wicked-looking whips, some with serrated edges on the leather. There were branding irons and piercing tools. Canes. Thin long strips of wood with holes drilled every few inches. Others with nails sticking out. A cattle prod hooked up to an electrical device was very prominent. The condoms the men had brought were scattered in plain view for them to see.

"We've got plenty of time. The clubs don't close down until two and then it's at least another hour until the others will bring us the night managers so we can work on them. Take your choice. Let's see what you got," Savage encouraged.

Destroyer looked over the various tools of the trade and chose a long, lethal-looking bullwhip. He tested the weight in his hand. "Nice." He shook it out and then cracked it.

Holler yelped, jumping, his skin jerking, and he hadn't been hit. Wings snickered, a nervous giggle escaping.

Savage chose a smaller, wicked whip, one that cut deep when wielded properly. He was a master at delivering a proper stroke. He indicated Destroyer start. "Warm up. He looks a little cold to me."

⌒

"We're looking at a first-class setup, Czar," Code said. "Cameras positioned every twenty to thirty feet, all trained on the entrances and exits to the clubs. There are new emails

exchanged between Haley Joico and the president of the
Sacramento chapter of the Diamondbacks. Assurances are
made that her club will be torched, and she'll sell to them
once she collects the money. She allowed them to install
cameras both outside and inside the club and she's been
feeding them information on what the Venomous club is
doing as well as the whereabouts of their managers. Of
course, she doesn't know they were picked up and delivered
to Savage and Destroyer. She's been their source in spite of
making money off the VC. She's playing both sides."

"She's going to end up dead," Czar said. "Diamondbacks know she can't be trusted."

"Look to your left. Pierce is there, up on the roof across
the street. He's not Sacramento chapter. Why would he be
here?" Code asked, not looking at Alena.

"Because he's screwing me," Alena said, before anyone
could answer. "They think he'll spot one of us before anyone else. They're wrong."

Czar glanced at Absinthe. Absinthe fucking hated it when
Czar gave him that subtle sign to check on one of their own,
but he had no choice. He shifted closer to Alena and kept his
eyes on her.

"Has Pierce heard anyone refer to you as Torch?" Czar
asked.

"No one calls me that ever unless we're together in the
clubhouse as just our family. You don't allow that anymore,
Czar," Alena pointed out. "As far as I know, no one's ever
broken that rule in front of him."

Absinthe waited until Czar again shifted his gaze just
for that millionth of a second and he nodded. Alena wasn't
lying.

"He's just doing his job for his club," Alena added. "The
same as any of us would do, Czar. He's not betraying me. He
has no idea I'm here. They want proof of what we're doing so
they can run us. That's all. We'd do the same thing."

"I didn't say he was doing anything wrong, honey," Czar

said gently. "You don't need to defend him. I'm asking to protect you, that's all. Your protection comes before anything or anyone else. That's the way it works in our club and that's the way it always will. You know that. You're getting too sensitive and I'm not sure why."

Alena ducked her head. "I'm not sure either," she admitted. "I'm feeling very scattered, all over the place. I think, sometimes, I just need to go somewhere quiet and be really still."

Absinthe flashed her smile. "I go to the library. You need to find your place, babe. Go to the beach alone. Cooking used to help you, but you turned it into your business. It won't work the same for you anymore. You need to find a new way to still your mind."

She nodded. "I know. I've known for a little while that I was starting to have trouble. I'll work on it, Czar."

"You need help, honey, you come to me," Czar said.

Ice slung his arm around his sister's shoulders. "I should have been paying more attention to you, Alena. I've been so wrapped up in Soleil lately, I haven't looked outside us. I'm sorry."

Alena rubbed the back of her head against her brother's shoulder. "Don't think that way. I love that you have Soleil. I love her for you. I want Storm to find someone that's equally that perfect for him." She looked up at the roof across the street. "When I'm around Pierce, I think things are good, but he's Diamondback and I'm Torpedo Ink. That's never going to change. There he is on that side and I'm over here."

"He doesn't have a clue what a fucking badass you are either," Reaper said. "That's the beauty of it. He sees us. He hasn't convinced Plank or the others what we are, but he's never, not one time, figured out that when he takes you to bed, you could end his life in a heartbeat."

"No, he doesn't give me that kind of respect," Alena admitted. "At first I thought it was a good thing. I'd always have the advantage. But now, there's a part of me that's a little bothered by the fact that he's been seeing me for a while and he still hasn't seen the real me. He hasn't looked that deep."

"Have you seen him?" Absinthe asked. "Are you certain you see the real Pierce, or are you taking him on the surface as well because for some reason he makes you feel still in your mind for just a little while?"

Alena sighed. "Hell if I know anymore, Absinthe. I think I'll join a nunnery. Do they even have nunneries? Are they called that?" She turned her attention to the job at hand. "How many Diamondbacks are out there waiting for us? Are we running a gauntlet, Code?"

"You're staying right here, Alena," Storm said. "You don't need to go near that club. Reaper will go in and make certain no one's inside. That's his forte, slipping past anyone unseen. We'll make certain he's safe. Once we know everyone's out, you torch the place from here. Make certain the fire department can't get it out until it's all the way to the ground."

"I like to make certain myself no one is in the building," Alena protested. "You know that. That way I know there isn't a mistake."

"Reaper will give you that assurance," Czar said in a tone that brooked no argument. "We don't want any other buildings to go up," he added.

"Czar, really?" Alena asked. "I'm not that distracted."

He grinned at her. "Just checking. The nearest building is across the parking lot and Pierce is on the roof. I thought you might just jump a flame or two his way to knock him off and shake him up."

"Now that you say that . . ." She laughed, but it was a little forced.

Ice ruffled the hair of her black wig. "Let's do it. Reaper's going in. Be a ghost, bro."

Reaper saluted and backed away from the heavy landscaping surrounding the mini-mall on the other side of the island that was the Felix Club. The mall was two stories high and had a small parking garage where they had stashed their vehicles.

Ice and Storm took vantage points high in order to cover Reaper. Pierce was their first target. He was lying on the roof across the street from the Felix Club, with a pair of binoculars. Another member of the Diamondbacks had taken up watch on the opposite corner, also watching the club with binoculars. The club was surrounded. They weren't alone on the parking garage either. They'd had to be careful, hiding almost in plain sight.

Ice and Storm, bring in heat lightning, just enough to make it seem natural to disrupt cameras.

No such thing, Czar.

You know what the hell I mean.

There was a little snicker, but at once in the dark overhead, lightning forked in every direction streaking across the sky, over and over.

Mechanic, I want every camera down. Every last one. You got that? In the club and out. I don't want Reaper accidentally caught on any camera, not even a shadow of him, Czar ordered.

No problem, Mechanic said. His body radiated enough energy to disrupt electrical signals and he'd learned to actually direct that energy. It had taken years of practice to be able to do so but he was very good at it.

He's in, Absinthe reported grimly. He detested not being able to have his eyes on his brother. Normally, Savage would be with him. Reaper had made it clear he preferred to go in alone, that anyone else would be a liability.

All they could do was wait. The Felix Club was large. Reaper had to search every room to make certain no one was inside, no janitor was working or sleeping in the basement. No homeless person had pried open a window and was using the basement as a place to rest. Fifteen minutes later, Absinthe spotted Reaper's shadow. He gave the thumbs-up and was back in the brush, moving with the landscape toward the line of parked cars.

Alena didn't waste time. If the club was suddenly on fire, it was the perfect distraction to provide, no one would be looking for Reaper. Everyone would be concentrating on rushing to the club itself in order to find whoever had torched the place. The Diamondbacks would want to retrieve the outside cameras before the fire department and police got there. They hadn't seen anyone enter the club or leave it. Alena didn't need to get near it in order to burn it to the ground. She had the fire burning hot, the flames rolling wildly, windows blowing out, the air feeding the hungry inferno until the roof was engulfed as well.

One by one the members of Torpedo Ink returned to their vehicles. They left before the place was overrun with police, fire and other emergency vehicles, and drove straight to the Devil's Palace to once again find they ran into the same setup, the Diamondbacks waiting for them.

They'd been set up by the club asking for help. Still, Czar ran their operation like clockwork. Once again, after determining that no one was inside, Devil's Palace was burned to the ground. The Diamondbacks would find that none of the cameras had been recording, including in the parking garages.

They were to meet Savage, Destroyer and Transporter with the six deceased members of the Venomous club at the Gypsy Club. This would be the most dangerous time for all of them. It wasn't going to be easy to get all six bodies of the managers into the club without the Diamondback sentries seeing.

Savage and Destroyer carefully transferred their equipment from their truck to Absinthe's car. Transporter would be driving the Dodge Viper home. Bringing the tools of the trade, weapons and the patches of the Venomous club would fall to Transporter. The weapons and patches would be turned over to the Diamondbacks. There would be nothing incriminating in the truck that Absinthe would be driving.

A few blocks from the Gypsy Club, the Torpedo Ink team parked their vehicles and slipped out, spreading out. Each had large oily blankets to create smoke. Czar went to the highest rooftop with Code and the night-vision high-powered binoculars.

Two on roof of the restaurant across the street from the Gypsy Club. The wind is blowing away from them. Ice, Storm, you'll have to deal with that. You've got two on the balcony of the two-story residence. I believe that is owned by Joico. All the windows are dark, but I caught a glimpse of movement on the lower story, front window. That might be a problem.

No problem, Czar, Storm replied. *Lightning flashes are blinding after staring into the dark. We'll light up the night when Savage is going in.*

Let's get it done fast then. Cameras need to come down, Mechanic.

On it, Mechanic replied with confidence.

Ice, Storm, start occasional lightning in the distance so the approaching weather front is believable. Savage, Destroyer, Transporter, be ready.

Standing by.

Torch, light the decoys. Ice and Storm, bring up the winds and lightning.

Within minutes the air was filled with smoke, covering the rooftops where the sentries were stationed. Lightning flashed bright and hot in front of the residence, nearly crashing right into the windows and onto the roof, shaking the structure and throwing the Diamondbacks to the ground. Savage, Destroyer and Transporter carried the six dead bodies of the day and night managers into the Gypsy Club, where Reaper waited for them.

They took the bodies straight to the stage and strung

Wings upside down on the pole exactly as the managers had Diane, leaving the other bodies on the stage floor with the emails of the step-by-step instructions of what they were going to do to the stripper to ensure all the other girls would comply.

We're done here, Reaper reported. *Bring us out.*

Czar gave the order and once more lightning flashed and the winds went wild. Smoke swirled around the buildings and rose into the air. Alena collected the oily blankets one by one, rolled them up to put out the smoldering ruins of material and placed them carefully in the disposable garbage bags she'd brought with her.

Torpedo Ink slipped into the various vehicles and began the four-hour journey home.

EIGHTEEN

"We've divided you children into groups according to where we think you'll be for weapons and self-defense training," Absinthe announced. "The older children will go with Lana, Preacher, Reaper and Maestro. Lucia, Benito, Kenny, Darby, the four of you go with them now and they'll take care of you. You'll be receiving more advanced training. The program we've put together calls for training every other week, but that means practicing on your part daily. You have to be dedicated. All of you, not just the older ones."

He waited until the older ones got up from where they sat in the grass and followed the four Torpedo Ink members across the field to where they would be working. The other children nodded at him, acknowledging that they would practice.

The little ones looked at him very wide-eyed and it took all he had not to smile. Little Emily was so cute it was heart-stopping. He decided he needed a little daughter just like Emily, with Scarlet's bright red hair.

"The middle group will go with Ice, Storm, and Ink.

Siena and Zoe and Nicia, you'll be with them. Again, whatever you work on, you'll have to practice at home and when you come back to class in two weeks, we expect that you'll have it down. Czar only gave us a week to practice and hone our skills before he gave us our next assignments, so you're getting extra time." He waved them toward Ice, Storm and Ink.

They'd decided ahead of time that it would be good to have one-on-one help. So each child would have an instructor to watch over them. The older and middle-aged children were going to be using deadly weapons and they wanted to ensure they were safe. He waited until they had gone with their instructors to their designated area at the corner of the field almost out of sight of the younger children. Absinthe thought it best if the younger children weren't so reliant on the older ones for comfort and aid. He wanted them to try to make their own decisions and work on their own during the time he had with them.

"Emily, you and Jimmy are with Alena and me. We'll be teaching you some very interesting techniques that will help you with all sorts of self-defense and weapons skills down the line. Give us a couple of minutes to set up."

He kept a watchful eye on Jimmy, Czar's newest son. The boy wouldn't meet his eyes and continually looked as if he might bolt at any moment. Emily, Czar's youngest daughter, sat close to the boy and held his hand. Jimmy clung to her but looked at the motorcycles and the various bikers and the colors they wore with a mixture of apprehension and hope.

"Where's Savage?" Alena asked as she placed a set of colored rocks in front of each child. "Shouldn't he be here? He said he'd come."

"Had a hard time lately," Absinthe said. "Knows an underground club in the Bay and decided it was best to go there for a day or two and get it out of his system. Said he'd be back tonight."

"And our newest member?"

"He went to watch Savage's back." Absinthe placed the wall Master and Player had built for him made up of wood with a multitude of small holes set at different heights across from the children. "Someone had to, and we had this gig. Savage knew he couldn't get back in time."

"I'll just bet he went to watch Savage's back. He's probably just like Savage, needing to fight in the clubs and then go after the women."

"There's nothing wrong with Savage, Alena," Absinthe said, keeping his voice low. "Any more than the rest of us. He thinks there isn't any hope for him, but he's saved my life more than once. I resented him for it too. I resented you."

"I *had* to save you, Absinthe. You were starving yourself to death." Her voice dripped with tears. She didn't pretend to misunderstand him, although the confrontation had been so many years earlier. "None of us could let you go. You're part of my soul. Part of all our souls."

"I know that now. I just didn't know that then." He slung his arm around her neck and brushed her cheek with his lips. "Thank you for saving my life. I didn't appreciate it then, but I do now. And just so you know, Savage is a good man regardless of what he thinks about himself. I see inside of him and I know what's there. He might have to battle demons in his mind, but in his soul, where it counts, he's golden."

Alena glanced down at her hands. "I didn't mean to imply I thought Savage was wrong for what he does. We all have our strange needs. They seem right to us, but weird to everyone else." She shrugged. "He's my brother. I guess, someday, Destroyer will fit with us too." She didn't sound as if she believed what she was saying.

"He didn't grow up with us, Alena, so it's bound to be much more difficult to accept him. That will come. Savage said Destroyer didn't shirk at all. That he took his back and no matter what was required of him, he did it without flinching. Although, I think both of them were more scared of these kids than they were of fucking up six members of the Venomous club."

Alena laughed and turned with him back to Emily and Jimmy. Absinthe sat down in front of the children and picked up one of the rocks, letting it slip through his fingers again and again to drop into his palm. "When we were kids, even younger than you, some very bad people murdered our parents and took us to an awful place so they could do bad things to us."

They had agreed that in order for the children to identify with them, particularly Jimmy, they would have to allow the children to know the same things had happened to them. They didn't know how to whitewash anything. They didn't have social graces or know how to talk gently to children. No one read them bedtime stories. They were going to try to help these children, but they were doing it their way. Bluntly. Following their path. What had helped them.

"Everyone has to decide for themselves what they're going to do when they find themselves in a situation where someone takes them from their home and family. We decided we needed to fight back. Czar taught us how. He was just a boy himself, but he figured things out using what we had right there. That's why he's president of Torpedo Ink and we all look up to him and listen to what he says."

Emily nodded. "That's why he's our dad, right, Absinthe?"

"That's right, baby. And that's why you always listen to what Czar says. His word is law. You don't keep things from him. You always tell him the truth. He can figure it out, even when you're scared. He might look scary mean, but he always comes up with a solution."

Emily nodded. "He kisses me good night. So does Mama Blythe." She squeezed Jimmy's hand. "They make things better."

Absinthe nodded. "Like I said, we didn't have much, we were just little kids, but we developed some wicked skills and I'm going to teach you those and the progression of each of the weapons you can make and how to use them if you need to."

That got Jimmy's entire attention. He suddenly turned his gaze fully on Absinthe. The kid was heartbreaking. He could see why Czar and Blythe were desperate enough to want Torpeko Ink to find a way to help them break through to the boy. He'd been taken by a man called "the Collector" and sold to a very wealthy pedophile who kept him for six years. Torpedo Ink had discovered him when Jimmy had been put up for auction online and they set out to find him and retrieve him.

The Collector found single parents, men or women without too many family members and very young children, babies even, took pictures of the toddlers and made up brochures. Those went out to exclusive websites, specifically those of very wealthy clients looking for children they could have without fear of interference. If they chose one of the Collector's toddlers, he murdered the family, took the child and was paid a fortune. Jimmy came from the Collector. The boy was new to the family. He'd only been with them a few short months and was still very nervous and unbelieving that he was safe.

Alena sank into the grass beside Absinthe. "The cool thing about these weapons is no one can ever detect that you even have them on you. Not ever. We started this way, with just little rocks and acorns to practice with until we became so accurate, we never miss. Never. And you won't either, if you practice the way we did."

She picked up one of the rocks, still sitting, half turned and sent the rock flying so fast it hummed in the air and shot right through one of the holes.

Emily and Jimmy both gasped, eyes widening and then exchanged grins. Jimmy reached down and picked up one of the rocks, his fingers moving over the smooth surface.

"Czar would have penalized me for showing off. We

were never supposed to make any noise. Not ever. You don't give yourself away. You don't want your prey to ever suspect you. You're the child. The innocent. Even if you're the only one in the room that could have done it, you have to perfect the look of innocence. Never be smug. Never have an ego. Never brag. Never show off. Never tell anyone that is not one of the brothers. That means Torpedo Ink. That's who you are. Torpedo Ink. This is your family and it always will be. What we say here stays here with us."

Emily nodded solemnly. "That's what Daddy Czar tells us all the time, right, Jimmy?"

Jimmy nodded. He looked as if he might say something, but he didn't make a sound.

"So, what we're going to do now," Absinthe said, "is start practicing. Emily has the red rocks because that's her favorite color. Soleil painted them for you. She put all those pretty little flowers on them, Emily. You'll be able to tell they're yours. You have twelve of them. Jimmy, you like blue. You've met Soleil. She's married to Ice. She painted the ocean on all of your rocks because Blythe told her you like the ocean. Each rock is varied, but all of them have various shades of blue and the ocean is acting different. You also have twelve."

Alena and Absinthe moved back out of the way.

"You're going to take turns throwing. You want to use a quick pitch, side arm. That's the first throw you're going to learn. At first your rock might not get to the wall and it can be frustrating. That's okay," Alena continued. "The point is to learn the arm movement. I'll help you with that. You need that very slight movement, so no one notices. You can actually practice it without anything in your hand. It just helps to have the rock in your palm. Sometimes, hold it without letting anyone see it." She demonstrated, concealing the rock in her fist and making the quick flick with her arm and wrist.

"Emily," Absinthe said. "You try."

Emily nodded solemnly and did her best. It was clear Jimmy couldn't wait to make his try. For being so young, the two stuck at it far longer than Absinthe thought they would. By the time the hour was up, they were actually hitting the wall with their rocks.

~

"What you're learning today, girls, is seemingly not a lesson in self-defense, but it really is. It's important to know. I'm going to tell you straight up that if you're caught using what we teach you for anything you shouldn't, like shoplifting, or stealing for personal gain, we will be very disappointed in you and the club will punish you in ways you don't ever want to know about. Am I making myself clear?" Ink said.

Nicia and Siena, Max's two girls, and Zoe, Czar's daughter—all three stared at him with wide eyes and nodded their heads solemnly, looking like they might faint. Ice had to turn his head away to keep from smiling. His little Zoe was always so somber. Nicia and Siena were as well. Ink could look very scary with his tattoos and his frowns.

"You need to learn to pick pockets. There might be times when someone will take your identity, or you will have to know theirs but will want to return it without them knowing. You have to be so good that you won't get caught. That means you have to be able to take a wallet or remove a weapon from anywhere on your enemy without them feeling you take it," Ink continued. "That's what you'll be practicing today."

Storm unveiled the three dummies they'd hung from several trees—two men and a woman. One was dressed in a business suit. One in jeans, T-shirt and vest. One in a dress with a purse. All of them had a multitude of bells hanging from various pockets and lapels.

"We have a list of items each of you will have to retrieve from each of the dummies without ringing the bells," Ice said. "I'm going to show you how to do it and then, one by one, you're going to try it. It can be frustrating, but the idea is to have fun with it. Don't get upset when you're not perfect first time out. Zoe, you always think you have to know what you're doing immediately. This isn't like that. It's a skill, which means it takes practice. You have to do it over and over to be good at it. Absinthe said you'll need to practice over the next two weeks before coming back to show us how good you are at it."

The three girls followed Ice to the first dummy and watched while he retrieved each item Storm called out to him to take from the "businessman."

"Each of you are wearing the jeans Lana sent you ahead of time," Maestro said. "At least you'd better be, or you can leave class now." He looked at the four kids sitting in the grass in front of him, waiting to see if any of them had disobeyed the dictates of the email that had been sent along with the delivery.

No one moved. Maestro nodded. "Good. We might as well just get to it. I know that Czar and Max have worked with you on shooting various guns. We'll train with knives, but today we're going to be working with garrotes. Lana sewed one into either seam along the sides of your jeans. The garrote is very thin and rarely can be detected."

Benito, Max's son, broke out into a huge smile, exchanging grins with Kenny, Czar's son. "Cool," Benito said. He felt along his jeans. Kenny did the same.

"It can't be detected," Maestro repeated, "otherwise it's useless to you."

"Is there a problem, girls?" Lana challenged as Darby and Lucia exchanged a look of concern. "If you would prefer to be excused, you can be. You don't have to learn this. Blythe and Czar made it a point that these lessons aren't mandatory."

Darby shook her head. "I want to learn. It's just that Blythe is so cautious with us all the time . . ." She trailed off. "I *definitely* want to learn."

"Me too," Lucia said.

"All of you, stand up," Preacher said, not waiting for any more explanations. "This takes finesse, not a bulldozer, Benito. You have to have the fingers of a pickpocket. You have learned how to pickpocket?" He made that half a question, half a statement. "If not, you need to go to the class Ice, Storm and Ink are teaching. You have to have that light a hand. No one can suspect you because you use this only in dire circumstances or if you're . . ."

Reaper cleared his throat and Preacher broke off abruptly. They weren't going to talk about assassination. That had been discussed ahead of time.

"We're going to teach the art of retrieval and then how to actually use a garrote. Of course, you won't be working with an actual garrote," Preacher continued. "We don't want anyone to accidentally kill Benito—er, someone."

Lucia laughed and nudged her brother with her hip. "Your reputation has preceded you, little brother."

"Drop your hand casually down to your side so that just your fingertips rest on the top of the seam of your jeans. You have to do this by feel. There will be a couple of stitches open. You have to be able to feel that with the pads of your fingers. Just rub back and forth until you feel it. Once you feel it on one side, do the same on the other with your opposite hand. Switch back and forth between sides until you're confident you can find those open stitches fast with either hand," Preacher instructed.

The four teens spent some time going back and forth feeling for the stitches. It was much harder than it sounded. A swipe over the top of a seam with the pad of one's finger didn't always allow for distinguishing at a quick feel the absence of a thread. One had to be very sensitive. It took the teens longer than they expected and they really had to slow down, concentrate, feel and then learn to do the same on the side they weren't as strong on.

"You have to build up both sides of your body. You can't just rely on being right-handed or left-handed. You don't know when you might be pinned down on your strong side. Or shot on that side. You always have to be prepared to use either hand," Lana said. "Once you get a feel for the absence of the stitches, you have to very gently use two fingers to push in and stroke upward. The ring is very small, but it's there and will slide through that hole. It has to twist as it comes through. You have to find the trick to move it with that pushing in and sliding upward and then twisting in one motion. You should feel the ring with the pads of your fingers."

"Retrieving that ring is the most difficult part," Reaper added. "It takes patience. No one does it the first time."

"No one even feels it first time," Maestro added. "The idea is you have to practice over the next two weeks until you get it. When you come back, we'll expect that you can do it. You'll also need to be able to rethread the garrote back into the seam."

Benito let out a snort of derision. "Lucia can do that."

Instantly Maestro spun around and took a menacing step toward him. "Why would Lucia do that for you? Are you incapable of doing it for yourself?"

"No." Benito drew himself up. "She's a girl."

"So you're telling us that threading a garrote into your clothing is beneath you? That women are somehow a lower status than men?" Maestro took another step toward him and he wasn't alone. Preacher and Reaper formed a solid wall with Maestro.

"What makes you think you're so damn much better than a woman? Because you have a fuckin' penis hangin' between your legs?" Reaper demanded. "We're one family. Torpedo Ink. Not one of us is better than the next. We treat our women with respect. Alena or Lana can take out an enemy with the same skill as any one of the brothers."

"You don't get that, Benito, you're not worth much to Torpedo Ink," Maestro snapped. "We're a family. We don't put one member down. We don't make them less. We never make them feel less. You need to be able to thread a garrote into your own fuckin' jeans just like Lucia has to be able to load her own gun. Essentially, it's the same thing. But don't you ever make the mistake of thinking you're more than a woman, because you aren't."

Benito nodded his head several times. "I'm sorry, Maestro. I tease my sister all time. I don't mean it. I really don't. I used to, but Max says the same as you, that we're equal, and never to think that way, so I don't."

"Then stop teasing that way," Maestro counseled. "If you tease that way, you might start thinking that way again."

Benito nodded again. "I hear you."

"Keep practicing, everyone," Lana said. "We've only got a few more minutes so let's get on to the actual way a garrote is used. It isn't as easy as it looks in the movies. There's a bit of a trick to it, especially if there's a height difference. We're going to use just some thin tubing so I can show you how it works, and you can practice with your partner. They'll sit in the grass in front of you."

Lana demonstrated on Preacher and then each of the instructors sat in front of one of the students and directed them step by step.

"What in the world is going on here?" Blythe's voice was a mixture of amusement, outrage and resignation.

"Please tell me you are *not* teaching these children to use a garrote," Airiana, Benito's adopted mother demanded. She shook her head and lifted her eyes to the sky. "That is the last thing that boy needs to know how to do."

"Ice, Storm and Ink were teaching the girls to *pick-pocket*," Blythe said.

"Naturally," Absinthe said, coming up behind them. "They have to be able to take away a weapon, keys, anything that will help them escape. They have to feel empowered. That's what turned us around. Especially Jimmy. He really responded to feeling as if he might be able to control something, *anything*. That's what Czar did for us. That's what we are doing for them."

Absinthe deliberately moved back away from the teens so the two women would follow him. "We make certain to tell them never to use what they learn outside of defending themselves from predators. We tell them Czar is the boss. He's the go-to man with the answers. We don't go outside our families. But they have to feel empowered. These are children who have had their parents and brothers and sisters murdered. They were brutalized. Their innocence torn from them. They can't get that back as much as you want them to. You couldn't reach them your way. You asked us to help you. We're trying to do that. Give us the chance."

Blythe took a deep breath and looked across the field. Jimmy and Emily were throwing rocks at a wall with holes in it, showing Zoe and Airiana's two girls what they could do. The girls immediately pleaded to try. Zoe managed to get one rock through a hole. Jimmy jumped up and down and smiled at her.

"He's never smiled before. Never." She bit her lip. "Okay. I'll trust Czar's judgment."

Airiana sighed. "Benito is a little demon child already. I suppose Max will just have to watch over him. He's going to laugh about this." She shook her head and walked off the field, following Blythe.

The moment they were gone, the Torpedo Ink members looked at Absinthe. He gave them the thumbs-up.

⌒

"Wanted to talk with you for a minute, Steele, if you don't mind," Absinthe said. He squeezed Scarlet's hand and then let go of that lifeline, patting her bottom, shaping it for just a moment, wishing she was naked and he had the comfort of his *kiska*, his pussycat. He needed that about now. "Go inside with Breezy, baby. This won't take long."

Scarlet's green gaze drifted over his face and then she nodded. Breezy was born into the club life and she was the wife of the vice president of Torpedo Ink. Her man nodded toward the bar and touched her face. She smiled at Scarlet immediately, hooked arms with her and went right up the stairs chattering as if they were old friends.

Absinthe walked away from the bottom of the stairs, not wanting to be overheard by the other members of his club. It was going to be difficult enough to say the things that needed saying to Steele, but he had to do it. The two went around the corner of the bar. Darkness had fallen, shrouding the night in a blanket of fog.

"What's up?"

"Hard to bring this up but can't put it off any longer. I keep having these flashbacks. They're getting bad and it put Scarlet in some danger the other night. Savage too."

"We're all dealing with post-traumatic stress, Absinthe," Steele said, his hand going back to massage the nape of his neck. "It would be impossible not to. You've got the biggest brain, you know that."

Absinthe wasn't going to pretend he wasn't the smartest man in the room. "Demyan and I had experimented with holding a path open between our minds. You know we were pretty strong at connecting with others. But the two of us were really strong together. We worked on it all the time."

Absinthe felt sick. He broke out in a sweat. He shouldn't have let Scarlet leave his side. She somehow managed to quiet the chaos that reigned in his brain when he thought back to that day—that horrible day when he felt everything his brother was feeling. The pressure in his chest was so tremendous he nearly went to his knees. He pressed both palms into the wide cement planter that wrapped around the back of the bar, trying to take deep breaths.

"I was supposed to hold him. Hold the bridge. I couldn't. I wasn't strong enough." He confessed the truth in a rush. "I blamed you, but it wasn't you. It was me. I lost him that day. I was so angry with everyone for so much, for keeping me alive after the kittens died and then when I lost Demyan. I knew it was me. All this time, I wanted to blame you, Steele, but it was me. I'm sorry, man. I should have told you."

His admission came out in a rush, the words stumbling over one another.

"Wait." Steele held up his hand. "Wait. You used the word *bridge*. You said *hold the bridge*. That day, I couldn't keep my eyes on him. They took him to another room. When I got to him, he was so far gone and he kept trying to tell me something important for you, but I couldn't hear him. He wasn't making sense. He kept saying he crashed the bridge. Tell Absinthe he crashed the bridge."

"He said he crashed the bridge?" Absinthe turned. He had to sit on the concrete wall abruptly. "Are you certain?"

"He was all but gone but he mumbled it over and over. Crashed bridge. Crashed bridge. I didn't tell you because I fuckin' let you all down by taking my eyes off of him."

"You were tied up. They wrapped you in barbed wire. You still have the scars," Absinthe said. "It's absurd to think you could have kept your eyes on him. He really crashed the bridge?" He rubbed his chest, trying to breathe.

Steele caught him by the nape of his neck and pressed his head down. "You're hyperventilating. Yeah. That's what he said. *Bridge. Crash.* Hell. He broke the connection between you because you were feeling everything he was, and he knew he was dying. You were keeping him alive."

"Damn that son of a bitch. He made me live when I didn't want to. When my guts were torn out." His lungs burned until he couldn't breathe, and he had to keep his head between his knees. His brother. Demyan.

Steele shook his head. "He wouldn't have survived. It

was impossible. I saw him. I'm a healer. They ripped him to shreds. I couldn't even touch him. I couldn't hold him. There wasn't a place on him to touch. He tried to spare you, Absinthe. He wanted to spare me. That was the way he was. You know that. If there was a connection between the two of you, he was the one to break it, not you."

It made sense. It was exactly what Demyan would do. He had done it. Of course he'd done it. Absinthe would have done it to spare Demyan, to spare any of them. He closed his eyes, trying not to let the burn behind them become anything more than his own. He couldn't take on Steele's grief, not when his was so visceral. That cut went so deep for both of them.

Steele sank down onto the cement beside him. Close, but not touching. "I'm sorry, brother. He was like you. Brilliant. The best of us. Sensitive. Willing to take on too much for all of us. I loved him with everything in me."

"I didn't know how to go on for the longest time," Absinthe admitted.

"I know you think you know you're one lucky son of a bitch to have found Scarlet, but brother, it's far more than that. We're, all of us, so fucked up and we're always going to be. We aren't like other clubs in that they put the brotherhood before their women. We don't do that. But somehow in that shithole, all of us, in order to survive, we had to take pieces of one another in order to make ourselves whole."

Absinthe nodded. He knew that. "It's true. When I'm in the room with everyone, I can feel the way we're mixed together. We're definitely one person, not eighteen." He hesitated. "The weird thing is, Destroyer doesn't upset that balance the way I thought he might. He fits with us."

"The point I'm making is that our women have to be able to not just fit into club life, but to fit into the way we are with one another. To be able to deal with our fucked-up ways and needs. Blythe, man, she puts up with all of us for Czar and she loves us. Soleil, she loves what Ice loves and gives him everything. Breezy was born into the life and she's down for it. Anya, she and Reaper deal with his shit. Scarlet, she just pleases you, Absinthe. She just does whatever the fuck you want or need because she loves the fuck out of you."

Absinthe knew Steele was right. He hadn't looked at it quite that way, but he knew Steele was telling him something important.

"That doesn't come along all that often. All of us, we hit the jackpot and the women we've got, we have to know what we have. You have to look at her and really see what she's worth. Know it in your soul. These women—Blythe, Anya, Breezy, Soleil and now Scarlet—they are what we live for. They're what Czar meant when he said we could turn our lives around. You see the way the others treat them. The way they accept them. They wouldn't do that if they didn't know what these women are. What they mean."

Absinthe nodded. "Savage scared the shit out of Scarlet in order to bring me out of my flashback. He was pissed at me like you wouldn't believe on her behalf."

"He doesn't want to fuck up his relationship with her," Steele said. "Any more than I'd want to. She's special. She's our sister. She matters."

Absinthe understood that because he felt those things for the other women. "I hear what you're saying, Steele. Demyan was my brother and I loved him. I looked up to him and admired him. I wanted him back after he was gone, and I blamed myself all these years. I was still that child and I knew that. I read psychology books all the time. Intellectually, I knew what I was doing, holding on to anger against you, Alena, Savage and even Demyan for leaving me. For keeping me alive after I'd lost so much. I knew, but I couldn't stop."

"You know the trauma won't go away because you figured the shit out, right?" Steele said. "Because I'm a fuckin' doctor and I've got this girl, my wife, and she gives me the world and I still can't make it stop. She makes it better, but it doesn't stop."

"No, it isn't going to stop," Absinthe agreed. "For any of us. It doesn't work that way, but we can all find better ways to cope."

Steele put a hand on his shoulder. "Thanks for talking to me about this, brother. I needed to hear what you had to say, and I needed to tell you what Demyan said. I never thought he was able to give me the message for you that was so important to him to say."

Absinthe ordinarily would have avoided physical contact in an emotional situation like this one, but he was grateful he didn't. He felt Steele's grief, but he also felt his genuine love for his brother, and also for him. It ran deep and allowed him to finally let go of the feelings of anger, betrayal and resentment he was harboring against Steele and just feel that shared grief and love toward him.

That sat together in silence for a few more minutes while more of their club gathered at the bar and music blared loudly. "I can't leave Scarlet alone for too long. She's new at this."

The two walked together around the corner to the front of the bar, where several of the members of Torpedo Ink had congregated on the stairs. Absinthe found himself viewing them differently. As his brothers—but just that little bit differently. Scarlet had already changed his life, just by talking to him, by insisting he work things out with Steele and the others, first in his head and then with them.

In the bar, she was standing in a small, tight circle of women, close to Breezy, who clearly was watching over her for Absinthe. Scarlet looked up, her eyes lighting up the moment she saw him, and then she smiled. His heart reacted, clenching hard in his chest. He went straight to her, threading his way through his brethren, nodding to all those greeting him, but his gaze was locked on hers. She searched his face, making certain he was all right after his talk with Steele. Clearly, Breezy was doing the same thing with her man.

The moment Absinthe got to Scarlet, he wrapped his arm around her waist and pulled her to him, gently brushing his lips over hers. "Missed you, baby. You all right? Breezy take good care of you?" He drew her away from the other women.

"She did," Scarlet said. "She introduced me to everyone I hadn't met. Lissa, Lexi and Airiana, who has been regaling us with tales about her son Benito and all of his antics as a mini-Max and assassin in training. Apparently, Blythe and Airiana had an entirely different vision of survival training than Czar and all of you. It was hysterical listening to her. She had us in stitches, although it was heartbreaking at times when she told us sometimes the children still come to their bedroom and crawl into bed with them because of nightmares."

He massaged the nape of her neck. "I still have nightmares and I'm in my thirties," he pointed out. "Steele was just telling me that our past doesn't go away because we want it to. Trauma like that sticks with you and the ramifications last forever."

Scarlet tipped her face up to his. "Are you good with Steele, honey?"

"Much better," he admitted. "Thanks for suggesting I talk to him. I did the same with Alena earlier. I feel better about a lot of things right now." He slung his arm around her neck and kissed her.

The moment she parted her lips, that strange electrical charge raced from her skin to his. Like putting a match to a detonator, an explosion went off. Fire raced through his veins straight to his groin. "Woman. Every single time." He pressed his forehead to hers, breathing deep. Taking her in while his brothers and sisters moved all around them setting up the tables and chairs to eat.

"Get a move on, you two," Czar said. "Eat now, dessert later."

Absinthe found himself laughing, feeling so much lighter, as if a great weight had been lifted off his shoulders. He helped fit the tables together while Scarlet helped bring out the trays of food. Fried chicken. Beef. So many side dishes. All the Torpedo Ink members were there, including Savage and Destroyer. They'd returned from the city only a half hour or so earlier. When Absinthe deliberately got close to him, he felt far less strained.

While Scarlet was putting plates, napkins and silverware at the end of the bar for everyone to use, Absinthe saw Savage go up to her. As always, Savage looked at ease, as if nothing bothered him. Scarlet straightened, her gaze immediately searching the room for Absinthe. He was a distance from her but when he started toward her, she motioned him off with a small shake of her head.

Savage faced his way so he could read his lips. "Just want to know we're good, Scarlet."

"I figured out, after I got over being scared, that I was mostly mad at myself."

"That doesn't mean you're okay with it."

"I love him, the same as you do. So, yeah, we're okay, Savage."

"Good." He started to turn away but then turned back to her. "Just out of curiosity. When you went for the gun, who did you plan to shoot? Me? Or Absinthe?"

"I thought I might wing both of you just to make myself feel better."

Savage shook his head. "I hope that man knows what he's got in his bed."

❦

Absinthe rubbed his hand along the base of Scarlet's spine. They sat in the shadows at the very back of the bar in one of the few booths, Scarlet in his lap. He felt like he hadn't been alone with her in days. The dinner had been fun, visiting with all the members of the club as well as the women. Most of the outsiders had gone home, along with Czar's wife and some of the newer women in the club—Casimir's wife, as well as Gavriil's woman. They weren't quite ready for what might be considered the wilder side of the Torpedo Ink parties. To the charter members, it was their normal.

"I wish we were home, *miledi*." Absinthe's hand moved up to Scarlet's ear, caressed her lobe over and over. "I want to fuck your brains out." He felt the shiver that went through her body. "We barely got married and didn't have a chance to have a honeymoon. It's all I can think about." He'd wanted a better start for them. He'd given that a lot of thought. If he couldn't take her off somewhere exotic, at least he wanted to be at their home and try to give her a honeymoon there.

She leaned into his hand. "Me too," she admitted. "We haven't really had time to be alone together with everything going on with the club."

At his insistence, she'd worn one of her librarian skirts, the butterfly one that had always made him crazy. It swung around her legs intriguingly, those butterfly buttons up the side making him mad to want to slowly undo them, one by one. Now he could. She had a little matching blouse, with the same butterfly buttons fluttering over her generous breasts, daring him to uncover her. She looked so prim and proper with the blouse closed and the swing skirt buttoned properly, not exposing her thigh.

He dipped his fingers below the hem and ran his nails up her knee. "This is one of my favorite outfits." She even wore the square purple glasses for him that matched. Her literary outfit. Prim and proper. "I wanted to sit you up on your desk, tear off your panties and devour you. I think I'm going to do that later. Eat some grapes right out of your hot little pussy. Or some of Alena's orange-spice dessert balls.

She serves them in these little sugar nets with strings I can tug right out of you." He teased her earlobe with his teeth. "How does that sound, baby?"

Alena had outdone herself, baking some of the specialty desserts, and Absinthe couldn't wait to try them with Scarlet, as long as she didn't object with the club around them.

"Fantastic. Sexy. I don't know. There's so many people here."

He laughed, his fingers massaging the nape of her neck. "Look in the corner, baby. Ice and Soleil are already going at it."

The lights in the bar were dim. They weren't expecting the Diamondbacks until the early morning hours. He caught Scarlet's head and turned her face toward the stage, where Ice was sitting on a stair, Soleil on his lap, her breasts in his hands, while she moved on him rhythmically. It was impossible to tell if he was pumping in her ass or pussy, but she was moaning, and he had his head thrown back.

Storm had a woman, it looked like Heidi, one of the club girls, busy sucking him dry while he watched. At the bar, Reaper suddenly pulled Anya over the top of the bar. She laughed while he dragged her clothes off and laid her out like a feast, reaching for the orange-spice balls, feeding one to Anya before devouring one himself.

"I guess you're right, no one is watching," Scarlet agreed.

"Alena," Absinthe called. "You have any of the orange-spice balls left for us?"

"Sure, babe." Alena came to the table with a tray.

"Thanks, honey." Absinthe took a generous helping. "She's going to love these. They're my favorite."

"I know," Alena admitted. She blew him a kiss and sauntered off. As she passed Savage and Destroyer, both grabbed several off the tray.

Absinthe lifted Scarlet onto the table facing him and slowly unbuttoned the little butterflies holding the blouse together over her breasts. As the two sides parted, the rounded curves spilled over her lilac bra, drawing his eye, her nipples peeking through the lace at him. His cock reacted with a hammering heartbeat. He opened the front of the bra so that her breasts spilled into his hands. At once his mouth was there, sucking her flesh into the heat, using his tongue, his teeth, grazing her skin, her nipples, her aureoles until her breathing was ragged and she was cradling his head to her, urging him to do whatever he wanted.

He loved being able to take her out of her head to a place where she wasn't aware of anyone else in the room with them or her surroundings. He began to slowly lift that little swing skirt, just the way he'd wanted to do at the library, on her desk.

"You're so fuckin' sexy, *ledi*." He pulled her thighs apart, rubbing them up high, massaging, sweeping his hand close to her heat, but not touching her. Not yet. "I fantasized about you in this skirt. On your desk. Library closed. My mouth between your legs. You screaming my name. Once I jerked off at the thought of you on your cushion, kneeling up on your library desk with your tail in, my little *kiska*, waiting patiently for me while I read my book. Another time, you sucked my cock while I read. And then I fucked you while I bent you over your library desk."

He felt her shiver. Goose bumps rose on her skin. He put his hand on her belly and pressed her down onto the table. "I have so many fantasies. I don't think we'll ever get them done in one lifetime. We'll need two or three together at least."

She moaned softly and writhed, a slow undulation he found sensual. Her little thong was already damp. He tugged it down her legs and pulled it off and then took one of the sugar nets with Alena's orange and spice balls. He pushed it slowly up inside her. She was slick and it went in, but the ball was fairly good sized and she cried out when it slid inside. He stroked her clit, looping the string over one finger.

"That feel good, baby? That spice is going to start mixing with your honey. Heat you right up."

"I'm already hot."

"When I eat you out, you're going to taste so delicious." He caught up a second net, licked at the ball and then slowly pushed it inside her, twisting the two strings together. "Think you can take a third one?" He bit down gently on her inner thigh and then circled her clit with his tongue. "I think you can, baby. My little *kiska* can do it."

Her hand went to his hair, fingers fisting in it as he pushed the third orange-spice ball inside her. Her little cries sent his cock into a frenzy of need. Absinthe rolled her skirt all the way up around her hips and shoved her legs wider. Lifting her bottom, he simply covered her slick entrance with his mouth and sucked at the spicy orange-honey-cream dripping from her. He plunged his tongue deep, drawing the sticky spice out of her, catching as much as he could, stroking along her clit, flicking, stabbing and teasing, driving her up and over again and again.

He ate the first of the orange-spice balls as the first of her orgasms crashed over her. It was a powerful wave that nearly took her off the table and jerked the hair out of his scalp. He devoured her thoroughly, never stopping, feeding the power of her second orgasm, allowing the spice in the orange-spice dessert to mix with her natural cream, creating an even more powerful wave as he consumed the sugar and spice and kept lashing at her with his tongue and fingers.

The sugar around the first spice ball was melting, just as it was supposed to do, and the ball was melting along with it in all of Scarlet's glorious heat, that natural inferno that was waiting to surround him. She writhed and bucked, nearly coming off the table as the spices were absorbed into her system. He sucked at the spicy, delicious concoction, one of Alena's masterpieces, and his particular favorite. He plunged his tongue into her over and over to get out as much as he could. He'd never eaten the orange-spice balls out of a woman before, but he would again, now that he had. Mixed with Scarlet's normal taste, they were addictive. He was definitely putting in a special order for them the moment he got home.

The next massive wave hit Scarlet and she screamed, her legs trying to close around his head, her hips coming off the table in a wild display as she tried to ride his face. Absinthe surged to his feet, freeing his cock with one hand, dragging her hips off the table with the other, and then he slammed home, throwing his head back as his cock found that tight, hot tunnel. So snug. Scorching. A fiery blaze surrounding him, squeezing down so viciously tight.

That fire. That slick spice was pure perfection as scorching hot as a burning volcano. He buried himself in her over and over, his head roaring. Thunder bellowed in his ears. Flames raced up his spine. Rolled in his belly. Became an inferno in his groin. The table rocked and slid toward the wall. He pounded himself deeper. Buried himself in her over and over as the flames streaked up his body, his thighs and back. He was wild. Out of control. Nothing had ever felt so good.

Before he could think to stop, to slow down, it was too late and her body had clamped down so hard on his that it was impossible to stop the explosion as that tight silken sheath surrounded and squeezed, stroked and milked. Hot semen splashed along the walls of her channel, mixing and blending with her spicy cream, bathing his cock in scorching heat so that his shaft pulsed and jerked wildly, sending those lightning strikes straight to his brain.

Her hot little pussy felt like it convulsed around him again and again, a crazy, beautiful ride that seemed never-ending—one he hoped would never end. His legs turned to rubber, and he had to collapse over the top of her, driving his sated cock deep as he did. The aftershocks rippling through her were strong and he felt every one of them as he buried his face in her throat, struggling to breathe.

Scarlet was doing the same, her arms winding around his neck, fingers sliding into his hair to massage his scalp. She was breathing hard, her soft breasts rising and falling fast, and he knew he was probably too heavy, but he honestly couldn't move.

Absinthe wrapped his arms around her as tight as he could without breaking her. "I love you, Scarlet. I don't know how else to say what I feel, and it's so much more. You've already given me more than I ever thought I could have."

He lifted his head to look into her green eyes. That look was there, the one that he didn't deserve—would never deserve no matter if he spent the rest of his life trying to make her happy. And that was exactly what he planned to do. He kissed her chin and then her throat.

"When we can move, we have to clean up. I've got a little more club business tonight. I want you to go with Breezy and a couple of the others to the clubhouse and wait for me. Then we can head home. This shouldn't take long." He kissed her throat again and then each breast and her belly button before adding several kisses to the little curls of fire on her mound.

"I'm going to try to get my legs under me and then under you. We can help each other to the bathroom. I'm sure we can make it."

She laughed and the sound added to that light feeling that seemed to be growing inside of him. She'd given him that and he was smart enough to want to keep it.

The roar of pipes was loud, announcing their visitors long before they turned off Highway 1 into Caspar. Instantly, Torpedo Ink was all business. They already knew the drill, each member going to their designated spot. They spread out. Up on the roof of the apartments above the bar, across the street to some of the rooftops of the businesses, rifles ready. Some in the parking lot where the bikes were.

The Diamondbacks came in, six of them, riding their Harleys and confident in their colors. They parked their bikes in front of the bar and came straight to Steele, who was waiting for them out in the open, with Maestro and Keys on either side of him. Absinthe and Destroyer had taken up residence on the stairs behind and just to the side of their vice president and his two guards. In the shadows, nearly impossible to see, but clearly there, again, boxing the six Diamondbacks in, were Mechanic and Ink.

Czar had specifically chosen Destroyer to be out in the open because he knew it would throw off Plank and whoever he sent not knowing the new Torpedo Ink member, and they needed Mechanic to ensure the Diamondback cameras weren't working on their phones. Even if they were, they wouldn't get much in the way of damning evidence.

Pierce led the others. Absinthe recognized a few. Judge, one of Plank's closest friends. Another called Trade, who always seemed to be near Pierce. The others he'd seen before but didn't really know well.

"Steele," Pierce said and let his gaze shift around the entire area. "Looks like you have things well under control." He let his gaze rest on Destroyer for a moment. "You have something for me?"

"Transporter picked up a package for you."

Steele held out his hand behind him without taking his eyes from Pierce. Absinthe stepped forward and placed a brown paper bag in Steele's hand. Steele didn't look at it but held it out to Pierce.

Pierce opened the bag, pulled the six patches out, dropped them back inside and closed the bag. "Got pretty creative on that stage. Want to tell me whose work that was?"

Steele just looked at him.

Pierce shrugged. "Only two clubs went down."

"Only two clubs were owned by Venomous. That was the contract."

Pierce sighed. "Can't argue with that. One last thing. Scarlet Foley. She's worth five million to a man named Holden. He sent word to Plank that you've got her here. Plank isn't okay with you taking the reward on this one. You're going to have to hand her over."

"She's Absinthe's old lady," Steele said, his tone mild. "She's not going anywhere."

"That certainly changes things." Pierce looked past Steele to Absinthe. "Plank will send the Diamondbacks to have a word with Holden."

Steele shook his head. "We appreciate the support, Pierce, but you tell him not to go to the trouble. Holden tried to kill her. That was a very big mistake on his part. Then he put a fuckin' price on her head. Just sayin'. You and I both know he won't be payin' out that five mil to anyone."

Pierce sent them a little half smile and salute, rolled up the paper bag with the patches and put it into a compartment in his Harley and signaled the others back onto their bikes. Until the sound of the pipes were just a faint memory in the distance, none of the Torpedo Ink members broke from cover.

NINETEEN

━◆◆◆━

Judge Benedict Calloway's home was modest on the outside. The house rose up between two other homes like a green environmental beacon with plants climbing up the sides of the three-story brick building. A wrought-iron fence and locked gate were the only things that might have given anyone pause to think that the inside could be a hidden treasure, but most of the neighboring homes also were behind very similar wrought-iron fences.

Calloway loved art. His weakness was art. He didn't collect art to brag or show off, he collected it because it was his obsession and he had to have it. He had to sit in a room by himself with a glass of the very best wine, listening to his favorite opera, surrounded by the most magnificent paintings others couldn't possibly appreciate the way he did, knowing nothing in the world would ever compare to them.

It was a thrill to be able to acquire a painting. It required a great deal of money, patience and knowing the right people. He had, over time, managed to put together all three components and then he'd built his private, temperature-controlled room where he housed his collection of stolen art. For him, the fact that he had acquired the paintings that way, targeted them and hired the right people to pull off a daring robbery of a museum to take the original painting from masses of people with no real concept of what they were looking at, or real appreciation of the masterpiece they were privileged to behold, made his collection all the sweeter.

He despised those who claimed they loved art when they had no real knowledge of the subject. They stared at some drawing and pretended to know the meaning because a teacher in school had quoted from a book and now they were parroting him or her. They couldn't think for themselves. Or have any real impression.

Calloway wandered through his home, admiring what he had done with the place. When he'd first moved into the house, he had seen the potential immediately. He had a good eye for space, and he wanted an upscale neighborhood, but not one that would stand out like that braggart Holden. He didn't need everyone to think he was a multimillionaire. He didn't want the aggravation of trying to explain where money had come from. Fortunately, he'd inherited a little bit from his wife, who'd died very early in their marriage, and he'd never remarried. He'd invested the money and doubled it and then doubled that. He'd been careful and cautious. That had paid off.

He moved through his house the way he did every evening. Walking slowly. Savoring the Bay Area setting sun pouring through the stained-glass windows set at just the right height to catch the rays and send them shooting through the rooms like stars to shine on the walls, giving him the feeling of walking in galaxies, he moved toward his hidden collector's room as he did most nights. He took his time, admiring the sculptures and modern art he had acquired and showed off to visitors who dropped by.

He'd made a few mistakes over the years. Holden was

one, but he couldn't really complain as he'd made quite a lot of his money from the repulsive man. It had been that one case he could never quite get out of his mind, that one blunder that preyed on him even now after his retirement. Scarlet Foley. She'd been a brilliant girl. Far more intelligent than Holden's weak-willed, entitled son. Holden had paid through the nose time and again to keep the psychopath he'd raised out of jail. Scarlet had been on her way to do great things; with her intelligent mind, she grasped concepts quickly.

Even at the very young age of seventeen, it was clear she understood what was happening, the lies and railroading going on. She had looked at her attorney and had known he was rolling over for Holden. She had looked at Calloway with those same too-intelligent eyes as well. He hadn't wanted to send her to prison, but at the time, there had been a Picasso he had needed more than his self-respect and he didn't yet have his art addiction under control. She had been the catalyst for him to find a way to stop his obsessive need to continually buy paintings. He'd slowed down after he had taken Holden's outrageous payout for sending an innocent teenager to prison.

She was a fighter. He would never forget that look she gave him. Steady. Those green eyes sometimes woke him up in the middle of the night, staring straight into his eyes. Intelligent. Knowing. It had been a terrible shame about her sister. He knew Holden's pitiful son and his friends had raped her and driven her to suicide. Foley's parents dead, murder-suicide that same night? That was awful.

Calloway sighed as he poured himself a glass of one of his favorite red wines. Two thousand dollars a bottle. He rarely opened that particular wine, but tonight he was going to listen to his very favorite Italian opera and sit in that room surrounded by his beloved paintings and let them take Scarlet Foley with her brilliant green eyes away so he wouldn't wake up the way he did whenever he thought too much about her.

She'd gotten out of prison, a female attorney had suddenly taken on her case, advocating for her, turning everything around, and Holden couldn't bribe her or scare her into giving up. She had uncovered the fact that the medical evidence had supported Scarlet's account, not Robert Jr.'s account. Somehow, she had found all kinds of facts that turned up evidence no one wanted to come to light, including his part in the entire mess. Scarlet's incarceration was over, and the city paid her money to keep her quiet. Holden was furious.

Calloway was very happy he had been allowed to retire with his pension. Scarlet left the country and disappeared. Calloway didn't blame her at the time. He had been afraid for her safety. Robert Jr. was a little pissant who would definitely target her again. She'd bested him and he couldn't take that. Now, her attorney had bested his father. She hadn't brought a civil suit against him, but it was hanging over Holden Sr.'s and Jr.'s heads and everyone knew it.

Fast-forward five years, Scarlet returned and moved a couple of hundred miles away, got a job as a librarian, minded her own business, and one by one, some killer murders the little pissant and his friends and Holden is absolutely convinced it's Foley. It didn't matter that the police investigated her thoroughly over and over at Holden's insistence and cleared her repeatedly until her attorney insisted it was harassment. Or that Holden got the Feds involved, and they cleared her, paving the way for her attorney to finally bring an enormous lawsuit against him.

Holden was positive that somehow Scarlet could be in two places at one time. Calloway had studied the photographs of the crime scenes. Scarlet wasn't a large woman. How could she have managed to kill three strong men even if she had found a way to be in two places at one time? He'd tried to talk to Holden once, but of course that man wouldn't listen. He knew everything, more than all the investigators. More than everyone. Now, he'd put a hit out on her. That was so like Holden. Things weren't going to end well either way and Calloway had distanced himself as best he could.

He slid open the door in the wall so cleverly hidden in the panels among all the intricate white cork sculpturing on the walls. It was quite breathtaking and all his friends had gotten up close to view the exquisite artistry, yet none had spotted the hidden door within the panel that slid inside the wall to allow him to enter the stairs leading down to his viewing room. He loved showing the beautiful walls in his home, each one a masterpiece all on its own, this one hiding a spectacular secret and millions of dollars' worth of precious artwork.

He carried his glass of red wine down the polished granite stairs, holding on to the curved bannister made of the finest polished wood over an intricate filigree of silver. He took his time, enjoying every step. No one else had ever made that journey with him. This beautiful place of solace he'd created was his alone and he never hurried. He didn't ever take a cell phone, nor did he have a landline in the room. He wanted no interruptions when he sat and listened to his opera and looked at his beloved paintings.

He pulled open the door to the room, a door that had once graced Teatro alla Scala in Milan. He had traveled to Milan on numerous occasions to sit in the world-famous opera house to listen to the best of the best perform. This room not only was temperature controlled for his artwork, but the acoustics were perfect for his operas.

He continued the slow, steady pace to his wide, comfortable chair that faced his most precious paintings but allowed him to tip his head back and look up at the ceilings, where more of his collection was displayed. He could close his eyes to savor the glory of the music, or simply study the beautiful lines and strokes of the visions on canvas.

Calloway filled the room with the extraordinary Italian voices rising in songs of hope and joy, of sorrow and compassion. The beauty made him want to weep. After the ugliness of listening to what humans did to one another day after day in his courtroom, the extraordinary beauty of the gifts these singers and musicians had, what the composers and visionaries had given to the world, never failed to move him. Coupled with the masterpieces surrounding him, the opera transcended him, taking him from the muck and mire he'd been in for so long.

"Hello, Judge Calloway."

Although the voice was very soft and musical, it jarred him out of the world he was used to floating in. He knew that voice. It haunted his nights. He turned his head slowly, reluctantly, uncertain if he was hearing things or hallucinating. She sat in the chair that had always been empty beside him, looking every inch a queen with her vibrant red hair and her vivid green, all-too-intelligent eyes.

"Scarlet."

"This music is incredible."

"It's my favorite."

"I can understand why. I learned Italian very early, and just hearing the way they sing the words makes me want to weep."

"Me too," he agreed. Of course she would know Italian. She was brilliant. He'd known that just looking at her those days in court. Hearing her speak. Looking at her records. She was a teen, but she hadn't been shaken by the prosecuting attorney or even her own double-crossing attorney. Not the testifying doctor or the friends who had deserted her.

It should have been Robert Jr. who had gone to prison, not this intelligent girl. She looked around the room with appreciation. Holden's boy would never have appreciated the masterpieces there, let alone the opera.

"Which one of these paintings did you purchase with my incarceration?"

She asked the question so mildly that he didn't even bristle. Her tone was just curious. Almost admiring. She looked at him from under the veil of her long lashes and then transferred her attention to the many paintings he had up on his walls and ceilings.

"The Picasso. Who gets the chance to get a masterpiece such as that one?"

She studied the painting. "*Le pigeon aux petits pois.* Amazing. This was stolen in 2010? Correct? I have to agree, it would be difficult to resist. A private collector offered it?"

He nodded. "Yes, but still, Robert Jr. was a worm of the lowest intellect. I knew after I acquired this painting that I had to curb my addiction. I'd gone too far. I let it get out of hand."

She sighed. "Yes, Judge, I'm afraid you did, and it cost me my entire family. You may as well have participated in the rape and murder of my sister and my parents right along with Robert, Beau and Arnold. They gang-raped a young teen. She was a virgin. Did you know that? She was like a little fairy princess. I loved her more than life."

She fell silent for a moment and continued to look at the masterpiece painted in 1911 by Pablo Picasso and taken from the world by a single thief in 2010.

"I had nothing to do with that, Scarlet. I just took the money. It was wrong, but it was only the money."

She sent him a little half smile. "You know better. You're no better than Robert and his friends. His father got him off over and over, allowing him to continue to do worse and worse things to women, and all of you saw it happening but were too greedy to stop him. That makes you accessories. You know that law. I know the law. I had thought to burn the painting as part of your punishment."

At his gasp she shook her head. "Don't worry. It's too beautiful. I can't deprive the world of something that incredible. You, however, have to pay for what you did to my family."

"Did you kill them? Was Holden right about you?" Calloway couldn't imagine it. Not even now when she sat right there in the room with him looking so calm and sweet, exactly like a little librarian.

She gave him a little smile. "Yes. One by one. I will kill Holden too. This persecution of me has gone on long enough. He started it by allowing his monster of a son to continue his crimes without paying for them. Robert's disgusting behavior escalated." She sent him another little smile. "I suppose my response has done the same."

Shadowy figures began to emerge from around him, stepping out into his theater, just as they might onto the stage of one of the great opera houses. Calloway thought it felt like he was an actor in one of the tragic dramas. The music swelled to a crescendo.

"I knew you'd come for me one day, Scarlet," Calloway said. "You were the one I regretted. I should have felt remorse for taking other bribes, but look around you. That money created this. No, you're my only regret. I knew you would come and I'm glad you have. I'm sorry for what happened to your family and the part I played in it. I was happy when Robert Jr. and his monstrous friends died the way they did. I thought they met with fitting ends. How shall I meet my end, Scarlet?" He took a sip of his wine, determined to go out like one of the most tragic heroes in the operas he loved so much.

"My husband will place a garrote around your neck and strangle you with it."

"You're married then?"

"Yes, recently. He insisted he take care of this one for me while I sit here and enjoy the opera. I do love this music."

"You must, one day, go to Milan and see it in person."

"I have on three occasions," she admitted.

He was proud of her. He'd known all along she was worth saving. His one mistake. He closed his eyes as he felt the garrote tighten around his neck. How amazing that he hadn't known the man was behind him. Or that the lethal weapon had been slipped around his neck like a noose of justice already. The bite was unexpectedly hard and fast, cutting off oxygen, taking him out of his fantasy world and into the realm of reality so that he realized he was actually going to die.

He dropped the wineglass and it fell to the floor, shattering, the red wine spreading out in an ugly stain, the pattern looking to his blurred vision like the outline of a dead man. His legs stiffened. His bladder let loose. That humiliated him, but he had no control. None. The thundering heartbeat in his ears drowned out the sound of his beloved music and his lungs burned and burned for air. He tried to fight, weakly reaching back to try to get to his executioner, but it was already too late, and he was losing consciousness.

Absinthe made certain Calloway was dead before he let the man go. "You all right, *miledi*?"

Scarlet nodded. "Yes, he wanted to justify his part in all this to himself. He just took the money. He was a judge, Absinthe. The law holds others accountable during the commission of crimes, yet he refused to be accountable, and he's a judge."

Alena wrapped her arm around Scarlet's waist. "He wanted to think he was better than Holden or even Robert Jr. because he has good taste in art. He's a snob, babe. Give up trying to figure these guys out. I stopped trying to figure out society a long time ago. Blythe keeps giving us lessons, but nothing makes sense to me."

"Me either," Ice agreed. "I say the word *fuck* or I prefer a Harley to a car, and no one wants me around their kid, but they let some asshole dressed all nice in the door and he's all over their kid. They don't even notice because he goes to church or he's got money. Go figure. I don't get it."

"Who's next?" Savage asked. He glanced at his watch. "We don't want to blow the time here. We've got to hit four more tonight."

Scarlet glanced up at him. "My original defense attorney. He was definitely in Holden's pocket. He rolled over for him. I've wanted to visit him from day one."

"Yeah, well, someone else did that for you," Absinthe said. "You must have mentioned that to Adrik." He watched her closely. He didn't know how to feel about Adrik. She couldn't change her past any more than he could. He was grateful that Adrik had chosen to return to Thailand after getting out of the hospital.

Scarlet shook her head, looking shocked. "I didn't talk to Adrik about my plans to go after Robert Jr. or the others. I wasn't certain if I would continue with the attorneys or judge later on either. I hadn't made up my mind."

"Someone not only killed your defense attorney and the prosecuting attorney who was in Holden's pocket, but also the medical examiner who testified in court about your injuries and the boys' as well. Each of the men were tortured and the true facts were pinned to their chests. They were strung up in their homes, each with a little card that said they were a wedding present to you from an admirer," Absinthe said. "Code received the detailed photographs and Czar agrees with me, it had to be Adrik just from the way they were killed. The bodies have yet to be found, but as soon as they are, we will run out of time on our end. Holden will hole up and the cops will come looking to talk to you. You'll need to be home with an airtight alibi."

"Where's Adrik now?" Scarlet asked.

"On his way to Thailand, according to Code. He was given the choice to join the Trinity chapter of Torpedo Ink, but he declined, said he was a loner." Absinthe kept watching her face.

His wife was gorgeous. Absolutely beautiful. She might fool others, but she didn't have a poker face, not to him. It was clear she wasn't asking about Adrik because she wanted to go chasing after him. Steele was right about their women. Absinthe had to come to terms with the fact that he still hadn't gotten to a place where he thought he deserved having Scarlet love him. He couldn't quite wrap his mind around it.

What the hell are you doing in there? Partying? We don't have all night. Code has drained Holden's bank accounts and will rescind the contract on Scarlet, but you have to get to him now before he's warned the others are dead. The timeline has been moved up.

Czar sounded annoyed, so Absinthe didn't make a snappy comeback. None of them did. They all recognized that tone. He was royally pissed with Adrik. The man might have made what he saw as a gesture, sending Scarlet a wedding gift by killing three of the men responsible for her incarceration, but it only called attention to her. Torpedo Ink always ensured reasonable suspicion fell on someone else. They couldn't do damage control on this one.

"Let's move," Transporter said.

The team did, keeping Scarlet in the center. She and Destroyer were new. They didn't know how the team worked yet and the others looked out for them, although Absinthe didn't think Destroyer needed anyone looking out for him.

～

Robert Holden Sr. tossed back the last of his scotch using the last glass made of Irish cut crystal his wife's father had given them on their wedding day. It had been in their family for a hundred years and she had fussed endlessly over it, reminding him continually not to use it unless it was a special occasion. He thought tonight, their anniversary, was a very special occasion. The scotch burned down his throat and felt like a furnace in his gut. He threw the glass as hard as he could into the stone fireplace, watching it hit the rocks and shatter, just as he had the other five glasses. The crystal splintered in all directions, scattering pieces across the hardwood floor to pick up the rolling flames of the fire, reflecting them all around the room.

He hadn't turned on lights because he didn't need them, not with a full moon shining through the thick walls of glass and the sliding door leading to the enormous outdoor pool. He swam laps nightly to stay in shape. He prided himself on his body, something his soon-to-be ex-wife couldn't say. She'd grown so complacent about herself. Putting on the pounds, waiting an extra week or two to color her hair, forgetting her Botox injections.

He was going to have to call his "security" company after his swim tonight and see what the holdup was on his wife's accident. She'd filed for divorce, but she hadn't yet made out a new will. He was still the beneficiary of her life insurance policy. He would still inherit everything if she died before the divorce went through. That had to happen.

Robert slid open the door and walked out to the pool in his sandals. Dropping his short robe on the lounge beside the pool, he kicked off his shoes and walked naked to the deeper end. Few men his age had his body. Women appreciated his looks. He got stares all the time. He didn't really need his cow of a wife. Just her money. That kind of bank account opened so many doors, paved the way for anything he wanted or could conceive of having.

"Hi, Robert."

Robert spun around at the sound of a soft, very gentle voice. A man's voice, but it somehow made its way right inside of him. Penetrating deep. The man was tall. Very good-looking. He wore jeans that rode low on his hips and a thin leather vest that was open over a chest that was all muscle. There were scars, a multitude of them stretching over his abdomen and running down his narrow hips. His hair was messy, his eyes a strange crystal blue.

"Who are you? What are you doing here?" Robert demanded, suddenly very aware he was absolutely naked and vulnerable. In spite of that soft, gentle tone, this man felt dangerous. Lethal even.

"Name's Absinthe. My club's Torpedo Ink." He half

turned and showed his club's colors, a tree with skulls buried in the roots and ravens in the branches. The top rocker proclaimed *Torpedo Ink* and the bottom said *Sea Haven–Caspar.*

Triumph burst through Robert. He didn't care about the indiscretion of penetrating his security or even how it was done. A club had found Scarlet Foley, and by the looks of this man, it was a very scary outlaw club. The little bitch hopefully got what was coming to her and now she was going to be delivered into his hands. He was going to make certain she suffered a long time before he sold her into human trafficking to live out the rest of her life in the worst places possible.

"I presume you're here about Scarlet Foley."

"Solokov." The voice was very mild.

"I'm sorry?" Holden frowned.

"Scarlet Solokov. Her name is Scarlet Solokov. Not Foley. She's married."

"I don't give a fuck if she's married or what her name is, the price is still the same. Did you come to collect the fee or not?"

"I have the money," Absinthe replied gently. "And you should care that she's married. She's my wife. I'm really pissed that you put out a contract on her. She was already pissed at you for bailing that worthless asshole rapist son of yours out of every crime he committed over and over, but she would have let it go after killing the little pissant. But then you just had to put that contract out on her. That was a stupid move on your part. Didn't it occur to you to do just a little research before you went that far?"

Robert's eyes lifted to the cameras that were trained on his backyard and the pool. His heart had accelerated to the point he feared a heart attack.

Absinthe smiled at him, but it was more the smile of a predator than one of humor. "Those cameras are useless to you. We took them over. If you're feeling vulnerable out here naked, we could go inside. Doesn't much matter to me where we talk. You go ahead and choose. Wherever you're more comfortable."

Robert indicated the house immediately. He had weapons and phones inside. Absinthe stepped back and waved him toward the house. Robert tried to hide his excitement and forced himself to walk slowly. Behind him, for such a big man, particularly one wearing motorcycle boots, Absinthe seemed to walk very quietly.

Robert took two steps inside, caught the slider and yanked, trying to force it to close as he took several running steps. Immediately he realized two things: the room held several people, and the broken pieces from all the glasses he'd shattered were lying all over the floor and he was barefoot. He yelped and tried hopping, bumping into the coffee table and then the low-slung couch. The couch was occupied by two men who looked exactly alike. They appeared to be eating from the exotic fruits he had laid out in his Irish cut-crystal bowl—part of the set he intended to smash tonight.

One looked up at him and smiled. "Take a seat, Bobby." He waved him to the chair opposite of him. "Your foot's bleeding everywhere. Looks like it hurts. Name's Ice. My brother Storm. That's Savage. He doesn't talk much, and you don't want him to, so don't piss him off."

He indicated one of the scariest-looking men Holden Sr. had ever laid eyes on. The man obviously shaved his head, had muscles and tattoos everywhere and the coldest, deadest eyes on him. Those eyes seemed to go right through Holden, as if he wasn't even a human being to the biker. It didn't escape his notice that there was a very large plastic tarp laid out in front of the bald man and the other one standing, unmoving, next to him, covered in what looked like Russian prison tattoos. Everyone in the room, and there seemed to be quite a few people, wore thin biker gloves. For the first time in his life, Robert felt both sick and a little faint.

He looked around for his clothes. Seeing none, he dropped into the seat opposite Ice and Storm and then tried to find a pillow to at least put over his lap, but even those were gone. There was a faint stirring and Scarlet was suddenly there, looking at him as if he were a distasteful insect she was about to squash.

"Your son, Robert, and his two friends did a lot of screaming, or at least they tried to. I taped their mouths closed and read books. I spent hours with Robert Jr. He had a lot to confess and seemed to want to talk, but in between his bouts with the clapper and his endless 'daddy' talks, I had time to study up on Arabic. It's a fascinating language. I'm much better at reading it than speaking it, and Robert Jr. made so much noise I really had to tape his mouth for some time. It was annoying, Holden. Not only did you raise a rat bastard of a son, but he was a coward as well. It will be interesting to see what kind of man you are."

"You want me to believe that you actually killed my son without the aid of your husband or these others?" Holden couldn't keep the sneer out of his voice. "Whoring yourself out to a club so they do your dirty work for you doesn't make you brave."

Absinthe caught him by his hair and yanked his head back, slapping him hard enough that for a moment his ears rang. The slap was very casual, and Holden would have much preferred to have been punched. It felt as if the biker had disrespected him, and judging by the grins on the other men's faces, he had. Scarlet blew her husband a kiss and smiled that same little half smile that was more of a smirk that he'd come to despise when she was in court. The one that told him she knew what was going on, but she didn't care—that she was already planning to retaliate.

"I didn't meet my husband until a year after I killed Robert Jr. We actually had to interrupt our honeymoon in order to take care of this little piece of business. I was going to let it go, but then you sent the other clubs after us and the

Diamondbacks were pissed at you and so was Absinthe, and now I am all over again."

She swung her gaze to Ice. "You're recently married. Wouldn't it upset you just a teeny tiny bit to have to interrupt your honeymoon because some sleazy-ass, hedonist, self-important, narcissistic, asshole stalker obsessed with you put out a contract on you? Wouldn't that just make you a little upset?"

Ice snickered. Scarlet turned her attention back to Holden, her tone still mild. "As if any woman would want to do you, Bobby boy, when your dick is so small. No wonder you're always paying for sex and your wife ran the moment she had a good excuse."

"You fucking whore," Holden burst out again. "I'm not obsessed with you. Not the way you make it sound."

Before he got another word out, a small silver object hurtled across the room so fast it whistled, the only warning. At the same time, Absinthe's fist settled in Robert's scalp again, jerking his head back, nearly breaking his neck. The very small knife cut perfectly into Holden's flaccid member, shaving skin off the left side. Blood poured out around the blade and ran down his leg onto the silk black-and-white damask cushion of the three-thousand-dollar custom-made chair. Robert screamed loudly.

Destroyer murmured something in Russian and Savage replied back immediately. Scarlet looked to Absinthe for an explanation.

"Destroyer isn't happy with Savage that he deliberately missed."

"I didn't miss," Savage denied, walking around the couch to retrieve the small throwing knife. "Hit exactly where I meant to hit. Shut the fuck up. You're not that hurt. I could start slicing inches off. You talk to my sister like that again and I will." He wiped the blood from the two-inch blade on the cushion of the chair and walked back to stand where he'd been, just in front of the shadows.

"I don't understand why you didn't just whack that teeny little dick off," Destroyer said. "He shouldn't talk to her like that. But you were very inventive on our last trip so I'm willing to learn."

"Go ahead, *moya literaturnaya ledi*," Absinthe encouraged. "Say your piece and then we're going home. Savage and Destroyer can handle this one for us."

Scarlet turned her head, her gaze meeting Savage's. "You look good, Savage. Very relaxed. Both of you do. I don't think it's necessary to carry this one out. Holden isn't worth it, not to me. He really is absolutely nothing. Nothing at all. I truly mean that. I won't lose sleep over him. Or think about him ever again. I don't want either of you to think about this night."

Savage shrugged, his broad shoulders rolling easily. "Your call, honey. You know it won't matter to me either way. I'll do it for you."

"I know you would and that's the most amazing gift of all, that all of you would." Scarlet turned her attention back to Robert Holden. "How sad for you, that you had everything, and you threw it all away."

She stood up and turned her back on him, moving gracefully through the bikers. Not just gracefully, Holden decided, but regally. In spite of the fact that he hated her, loathed her, *despised* her with every breath he took, he knew she had somehow bested him again. It made no sense because she was nothing. Absolutely nothing, and yet she was walking away, dismissing him, not even delivering the last blow, as if he wasn't even worth that much.

Robert Holden Sr. wanted to scream at her to come back, to shoot him, to torture him, to do something, but the bikers were filing out after her. All but one. All but her husband, who had looped something thin and sinister around his neck and was slowly tightening it to the point that he couldn't breathe.

Absinthe leaned down so that his warm breath was in

Holden's ear, almost soothing the pounding of his wild, erratic heartbeat. "I'm not quite as nice as she is. You put a contract out on my wife, you worthless son of a bitch. She single-handedly killed that pussy son of yours and his little pissant friends. You did it because she bested you. And you couldn't take it."

As he spoke, that voice nearly gentle, mild, even soothing, the noose tightened by slow increments, cutting off Holden's air supply so that his body began to thrash in protest. It didn't matter. The man behind him was too strong. Without mercy.

"The contract on your wife has been called off. She won't inherit your money because you're penniless. Your money now belongs to my wife and is completely untraceable. The cash you kept hidden belongs to Torpedo Ink and Scarlet, but your woman gets all those properties you purchased on your own and hid from her so you could have your fun with other women, and of course, your life insurance policy."

The noose continued to tighten slowly, relentlessly. Holden's heels drummed on the floor, spilling blood from the deep cuts from the crystal glasses he'd deliberately shattered against his fireplace and then carelessly stepped on.

"Scarlet will live a happy, full life. Everyone will know what lousy, filthy human beings you and your son were. They'll know how you manipulated the courts to convict a young teen after your son and his friends tried to rape her and that you knew they had but because she defended herself, you wanted her in prison. They'll know how your son and his friends gang-raped her sister, driving that child to suicide, and even then you defended him and tried to keep Scarlet in prison. No one will ever want to be associated with your name. And Scarlet? She'll be happy. Living her life."

There was pain, anguish, a terrible raw burning in his lungs, but no strength in his arms when he tried to lift them to pry the deadly noose from his throat. It just cut deeper and deeper until the blackness took over and he couldn't see or breathe and the world around him faded and was gone.

Transporter will take you and Scarlet back, Absinthe. Move it fast. The others will set the stage for the cops, Czar ordered. *The moment that any one of these bodies are found, the cops will come knocking on your door and you'd better be home and in bed looking like honeymooners.*

~

Absinthe considered that they were very lucky for a variety of reasons. Transporter handled the Viper like a race car, shaving significant time from the three and a half hours it would take the majority of people to make the drive in the middle of the night with no traffic. One of his gifts, which Absinthe could never quite figure out, was how Transporter managed to know when they were coming up on cop, or when one was in the vicinity at all. He seemed to be a human radar detector. He always slowed and obeyed all traffic laws.

Transporter delivered the two of them to their front door and with a wave was gone, leaving Absinthe alone with Scarlet, and he immediately lifted her into his arms and carried her over the threshold, nuzzling her throat. "Should have done this that first night, baby. Don't want evil demons following us around anymore. We've had our share."

She settled her arms around his neck. "Yes, we have."

"Clothes off," he ordered, nibbling on her neck.

She unbuttoned her blouse and he carried her through the house, peeling off her clothes as she unfastened them, leaving a trail to the back deck where the hot tub was. She was naked by the time he got her there. Naked and laughing. He loved her laugh. Loved the way her eyes lit up. The moonlight spilled down on her red hair, turning it into a blaze of fire. She already had the silken mass piled on top of her head, twisted into some kind of knot.

He liked very hot water, so his outdoor tub was blazing hot and she gasped as she sank down into it. "Absinthe. This could take your skin off."

"Or take all the kinks out." He scattered his clothes down the hall from the front room to the outdoor deck almost on top of hers, making it seem as if they had come through their living room and couldn't quite make it outside before they were all over each other.

She rolled her eyes. "I don't think that's ever going to happen. You're always going to be a little kinky and I like you that way."

He caught her around the waist and pulled her onto his lap, cupping the weight of her breasts in his hands, kissing her upturned mouth. "That's a good thing, baby, because I'm crazy in love with you."

⟜

The doorbell was loud and demanding. Absinthe went from a deep sleep to instantly alert. His body was curled around Scarlet's, his arm locked around her waist, his cock snuggled in the seam of her cheeks. She rolled with him.

"Cops," he announced, peering into the security screen, which clearly showed the two men at the front door. "Don't get dressed, baby. Put that nearly transparent long shirt on, as if you hastily threw it on. Wear a thong. Come out right after me, hair falling down, very messy, and look sleepy as hell." He'd marked her skin, so she looked well used and very his.

He dragged on a pair of the silky drawstring pants and called into the intercom. "This better be important, Jonas. I'll be right there." He strode down the hall leading to the main part of the house. When he opened the door, he was barefoot, bare chested, hair rumpled from sleep, and he wore only the thin drawstring pants.

Jonas Harrington, the local sheriff, and Jackson Deveau, the deputy, both stood on his verandah, eyes sharp, taking in every detail, including his woman's fingernail scratches at his shoulders and the little bites at his neck.

"What's wrong?" Absinthe demanded, waving them inside. "Is everyone all right?" He looked around for his phone. "Damn it. Blythe? Czar? The kids?"

There was a little whisper of feet and Scarlet rushed in, looking sexy, disheveled and very upset. Beneath the long boyfriend shirt she'd "thrown on" hastily, her full breasts were bouncing as she ran. Her red hair tumbled around her face, falling in a mass of silk, yet anyone could see the marks of his possession on her neck and down to the curves of her breasts. Bite marks, strawberries, an obvious night of wild possession.

"Honey? Is something wrong? Someone hurt?" Scarlet skidded to a halt, one hand going defensively to her throat when she saw the two uniformed men. She backed up a couple of steps. "I thought it was Czar."

Absinthe picked up one of the throw blankets on the chairs and wrapped it around her, covering her body. "It's all right, *miledi*. They were just about to tell me why they're here. Scarlet, this is Jonas Harrington and Jackson Deveau. They're law, but they're good guys. My wife, Scarlet." He waved the two men to a seat and sank down in the widest chair, pulling Scarlet down on his lap. He wrapped his arms around her, locking her to him, his chin on her shoulder, eyes on the two men. "Get it done, gentlemen. I left my phone in the bedroom. If it's one of my brothers I want you to just spit it out fast."

Jonas shook his head. "Everyone's fine as far as I know, Absinthe. We're here on another matter. It's nice to meet you, ma'am, and we're sorry to disturb you, but we received a call from a police department in the Bay Area. Several bodies were discovered tonight. Calloway, the judge who presided over your trial; your defense attorney; the prosecutor; a doctor who was a witness for the prosecution; and Robert Holden Sr. Three of the bodies had cards pinned to their chests made out to you, Ms. Scarlet."

Jonas leaned forward, looking right into her eyes. Absinthe kept his arms around her. She let out a small distressed sound and looked back at him over her shoulder. "I swear this nightmare is never going to end." Her voice trembled, a thread of sound, barely there. So genuine.

"The card said the men were killed as a wedding present to you from a fan. Calloway was murdered in a hidden room housing stolen masterpieces, artwork that belongs in museums. Holden was killed in his house in the same manner, a garrote," Jonas continued.

Jackson, as usual, didn't say anything, preferring Jonas to do all the talking. His gaze didn't stray from Scarlet's face or her body, although Absinthe did his best to break up the way the other man could see her, using his arms and chin. Torpedo Ink had studied the two law enforcement officers very early on when they knew they were going to settle in Caspar. Jackson was their human lie detector just as Absinthe was Torpedo Ink's.

"It's over," Absinthe assured. "Whoever did this has nothing to do with you, Scarlet. You're safe with us. You've got a life here with me." He pressed his lips right over the pulse in her neck. It wasn't even elevated. She was damn good at what she did. He was proud of her.

"How do you know this person hasn't fixated on me and isn't going to try to kill you or . . ." Scarlet trailed off and waved her hand vaguely in the direction of the clubhouse.

"I'm sorry, Absinthe, Scarlet. We have to ask a few questions and then we'll get out of your hair."

Jonas was skilled at interrogation, sounding friendly, asking Scarlet questions about anyone she knew who might have shown interest in the trial and/or thought it had been unfair. Had anyone written to her in prison on a regular basis? The interview lasted nearly an hour. In all that time, Scarlet acted by turns frightened or upset.

In the end, Jonas and Jackson seemed satisfied that they knew nothing at all about the murders and that there was no way they had been anywhere near the Bay Area during the time the men had been killed. Jonas told them that detectives from the Bay Area assigned to the case most likely would want to talk to Scarlet themselves at some point in their investigation, but not to worry too much about it.

Absinthe walked the two men to the door, accepted their apologies and took his wife back to bed, grateful he'd been awakened in the middle of the night so he had the chance to take his time making love to her.

TWENTY

—◆—

Scarlet was so excited she was nearly jumping up and down, waiting for him to sling his leg over the Harley and make his way up to the house. Perversely, Absinthe wanted to take his time and just enjoy the show she was putting on for him. She looked so beautiful, her face lit up, happiness giving her a carefree, even younger appearance.

He had taken his time making his way on the bike from the clubhouse to their home, using the twisting back roads rather than utilizing Highway 1 to take a shorter route. Normally, Scarlet loved every moment she could have on the motorcycle with him, her arms locked around him, hands at his waist, sometimes sliding lower to tease him, but this time, she hissed in his ear to hurry, which only made him slow down, joy spreading through his gut at her reaction.

Her entire body vibrated with eagerness. She was nearly as coiled with tension and ready to explode as when he played deliberate sexual games with her body. He loved playing. Prolonging that tension. Stretching that time out until he could hear and see and feel her need for him. Right now—and it had never happened before without sex being involved—the tension felt the same way. Whatever Scarlet had done for him mattered so much to her that he knew even if he didn't like it, he was going to find a way to love it because she had cared this much to give it to him.

Scarlet had talked him into staying at the clubhouse with her for the last three weeks while Maestro, Master, Player and Keys renovated their house at her direction. He hadn't been allowed to go near it. His brothers had been closed-mouth, refusing to tell him one single thing about what she was up to with her surprise remodel. She'd been the one to design everything and had worked closely with his four brothers. They grinned at him a lot, but they continued to be tight-lipped even when he'd made a halfhearted attempt to bribe them.

She said the renovation was a birthday gift. He reminded her his birthday was a few months earlier. She just laughed and said that didn't matter, that only meant it was a *belated* birthday present and she just owed him all the more. Now, watching her hop from one foot to the other while he strad-dled the Harley, pretending to fiddle with one of the compartments while she was bursting with impatience, it was all he could do to keep a straight face.

"Absinthe."

He glanced up. Casually. One eyebrow lifted. *Bog.* She was so beautiful she took his breath. The sun hadn't yet set, although the fog was beginning to creep in, little fingers of mist drifting on the wind. The rays of the sun caught the brilliant red of her hair, turning it into flashes of ruby, re-minding him of the gemstones in the furred tails Ice had made for them. He wasn't certain she would ever play his *kiska* again for him and he knew he needed that kitten in his bed at times. He hadn't brought himself to talk to her about it, not after the disaster of their wedding night.

Scarlet stepped close to the bike, her hands framing his face. "What is it, honey? You suddenly looked so sad."

He hadn't thought to keep his emotions off his face. This was her moment and just like that he'd changed her mood. She was that tuned to him. He should be grateful for their close connection. It was growing all the time, but it also made it more difficult to keep anything from her. He had always thought he would be able to know her every thought, every worry. He hadn't expected it to be a two-way path. She was becoming very adept at reading him. They'd promised each other the truth. In any case, she would hear a lie. Communication was necessary in a relationship like theirs. Sometimes, it was all they would have.

He turned his face so his lips slid along her palm, pressing a kiss into the center. "I was wishing I wasn't quite so fucked up in my needs."

She leaned into him, kissing his forehead and then straightening and stepping away from the bike. "Aren't we both a little fucked up? If you're talking about me being your little pussycat, I have to admit, I miss being her. I missed our privacy and our home. I hope you like the changes and what I've created for us."

His heart kicked into overdrive at the casual way she announced that she missed being his little pussycat. He decided to take the chance and push it just a little. Swinging his leg over the bike, he stood up and held out his hand to her. "I'm happy to hear you miss being my *kiska*. That's never going to go away. Demyan planted that need so deep in me that no matter what, along with the training of my childhood, it's there for the rest of my life. In reality, I've not only accepted it, I enjoy it."

She took his hand and let him draw her close, right under his shoulder as they walked up the stairs together to the front door. He would have to put his bike up later. Torpedo Ink rarely left the motorcycles out in the saltwater air for too long. The Harleys were protected every bit as much as they protected one another.

"I've continued to read about it from a kitten's point of

view," Scarlet said. "And I watch videos. I pride myself on always being the best for you. You're going to have the best pet ever."

He punched in the new security code and stepped back to allow her to precede him so she wouldn't notice that just her saying that could bring him to his knees. She could do that so easily with her honest, casual statements. She studied how to be a better kitten for him because she wanted to be the best pet possible. For him. How many women would do that for their man? He doubted if there were many. Most would think he was far too fucked up to bother with.

He walked into the entryway behind her and stopped abruptly. The living room had been completely renovated. The huge glass wall facing the ocean was still there, letting in the light from the waning sun and showcasing the creeping fog as it began to move faster toward them, spreading out like an eerie gray blanket. Where the fireplace had been was a floor-to-ceiling thick glass wall filled with bubbling water that looked like a perpetual waterfall, but obviously housed something behind it.

She took his hand and tugged. He went with her to see her lay her palm on the plate that was a golden inset into the glass. The bubbling wall slid to one side, revealing a large rectangular glass cubicle stretching out into the inner courtyard garden. All four of the walls contained those same bubbles inside the very thick glass, creating a sound barrier between the inside and the outside world.

The floor inside the spacious room was carpeted a thick soothing gray with thin black circles. A single chair was there, clearly designed for comfort, sitting beside a small table to set books and a drink. One wall could be opened to the outside and a screen could drop down to keep insects out, or a large screened window could be utilized for cooler air.

Beside the chair was a thick square cushion. The cushion matched the soothing colors of the carpet and was built for the long-term comfort of his pet to wait for him in silence, either curled up sleeping or head on his thigh so he could pet her or kneeling between his legs, sucking his cock. The front of the cushion simply proclaimed *Yego kiska*—His pussy.

He knew Scarlet had thought to ask Lana to help her as well. The chair, the table, the cushion. That had all come with Lana's help. The room clearly was built for one reason only. His pleasure. His solace. Scarlet knew that he would always have demons and he needed places to escape to. She already knew he would need his *kiska*. He didn't have to tell her. She had removed the fireplace, a trigger for his flashbacks, and given him the gift of this to enter when he needed somewhere quiet to go.

It was no wonder he wanted to fall to his knees and worship her. How could he not? He couldn't look at her, not yet. Not with his eyes burning like hell. He just stood in the middle of the room, looking around at the stark beauty. Hearing the silence. Seeing the rolling bubbles, the various shades of green in the garden in their courtyard. He looked down at the cushion beside the chair. Slowly he turned to look at Scarlet.

His wife looked so anxious, those green eyes of hers searching his face, causing his stomach to do a slow roll and his heart to turn over. He stalked across the room to her and framed her face with both hands, leaning down to take her mouth. She even tasted like love. Like sweet fire.

"I love you so much, *moya literaturnaya ledi*. You have no idea what this means to me."

"You like it." She let out her breath.

"I would never have thought of this, not in a million years. I don't know how you did, but I'm grateful. This is going to top the library and I didn't think anything could."

She gave him a little smirk. "We're not finished yet."

"We're not?" He rubbed his palm over his heart. "You've already given me more than anyone ever has, Scarlet. I don't know if I can take more."

"They all helped. Your brothers and sisters. I couldn't have done it without them," she confessed. "I'd like to take all the credit, but they all helped me."

He knew they had to have done so, because this room alone with the extraordinary glasswork should have taken months. Scarlet took his hand and led him out of his quiet room and down the hall toward their master bedroom. He wasn't positive what to expect, but anticipation was building fast. She opened the door and stepped back to allow him to enter. He saw one hand go up to cover her mouth, her fingers pressing tight to her lips. She really was nervous.

He stepped inside their enormous bedroom. Like the living room, the bedroom had also been transformed. The fireplace had been removed and in its place was a floor-to-ceiling bookcase. The entire wall was taken up with the case. In front of the shelves was a solid oak desk, almost a replica of the one she sat behind at the library, only this one was much more suited to him and his fantasies.

There was a very large space under the desk where his *kiska* could be hidden while he sat working late. There was a cushion on top of the desk, this one matching the color of the carpet in the bedroom, with the same *Yego kiska* embroidered on the front of it in flashy letters. A golden stand sat to one side of the desk holding several jeweled collars.

The closet doors were open, and he could see that another wardrobe had been added. She took him over to it. Inside was an array of her library clothes. Her pencil skirts. The swing skirts. The prim tops. On a shelf above was an array of glasses in all colors to match the various clothing. Boots and high heels were in a separate stand beside the prim clothing.

His woman could give him whatever he wanted, his librarian or his *kiska*, or, if he preferred that night, his sexy woman in her sensual lingerie.

"I stocked the shelves with a few books I thought you'd be interested in based on what you were reading at the library," she explained. "I also included some interesting studies on sadism, which, by the way, Savage doesn't really fall into the true meaning of a sadist. I thought if we came at his problem from a strictly intellectual view, we might find ways to help him. You said you subtly influenced him over the years to be the way he is. Is it possible to reverse that need just as subtly?" She shrugged. "We can't know until we try it, right?"

"Babe." He had to sit down. Not only had she removed one of his biggest triggers, but she was trying to find ways to help Savage even after he had really frightened her. "I've tried. I don't know if it lessens for him or not, I can't tell, and I don't ask him because then he'd know what I was doing and it wouldn't work."

"I've thought a lot about the things I really want as well in our relationship. Not just want from you, but need to make us work, Absinthe." Scarlet sat on the bed. "Savage is a huge problem for you. You take on too much with him. And now there's Destroyer adding to the mix of really ugly memories that will run around in your head. I want some assurances from you and I honestly don't think they're too much to ask."

Absinthe sank down onto the bed beside her. "You're wearing too many clothes. You're in our bedroom. If we're going to have this discussion and you don't want to be naked, we have to go somewhere else."

She reached down and pulled off her T-shirt. Her nipples were already hard pebbles. "I've waited as long as you have to come home. Remember, I've known what I was coming home to. Which do you want first? Librarian? Sexy wife? *Kiska?*"

He'd had three weeks of his sexy wife and his librarian in the compound. He was desperate for his kitten. "I want *moya malen'kiy kiska*. So, talk fast. You won't be talking for a long time." He removed her bra and crouched down to take her shoes from her feet.

"When Savage is having a difficult time, when any of them are, and you need to help them by influencing them the way you do, I want to be with you. I help you. You know I do. You can touch me, and it lessens the impact on you."

"I don't like that you see what happened to them. It's . . ." He tried to search for the right word. "Invasive. It gets in your head and it also strips away their privacy."

"I realize that," Scarlet said. "I probably won't get half of what you do from them."

He shook his head immediately, going back on his heels. Retreating fast. "What I love most about our relationship is the absolute honesty between us, Scarlet. You know what's real and I do too. You'll feel their demons in your head every time. If you want this, you have to accept the consequences. If I allow it, I do as well."

She nodded and stood to slide the jeans down her hips and off her legs. He followed her to the shower. He stripped and joined her.

"We're a partnership, Absinthe," Scarlet continued. "If you continue to take on every one of your brothers' and sisters' demons, and they have so many, you're going to burn out. You know it. You have enough of your own. You need me. I take that away for you. I think my mind kind of throws it away or burns it up. I don't have Savage's images running around in my head anymore. I did for a few days and then they were gone."

Absinthe closed his eyes for a long moment, turning what she said over and over in his mind. He knew she was different than he was, that her brain worked differently. "Then yes, Scarlet, I think it's a good idea. It would be ridiculous to turn that offer down. You're intelligent and you know your own limitations just as I do. You've given me so much. This house has been transformed into something so incredible and beautiful. A place of peace. Of solace. Thank you. I love you, baby, I hope you always feel that from me in everything I say and do for you."

She nuzzled his neck and kissed his chest as he turned off the water. She reached for his cock, signaling she wanted to play. Absinthe closed his eyes and let her magic hands stroke and caress him before he stopped her, turning her around to face the wall. She hadn't been his *kiska* for quite some time and she hadn't forgotten what he liked. The playing. The satisfaction he received over and over from his little kitten while he petted and played with her. The caring she received at his whims. He kept one hand on the nape of her neck while his other slid down her spine to her wet cheeks.

"My little *kiska*. Looks bare without her pretty bushy tail. So pale. Too white. You need color, little pussycat." He smacked her wet cheek with his free hand, watching the color come up with satisfaction, then slid his fingers to her clit, flicking the little bud. "Come on, *kiska*, let's get out now. You can crawl out. I'll get your towel, collar and tail and meet you in the bedroom. Remember to behave yourself. I'll be very disappointed if you've forgotten how to behave."

Absinthe left her there, nabbing a towel as he vacated the large shower, not daring to look back. His heart raced, adrenaline pouring through his veins. He had to calm himself, let the fact that he actually had his pet back with him sink in, let that bring him peace. Toweling his body off as he walked into the bedroom and took another long look around at what his wife had done to their room for him, he let himself be overwhelmed with love for her, knowing that Scarlet was a gift beyond any price.

She got him. She knew him. She loved him without judgment, and she didn't try to change him. She not only tried to find ways to make his life better, but she tried to find ways to enjoy the lifestyle he needed. She'd given him choices in their bedroom, all of which he loved. He went to the desk and touched the collars. By using the club members to help, and openly exposing them to what she needed help with in their bedroom, she was acknowledging that they all knew his fetish for kitten play. That excited him.

He did want to show off his kitten occasionally. Never to outsiders, but once in a while he would like to bring her to a party, or if someone dropped by late at night for a drink and she was already out, he wouldn't mind displaying her. She was beautiful. Gorgeous. And he was proud of her. Showing her off was a big part of playing, although he could live without that side of it if she never got there. Looking around at the cushion on the library desk and knowing about the one in the glass room, he thought perhaps she was signaling she was very close to accepting being put on display at a Torpedo Ink party.

He drew on his silk drawstring pants, the ones that gave him room for his already hard cock to expand and allowed his little *kiska* to easily pull them down when she needed to get to her salty cream when she was hungry. The larger toy chest was in his closet and he took the tail he preferred, the last one she'd been wearing, the one with the fluffier fur and rubies and diamonds. The plug was a little wider and curved to accommodate the natural shape of her body for comfort, and a little longer in order to push her boundaries just a bit.

He laid out the tail and bottle of special lubricant on the bed. He hesitated over the harness. He loved the way it looked on her body, but he also liked the way her skin looked so pristine, muscles rippling suggestively, so feline and sensual as she crawled toward him or away from him, nothing marring his view of her.

Movement caught the corner of his eyes. Scarlet peeked around the corner of the doorway, head low to the ground, just the way a little kitten might cautiously survey a room before entering it. Every nerve ending in his body went on high alert, so aware of her and every nuance, every expression. She cocked her head from side to side, her jeweled eyes meeting his, and then she retreated fast, pulling her head back from the doorway.

"Kiska." He kept his voice gentle. That smooth velvet that caressed and soothed. "Come here to me now."

Her head slipped back around the door to study him for a moment, lashes fluttering in hesitation, and then she began that slow, sensuous crawl that was sexier than even his brain had remembered was so fucking amazing because she was even better at it. Lower to the ground, slower, almost a slow-motion freeze-frame, but not quite, still always in motion. Her hips swayed. Her breasts rocked. Her shoulders undulated as she put one hand slowly in front of her on the carpet, moving the opposite knee.

He sank down onto the edge of the bed. Spread his legs wide and patted his lap. "Crawl up here, *kiska*. You look naked without your tail and collar."

Little droplets of water clung to her, enhancing the way the waning sun shone on her skin. Already the fog was drowning out the last of the rays, but he had always enjoyed the way the mist closed in, muffling sound around the house, turning his home into what seemed like a private estate. Now, sharing his world with Scarlet, he wouldn't mind if they lived on a private island where no one could find them for days on end.

Scarlet wove her body in and out of his legs just like a little cat, rubbing her head along his thigh before she crawled up onto the bed and finally stretched herself out over him, making certain her bottom lay across his lap. Feeling her tremble, he rubbed the backs of her thighs and then her buttocks.

"You like this, *malen'kiy kiska*," he soothed. "The lotion warms you. You just stay still for me." He bent his head to press a kiss to the base of her spine. "I'll take care of you."

He poured the oil into his palms and began to rub it into the backs of her thighs, moving his hands in circles, pressing deep, going up her legs to the seam under her buttocks. "Remember how good it feels to wear your tail? How stretched and full you feel? This tail fills you and vibrates. It can do so much more than that."

He rubbed the oil on the inside of her thighs and then between her legs, wickedly painting her clit, circling it and then fucking her gently with an oil-coated finger. He painted her pussy lips and then began to rub the oil into her cheeks, his thumbs making loops into the seam, pressing deep and pulling her cheeks apart. He pressed his thumb into the little star and poured the oil directly into that little entrance, using his thumb to press in and out and then his finger, pushing deeper and deeper. The heat was beginning to grow into something else and his little pussycat began to squirm in spite of his command not to move.

He smacked her immediately. "If you're a bad kitty, I'll have to take some of your privileges away."

She meowed loudly when he smacked her, her little nails biting into his thigh.

"We haven't even started for the night," he cautioned. "I want you to stay still, *kiska*. I suppose it has been a long time and your training had just begun, but that isn't any excuse. We haven't even gotten your tail in."

He painted the glass base of the tail with the oil and began to insert it slowly, his cock jerking hard as he watched it disappear into that forbidden little star, preparing her for him. The furry tail rose proudly, rubies and diamonds scattered among the red fur. He loved the way it looked rising above her firm cheeks.

"So nice, *kiska*." He inserted one finger into the heat of her slick pussy, his heart already beating fast as he slowly stroked her tight little channel into need. "Kneel up, baby. I want to put your collar on you."

She crawled off his lap, a sensuous kitten, displaying her tail, and wound around his leg before coming to kneel in front of him. He buckled the thin gemmed collar loosely around her, not wanting her to have any reminders of their disastrous wedding night. She didn't so much as flinch.

"Tonight, I want to take advantage of the new room. I feel like reading for an hour or so. We'll see how good you can be for me while I do a little relaxing."

Scarlet purred and rubbed her face along his thigh to show her approval. He stroked her hair, loving the feeling of peace stealing into him that always came with having his pet close.

He couldn't wait to use the new room in the living area. It looked like a spacious retreat, one he might need when his demons tried to get the better of him. She had designed it for quiet and calm, surrounding him with the sounds of water and nature yet giving him silence away from the outside world.

By setting only one chair in there, Scarlet had made it clear that the room was his space and he could invite her in as his pet or he could enter alone. Their bedroom was set up to play and love in any way they chose together. The room was his, her gift to him. He wanted to get the feel of it once he was closed inside.

He settled the leash onto the ring on the collar and led his kitten down the hall back to the main part of the house. She moved exactly like a feline, every slinky muscle rippling beneath her skin as she crawled beside him. The movement of her body excited him, bringing every nerve ending in his body to life. He slowed the pace deliberately just to watch the play of her muscles, surprised that she'd put so much work, so much effort into learning how to move like a cat for him. Love for her welled up all over again, overwhelming him.

The bubbling wall slid aside to allow them entrance into the large rectangular space. He was shocked at how, once inside, with the wall closed, the room felt open because it was all glass. The bubbles rose in waves inside the thick walls of glass, rising and falling in a mesmerizing and very soothing pattern. All outside noise was completely drowned out. There was a small refrigerator in the very corner of the room closest to the inside wall, the door transparent so he could see the rows of ice-cold water bottles, the temperature exactly what he required.

The rug beneath his bare feet was thick, the color soothing to his mind. He walked his pet to the cushion beside his chair and indicated for her to kneel on it. She did so immediately, looking beautiful and poised. He retrieved a bottle of water, looked over the titles of books tucked into the little book rack built under the table and selected one before he loosened the drawstring of the silken pants. His cock was as hard as a rock.

He sank into the chair and instantly recognized Lana's influence. Soothing. Calm. So comfortable. Already he could feel that this room was going to be the place that would be his salvation when the others were struggling with their demons and needed him to siphon some of the rage and pain away.

He picked up his book. Uncapped the water. Looked around the perfection of the room. A small remote allowed him to open windows, slide back walls or bring down screens.

Scarlet had thought of this. Not only had she thought of this for him, but she'd taken that a step further and actually had it made for him. He looked at her kneeling there. His pet. His beautiful *kiska*. Waiting. Vivid green eyes on his face. Devoted. Adoring. Scarlet. The love of his life. Giving him everything he could possibly want or need. He would never deserve her. Never.

He put down the book. "Come here, baby," he whispered. Love was so strong it was almost painful.

She crawled between his legs, kneeling up. He framed her face with both hands and kissed her, needing her to know how he felt. Unable to voice the emotion that had welled up so strong that it shook him. He could only kiss her over and over and hope she understood how much she meant to him. He swore to himself that he would do everything in his power to see to it that she was always as happy as she had made him that day because he couldn't conceive of ever being happier.

TERMS ASSOCIATED WITH BIKER CLUBS

1-percenters: This is a term often used in association with outlaw bikers, as in "99 percent of clubs are law-abiding, but the other 1 percent are not." Sometimes the symbol is worn inside a diamond-shaped patch.

3-piece patch or 3-piece: This term is used for the configuration of a club's patch: the top piece, or rocker, with club name; a center patch that is the club's logo; and a bottom patch or rocker with the club's location, such as Sea Haven.

Biker: someone who rides a motorcycle

Biker friendly: a business that welcomes bikers

Boneyard: refers to a salvage yard

Cage: often refers to a car, van or truck (basically any vehicle not a motorcycle)

Chapter: the local unit of a larger club

Chase vehicle: a vehicle following riders on a run just in case of a breakdown

Chopper: customized bike

Church: club meeting

Citizen: someone not a biker

Club: could be any group of riders banding together (most friendly)

Colors: patches, logo, something worth fighting for because it represents who you are

Cut: vest or denim jacket with sleeves cut off with club colors on them; almost always worn, even over leather jackets

Dome: helmet

Getting patched: Moving up from prospect to full club member (you would receive the logo patch to wear with rockers). This must be earned, and is the only way to get respect from brothers.

Hang-around: anyone hanging around the club who might want to join

Hog: nickname for motorcycle, mostly associated with Harley-Davidson

Independent: a biker with no club affiliation

Ink: tattoo

Ink slinger: a tattoo artist

Nomad: club member who travels between chapters; goes where he's needed in his club

Old lady: Wife or woman who has been with a man for a long time. It is not considered disrespectful nor does it have anything to do with how old one is.

Patch holder: member of a motorcycle club

Patches: sewn on vests or jackets, these can be many things with meanings or just for fun, even gotten from runs made

Poser: pretend biker

Property of: a patch displayed on a jacket, vest or sometimes a tattoo, meaning the woman (usually old lady or longtime girlfriend) is with the man and his club

Prospect: someone working toward becoming a fully patched club member

KEEP READING FOR AN EXCERPT FROM THE NEXT
CARPATHIAN NOVEL BY CHRISTINE FEEHAN

DARK SONG

AVAILABLE SEPTEMBER 2020 FROM BERKLEY

Sound woke her. Elisabeta Trigovise didn't want to be awake. She wanted to sleep forever, but those weeping notes refused to allow her to succumb to her need to hide from the world. Like drops of rain drumming softly into the earth, feeding the soil, those notes slipped into her mind with a song of rising. More and more that gentle melody awakened her on each rising, became more insistent that she comply more fully. That she do more than just wake to feed and go straight back to slumber.

Whereas before the song was in her mind, now it sank into her body, her blood and bones, her heart and soul, calling to her persistently, and she knew it was the call of her lifemate—one she couldn't ignore. She didn't dare ignore. It didn't matter how terrified she was of him. She had to answer.

There was safety beneath the ground. Solace. No one could get to her. She was alone and no demands could be put on her, but she had known all along it wasn't going to last. Every rising, each time the sun set, the danger began.

She tried to sleep, but they came to feed her. At first many had come. Different ones. That had been frightening, but the blood had revived her, made her stronger, and no one had asked anything of her. She was allowed to go back to sleep in the healing soil to repair her body and fractured mind. Now, only *he* gave her blood.

Elisabeta tried not to waken, but it was too late, the song had played through her mind, those beautiful weeping notes of rain. The sun had set, and the moment it did, her body had tuned to it. She was Carpathian, that ancient race paralyzed during daylight hours and needing blood to sustain their lives. There were few of them left in the world and the fight to keep from dying out was made worse by the vampires trying to kill them.

A little shudder went through her body. Elisabeta had been tricked by a friend when she'd been young and naïve, and she'd been kidnapped, taken from her home and family and hidden away by one such vampire for centuries. She no longer remembered that young girl, or her family. She'd been reduced to this woman, who hid herself away in the ground, too terrified of everything and everyone to show herself. Sergey Malinov, the master vampire, would come for her and he would use her to destroy everyone who had shown her any kindness because that was what he did. He would never let her escape him. Never.

The moment she surfaced, he would use her, and they had no idea how powerful he was. They had rescued her, and he was angry, whispering to her, trying to get past the barriers and shields they had erected to protect her, but he was there, crouched and waiting to strike. She knew him, knew he was wholly evil. There were children in this compound, this place her rescuers thought safe. No one was safe from Sergey, least of all children.

The world had passed her by while she lived in a cage, with only her sadistic captor for company. One moment he could be falsely sweet; the next, savagely ugly, torturing her, starving her, hurting others in front of her. Leaving her alone for long periods of time so that she thought she would slowly starve to death and even welcomed that end. He was her only company. She couldn't speak unless he gave her permission. She made no decisions for herself, and after centuries, no longer knew how to make them.

She had been rescued, put in the healing ground to recover from the wounds to body and mind, but there was no recovery from centuries of captivity. She had no idea how to fend for herself. She was terrified of having to talk to strangers. They had told her she had a brother and that he had searched for her for centuries. She had thought of that often, ashamed that when she tried to remember him, her mind seemed to explode with pain, rejecting the idea of her past. She knew they would expect her to remember him, but she didn't.

She didn't remember herself as a young Carpathian woman, nor did she remember her parents. Her mind had been fractured and no amount of healing in the earth was going to change that. She wasn't that same girl who had been taken from her home. She was—nothing. No one. She wanted to remain where she was, hidden away from everyone, but she knew her time was fast running out. Her lifemate had found her. Just thinking of him made her heart pound out of control. She knew better. She knew to control herself. That simple sound would alert him, and of course it did.

Elisabeta.

His voice filled her mind. Calm. Soothing. A masterful voice. One always in control, unlike her. Her heart accelerated even more. Panic began to set in. At once the ground above her opened before she could begin to struggle for air. He did that for her. She hadn't done it for herself and it shamed her that she always had to be taken care of. The least little detail of her life had to be arranged for her because she didn't know how to do it.

She couldn't provide herself with clothing, and if her lifemate knew, he might be angry. If she spoke without permission, he might be angry. Punishments could be terrible. She didn't know the rules in this new world or with this man. She only knew what she sensed of him—that he was an ancient, far older than Sergey and much more dangerous. He terrified her on so many levels, but then everything did.

She had been befriended by Julija, a strong woman who walked her own path, walked beside her lifemate and made her own decisions. Elisabeta had dared to defy Sergey and secretly talked with her. She wanted to be strong like Julija but knew she never would be. Hundreds of years of captivity and silence, of having someone telling her what to do, of punishments and fear, had shaped her into this terrified being she had come to despise. She no longer knew who or what she was, only that she had no purpose, and she was so tired of being afraid.

She stayed very still and remained silent, terrified of being tricked. She kept her eyes closed tightly, even with the ground above her open, afraid of seeing where she was. She hadn't been out of a cage in hundreds of years. Open spaces made her feel sick and disoriented. She didn't know how to process space.

Speak to me, lifemate.

Her heart sank. That was a direct order. The first he had ever given to her. It mattered little that his voice was so different from Sergey's. He was her master and could torture her, deprive her of food, kill others in front of her. Her heart pounded out of control. *What would you have me say?*

There was a small silence that terrified her even more. Had she angered him? She really didn't know what he wanted from her.

Elisabeta, listen to my heartbeat. You are panicking for no reason. We are merely having a conversation. Breathe with me. Listen to my heartbeat and follow with yours.

She made the mistake of lifting her lashes, just for a

second. Surrounding her, she could see what appeared to be balconies where people could stand and look down onto the healing grounds where she lay. They could see her. Full-blown panic had taken hold and she couldn't find air. Her body nearly convulsed. She tried to curl into the fetal position, to sink deeper into the healing soil, allowing the rich minerals to blanket her body and hide her from any prying eyes.

She sank into waiting arms. Strong arms. She had always fantasized about being held when she needed it most. She longed for human contact—was often desperate for it—and now, somehow, she had made her fantasy so real she felt a very hard male body surrounding hers, holding her safe. With her eyes closed tight, she felt him surround her with his warmth, his heat. His breath was in her ear, his chest rising and falling behind her back.

Breathe with me, piŋe sarnanak, follow the rhythm of my heart.

Her heart tuned almost automatically to his before she could do so intentionally. The breath moved in and out of her starving lungs, pulling air into her. The air smelled of rain, of rich soil and unexpectedly of juniper and allspice mixed together. He had called her *little songbird.* That didn't seem so bad, an endearment in the ancient Carpathian language. Her heart stuttered a little at the gentleness in the way he treated her.

That's good, Elisabeta. Now tell me, while you feel safe, what is your greatest fear of rising?

She did feel safe. She burrowed deeper, imagining being held in those strong arms, feeling them tighten around her, feeling the warm breath in her ear, so steady. Breathing in and out. His heart rate never faltered. Never rose or slowed but remained that same steady rhythm as if he could always be counted on. Did she dare voice her concern aloud? Already she was terrified that she had been awake long enough to alert Sergey.

He will never give me up. He will use me to kill everyone who helped to take me from him. He's so cruel. If I don't go back to him, he will burn this place to the ground with everyone in it right in front of me.

As soon as she gave voice to her concerns, even if it was only in her mind, panic again began to burst through her. What if Sergey heard? What if he was able to monitor her in spite of the safeguards the Carpathians had so carefully woven around her? She didn't dare utter his evil name just in case the vampire was able to latch on to that.

A hand pressed into her hair, a soothing stroke down the back of her head. Like a caress. It was so strange, so unusual, such a rare, shocking feeling she'd never experienced, it stopped the welling panic before it could take her over.

Thank you for telling me your greatest fear. I know it frightened you just to tell me. What else has upset you? Be truthful with me, Elisabeta. You will not be punished for telling the truth to me no matter what you say.

Could she believe that? She had to answer him truthfully, no matter if she was punished or not. One didn't lie to one's lifemate. He would know. She took a deep breath. *You did not claim me as your lifemate. You know I am not worthy. I accept that, and I understand. I am not the same woman I was born to be. I have been corrupted by the vampire who took me and held me captive for so many years. I do understand but . . .* She broke off.

It was the truth. She didn't even know if she wanted to be claimed because she had no idea what she would do as a lifemate. Carpathians only had one. When a man was born, his soul was split in half. He carried all the darkness in him. The light was placed in a woman who was born either at the same time or later. Around the age of two hundred, Carpathians males began to lose their ability to see in color and emotions began to fade. As time went on, if they didn't find their lifemate, their world became gray and emotions retreated completely.

Men were born with the ritual binding words imprinted on them. Once they found their lifemate, their emotions and color were restored to them. They said the vows to the woman when they found her, binding them together. No man waited, especially an ancient hunter who had lived long and suffered greatly.

Still, she *did* understand. She was conflicted about her feelings. If he claimed her, it would be another layer of protection for her against Sergey. Ferro Arany was a very dangerous man. She could feel that even beneath the ground. He was older than so many of them, and most had been on earth a long time. He was a skilled warrior. She was a little humiliated that he didn't want her, even if she did understand.

It had been drilled into her almost from the moment of birth that somewhere was her other half and he would be actively looking for her. Always looking for her. To know that he found her and didn't want her was another blow to her. Although, if he had claimed her, she would have been even more terrified, so that made no sense at all. She just needed to stay in the ground where she could lose herself and not have to face the world she didn't understand.

I intend to claim you now, piŋe sarnanak. You are going to leave this healing ground, and to do so, you will need my protection. I feel your fear of the unknown beating at me and wish to protect you from that, but most of all from him. He cannot get to you here, and he will know, once we are bound together, that he cannot have you unless he destroys our bond. He can only do that if he kills me. With me protecting you, and shielding you, this vampire cannot use you to harm anyone here at the compound. You have no need to worry about him using you to that end.

His heart rate never rose. His voice was as calm as ever. He didn't seem to fear Sergey in the least or to be impressed that the master vampire had outsmarted his four older siblings and even powerful mages. The vampire led an army against the Carpathians, yet Ferro seemingly wasn't worried about him.

I do not know what a lifemate does. I have forgotten so much.

He was claiming her to protect her from Sergey. While his last statement brought tremendous relief, it also brought her clarity. He was an ancient hunter. He had spent several lifetimes sacrificing for his people. Binding himself to her would be nothing in comparison to what he had suffered on behalf of the Carpathian people. That made perfect sense to her.

I will have no trouble telling you what I expect from you.

She hoped so, because she wasn't good at thinking for herself. Julija was trying to help her with that. Julija told her she had a couple of friends who would love to meet her, and they would be as welcoming as Julija, but even that scared Elisabeta. Everything scared her.

Hands circled her arms and began to rub up and down them. *You are shivering. There is no need to be so afraid, piŋe sarnanak. You have only to look to me and I will help you when you feel you cannot find your way.*

She wanted to cry, but she had long ago run out of tears. *I lost my way a long time ago. I have no knowledge of any way. I cannot talk without permission. I do not dress myself or know how. I cannot do my hair or find my own food. I cannot be out in the open. I am lost, a burden to a man who does not want the responsibility of a prisoner.*

Sas, piŋe sarnanak. I am an ancient, not a modern warrior. I am your lifemate. My soul calls to yours. When you have a question, you are to ask me immediately. That is an order. Do you understand?

Without permission?

You always have permission to talk to me or to your female friends. If the vampire tries to reach you, and for some reason I do not feel him, you must come to me im-

mediately no matter what he threatens. That is an absolute rule. Do you understand?

She swallowed hard. The rules were certainly different, but she felt better that there were rules. She understood structure. *Yes. I will obey.*

Once she gave her word, she would never go back on it. She liked that he gave her permission to talk to Julija. She wouldn't have to sneak, and she would have tried to. That would have been difficult. Once he tied them together, he would have been slipping in and out of her mind easily. She wouldn't always know he was there.

Te avio päläfertiilam. You are my lifemate. Éntölam kuulua, avio päläfertiilam. I claim you as my lifemate.

Her breath caught in her throat. The ritual binding words. His arms were real. She felt him there, surrounding her, but she still didn't have the courage to open her eyes and look at him, to see what her lifemate looked like. He felt big. All muscle. When her heart began to hammer, his immediately tuned to hers and once more slowed her rhythm.

Ted kuuluak, kacad, kojed. I belong to you. Élidamet andam. I offer my life for you. Pesämet andam. I give you my protection.

His lips slid into her hair, nuzzled the side of her neck right over her pounding pulse. His tongue touched her skin. It felt . . . erotic. Her pulse jumped. He made her feel things she didn't know were possible. His arms felt safe when she'd never been safe, not even in her own home.

Uskolfertiilamet andam. I give you my allegiance.

Was that even possible? It was a vow. More than a promise. A vow between two souls. His allegiance was to her. Her eyes burned. More than anything she wanted to be strong for herself. To stand on her own two feet and be a partner to her lifemate. Maybe not the kind of partner Julija was, but at least someone Ferro could be proud of. Not some shrinking ball of terror hiding under the ground.

Sívamet andam. I give you my heart. Sielamet andam. I give you my soul. Ainamet andam. I give you my body. Sívamet kuuluak kaik että a ted. I take into my keeping the same that is yours.

His heart was given to her. His soul. His body. And he took hers in return. Her mouth went dry. She could handle it if he took her heart and soul, but her body? Even the vampire hadn't taken that. He couldn't. That was all she had left of herself that belonged to her. Her pulse jumped under his touch and he soothed her with a soft brush of his lips. His hands continued to rub her arms gently.

Ainaak olenszal sívambin. Your life will be cherished by me for all time. Te élidet ainaak pide minan. Your life will be placed above mine for all time. Te avio päläfertiilam. You are my lifemate. Ainaak sívamet jutta oleny. You are bound to me for all eternity. Ainaak terád vigyázak. You are always in my care.

His lips wandered down the side of her neck, and then he was suddenly shifting his body out from under her, so she lay in a fine mattress of rich minerals with his heavy body blanketing hers. His lips kissed both closed eyelids.

"Are you ever going to look at me and see your lifemate, *piŋe sarnanak*?" There was the faintest trace of amusement in his voice.

She pressed her lips together. *Only if you command me. I mean, yes. But . . .* She couldn't. Not yet. As long as she had her eyes closed, she could enjoy his touch. Pretend her world was going to be all right. If she opened them and the world was too big or she panicked, and everything frightened her, he would realize just what he had tied himself to for all eternity.

He didn't command her to open her eyes. His lips continued a slow travel from her eyelids along her left cheek to the corner of her mouth. Her heart stuttered as he brushed across the curve of her lips and then down her chin and throat. He continued lower over the curve of her breasts.

For a moment she thought to bring her hands up to cover herself, but it seemed a little silly. Her body belonged to him. She had scars. He had already seen them. He had already seen how thin she was.

His lips moved back and forth in a mesmerizing way, pushing out coherent thought. She didn't know what he was doing. She was feeling, but she wasn't quite certain what. She wanted to bring her arms up and touch him, to put her hands in his hair. She could feel it sweeping over her skin, a thick mass sliding over her, sending ripples of awareness and adding to the slow heat building in her veins caused by his mouth moving on her body. The scrape of his teeth sent a dark shiver down her spine. Unexpectedly, her sex clenched. In all her years of being alive, that had never once happened. It was shocking. Maybe even a little mortifying, mostly because she didn't know what it meant.

His teeth sank deep and she bit back a gasp at the shocking wave of pain that instantly turned to erotic pleasure, spreading flickering flames through her body. She could have sworn flames licked at her skin and the insides of her belly, smoldered between her legs and threatened to build an inferno in her deepest core that could never be put out if he didn't stop.

She couldn't stop her arms from creeping around him, no matter how hard she tried. She cradled his head to her, needing him to feast on her, to sate himself on her blood. Nothing in her life had prepared her for the way it felt with him taking her blood. He could drain her dry and she would be happy. When Sergey had taken her blood, it had been painful; a terrible, torturous experience. With Ferro, it was a wonderful, sensual, shocking encounter. He held her in his arms as if she meant something to him. His mouth moved over her like she was priceless.

Again, her eyes burned, when she had no tears to shed. No one had ever treated her the way he did, not that she could remember. If she had to have a new master, no matter if he turned cruel later, she had this moment, this one moment, to hold on to and treasure. Did she believe that he would stay kind to her? No. Not really. She'd lived with terror for so long that she didn't know how to live without it, but she was determined to hold on to every decent moment life gave her. This one was unexpected—a true gift.

His tongue swept across the pinpricks, closing them, and he shifted back and to one side, taking her with him, lifting her as if she weighed no more than a feather and settling her onto his lap. He swept her hair back and pressed her face to his chest.

"Drink, *piŋe sarnanak*. You need to take my blood in the way I took yours."

Her eyelashes fluttered before she could stop them. Curiosity was one of her worst traits. It always had been. Sergey Malinov had known that about her. She had tried so hard to suppress that need to find out every little thing, and she still couldn't help herself at times. Like now. Her lashes lifted and she found herself staring into her lifemate's face for the first time.

She had known he was dangerous. Lethal even. His face could have been carved from stone, etched out of the hardest rock known to man. His jaw was set, stubborn, his eyes the color of iron ore, a light, almost silvery color, although she could see streaks of the lightest blue and just the faintest jagged lines of rust spread through the irises. His lashes were dark like his hair, although his hair had streaks of silver running through it. He had high cheekbones, an aristocratic nose and a dark shadow along his jaw where most Carpathian men were clean-shaven.

His gaze drifted possessively over her face. He didn't smile at her, but he bent his head and his lips moved over her eyes, pressing kisses over them.

"You're very brave, Elisabeta."

She wouldn't call it bravery. The moment she opened her eyes and saw his face, saw all that male power, she knew she was in trouble. She'd had to fight her first inclination to hurl herself to the ground and try to burrow into the soil fast. She knew from experience there was no running away. She was always captured, and the repercussions were terrible. Still, the admiration in his voice, that respect, was totally unexpected and caught her off guard.

"Take my blood, *piŋe sarnanak*. You are very pale. I can feel your hunger beating at me."

She was so used to being hungry she barely noticed it anymore if she hadn't gone weeks without blood. He pressed the back of her head very gently, urging her face toward his bare chest. She transferred her gaze there. He had a thick chest, with heavy, defined muscles. He wore ancient ink, the kind etched into his skin. It was difficult to tattoo a Carpathian. Ink didn't stay. Carpathians rarely scarred. Ferro had ink pressed into scarring on his chest, arms, shoulders and, she was certain, his back.

The back of her head fit into his palm easily and he pressed her close to his skin, to those heavy muscles. At once she caught his intriguing scent and drew it deep into her lungs. Something about the way he smelled got to her on a molecular level. She instantly wanted to taste his skin— no, *needed* to taste him. Without thinking, her tongue lapped at him. An exotic, perfect flavor burst on her tongue and slid down her throat, bringing a heat to her belly. She almost keened with delight. Nothing tasted like he did. Nothing.

Her teeth scraped back and forth over his pulse while she contemplated what his blood would taste like. Would it be that good? Would it live up to the promise of his scent? The mere flavor of his skin? He had fed her before, when she was beneath the ground and he slept above her, but he hadn't claimed her, hadn't joined them together. Was there a difference? She had been too terrified to notice then. She was terrified now, but . . . He groaned. It was just a soft sound, but it went straight to her sex. Like an arrow.

"Elisabeta, take my blood." He growled the command at her. His voice was velvet soft, but still, it was a growl. An order.

She sank her teeth instantly. Deep. Without preamble. Shocking him. Shocking her. He threw his head back, his hand locking her head to his chest while the other pinned her hip to his, holding her still, forcing her to realize she was squirming on his lap, her bare cheeks sliding over his fully erect cock. She would have been mortified, but already his blood was in her mouth. Not just any blood—an aphrodisiaic, the finest thing she'd ever tasted in her life.

Ferro would never have enough blood to give to her. Never. She would forever crave his blood. Nothing would taste this good and she knew it. She tried not to be greedy. She'd been trained not to take what she needed. If she tried, Sergey beat her into submission. Twice, she tried to pull back, but Ferro murmured his displeasure and held her to his chest. She continued feeding, grateful he allowed it, grateful for the rich sustenance from a true ancient, but more importantly, the amazing gift a lifemate's blood provided.

"That's enough, Elisabeta," Ferro said finally, gently stroking her hair. "In all the years of my existence, no one has ever tasted the way you do. I hope it was the same for you."

She reluctantly slid her tongue across the pinpricks to close them and lifted her head away from temptation. She nodded. "It was."

He continued to stroke her hair. "That is a good thing. I want you to come to me when you are hungry. If you can't find me, reach out to me. Don't wait until you feel starved. You will need extra feedings for a while."

At once panic set in. "I won't be with you? If I'm not with you, won't I be in the ground? I can't be on my own. I won't know what to do." Her heart rate had gone crazy and her lungs burned for air. She couldn't do this. She really couldn't. She couldn't even look around her, let alone be on her own. Just because he held her and gave her blood and gave her permission to speak didn't mean she could maneuver her way through a world she didn't know or understand.

She clapped a hand over her mouth to keep from blurting out another word. It was already far too late. He could read her mind anyway. She'd gone from appearing half-normal— or at least she hoped she looked that way—to looking insane. He was stuck with crazy. She did try to crawl off his lap back to the welcoming soil. It was impossible to move when Ferro didn't want her going anywhere. He simply clamped his arms around her and held her to him.

"You are having another panic attack. Breathe. I am not going to leave you on your own until you are ready. Stay still, *piŋe sarnanak*. Just breathe while we go over a few more rules."

She could do that. Rules made her feel safe. She liked rules. He stroked her hair in that soothing way he had, and she found herself following his breathing pattern. She liked that he called her "little songbird." It sounded a little like an endearment. He wasn't making fun of her, or taunting her. He seemed only gentle when he could crush her so easily.

"I know that you are very afraid of Malinov attacking this compound."

She gasped at his audacity in naming the master vampire. She even put her fingers up to cover his lips before she could stop herself. It was a terrible transgression, and the moment she did it, she knew she should be punished. She dropped her hand into her lap and bowed her head.

"I'm sorry. Truly. I shouldn't have touched you without permission. There is no excuse. Whatever you deem is a fit punishment . . ."

Ferro caught her hand and returned her fingertips to his lips. "I am your lifemate. You are allowed to touch me when you wish or have need. Sometimes those needs will be for comfort, other times they might be sexual. You might just want to feel close. Whatever the reason, there is no need to ask for permission. I intend to touch you at will."

She was confused, frowning at him. "But I belong to you. You have the right to touch me when you desire to do so."

He shook his head. "I belong to you as well, Elisabeta, but we are lifemates, not master and prisoner. Not master and slave owner. Not vampire and captive. Those days are over for you. He will not get you back. You have every right to say no. To me or to anyone else."

Elisabeta was more confused than ever. Shocked even. She didn't understand what he was telling her. It sounded so farfetched she was afraid he was trying to trick her. The inevitable panic began to well up and she pushed her fist into her mouth, biting down hard on her knuckles. She didn't understand anything. The cool earth looked so good to her. She understood the richness, the wealth of the soil. The way it surrounded her body and eased the pain in her joints the tiny cage had caused when she couldn't exercise properly or get enough blood to sustain her. This world she found herself in now was so foreign to her that she didn't understand even one small part of it.

Ferro stroked more caresses in her hair, soothing her. "We are going to start with simple things. Do you remember how to clothe yourself or is this something the vampire insisted he do?"

That shamed her. "He did if he allowed clothing. He always made decisions."

"Do you prefer to wear dresses or trousers?"

Her heart accelerated. Was it a trick question? What did he prefer? She'd never worn trousers in her life. Not once. She knew Julija wore them, but they looked as if they might be uncomfortable. Would Ferro want her to wear them?

"Do you want me to wear dresses or trousers?" she countered, trying not to sound as timid as she felt.

"This is about what you want. There is no right or wrong answer, *piŋe sarnanak*, only what you would really prefer."

She couldn't possibly choose. There was no way. She hadn't made a choice in hundreds of years. Not one single choice. She shook her head, refusing to look at him, refusing to answer.

Elisabeta expected him to be angry, frustrated, to lose patience with her, but his hand continued the gentle strokes in her hair. She realized her long, thick hair—hair that had never been cut—was clean, and as he burrowed his strong fingers into it to massage her scalp, the strands slid through his fingers free of tangles.

"I prefer dresses, but I am an ancient warrior, Elisabeta, not at all modern. I have not had time to catch up to this world. I do not want to color your choices with my own. Still, if you prefer me to choose for you at this time, I will show you two different dresses that I really like, and you can decide which one to wear this evening and which you will wear next rising. Is that acceptable to you?"

She would still have to make a choice, but he liked both dresses and, in the end, she would wear both of them. Her only choice was which to wear tonight and which one the following rising. The thought of making that decision was still difficult, but exciting. It was a decision. *Her* decision. Ferro was letting her choose.

"Yes, I like the idea very much," she agreed.

"But it is still a little scary to you," he said.

Of course, he would know. There was no hiding her pounding pulse from him. She bit her lip and nodded slowly, daring to lift her lashes and sneak a peek at his face to see if he was exasperated with her. She wouldn't blame him if he was. He looked so invincible, as if nothing in the world had ever frightened him. Nothing. How could he sit there so calmly in the middle of the healing grounds, taking his time as if he had nowhere else in the world to be but right there with her, sorting out the terrifying new world she found herself in?

"When you get very frightened, *piŋe sarnanak*, always

remember that you have only to look into your mind and I am there with you. You can hear our song. It soothes you every rising. The sound of the rain calling to you to awaken. When you hear that, it is our combined heartbeat. No matter even if I am holding you, if you wish to soothe yourself first, our song is there in your mind. I will admit, I prefer to be the one to care for you, but I want you to know that you are capable of standing on your own two feet always. The vampire took that from you, but I intend to give it back to you. You are not without your own power, Elisabeta. You will learn, with time, to believe in yourself. To know you're strong. I want that for you."

She was his lifemate. More, she had spent centuries tuned to the slightest nuance of her master's voice. His body language. His breathing. "You do want that for me, but you do not want that for you." It was utterly daring of her to state what she knew to be truth aloud, to basically contradict him. Had she done so with Sergey, it would have earned her such a beating she wouldn't have been able to move for a month. Maybe she was testing Ferro's limit. The truth of his rules.

To her utter astonishment, he nuzzled her shoulder, turning his face into her neck, his breath warm against her wildly pounding pulse. "I am ancient, Elisabeta, and more, I have always thought my woman would obey my every wish. That is what you see in my mind. Having seen what this vile creature has done to my lifemate, I am determined that the two of us will learn more modern ways. We will not be as the others living in this compound, perhaps. We will find our own union, but we will not be as I envisioned long ago because I no longer want that for either of us."

She turned his statement over and over in her mind. He was willing to change. To grow into someone different. She had to find the courage to do the same. She took a deep breath. "I would very much like to see the dresses, um . . ." What was she supposed to call him? How was she supposed to address him?

"Ferro," he supplied. "I am your wedded spouse. You will call me Ferro."

She pressed her lips together to keep them from trembling. He was her wedded spouse. He'd said the ritual binding words and there was no going back from that. Not ever. He'd tied them together for all eternity. For whatever reasons, they were bound together.

"Say it, *piŋe sarnanak*, say my name. I wish to hear how it sounds coming from your lips." His mouth was against her ear, his breath warm, teasing, wreaking havoc with the blood in her veins.

Elisabeta wasn't certain she wanted to call him by his given name. "Ferro," she said softly. "But you call me *piŋe sarnanak*. I think you are *kont o sívanak,* strong heart, and this songbird will learn to fly because you have a heart big enough for both of us." She felt very daring to tell him what she was thinking.

Deep inside, she was desperate for it to be true. They were lifemates and she could look into his mind, but she wasn't brave enough for that yet, nor was she strong enough, if he deliberately kept her out, to push beyond any shield. She had learned, over the centuries, to do so with Sergey, but subtly, so he was unaware. She had the feeling that Ferro would always be aware.

His teeth tugged at her earlobe and then released her just as abruptly, but not before the sudden gentle bite caused a spasm in her sex that sent a shock wave through her entire body.

"Take a look at these dresses. Lorraine, lifemate to my brethren Andor, had several books she called catalogues she allowed me to look through for clothing styles. She has been very helpful."

Elisabeta tried not to stiffen at the underlying affectionate note she heard in his voice. Up until that moment, Ferro had little expression in his voice. It was by turns gentle or soft or commanding, but there was definite affection for this woman. Another woman. Not his lifemate. She didn't like it.

His hand waved in the air and two dresses floated in front of her. She tried not to gasp, but—well—they were just a little bit formfitting. She had rarely been seen by anyone other than Sergey, and then he had covered her body in shapeless gowns. She'd never worn anything like either one of them. It wasn't that they wouldn't cover her adequately—they weren't low in the front, they went to her ankles, and both had three-quarter-length sleeves—but they weren't the shapeless, boxy dresses she was used to wearing.

One was a soft shade of cool forest green with accents of a lighter green in blocks on the bodice and skirt, the material thin and clingy so she knew it would emphasize her curves. She was thin, and not all that curvy, so maybe her bones would show more than her curves, but it was still a little risqué.

The second dress was black with gray accents. It was also made of a soft material she'd never seen before. The bodice came to a vee at the waist and the skirt dropped in a series of lacy ruffles to the ankles. It was the bodice that gave her pause or she would have chosen it immediately. She wasn't certain how comfortable she would be in a dress that clung to her body that closely.

Ferro didn't hurry her. He waited patiently. In fact, he seemed more interested in her hair and the nape of her neck than he did the dresses and her dilemma. He kept distracting her with his breath, with his lips moving against her pulse, with the way his fingers on her skin and scalp felt, until she was desperate to stop the unfamiliar feelings he flooded her body with.

"The black-and-gray one," she said. "I'll wear that one."

"Excellent choice."

His large hands spanned her waist and he lifted her off his lap and to her feet, setting her to one side. When he stood, he was fully clothed. He waved his hand and she found herself in the long black-and-gray soft dress. The material clung, just as she knew it would, but there were undergarments, just as soft, providing a buffer.

"You look beautiful, Elisabeta. Are you used to wearing shoes at all?"

She looked down at her feet and shook her head. "I was never allowed to leave the cage for any length of time."

He waved his hand again. "If these shoes become uncomfortable you are to tell me immediately. That is an order. Am I clear on that?"

She nodded and looked down at the slipper sandals on her feet. They were black and gray to match the dress she wore. She had no idea what they were made of, but it didn't feel like stiff leather. Whatever it was, they were comfortable, and she wiggled her toes. His hand brushed hers. She looked up at him expectantly.

"Take my hand, *piŋe sarnanak*," he said. "We're going to walk around the compound together. I want to show you where everything is and where we'll be staying."

She blinked at him, trying to process what he'd just ordered her to do. What he'd just said. He wanted her to let him take her hand. He was going to walk with her and take her outside the safety of the healing grounds. Outside, where there were people. Walk. When she didn't know how. She swallowed hard and tried to remember the mechanics. She'd seen it enough times. She was intelligent. She could shuffle along.

"Ferro . . ."

He reached for her hand, curling his fingers around hers, bringing her palm to his chest. "You will be with me, Elisabeta, and therefore safe at all times. My brethren will be close, and they will protect you as well. Julija, your friend, is here with her lifemate. Lorraine, my sister-kin, is here and anxious to befriend you."

She remained frozen, staring up at him, too terrified to move. He brought her fingers to the warmth of his mouth, his strong teeth scraping the very tips of them, sending spirals of heat dancing through her veins.

"If you become overwhelmed, just look to me. I will shield you. I am your lifemate, Elisabeta. Everyone we come across, including my brothers, will expect me to be old-world and overbearing." He showed her his teeth again, this time looking for all the world like a predator. "We can communicate as we did this morning, just the two of us. You tell me what you need, and I will provide it. I do not expect you to suddenly, after centuries of captivity, know how to speak with strangers or handle situations unfamiliar to you. I am proud of you for just choosing to rise and face your lifemate. I am told I am quite intimidating."

She glanced up at his face. He was walking her across the healing ground toward the exit, not striding fast but setting a leisurely pace, enough that she could slide her feet, one in front of the other, not lifting them, her heart beating as if it might fall out of her chest. His tone invited her to find amusement in his statement. She wished she could laugh, but she was too scared. Still, just having him so close gave her courage. Thus far, Ferro had shown her nothing but kindness. She had to believe he would continue to do so.

#1 *NEW YORK TIMES* BESTSELLING AUTHOR

CHRISTINE
FEEHAN

"The queen of paranormal romance...
I love everything she does."

—J. R. Ward

For a complete list of titles,
please visit prh.com/christinefeehan